Truly ✧ **P9-CFT-362**

Daniel, ninth Duke of Sussex, has big plans—and they don't include marriage. A member of the covert Free Fellows League, he's determined to become one of England's greatest war heroes. All his ambitions are temporarily dashed, however, when he's injured during a mission.

Known as society's perpetual bridesmaid, Miranda, Lady St. Germaine, agrees to let Daniel recuperate privately in one of her father's homes. But soon enough, all the ton is abuzz with gossip—gossip about Miranda's mysterious lover . . .

Realizing his stay has compromised Miranda's reputation, Daniel goes against his better judgment and proposes marriage. But Miranda will have nothing to do with a marriage of convenience—especially with the one man she's always privately adored. Unless, of course, she can convince him to make her truly his wife—with all his heart and soul . . .

"Rebecca Hagan Lee taps into every woman's fantasy."
—Christina Dodd

Don't miss the first three novels of the Free Fellows League

Barely a Bride
Merely the Groom
Hardly a Husband

and

The Marquess of Templeston's Heirs Trilogy

Once a Mistress
Ever a Princess
Always a Lady

Turn the page for more acclaim for Rebecca Hagan Lee . . .

Truly a Wife

Rebecca Hagan Lee

BERKLEY SENSATION, NEW YORK

THE BERKLEY PUBLISHING GROUP
Published by the Penguin Group
Penguin Group (USA) Inc.
375 Hudson Street, New York, New York 10014, USA
Penguin Group (Canada), 10 Alcorn Avenue, Toronto, Ontario M4V 3B2, Canada
(a division of Pearson Penguin Canada Inc.)
Penguin Books Ltd., 80 Strand, London WC2R 0RL, England
Penguin Group Ireland, 25 St. Stephen's Green, Dublin 2, Ireland (a division of Penguin Books Ltd.)
Penguin Group (Australia), 250 Camberwell Road, Camberwell, Victoria 3124, Australia
(a division of Pearson Australia Group Pty. Ltd.)
Penguin Books India Pvt. Ltd., 11 Community Centre, Panchsheel Park, New Delhi—110 017, India
Penguin Group (NZ), Cnr. Airborne and Rosedale Roads, Albany, Auckland 1310, New Zealand
(a division of Pearson New Zealand Ltd.)
Penguin Books (South Africa) (Pty.) Ltd., 24 Sturdee Avenue, Rosebank, Johannesburg 2196, South
Africa

Penguin Books Ltd., Registered Offices: 80 Strand, London WC2R 0RL, England

TRULY A WIFE

A Berkley Sensation Book / published by arrangement with the author

PRINTING HISTORY
Berkley Sensation edition / April 2005

ISBN: 0-425-20194-5

BERKLEY® SENSATION
Berkley Sensation Books are published by The Berkley Publishing Group,
a division of Penguin Group (USA) Inc.,
375 Hudson Street, New York, New York 10014.
BERKLEY SENSATION and the "B" design are trademarks belonging to Penguin Group (USA) Inc.

PRINTED IN THE UNITED STATES OF AMERICA

10 9 8 7 6 5 4 3 2 1

For my mother,
Alice H. Bolstridge,
who wants only the best for her children,
who knows that the chain of a mother's prayers
can link her child to God,
and who understands and shares my writer's soul.
With love.

Prologue

"Perfect courage is to do without witnesses what one would be capable of doing with the world looking on."

—François, Duc de la Rochefoucauld, 1613–1680

HAVERSHAM HOUSE
Spring 1813

*H*e had wanted to be a Free Fellow since he was seven years old. He had wanted to join their ranks and be a member from the first moment his cousin, Manners, had told him of the League and how it had come to be.

He had listened in rapt silence as Manners had confided his secret knowledge of the little band of blood brothers—all students at the Knightsguild School for Gentlemen—and their grand schemes and glorious purpose. The Free Fellows—Griffin, Viscount Abernathy, Colin, Viscount Grantham, and Jarrod, Earl of Westmore, had sworn an oath to remain unmarried for as long as possible in order to preserve their freedom so that they might fight for king and country against Napoleon and become England's greatest heroes. He had listened to his cousin recount the League's adventures, and Daniel, ninth Duke of Sussex, had vowed to become a Free Fellow no matter the sacrifice or how long it took.

And Daniel had kept the promise he'd made to himself so

long ago. He had sat alone in his room at Eton and pretended he was part of the glorious circle of heroes-in-the-making at Knightsguild, paying no heed to the fact that the Free Fellows League was closed to all but the founding members. He bribed Manners for every scrap of information about the Free Fellows League the other boy could uncover, ultimately following Manners's example by beginning to train for his first mission.

Daniel smiled. It had taken eighteen years, but he had finally earned the Free Fellows' trust and become one of them. Nearly three years after being granted provisional membership in the Free Fellows League, he was about to assume command of the Channel operation. He was about to become a regular member of the band of smugglers he, Jarrod, and Colin had put together to cover vital operations.

That meant he would spend many long nights crossing the English Channel.

Unfortunately, that meant long hours in a boat. And Daniel hated boats. He didn't mind water. And he truly enjoyed the seashore. But he hated boats. Any boat. Every boat. With a passion usually reserved for defilers of small children and animals.

But he hated weakness more—especially his own weakness. Daniel had yet to conquer the queasiness that assailed him each time he set foot in a boat.

Which was why he was about to spend the afternoon sailing the lake at his country estate.

He had become a member of the League, but he had one last fear to conquer before he could think of himself as a true Free Fellow, or a true hero . . .

Chapter 1

"But screw your courage to the sticking-place
And we'll not fail."
—*William Shakespeare, 1564–1616*
Macbeth

ENGLISH CHANNEL
A fortnight later

"Bloody hell!" Daniel, the ninth Duke of Sussex, cursed aloud as a rifle ball whizzed over his right shoulder, past his ear, and plopped into the choppy waters of the English Channel off the starboard bow of the *Mademoiselle*.

"The coast watch has spotted us, sir!" Billy Beekins, the grizzled old boatswain, shouted as the watch crew fired another rifle volley toward the skiff. "The bloody frogs are firing at us!"

Daniel glanced over his shoulder. It didn't seem possible. The night was perfect for smuggling. It was after midnight, but the moon hadn't risen and the stars were hidden behind a veil of clouds. The only light on the water came from the faint glow of the phosphorescent sea life below the surface. The crossing had been a little choppy, but the mission had gone without a hitch until now. His little band of smugglers had slipped silently into a sheltered cove south of the French port of Calais and deposited their colleague on the beach, retrieved the secret cargo and the military dispatches Colonel Grant had left for them, then began the return crossing.

He and Jarrod had meticulously planned the mission, and Daniel and the crew had executed it flawlessly until moments before, when they'd come under fire from the French side of the Channel.

Another rifle ball zinged past him—from across the port bow. "They're not shooting at us," Daniel shouted, pointing ahead toward the dark hulk that sailed into view. "They're shooting at them!"

"Mary, Mother of God!" Billy Beekins crossed himself, as a British frigate—one of many such vessels assigned to patrol the stretch of coast between Dover and Brighton—glided out of a patch of fog, its bow slicing the waves as it cut through the rough water.

The little skiff was caught in the exchange of rifle fire between a British Navy frigate and the French coast watch, and now the frigate was bearing down on the smaller vessel.

He thought, at first, that the frigate had seen them when the clouds had suddenly lifted, but Daniel quickly realized that that wasn't the case. Still, their choices were bleak. If the *Mademoiselle* stayed on her present course, the heavy frigate would ram her, but if she moved off course in either direction, it would be into the rain of rifle and musket fire from the sailors on board the larger ship and from the coast watchers on the French coast. "Hard, starboard!" He shouted the warning to the other members of the crew, then ducked as another ball whizzed past his shoulder.

"It's going to be close!" Beekins leaned on the rudder.

"Everyone down!" Daniel instructed. "Brace yourselves!"

The *Mademoiselle* swerved hard to the starboard side to avoid colliding with the bow of the frigate. The wake from the frigate sluiced over the sides as the smaller vessel tipped, tilted, came perilously close to capsizing, then finally righted itself. The repeating flashes from the muzzles of the rifles on the French shore and from the deck of the frigate colored the night sky seconds before the sound of the balls whistling through the air all around them warned them of the danger.

"Jesus, Joseph, and Mary," the boatswain swore as the muzzle flash along the rails of the frigate tripled. "We're on their side!"

They were. But the Royal Navy had no idea the skiff or its crew existed. And Daniel knew they'd be arrested and charged with smuggling if it did. The fact that the English Duke of Sussex was captaining this particular boat and this particular band of smugglers at the behest of the British government wouldn't make any difference to the captain of the frigate. The frigate's mission was to stop all suspicious vessels and put an end to smuggling. And a small boat carrying a crew of four across the channel in the dead of night qualified them as officially suspicious.

They were smuggling for the good of the nation, but they were smuggling all the same. And they would suffer the same fate as any other band of smugglers apprehended by the British Navy. For the handful of gentlemen and government officials who knew of their existence would deny all knowledge of it should the *Mademoiselle* and her crew be captured.

Straining as he pulled the oars, Daniel listened as the heavy balls plopped into the water, sizzling as the seawater cooled the hot metal. He sucked in a breath as one heavy lead ball missed the channel and seared a path through his thick wool jacket, his waistcoat, his linen shirt, and the tender flesh of his side, tearing skin and muscle, pushing bits of wool and silk and linen into the groove along his ribs. The wound hurt like hell and burned twice as hot. Daniel bit his bottom lip to keep from yelping in pain as the lead ball exited his body and thudded against the floor of the boat. He felt the hot rush of blood fill the wound and soak his clothes as a sheen of perspiration coated his skin.

He slumped down against the side of the boat, praying for strength as the skiff rode out the storm, skimming over the waves and the hail of falling lead, praying they would remain undetected as the frigate directed its firepower toward the French coast.

"We're clear, sir," Beekins announced as he put distance between the sloop and the frigate and left the skirmish far behind.

"Anyone hurt?" Daniel asked, pushing himself up and onto his seat, gritting his teeth and groaning as he did so. He slipped his left hand inside his jacket and pressed it against the right front of his waistcoat, frowning at the size of the hole marring the brocade and the liquid warmth staining it.

"Shavers caught one through the flesh of the arm, sir," the boatswain answered, "and Pepper's got a new part in his hair, but the rest of us are fine."

"Good," Daniel pronounced, in a strange-sounding and embarrassingly weak tone of voice.

"What about you, sir?" Beekins inquired, a note of alarm in his voice in response to the Duke of Sussex's thin reply. Of the four-man crew paid to smuggle upon request, only Billy Beekins knew that the man known to the crew as Danny Arthur was, in fact, Daniel, ninth Duke of Sussex.

"I took a ball in my side," Daniel answered, sucking in another breath at the pain, then releasing it in a low hiss.

"How bad?" Beekins asked.

"I'm fairly certain it missed my vitals, but I'm losing quite a bit of blood." For the first time in his life, Daniel was afraid he might disgrace himself by swooning, but he fought to maintain control and kept his hand firmly pressed against his left side to staunch the flow of blood.

"Pick up your oars," Beekins ordered the rest of the crew. "And put your backs into it, boys. We need to make shore as quickly as possible, for Danny Boy needs a surgeon."

"No," Daniel said.

"But, sir . . ." Beekins began.

"No surgeon," Daniel repeated more firmly. "Not here."

"But, sir . . ." Beekins renewed his protest and tried again.

Daniel cut him off. "Are you acquainted with a trustworthy surgeon?"

"No."

"Then, it's out of the question," Daniel told him. "The risk is too great. We don't know whom to trust, and it's imperative that our cargo reach London as soon as possible."

"You intend to travel all the way to London?" Beekins was aghast at the idea. "Tonight?"

"I must," Daniel explained. "I have obligations I cannot shirk."

"Someone else can accompany our cargo to London," Beekins told him.

"Delivering the cargo isn't my only pressing obligation," Daniel insisted. "I have a social engagement later this evening that demands my presence." Not to mention the marchioness to whom he'd extended his personal invitation.

"But your wound . . ."

"If your good wife will bind it well enough for me to make the journey back to town, I'll find someone there to tend it." Although he couldn't see him in the darkness, Daniel turned toward the boatswain. "I have to return to town. I cannot miss this particular engagement." Inviting Miranda to enter the lioness's den, then leaving her alone to fend for herself, was unconscionable. Not that she couldn't . . . He managed a brief grin despite the pain at the thought. Miranda was more than a match for the duchess. But he'd invited her to the party, and it was up to him to see that she enjoyed herself while she was there. And she would no doubt have his guts for garters for abandoning her when she caught up to him, because the dancing at the Duchess of Sussex's gala was unrivaled and there were only a handful of men in London, of which he was fortunate to be one, with whom Miranda could dance without feeling awkward and graceless at towering over them. And as far as Daniel could tell, the only thing Miranda enjoyed more than dancing with him was sparring with him.

Beekins shook his head. "You'll not be in any condition to enjoy it," he warned.

"I don't have to enjoy it," Daniel told him. "But I do have to attend."

Beekins blew out a breath. "If you insist."

"I do."

"Then I'll see to it that the missus patches you up and that you've someone you can trust traveling alongside, watching your back." Beekins thought that nothing short of an order to appear before the King or an invitation to dine at Carlton House with the Prince Regent could induce him to travel all the way to London after crossing and recrossing the Channel and being shot while doing it, but he wasn't an aristocrat, and he wasn't burdened by any of the social obligations or responsibilities young Sussex faced.

"Good enough. Thank you, Beekins." Daniel closed his eyes and concentrated on the soft slap of the oars against the water as the crew of the *Mademoiselle* made its way to shore.

He only meant to rest his eyes a moment, but when he next opened them, it was to find Mistress Beekins staring down at him. Jolted awake, Daniel attempted to sit up. He still wore his boots and breeches, but he was missing his shirt, waistcoat, and jacket. "Where am I? How? What . . . ?"

"Not so fast, sir," Mistress Beekins commanded. "I've another stitch or two to finish before I begin with the wrapping." She finished sewing and carefully knotted and clipped her thread before she glanced back over her shoulder. "Here, help me get him up so I can wrap the bandage around him."

"Beekins," Daniel breathed as the boatswain and a young man he had never seen before hurried to oblige.

"Aye, sir," Beekins replied, lifting Daniel into a sitting position, steadying him while Mistress Beekins wrapped

a length of white fabric over the wound she had spent the
better part of an hour cleaning and stitching. The young
duke was lucky to be alive. The rifle ball had ripped a nasty
gash along his right side, entering at the back and exiting at
the front below his ribs, leaving an ugly hole in its wake.
Beekins nodded toward his wife. "You know my wife. And
this is my son Micah."

"Madam. Micah." Daniel's face lost color, and perspiration dampened his entire body, as Beekins' wife worked
over him. "How long was I unconscious?"

"A little over two hours," Beekins answered. "I brought
you home with me," he explained. "I carried you on my
back."

Daniel grunted in pain. "Where's the cargo?"

"The pouches are here," Beekins said. "As are your personal items." He nodded toward Daniel's leather purse and
pocket watch lying on top of the bedside table. "And I
stowed the rest of the cargo in the compartments in your
coach." The boatswain held up his hand to forestall the
protest he knew was coming. "Rest assured, sir. My other
son, Jonah, is standing guard to keep it safe."

Daniel breathed a sigh of relief. "I must be going."

"You would do better to stay here and rest," Mistress
Beekins cautioned as she pulled the bandage tight around
his chest and around his waist before gathering the ends to
tie it into place. "I cannot be sure, but I suspect the ball
cracked one of your ribs." Mistress Beekins concentrated
on fastening the ends of the bandage into a secure knot.
"You'll do best not to lift your arm for a few days or you'll
ruin my needlework."

Daniel nodded, acknowledging the wisdom of her
words before stubbornly reaching for his shirt.

"Not that one." Mistress Beekins removed Daniel's torn
and bloody shirt from the foot of the bed. "I didn't spend
all that time cleaning the wound so you could put a filthy
shirt back over it." She pulled a sea chest from beneath the

bed and opened the lid, then took out a clean white shirt and dropped it over Daniel's head. "It's not nearly as fine as yours, but it's clean."

"Thank you," Daniel said softly. "For the shirt and for your tender care."

"See that you don't spoil the shirt by tearing open your wound and bleeding all over it," she fussed. "And see that you don't waste my tender care by dying on the way back to London."

Daniel managed a slight smile as she buttoned his shirt for him and helped him into a plain black waistcoat and jacket that belonged to her son. "I'll do my best."

"You'll be needing these." She handed him his heavy leather purse and watch, then thrust a pewter flask into his hand.

Daniel arched an eyebrow in query at the flask.

"It's whisky. For the pain. And I suggest you drink all of it."

"And if you need more, ask Micah," Beekins added. "He'll be going along with you to watch your back."

Daniel struggled off the bed and onto his feet. He faltered when his knees buckled beneath his weight, but forced his body to do his bidding. Offering his hand to Billy Beekins, Daniel said, "Thank you again." He looked from Beekins to his wife and son, then reached into his purse, removed three gold guineas, and presented them to the boatswain's wife. "For you, madam. For my care and the loan of the clothes."

"There's no need—" she began.

"Please," Daniel urged, "accept it as a token of my thanks and my esteem."

"Thank you, sir." She bobbed a curtsey.

"And you, Beekins," Daniel said. "Is there anything you would like? Anything I can do? Anything I can bring you from London?" Although Daniel had paid the crew a princely sum before the mission, he wanted to do more, for Billy Beekins had proven himself more than trustworthy and capable; he had proven himself a true friend and ally.

Beekins grinned. "There is one thing, sir."

"Anything," Daniel replied.

"Call it curiosity." Beekins looked down at the tops of his shoes, then back at the duke. "But I'm itching to know what sort of social engagement is so important you're willing to risk your life in order to attend. Will you be meeting the Prime Minister or dining with the Prince Regent?"

"No." Daniel shook his head, then immediately regretted it. "Someone far more important and far less forgiving. The Duchess of Sussex is hosting her annual gala this evening." And the Marchioness of St. Germaine would be there waiting for him.

Beekins frowned. "But, sir, that's your mother."

"Indeed, she is," Daniel admitted. "And she would never forgive my absence, or rest until she uncovered the reason for it." And neither would Miranda. He met Beekins's gaze. "So word of my midnight activities must never reach her ears. . . ."

Chapter 2

"Do not bite at the bait of pleasure, till you know there is no hook beneath it."

—Thomas Jefferson, 1743–1826

LATER THAT EVENING
Sussex House, London

"Good evening, Miranda." Daniel pushed away from the marble column he'd been leaning against and gave the Marchioness of St. Germaine an awkward little bow as she left the dance floor, then spared a nod for Lord Hollister, her dancing partner and escort. "Hollister. Fancy meeting you here."

"Your Grace," Lord Hollister acknowledged, as the last strains of music died away.

"May I?" Daniel reached for the dance card dangling from Miranda's wrist, opened it, and lifted it high enough for him to read without bending. "I believe this was my dance. . . ." He did his best to keep from sounding disappointed. Miranda always granted him the first and last dances at the duchess's annual gala.

"You were late," Miranda told him. "And Lord Hollister kindly took your place."

Daniel watched as Miranda smiled at the recently widowed viscount.

His gut knotted at the sight.

The pain had nothing to do with his wound and everything to do with the way Miranda was looking at Patrick Hollister. And the way Hollister was looking at her.

Turning slightly, Daniel brushed his lips against Miranda's gloved hand. He'd seen Miranda smile at other men. He'd admired her as she danced with other men on countless occasions. But this was different. Miranda stood three or four inches taller than Hollister and hadn't appeared bothered by it in the least. Nor had she seemed bothered by his own tardy arrival, despite the fact that until tonight she had never danced the first dance with anyone but him. Holding her hand a fraction longer than was necessary, Daniel stared over the top of it and met Hollister's gaze. "Then I'm indebted to you, my lord, for standing in my stead and accompanying Lady Miranda onto the dance floor."

There was no mistaking the ducal dismissal, but Lord Hollister refused to go silently. "Not at all, Your Grace," he murmured. "I didn't consider that I was standing in your stead. For, if truth be known, I took advantage of your absence to dance with the lady of my choice." Hollister gave Miranda a smile. "And I was honored by her acceptance."

The knot in Daniel's stomach grew tighter. He met Hollister's gaze as he pressed his lips against Miranda's hand once again, then stepped closer and tucked it into the crook of his arm. "Then I'm certain you won't object if she honors me with the next dance."

"No," Lord Hollister agreed, glancing from Miranda to Daniel and back again. "I don't suppose I will. Thank you for the dance, Lady Miranda."

"Thank *you,* Lord Hollister," she answered. "For coming to my rescue."

Hollister bowed to her, then slowly stepped away, leaving her in the Duke of Sussex's care.

"Your rescue?" Daniel arched an elegant brow at her.

"What would you call it?" she demanded, glaring at him

when Lord Hollister moved out of earshot. "Your mother was very surprised and none too pleased to see me."

He grinned.

"This isn't funny, Daniel." She jerked her hand out of the crook of his arm. "The duchess made it quite clear that my name was *not* on the guest list."

"Not on *her* guest list," Sussex corrected.

"Your mother's guest list is the only one that matters," Miranda snapped at him.

"Not to me," he countered, lowering his voice as he stared into her eyes. "And I invited you."

"Then you should have had the decency to inform your mother, because hers is the guest list they use at the front door."

He winced.

Miranda frowned. "You do this to me every year, Daniel, and you know she doesn't like me crashing her party."

It was true. His mother had never liked or approved of Miranda. There was, the duchess always said, something unsettling about a girl Miranda's age inheriting her late father's title and becoming a peeress in her own right. There was, she said, something shocking about a young woman who considered herself the equal to male peers. Daniel suspected his mother might be more jealous than disapproving, for the duchess had been born an honorable miss and had gained her lofty title by marrying a duke, while Miranda had rightfully inherited hers. So Daniel invited Miranda to the annual gala every year knowing his mother had deliberately omitted her name from the guest list.

It began as a way to right his mother's injustice, but Daniel had continued to invite Miranda year after year because he enjoyed her company. He had wanted to see her again, to hear her voice and resume the verbal sparring they'd enjoyed during their brief courtship—a courtship that had come to a rather abrupt end when he'd been a few months shy of his majority and certain his dream of becoming a member of the Free Fellows League was within his grasp. Miranda had just inherited her title, and his attraction to her had scared him.

He'd been looking for companionship and a light flirtation.

But Miranda deserved so much more than he could offer her. She had the air of permanence about her. He'd wanted her, but she was a lady and he couldn't, in good conscience, take what he wanted from her without offering her a wedding ring in return. Nor could he find it in his heart to ask her to wait for him or settle for anything less. He told himself he was doing what was best for both of them, told himself that he had to stop calling on her *before* he fell madly in love with her, before he went so far as to propose matrimony when he was not ready to settle down, do his duty, and be the sort of husband Miranda deserved.

And when Daniel stopped calling, he and Miranda had gone from would-be lovers to complete adversaries almost overnight.

He should have let her go completely and done everything in his power to forget her. He should have ignored his mother's pettiness and let Miranda handle the duchess in her own way. But he'd seized the opportunity to intervene instead. Every year he invited her to his mother's society gala, and every year Miranda responded to his invitation. And Daniel was convinced it wasn't just to avoid the humiliation of having everyone else in the ton know that hers was the only prominent name that didn't appear on the duchess's guest list. She looked forward to seeing him, being with him, verbally sparring with him, every bit as much as he did.

"Yet, you came," he mused.

"I must be as daft to accept as you are to invite me," Miranda admitted. "And I promise you it won't happen again, because this year, Her Grace issued an edict against me and anyone wearing St. Germaine livery." She looked up at him. "If Lord Hollister hadn't graciously offered to escort me inside, your mother would have had her footmen escort me back to my carriage."

"Then I'm doubly indebted to Hollister," he murmured.
"For if she had, it would have marked the end of my
mother's gala evening and her role as hostess here at Sussex House."

Miranda glanced up at him. A thin line of perspiration
beaded his upper lip, and the look in his eyes was hard and
implacable. "Daniel, you can't mean that."

Daniel softened his gaze as he looked at her. "Oh, but I
can," he said. "After all, this is my house. And as long as
I am the duke, you will always be welcomed in it."

Miranda felt her heart flutter in her chest as she recognized the sincerity in his voice. "It may be your house," Miranda reminded him, suddenly prepared to be high-minded.
"But your mother has had it longer. And she is the duchess."

"Dowager duchess," he corrected.

"A duchess all the same." Miranda sighed. "I grant that
your mother dislikes me, but she is your mother and I really don't enjoy coming here uninvited."

"You didn't."

"How many other guests did you invite?"

"None," he answered truthfully. "Only you."

"Why am I the only recipient of the Duke of Sussex's
largesse?"

Daniel smiled at her. "You're an intelligent woman,
Miranda. Surely that shouldn't be difficult for you to
discern. . . ."

He slurred the last word ever so slightly, but Miranda's
heart was thundering so loudly at the look in his eyes and
the husky note in his voice that she barely detected it. She
giggled softly. "Because everyone else received an invitation from the duchess and you didn't want to suffer alone?"

The sound of Miranda's uncertain laugh enchanted him.
It was so thoroughly out of the realm of his experience
with her. Miranda was never nervous around him. She was
never girlish or coy. He knew she expected him to argue,
but Daniel leaned closer, suddenly wanting . . . needing . . .
more from her. "Let's not argue anymore, Miranda."

"We always argue," she told him.

"Not tonight."

Miranda chuckled again, a wonderful, throaty sound that filled his head with images of her naked and smiling up at him.

She shrugged, thrown off guard and more than a bit captivated by Daniel's astonishing change from the maddening antagonist with whom she'd clashed during the past few years to the devastatingly attractive gentleman with whom she'd once fallen hopelessly in love. "I'm not quite sure where that leaves us." She looked up at him. "What shall we do instead?"

"I'm here," he said, reaching for her hand. "You're here. And the orchestra's here. Why not do me the honor of a dance?" He nudged her onto the edge of the dance floor.

Miranda blinked up at him, not certain she'd heard him correctly. "You're asking me to dance?"

"I am." Lifting the dance card and tiny pencil dangling from her wrist, he penciled in his name for the current dance and all the others that followed, blithely crossing out the names already listed and adding his own. Although Lord Hollister's name was written on the first line, his name had been written beside the last dance of the evening. He looked up at her. She hadn't given up on him entirely. "And it seems I've done so in the nick of time, before your card was completely full."

"You want to dance to this?" She frowned. The orchestra was playing a quadrille, and in all the years she had known him, Miranda had never seen Daniel Sussex partner anyone in a quadrille.

"You know better than that." He gave her his most devastating smile. Turning in the direction of the orchestra, Daniel held up three fingers, then four, designating the three-quarter time of the waltz.

"Daniel, you can't!" Miranda protested as soon as she realized his intention. "You know your mother doesn't allow waltzing at her galas."

"She'll allow it at this one," Daniel replied, signaling for the waltz once again. The orchestra leader glanced at the dowager duchess before giving Daniel an emphatic shake of his head.

Miranda turned to Daniel with a smug, I-told-you-so expression on her face.

But the Duke of Sussex was undaunted. "I've no intention of admiring you from a distance as we step our way through an interminable number of old-fashioned squares. Tonight, I'm going to put my hand upon your waist and feel the warmth of your body as we dance."

Her smug expression died a swift death as he gave voice to his intentions. Her breathing quickened and her heart began a rapid tattoo when Daniel lifted his right hand high into the air, indicated the signet ring bearing the ducal crest, and signaled once again for a waltz in three-quarter time. He kept his hand aloft until the orchestra leader nodded his acquiescence, then slowly lowered his arm, wincing as he did so. "There. See, Miranda?" He turned to her and smiled a wicked smile that sent anticipatory shivers up and down her spine. "With the right incentives, one can accomplish the impossible."

"I hope so," she murmured, "because as soon as she hears the music, your mother is sure to put an end to it."

"Then it's our only chance."

"Chance for what?"

"To escape."

"Escape?" Miranda frowned.

"Into each other's arms," he added, leaning close enough for his breath to feather the tendrils of hair at her temple.

She sighed, fighting the almost overwhelming urge to do as he suggested and melt into his embrace. The thought of being held in his arms while they circled the room at a romantically breathtaking pace thrilled her. Daniel was wickedly handsome, and Miranda knew he could be quite charming when he wanted to be. And she knew he had a healthy sense of humor—she'd seen and heard him poke fun at himself and his lofty position in society on a number of occasions. But this was something new. In all the years she'd known him, Daniel had always been in complete control, had always behaved as a consummate gentleman.

She'd never seen his dangerous side before, or experienced this blatantly naughty flirtation. And heaven help her if he decided to put her attraction to the test. Miranda was intrigued and more than a bit excited. She was drawn to him like a moth to a flame, more than willing to singe her wings . . . until she caught a whiff of his breath. "Daniel, you're foxed!"

"I am," he confirmed, swaying on his feet, admiring the depth of her décolletage even as he fought to keep his balance.

"But why?"

"Because I've been drinking."

"Yes, you have." Miranda struggled to keep from smiling but lost the battle. "My guess is whisky. Quite a bit of it."

"Quite." Daniel nodded, swaying on his feet once again. "Lucky for me, I've always been able to hold my liquor."

"Yes, isn't it?" Miranda put out a hand to steady him and felt dampness against his waistcoat. He groaned in obvious pain. "Daniel?"

Daniel glanced down. "Bloody hell." He reached inside his waistcoat and cursed beneath his breath. "Mistress Beekins won't be pleased. She told me not to lift my arm."

Miranda's ears pricked up at the sound of an unfamiliar female name. "Who is Mistress Beekins?"

"The lady who sewed me up," Daniel replied matter-of-factly.

"Sewed you up?" Miranda wrinkled her brow in confusion.

Daniel nodded. "In nice, neat stitches." He frowned. "But it appears to be for naught, because I seem to be bleeding again." He fought to keep his feet, leaning heavily on Miranda for balance. "There's the end of the quadrille. Come, Miranda, I want to waltz with you. *Now*."

"Have you lost your senses?" she demanded, digging in her heels as he attempted to steer her onto the dance floor. "You've been hurt badly enough that someone had to sew you up, and you want to waltz?"

"Sssh!" Daniel warned. "Someone might overhear you."

She glanced around to make sure no one had overheard her, then lowered her voice. "You said you're bleeding *again*. What happened? How badly are you wounded? What sort of trouble are you in?"

"None that I can't handle," he replied. "So long as I manage to leave this ballroom without anyone else finding out."

"Without anyone else finding out that you're foxed? Or that you're bleeding and in obvious pain?" Miranda whispered fiercely.

"Yes," he managed, through tightly clenched teeth, as he offered her his elbow. "Shall we join the others on the dance floor?"

"Good heavens, Daniel!" She looked closely and saw the sheen of perspiration on his face. "You're in no condition to waltz."

"Don't you want to dance with me?" he cajoled.

"Of course I do," she answered.

"Because I want to dance with you. . . ."

"That's not the point," Miranda said. "You shouldn't be here."

He looked as if she'd hurt his feelings. "Of course I should be here. What sort of gentleman would I be if I invited you into the lioness's den, then left you alone to become dinner?"

"Oh, Daniel . . ."

He stared down at her exposed bosom. "Though I'm sure you'd be a very tasty dinner."

Miranda gasped, aware that his words had another meaning. She forgot what she intended to say, then remembered. "You ought to be in bed."

Daniel grinned wickedly. "I'm doing my damnedest to get there."

"I'm serious," Miranda replied, her tone laced with concern and the tiniest hint of disapproval.

"So am I," he replied. "I'm willing to go to bed—just as soon as you waltz me out of here and into the carriage I hope to God you left waiting." He looked her in the eye. "Tell me, sweet Miranda, will you take me to bed?"

Miranda blushed. How he managed to make his words sound so suggestive when he was barely able to keep his feet was beyond her. "*Your* bed is upstairs, Your Grace."

"Up sixty-eight stairs I can't negotiate," he admitted. "And even if I could get to my bed without anyone down here noticing, how long do you think it would be before word got around upstairs that I was in my bed instead of at the party? How long before *she* discovered the reason for my absence?" He leered at her. "Unless you're willing to join me upstairs and give me a better reason for abandoning the party. . . ."

"Daniel!" Her blush was hotter this time. "She's your mother," Miranda reminded him. "She should know you're injured."

"No, she should not." He ground out the words. "No one can know." He leaned forward, pressing his forehead against the top of Miranda's head. "No one except you."

"Why me?"

"Because I trust you," he told her. "And . . ."

Miranda's heart swelled with pride at his admission. "And?"

"You're the only woman tall enough and strong enough to manage."

Miranda's romantic dreams dissolved in a burst of white-hot flame that tasted of ashes. "Thank you for informing me of that, Your Grace." Miranda's reply was sharper than she intended, but she was struggling to keep her hurt and the tears that stung her eyes from showing. "No doubt I needed to be reminded that I'm always the biggest, clumsiest, most awkward girl anywhere," she muttered.

His words had come out all wrong. He hadn't meant to

hurt her. All he'd meant to do was answer her question. Daniel frowned. He'd learned years ago that he was able to consume a great deal more liquor than most men of his acquaintance. He could drink to excess and keep his feet, even dance if necessary. He could gamble and retain his card sense. He could sit a horse without falling off, and drive his phaeton if necessary. He had the ability to drink heavily and still go about his normal routine generally none the worse for having done so and with no one the wiser.

Among his friends, his ability to hold his drink was legendary.

Daniel wished he possessed the same ability to hold his tongue and subdue his more amorous instincts while under the influence. But that wasn't the case. He could make love and perform admirably, if not exceptionally, while drunk, and he had a tendency to reveal and caress as much of his partner's naked flesh as possible without regard to rules of society or propriety, and to talk the entire time—traits most disconcerting to a man who prided himself on his judgment and restraint.

The alcohol that had dulled the pain in his side tonight had also dulled his inhibitions and his good manners. And unfortunately there didn't seem to be a thing he could do about it except try to say as little as possible and keep his hands to himself until he sobered up. Daniel exhaled. "Miranda . . ."

"No," she answered, avoiding his gaze.

"I'm sorry."

His apology sounded so genuine and heartfelt that Miranda looked at him, but her expression was doubtful.

"My words came out all wrong."

"That's odd," she said. "Because I heard them quite clearly."

"You heard what I said, not what I meant."

"Then suppose you explain yourself."

"Waltz me out of here and I will," he pleaded.

She hesitated.

Daniel pressed his advantage. "Please, Miranda, I can't walk out of here on my own, and I bloody well can't quadrille out. Waltzing is the only way I can get to the terrace. . . ."

The terrace. Waltzing beneath the stars with Daniel on the terrace. . . . There was nothing romantic about the way he presented it, but suggesting that she waltz him outside was so out of character and so daring that Miranda was willing to do it. Despite the consequences. Because if she was seen waltzing outside and onto the terrace with Daniel, she might as well bid her good name and her reputation goodbye.

The Sussex House gardens lay beyond that terrace, and its vast landscape of formal gardens surrounded by hedges and decorated with a myriad of statuary provided numerous opportunities for stealing kisses or a quick rendezvous despite the fact that the duchess had ordered it illuminated with torches and gaslights. "You're an ass, Your Grace. . . ."

"I know," he answered as the orchestra began the waltz. "But if you hold on to me and I hold on to you, I know we can make it. . . ."

"Because I'm the 'only woman tall enough and strong enough to manage,'" she reminded him, as he took her in his arms and guided her into the first steps of the dance. "You're lucky I don't leave you bleeding all over your mother's marble floors."

"I know." His ability to force his body to do his bidding was ebbing at an alarming rate. Daniel inhaled deeply, gathering his remaining strength. "You are the only woman tall enough and strong enough to manage me," he replied softly. "But I've never found you awkward or clumsy. I've always found you to be the personification of grace and elegance."

Miranda's breath caught in her throat. "That's because

you're so tall and graceful. You should see me with other partners."

"I *have* seen you with other partners," Daniel reminded her. "And I've never seen a more graceful woman." He gave her a rueful smile as he labored to dance and converse. "But I'd advise you to reserve judgment about my own achievements in that area."

Miranda felt the trembling in his arms and carried as much of his weight as she could. "Good heavens, Daniel, you weigh a ton."

He grunted in reply and did his best not to lean so heavily on her. But he was fighting a losing battle, and they were both keenly aware of it.

Miranda could only guess at the effort it took for him to appear to waltz so effortlessly, and she did the only thing she could think to do to keep him upright and moving. "If you stumble and fall or step on my feet, I swear to God, I'll leave you where you lie and let Her Grace deal with you."

Squeezing his eyes shut against a wave of dizziness, he faltered.

Miranda felt the slight breeze from the open terrace doors and realized victory was within reach. She moved closer, taking on more of his weight as she whispered, "Hold me tighter."

"Too . . . tight . . . already . . ." He fought back a wave of nausea as he ground out each word. "Your rep—"

"Hang my reputation! You're bleeding through your waistcoat and onto my new ball gown. So don't give up on me now, Daniel. Because when this is over and you've recovered, you're going to accompany me to my dressmaker's and buy me the most exquisite ball gown anyone has ever seen. . . ."

Daniel barely spared a glance for her pale green dress. "Help me and I'll buy you a ball gown fit for a queen," he promised.

"You'll have to do better than that," she warned. "This

ball gown *was* fit for a queen." Miranda realized that Daniel's face was grayish white, his upper lip dotted with perspiration. Fearing he might pitch face-forward onto the hard marble floor at any second, Miranda wedged her knee between his and nudged him through the terrace door. "The queen and I share a dressmaker."

The night air helped cool his feverish brow, and Daniel murmured a brief prayer of thanks as he lowered his gaze and found himself staring at the cleavage Miranda had pressed against his chest. The view was spectacular, and he was relieved to discover that, despite the fog of pain surrounding him, he could still appreciate the sight of the truly magnificent bosom pressing into him. "I've no doubt your seamstress is thrilled to have your patronage, for I doubt that dressing the queen compares to dressing you." Or undressing you, he silently added.

"Flattery isn't going to get you out of this, Daniel," Miranda advised. "You think I'll take pity on you and allow you simply to pay the bill because you were foxed and injured when you made the bargain. But no matter what you say or do, when you're recovered, you're going to *accompany* me to my dressmaker's and buy me the gown of my choosing."

Daniel squeezed his eyes shut, trying to block out the sight of Miranda's cleavage as much as the burning pain in his side. "So long as you live up to your end of the bargain and help me out of here." He would happily accompany her to the most expensive dressmaker on earth so long as she got him away from Sussex House before he fell flat on his face. Daniel opened his eyes and blinked several times before he managed to focus on her lovely face—*both* her lovely faces.

"Hold on," she ordered, dropping her hand from his shoulder to his waist, and wrapping her arm around him.

Daniel tried to muffle his groan of pain but failed.

"I'm sorry," she whispered as she tightened her grip,

feeling dampness at the back of his jacket as she half-pushed, half-carried him across the terrace.

He stumbled twice and nearly sent them tumbling down the steps that led from the terrace to the garden, but Miranda managed to keep them upright as they made their way along the gravel path through the garden to the street. For once, she was grateful for the fact that she towered over most of her acquaintances. But she was trembling from exhaustion and perspiring through her silk ball gown despite the heavy mist and the cool breeze that blew her skirts against her legs. "I take it back," she complained. "I take it back, Daniel. You weigh a ton and a half."

"It's a good thing you're no featherweight yourself," he murmured.

"Insult me again and you'll be buying me jewels to match my new gown."

"I didn't insult you," he said.

"What do you call it when you tell a lady she's bigger and heavier than average?" she demanded.

"A compliment." Daniel sucked in a breath. "The fact that you're no featherweight is one of the things I like best about you. You give the appearance of being solid and reliable and trustworthy."

"Instead of beautiful and mysterious and romantic," Miranda murmured.

"The world is full of beautiful, mysterious, and romantic women," he said. "Solid, reliable, and trustworthy women are rare."

"Take it from me, Your Grace," she informed him. "That is *not* a compliment."

"It should be," he muttered, aware that Miranda was the only thing keeping him upright. "Thunderation, Miranda, don't you know you're beautiful? Have I been so remiss? Haven't I ever told you how beautiful you are?"

Had she heard him correctly? Did he think she was beautiful? She stopped suddenly, and Daniel leaned on her to keep from falling. "No, Your Grace," she answered. "You've never so much as hinted you think I'm beautiful. Suffice it to say, you've been extremely remiss."

Miranda thought she'd already born the brunt of his weight, but until a few moments ago, Daniel had supported more than she'd realized. That no longer being the case, Miranda gave an unladylike grunt as Daniel's strength abruptly deserted him and the pressure on her shoulders increased tenfold. "Allow me to rectify the error." He tried to bow and nearly tipped them over. "Miranda, you are beautiful. From the top of your auburn head to the tip of your toes and everywhere in between." Leaning forward, Daniel peered down the front of her dress and grinned appreciatively. "Not that I've seen everything in between . . . But I'm a man with extit . . . exquistit . . . *good* . . . taste, and I can tell from looking at these lovelies that everything else is just as nice."

Miranda blushed.

Daniel frowned. "Now," he asked, "how much farther?"

"About ten feet," she answered.

Daniel braced himself for another wave of pain and nausea. "I think I can make it."

"That makes one of us," Miranda replied bluntly. "Because I'm not certain *I* can." Her knees were shaking and her heart raced from physical exertion and the effect of his words. "Especially across the lawn in full view of the late arrivals." She pushed him down onto a stone bench and sat down beside him.

Daniel groaned once again. Damn, but he'd forgotten about late arrivals! "You must," he ordered. "I can make it with your help. I can't make it alone."

Miranda took a deep breath—as deep as her half-corset would allow—and forced herself to her feet, then turned and faced him. "Then wait here," she instructed, "while I go back inside for help."

Daniel's face must have mirrored his alarm, for Miranda gave an exasperated sigh. "I understand the need for discretion, Your Grace, but we need help, and Alyssa told me she and Griff were coming tonight. If I can't find Alyssa and

Griff, I'll look for Lord Grantham or Shepherdston, or your cousin Barclay. They're sure to be here." She named the men with whom she knew Daniel associated, the men she knew he trusted, the men she knew the dowager duchess wouldn't exclude from the guest list. "Rest a bit," she urged. "I'll be back as soon as I can."

Shaking his head slightly, Daniel reached inside his jacket and removed a pewter flask.

Miranda looked askance at the flask. The plain pewter vessel was at odds with Daniel's otherwise elegant attire, as was the fact that he carried a flask at all. She'd never known him to carry one before—even on cold mornings in the country, where riding and tramping the moors for grouse and pheasant were the local pastimes. And if he carried a flask, Miranda somehow would have expected the Duke of Sussex to carry a silver one.

"What is it?" he demanded, uncapping the flask and taking a long drink from it.

Miranda spoke her thoughts. "In all the years I've known you, I've never seen you carry a flask."

"In all the years you've known me, you've never seen me shot and bleeding like a stuck pig despite Mistress Beekins's best efforts. Besides—" He drawled, frowning at the flask. "It's almost empty."

"Shot?" Miranda's voice rose an octave. "You complained of tearing some stitches," she accused. "You didn't say anything about being shot."

"If I hadn't been shot, I wouldn't *have* any stitches to tear." He took another long swallow from the flask and returned it to his inner pocket, amazed that he had the dexterity to do so. He'd consumed an inordinate amount of whisky during the past twelve hours. He'd needed it in order to sleep through as much of the journey to London as possible, but Daniel had still been awakened by the pain during the trip inland and asked Micah to refill the flask several times. And now Daniel remembered Micah refilling it once more before leaving him at the side entrance to Sussex House, departing to deliver the leather pouches to the Marquess of Shepherdston's London residence.

Daniel was foxed, but not so foxed that he couldn't feel pain and know that the wound in his side wasn't going to be the only part of him aching on the morrow. His head would feel the size of a melon and be accompanied by a full company of drummers.

He focused his gaze on Miranda. There were still two of her, but he was able to see both of them clearly. "What did you think happened?"

"I don't know what I thought," she admitted. "That you'd been in an accident of some sort. That you'd cracked a rib, or cut yourself climbing a trellis up to the mysterious Mistress Beekins's bedroom. . . ." She stared at him. "I never dreamed you'd been shot."

"Cracked ribs don't bleed, Miranda. And although a cut generally bleeds, I've never had to climb a trellis to gain entry to any woman's bedchamber. And even if I had, I doubt a cut from a climb up a trellis would bleed like that." Daniel nodded toward the blotch of crimson marring her bodice and trailing down onto her skirts.

"Good heavens!" Miranda stared down at her dress. The bloodstain on her ball gown had spread. It had grown from a stain the size of a coin and blossomed into a stain the size of a man's hand. Staring down at her bodice, Miranda realized there were, in fact, two stains on her dress—the original one and a nearly perfect impression of Daniel's bloodied handprint on the curve of her waist and hip. They had known he was bleeding through his waistcoat, but she was certain that neither she nor Daniel had realized he was bleeding so profusely.

"Surprised you, didn't it?" He looked at his waistcoat. The blood wasn't visible on the black brocade, but the garment was wet with it. "Surprised me, too."

"You need help." She let out the breath she hadn't

realized she'd been holding. "Someone experienced. Someone who knows what they're doing . . ."

"You can't go back in there to get it," he said, glancing toward Sussex House. "Not looking like that. Not without attracting attention."

"But, Daniel, you need . . ."

"The ball went through the back and out the front, and Mistress Beekins cleaned and stitched the wound," he said. "I'll be fine with some rest."

"Not if you bleed to death first."

Daniel winced. "I won't. Not as long as I rest. But rest is the one thing I won't get if anyone in there suspects I'm injured. All I'll get is questions I can't answer and a stream of curious callers I'd rather avoid." He reached out and took her hand. "You've got a good head on your shoulders and you spent an entire summer helping Alyssa Abernathy devise all sorts of healing concoctions. I know you learned something, and despite our past differences, Miranda, I trust you to keep this *our* secret."

"Daniel, I can't," she faltered. "I can't keep a secret that might endanger your life. I won't use the front entrance. I'll go around back to the service entrance and ask to speak with your mother. . . . I'll tell her it concerns you. . . ."

"You'll be wasting your breath." Daniel sighed. "My mother won't believe anything you have to say. . . ."

"She can't deny the blood on my dress," Miranda argued.

"Of course she can." Daniel attempted a lopsided smile. "Her son is a duke, and everyone knows that a duke's blood is royal blue."

"Daniel, this isn't a joke."

"No, it isn't," he agreed. "It's a matter of life or death. *My* life or death, and believe me, my dear Lady St. Germaine, my life won't be worth a penny if word of my injury gets around. And it *will* get around if you return to the house like that. Someone is bound to notice and ask questions I cannot afford to have asked, much less answer."

Miranda knew he was right. She couldn't return to the

party with bloodstains on her gown, and she had nothing with which to cover them. She hadn't worn a wrap, and her evening cloak was hanging in the cloakroom along with a hundred other evening cloaks deposited there by the footmen and maids collecting them at the door as the duchess's guests arrived. Without her cloak, there was no way Miranda could hide the damage that had been done to her dress, and the only other option was to dispense with her gown and go back inside Sussex House in her undergarments.

As a peeress in her own right, Miranda had always been a bit more independent and daring than was considered proper for an unmarried lady. She had garnered her share of gossip since she'd made her curtsey, and had earned a reputation as the ton's perpetual bridesmaid. She was unconventional in many ways, but Miranda was a lady to her core, and dispensing with her ball gown wasn't an option she could seriously consider. Unfortunately, a bloodstain the size of the one on her dress was nearly impossible to disguise.

Nor could she dismiss Daniel's concerns. He knew the situation better than she, and Miranda would never forgive herself if what Daniel said was true and some eagle-eyed member of the ton raised a hue and cry and demanded to know what had happened. Or if someone recalled the fact that the Marchioness St. Germaine's exquisite ball gown hadn't been stained until *after* she'd accepted the Duke of Sussex's invitation to dance the waltz—an unprecedented occurrence at his mother's annual gala.

Miranda gritted her teeth in frustration. If only she'd realized how foxed he was before he'd asked her to dance, before he'd ordered the orchestra to play the waltz, she might have persuaded him to make his exit in a less noticeable manner, but she'd foolishly succumbed to the temptation of being held in Daniel's arms once again, and now they were both going to suffer for it. But once they were safely away and Daniel was settled into bed with someone to look after him, Miranda was going to demand an explanation.

She looked at Daniel. "You're right," she stated matter-of-factly, extending her hand to him in order to pull him to his feet. "Unfortunately, we've no choice but to make a run for it. So, let's be about it, Your Grace, before you're too weak to support your weight or before you expire on the spot."

Chapter 3

"Now or never was the time."
—*Laurence Sterne, 1713–1768*
Tristram Shandy

Daniel took a deep breath, steeling himself for the ordeal ahead. He pressed his hand against the front of his waistcoat in a vain attempt to suppress the ache and offered Miranda his arm as they left the gravel path. "I can't promise I'll succeed," he said, stepping onto the lawn before removing his hand from the front of his waistcoat and reaching into his jacket pocket for a handkerchief. "But I'll do my utmost to prevent you from having to bear the bulk of my weight."

"You'll succeed," she returned in a no-nonsense tone she hoped masked the terror she felt. "You've no choice. If you falter, I will leave you where you lie and go for help." She glanced at him from beneath her lashes, watching covertly as Daniel dabbed his handkerchief along his brow, mopping up the beads of perspiration that dotted it.

"What happened to your resolve not to endanger my life?" he asked, frowning at the crumpled square of handkerchief linen that bore smears of blood where he'd gripped it.

"The way I see it, your life is in danger either way. You started this by insisting that we waltz out of the ballroom in order to get you safely out of the reach of prying eyes," Miranda reminded him. "And until we succeed in getting you away, you're going to act a part worthy of the Bard and carry yourself like the duke you were born to be. You're going to cross the lawn as if you hadn't a care in the world. And if we encounter any late arrivals or early departures, you're going to protect yourself by living up to your reputation as a quick wit or by being fast on your feet. Whatever seems most appropriate."

"I'm muzzy-headed, but believe it or not, I comprehend the situation, Miranda," he murmured dryly, still clenching the handkerchief in his fist. *And the danger.* "I am, after all, the one bl—"

"Good evening, Your Grace."

Daniel froze at the greeting, and Miranda took a step back, hoping to hide her dress from the other man's view.

But it was next to impossible to hide anything at Sussex House tonight. The place glowed with light like a birthday cake covered with candles—and all for the benefit of the guests attending the Duchess of Sussex's annual gala.

The entire house was blazing with hundreds of candles, and the gardens and grounds were equally well-lighted with an almost equal number of lanterns. The duchess had insisted on installing a series of gas lamps along the front and side entrances to Sussex House after thieves had accosted Lady Gentry and her daughter at knifepoint earlier in the season as they'd returned home from the opera. The fact that the Gentrys lived on the opposite end of Park Lane from Sussex House hadn't seemed to matter to the dowager duchess.

She had had workmen from the Gas-Light and Coke Company working day and night to lay the gas pipe and install the lamps in time for the gala. The duchess had also hired a veritable army of footmen, and lamp- and lantern-lighters and tenders, whose job it was to light and tend the candles and oil lamps inside Sussex House and the gas lamps and oil lanterns outside, and to keep everything glowing until half past two in the morning, when every light in the place would be extinguished so the duchess could delight in waking the rest of London with a show of three a.m. fireworks. And after the fireworks, the army of lighters and tenders would be put back to work illuminating the way for the departing guests.

It was costing Daniel a bloody fortune. But no expense was spared, no whim was too extravagant when it came to the Duchess of Sussex's Annual Gala.

Daniel almost pitied the pickpockets, cutpurses, house-breakers, and footpads seeking the shadows of Park Lane tonight. There were no shadows around Sussex House—for thieves or for the amorously inclined. Heaven forbid that the duchess's party be marred by robbery, by scandalous behavior, or by her blue-blooded son's clandestine activities.

He gritted his teeth, allowing the breath he'd been holding to escape. He'd known all along that the optimal time for escaping the party was the golden hour and a half between the extinguishing of the lamps for fireworks and the relighting of them to aid the departing guests, but that meant enduring the entire evening, and Daniel was quite sure that suffering through his mother's party was not something he was prepared to do—not if he wished to keep his injury a secret.

Daniel had intended to ask his cousin and Free Fellow colleague, the Earl of Barclay, for assistance, but he'd deliberately delayed his entrance to avoid being pressed into duty standing beside his mother in the receiving line. Because he'd been engaged in the business of avoiding his mother, Daniel had missed Jonathan. And although he'd spotted his cousin several times, Daniel hadn't the energy to leave his cozy hiding place and make his way through the growing crush of people to reach him. He'd decided to lie in wait until Jonathan or someone else he knew he could trust made their way close to him.

Miranda's timely arrival had been a godsend.

Daniel had invited her knowing there was a very good
chance she wouldn't appear. But Miranda hadn't disappointed him. She'd accepted his invitation.

Daniel had breathed a sigh of relief when he'd seen her—
even though she'd been dancing the first dance of the evening—his dance—with Patrick Hollister. And he'd breathed
an even bigger sigh of relief when she'd agreed to waltz
him out of the ballroom. Making their way across the lawn
without being seen had been trickier, but their luck had
held, and he and Miranda were nearly home free.

But luck was fleeting and theirs seemed to have run out
as they approached the long line of vehicles parked along
both sides of the street and came face to face with Lord
Espy exiting his coach.

After coming face to face with the man, Daniel couldn't
ignore him. He was acquainted with Espy. The viscount was
one of Lord Bathhurst's secretaries and was often called
upon to act as liaison between Bathhurst and the Prime
Minister's government. Daniel couldn't pretend he hadn't
seen or heard him, couldn't pretend that Lord Espy was ad-
dressing someone else. Not when it was quite clear that
Daniel was the only gentleman within hearing and that
Lord Espy had directed his greeting to him.

"Evening, Espy." Daniel returned the greeting, hoping
that by doing so, Lord Espy would refrain from attempting
further conversation.

"Lovely night for a party."

"Quite." Daniel nearly groaned aloud. He focused his
attention at a point above the other man's shoulder, on
the rather ornate lanterns decorating the coach. His short,
clipped answer was designed to send a message to Espy to
take the hint.

But Espy seemed bent on conversation and took no notice of Daniel's one-word reply. "I didn't expect to see you
here this evening."

"Why not?" Daniel asked. "I attend the duchess's gala
every year."

"And the duchess's annual gala far outstrips all the other events of the season. Mayfair is packed with partygoers, and the whole of London is buzzing with excitement. I believe the party is just getting under way." He stared at Daniel. "I would have arrived at the appointed hour myself, but I lost precious time waiting for my brother to dock his ship. Still, I made it in good time all the same. Couldn't outstrip you, of course, but the night is still quite young, and I vow it was impossible to think of missing the duchess's gala. Surely you aren't leaving already? It's such an honor to receive an invitation that I eagerly await its arrival every year. . . ."

Miranda gave a low, almost inaudible snort.

Daniel clenched his teeth so hard a muscle in his jaw began to tic. He should have known Miranda wouldn't go unnoticed for long. She stood a head or more taller than most of the other women present, and that and her auburn hair made her instantly recognizable. And asking her to remain completely quiet was like asking the stars not to twinkle at night.

"Great Jupiter!" Espy exclaimed, staring at the front of Miranda's gown. "Pardon my language, my lady, but your gown! Is anything amiss? Are you injured?"

"Nosebleed," Miranda announced to Lord Espy, snatching the handkerchief Daniel held clutched in his fist and hastily covering her nose and mouth with it. "My family has long been prone to nosebleeds, and I'm afraid I suffered a rather severe one while dancing with His Grace."

Lord Espy gave Miranda a sympathetic smile.

"And he kindly offered to see me home," she continued, the handkerchief muffling her words as she stepped closer to Daniel.

Lord Espy stared at Daniel, aware that the Duke of Sussex had gallantly refrained from embarrassing his companion by introducing her while she was indisposed, but Espy recognized her nonetheless and admired the duke for his forbearance. Everyone who was anyone in the ton understood that there was no love lost between Daniel, Duke of Sussex, and Miranda, Marchioness of St. Germaine. Although no one knew what had caused their enmity, the duke and the marchioness had been thorns in each other's sides for years. Their public disagreements and verbal sparring matches were the stuff of legends and no doubt quite capable of provoking a massive nosebleed. And probably no less than the marchioness deserved. Rumor had it that she was never invited to the Duchess of Sussex's annual gala, but resorted to sneaking in like a common gate-crasher. And it was said that the duke had had the unenviable task of escorting her off the premises on more than one occasion.

"A shame," Espy clucked his tongue, "for you to miss the grandest party of the season, my lady."

"Indeed," she murmured.

"And a disappointment for you as well, Your Grace," Lord Espy continued.

Daniel focused his gaze on the older gentleman, amazed to find that the other man honestly imagined he regretted missing his mother's party for any reason—especially for an indisposed companion.

What Daniel regretted was the fact that Espy obviously didn't understand his true measure as a gentleman.

Miranda wasn't indisposed. *He* was. But Miranda was proving to be an exceptional actress, and Lord Espy had believed her story. If the reverse had been true and Miranda had been indisposed, Daniel would have gladly volunteered to see her safely home from his mother's party or from any other social function without a single hesitation or regret. "Quite." Daniel understood, even if over half the members of the ton did not, that the people attending them were always more important than the functions. "If you'll excuse us, Espy," Daniel replied firmly, taking hold of Miranda's arm and gripping it harder than he intended in an effort to steady himself. "I'm sure the lady would like to be on her way."

Miranda nodded.

"Yes, of course, Your Grace." Espy stepped aside to allow them to pass. "Please remember me to your lovely mother, Lady St. Germaine."

Miranda stared at Lord Espy over the top of Daniel's handkerchief, bristling at the older man's audacity in using her name when Daniel had quite purposefully not introduced her. Miranda braced herself against Daniel's weight in an effort to maintain the fiction that she was indisposed instead of him.

"Since I am sure you understand how the young lady might find her condition to be somewhat *distressing* and . . ." Daniel continued.

"Mortifying," Miranda corrected, her words muffled by the handkerchief.

"Embarrassing," Daniel replied. "I trust that we may count upon your gentlemanly discretion should you hear any remarks about it or should anyone question our early departure." He leaned a fraction closer to the man. "I shouldn't like to upset Her Grace, the dowager duchess, by letting it be known that I missed a single moment of the extraordinary festivities for any reason."

Miranda gasped into the crumpled folds of the handkerchief.

Daniel was taking a huge gamble in leaning close enough for Lord Espy to discover how well and truly foxed he was. Or how physically weak he was.

"Indeed, Your Grace," Espy assured him. "You may stake your life upon it."

Daniel managed a grin. "I trust that won't be necessary."

Chapter 4

"Something between a hindrance and a help."
—William Wordsworth, 1770–1850

"*A nosebleed!*" *Daniel marveled as soon as Lord Espy* was out of earshot and he and Miranda finally made their way through the jumble of carriages to her coach. "Quick thinking, my lady."

Miranda smiled. "Thank you, Your Grace."

"I confess to being nonplussed," he said. "Pleading a nosebleed was brilliant."

"I'm not so sure," she admitted. "It isn't enough that I'm cursed with red hair and stand head and shoulders above nearly every eligible man we know. I've just announced that generations of my family members suffer spontaneous nosebleeds. How attractive! Now I'll have every eligible bachelor in London believing that in addition to outranking, outweighing, and looking down upon most of them, I also bleed upon them whenever I'm asked to waltz. I thank you for the praise, Your Grace, but I believe I've just ruined whatever chances I may have had to walk down the aisle at season's end, as someone's bride instead of someone else's *bridesmaid*."

"It was damned quick thinking on your part," Daniel replied, retrieving his handkerchief and pressing it against his brow once again. "Especially in light of my muzzy-headedness."

"You're very foxed," Miranda reminded him, "and very muzzy-headed, or you wouldn't have leaned close enough for Lord Espy to smell your breath. Has the pain driven you stark-staring mad? Or are you deliberately trying to drive *me* so?" She didn't wait for his answer, but instead propped him up against the side of the coach parked beside hers. It had taken longer to reach her coach, but Miranda was glad her carriage was parked at the end of the long line. It meant that she and Daniel could leave quietly without waiting for a hundred other vehicles to make way, and it was one of the few advantages to knowing she had come without the duchess's invitation. "Here. Rest a moment while I get Ned to help you."

"Who's Ned?" Daniel demanded.

Miranda thrilled at the barest hint of jealousy she thought she heard in Daniel's voice and was tempted to announce that he was her lover. But she reluctantly settled for the truth. "My footman."

"I don't need your footman's assistance," Daniel protested, disliking the mere idea of anyone else seeing him in his current state.

"Ten minutes ago you were certain you couldn't make it without assistance."

"*Your* assistance," he replied, wearily aware that he and Miranda were doing what they did best—arguing. "No one else's."

"I'm afraid I cannot accommodate that request, Your Grace," Miranda said softly. "You may think you can do without Ned's assistance, but I happen to know differently. And in any case, I require his help even if you do not." She knocked on the side of her coach and gestured for her footman.

Embarrassed by his selfish disregard for the discomfort he'd put her through, Daniel reached out a hand and caressed

Miranda's face with surprising tenderness. "Forgive me," he said, before bending close enough to press his lips against her forehead.

Enjoying the feel of Daniel's cool lips on her face and the brush of his breath against her hair, Miranda gave in to desire and leaned against him just as Ned alighted from the coach. Tripping over her feet in her haste to put some distance between them before her footman caught them in an intimate embrace, she stepped away from Daniel and the temptation he offered. "My lady, what happened? Are you all right?" Her footman's eyes were round as saucers when he caught sight of her dress.

"I'm fine, Ned," Miranda assured him.

"But your gown . . ."

"An unexpected nosebleed," Miranda prevaricated. "I'm quite recovered, but His Grace is not quite the pink." She wrapped her arm around Daniel's waist. "Please help me assist him into the coach."

Miranda's assessment of his condition was an understatement. His Grace *wasn't* quite the pink. He wasn't anywhere *near* the pink. Whatever and wherever that was. Daniel sucked in a breath, releasing it in a slow, painful hiss as Miranda and her footman boosted him into the coach. If he had to compare himself to a color, he could only surmise that he was closer to ash gray than to pink. And becoming more ashen with every passing moment.

"Mind his side!" Miranda warned, releasing her hold on Daniel in order to hurry around the rear of the coach to the door on the opposite side. Hiking up her skirts, Miranda climbed into the coach. "You push and I'll pull," she ordered, as she and Ned worked to get Daniel onto the bench.

Daniel groaned, unable to fully appreciate the sight of Miranda baring her lace-trimmed chemise and drawers as she scrambled over his legs and released the curtain covering the window before propping him up against it, angling his body so he could extend his legs. "You might try helping a bit," she suggested as she climbed back over him in order to lift his legs onto the opposite seat.

Daniel closed his eyes and rolled his head from side to side against the velvet-covered squabs. "Can't," he said. "I'm all done in."

Miranda lifted his legs onto the opposite seat, then settled on the bench beside him and gestured for Ned to close the door.

"Where to, my lady?" the footman asked, ready to relay her directions to Rupert, the driver.

Miranda glanced at Daniel. "Daniel?"

He grunted in reply.

"Where do you want to go?"

"Away from here," he muttered. "Someplace far away from prying eyes."

"Haversham House?" Miranda asked, suggesting Daniel's country house in Northamptonshire.

He rolled his head from side to side once again. "Too far," he breathed. "Can't leave town."

Miranda shook her head at the irony. They were sitting in a coach on the street beside Sussex House—*his* house—trying to decide where he could go to rest and recover in private. "I think we should simply drive around back and carry you up to your apartments."

"No."

Miranda frowned, then pursed her lips and tapped them with the pad of her index finger. "Well," she drawled, glancing up at him from beneath her lashes. "I could take you home to Mother, but that would mean announcing our nuptials in all the papers on the morrow and . . ."

His eyelids weighed a ton, but Daniel managed to open them long enough to look at her.

"I didn't think so," she said softly.

"It's not you," he whispered. "It's me. Any man would . . ."

Miranda held up her hand to stop his words. She knew what he was going to say before he said it. Any man would be honored to marry her. . . . Any man would be glad to share his name with her in exchange for a share in her fortune. . . . Any man would be pleased to have such a big, healthy woman bear his children. . . .

Any man except the ninth Duke of Sussex.

But knowing he wasn't in the market for a duchess didn't make his rejection any easier to bear. She understood his reluctance to relinquish his freedom, understood that he was quite satisfied with the status quo. She knew his rejection wasn't personal. Her *head* knew his rejection wasn't personal. Her tender heart felt differently. Miranda wasn't surprised to learn that Daniel hadn't changed his mind about marriage. What surprised her was how much the knowledge pained her and how much she'd wanted to hear otherwise. She sighed. How long would she continue to wear her heart on her sleeve for him? And how long would he continue to pretend he couldn't see it? "Yes, Your Grace, I know," she said wearily. "I'm perfect and you're a perfect ass."

Miranda's footman gasped at her audacity in calling the duke an ass.

"Don't worry, Ned," she assured her employee. "I'm not spilling state secrets, and His Grace doesn't take offense at the truth. His Grace knows he's a perfect ass. He works quite hard to retain the title."

Daniel couldn't muster the energy to reply. The best he could manage was the faint curving of his lips.

The heavy mist that had hung in the air for the past quarter hour had dissolved into a steady rain. Miranda bit her lip to keep her teeth from chattering as the cool damp of the night air penetrated the silk of her gown. She rubbed her hands up and down her arms to warm them, then leaned close to Daniel—close enough to notice that it took a great deal of effort for him to respond and that despite the chill in the air, beads of perspiration continued to dot his brow and his upper lip. "So, we stay in town. What's it to be, Your Grace? Shall I drop you off at Griff and Alyssa's? Or at Colin and Gillian's?" She named the most logical choices, for she knew Griffin Abernathy, the first Duke of Avon, and Colin McElreath, Viscount Grantham, were attending the Duchess's party with their wives—or, she knew Griff and Alyssa were attending, and Miranda assumed Lord and Lady Grantham were there as well—for the couples had become close friends, and the Duchess of Sussex's gala was the most coveted invitation of the season. It seemed unlikely that anyone who received an invitation would choose *not* to attend, except Jarrod, Marquess of Shepherdston, of course. And he was known for refusing coveted invitations, preferring to keep a healthy distance between himself and society mothers hoping to snare a wealthy marquess.

"No."

"Why not?" she asked. "You have to go somewhere, Daniel. You can't hide in my coach all night."

Daniel knew Miranda was right. He should go to one of his fellow Free Fellows' houses. But he was reluctant to do so. Despite the fact that he despised boats, Daniel thrilled in anticipation at the thought of another mission, and Jarrod had made no secret of the fact that he hated sending Daniel out on them. Sitting dukes were rather scarce, and the Crown and the ton took note of the Duke of Sussex's comings and goings. They would be sure to notice his absence from town at the height of the season—especially if he failed to appear at the major events. Which was the primary reason he'd nearly killed himself racing back to town in time for his mother's gala. If Jarrod discovered he'd been seriously injured, Daniel's participation in the smuggling runs would be curtailed and he'd be reduced to arranging and financing the missions from the safety of his Sussex House study instead. And all the time he'd spent sailing and rowing in order to learn to control the violent heaving of his stomach he suffered whenever he set foot on a boat would be for naught. Of course, he'd never have to set foot in a boat again. But to be relegated to the role of onlooker once again would be intolerable.

It would be so much simpler if he could tell Miranda about the League. . . .

But he was sworn to secrecy—even from her. He didn't believe for a second that Miranda would ever betray him, especially since she was risking almost as much as he was by putting her reputation in jeopardy in order to help him. But one slip of the tongue—one word about his clandestine activities to the wrong person—and the work of the League would be in grave danger.

But keeping her in ignorance was going to be a problem. . . .

Miranda had known him too long and too well to be put off by trifling excuses. He trusted Miranda more than he'd ever trusted any woman, and he knew she cared about him. She'd never made any secret of the fact that she'd been terribly hurt when he'd abruptly ended his courtship of her.

If only there were a way to ensure that he and Miranda would remain on the best of terms . . . A way to protect her as well as himself . . . If only there were something he could do . . . Some way to ensure that Miranda's guilty knowledge of his injury wouldn't do either one of them any harm . . .

If only . . .

Daniel suddenly recalled the look on Miranda's face when she'd told him, "that would mean announcing our nuptials in all the papers on the morrow." Recalled the way she'd looked when she'd read the expression on his face and confirmed it. "I didn't think so."

There *was* a way. A way that offered them the protection they would need if anyone learned his secret.

No matter that it wasn't his first choice—it was the best one. For Miranda deserved all the protection he could give her.

His friends and the work of the league deserved all the protection he could give them.

"Bloody hell!" His whisky-soaked brain latched onto

the idea and refused to let go. He could give Miranda what she wanted and protect himself at the same time.

"Daniel, what is it? What's wrong?"

"Everything," he said. "But it's going to be all right." He gave Miranda a drunken smile. "Everything is going to be all right."

She did her best to return his smile and almost succeeded. "Are you certain?"

Daniel didn't trust himself to speak, so he nodded his head instead.

"Have you decided where you want to go?"

"Number Four St. Michael's Square."

"Number Four?" Miranda frowned. "That's . . ."

Daniel nodded. "St. Michael's Palace." He had been christened at St. Michael's Church, which stood beside the palace. It was the church to which he belonged and the church to which the dukes of Sussex had been patrons for as long as anyone could remember.

Miranda reached out and placed her hand on his forehead. "You're feverish. You need a doctor. I think I should take you to hospital."

Daniel opened his eyes. "No hospital. No doctor. Just the Bishop Manwaring and you."

Miranda's mouth formed a perfect "O" of surprise. "You're foxed, Daniel. Very foxed. You don't know what you're saying or what you're doing."

"I am foxed," Daniel agreed. "Very foxed. But I know what I'm saying and I know what I'm doing."

Miranda shivered involuntarily, and her voice quavered when she whispered, "Please, Daniel, don't." She bit her bottom lip and looked down at her hands, tightly clasped in her lap. "Don't make things worse than they already are."

"Worse?" He winced. "How can making things right make anything worse?"

"I became an object of pity and the ton's perpetual bridesmaid when you ended our last courtship so abruptly. If word of this got out, it would be far worse. And it isn't something you can take back, so please, don't say it unless you mean it."

"Marry me," he said. "Now."

Miranda shook her head. "You won't remember this in the sober light of morning," she warned.

"I'll remember."

"If you do," she predicted, "it will be with regret."

Daniel looked her in the eye. "I promise I'll have no regrets unless I read about it in tomorrow's papers," he told her. "I want you to marry me."

"Tonight?"

He nodded. "And it must remain a secret for a while."

"How long?" she asked.

"I don't know," he answered.

Miranda was afraid to hope. Afraid to dream. Afraid to believe he might really mean it. "Why?"

"Why?" he echoed.

She nodded. "Why do you want to marry me?"

Daniel hesitated, debating whether to tell her the truth or the fairy tale. The truth was that he'd always felt badly about ending their first courtship and reducing her to an object of pity in the circle in which they moved. The truth was that as a gentleman, he was expected to sacrifice himself upon the matrimonial altar in order to preserve her good name and reputation since he'd been the man who'd recklessly jeopardized them. Not just tonight, but once before.

The truth was that marrying her immediately offered privacy and protection for both of them. A wife could not be compelled to bear witness against her husband if the nature of his injury or the reason for it became known. But the truth was calculating and not the least bit romantic, so Daniel opted for the fairy tale. "I thought all young ladies dreamed of eloping with a duke."

"And I thought you'd learned better when Alyssa Carrollton chose Griffin Abernathy over you."

"Alyssa was the exception," he admitted. "She didn't want to be a duchess."

The irony, of course, was that Alyssa had chosen a viscount over a duke, only to have her viscount elevated to the rank of duke when he returned from war a national hero. "She's perfectly happy as Griff's duchess," Miranda reminded him. "She didn't want to be *yours*."

"What about you, Miranda?" he whispered suggestively. "Can you honestly say the same?"

She couldn't. And Daniel knew it.

"What's the matter?" he asked. "Cat got your sharp little tongue?"

"When did you become so cruel?" Miranda asked.

"I'm not being cruel." He reached inside his jacket, fumbling to get his hand in one of the inner pockets. "I'm offering you your heart's desire."

Miranda watched as Daniel produced his pewter flask, uncapped it, took a long swallow, then laid the flask aside. "I'm sure the bishop will sell us a special license. Think about it, Miranda. I've decided to take a duchess. Now. Tonight." He paused, collecting his thoughts, cringing even as he spoke them. "Wouldn't you like to be a bride? Or are you content to walk down the aisle at season's end as someone else's bridesmaid?"

She looked over at Ned. "Take us to Number Four St. Michael's Square."

Chapter 5

*"Where love is, no disguise can hide it for long;
Where it is not, none can stimulate it."*

—François, Duc de La Rochefoucauld, 1613–1680

Rupert pulled the coach to a halt in front of Number Four St. Michael's Square a little past midnight. The bishop's residence was called a palace, but it wasn't appreciably larger than any of the other houses fronting the square. It was a stately red brick house that had housed the bishops of St. Michael's for over a century. The other houses on the square were dark and quiet, and the streets around and behind it were empty of vehicles and pedestrians.

It was, Miranda had to admit, the perfect setting for a secret wedding, even if it wasn't the wedding of her dreams. She waited in the coach with Daniel as Ned hurried up the walk to ring the bell, rouse the bishop, and bring him to the coach.

"Aren't we going in?" Miranda asked.

Daniel lifted the leather curtain and looked out the window of the vehicle. He gauged the distance between the street and the front door, counted the number of steps, and then slowly shook his head. " 'Fraid not. I don't think I can make it inside under my own power, and I refuse to be carried inside. I don't intend to give Bishop Manwaring a reason to refuse us a license."

"What reason could he have?"

"Coercion," Daniel replied, slurring the word ever so slightly.

"Of whom? You or me?"

Daniel's attempt at a smile turned into a grimace as he shifted his weight on the seat, trying to find a more comfortable position. "I'm the only one sporting a wound."

"I can see it in the papers now," Miranda said. "Mad Marchioness Wounds Dashing Duke in Desperate Bid to Force Him to Wed."

"Pray we don't see it in the papers," Daniel managed. "Since scandal is what we're hoping to avoid."

Miranda smoothed the wrinkles from the front of her bloodstained silk dress. "That's not all we're trying to avoid. Is it, Daniel?"

"I'm doing my damnedest to avoid the grim reaper. . . ." He gave her a ghost of his usual charming smile, and Miranda suddenly realized just how weak he was. "And avoiding both our mothers is an equally challenging and worthy goal."

"I understand why you want to avoid your mother," Miranda told him. "But I don't know why you want to avoid mine. *My* mother is warm and welcoming and approves wholeheartedly of you."

"Most mothers approve of me, my dear marchioness," he drawled. "I'm a duke."

"Cumberland's a duke," Miranda reminded him. "And Mother despises him."

"Your mother is a paragon of good judgment," he conceded. "Unlike mine, whose taste in all things fashionable is unparalleled, but whose ability to judge character is questionable at best."

"Her Grace is an excellent judge of character," Miranda disagreed. "That's why she doesn't like me."

Daniel pretended to be shocked. "Are you saying you've no character, Lady Miranda?"

"I'm saying I've too much character and that your

mother wishes I had less." Miranda sighed. "She only wants what's best for you, and she believes that a beautiful, petite, malleable young bride is the best choice."

"Like I said, my mother's ability to judge character is questionable at best, especially if she believes that that sort of girl is what I require in a duchess. It's what *she* requires, not I." He paused to press his arm against the wound in his side. "Fortunately, I have the final say."

"Yes, and think how delighted Her Grace is going to be when she learns of your choice."

"You're more than equal to the task of managing my mother," Daniel told her.

"Let's hope so," Miranda breathed, peeking through the curtain in time to see Ned holding an umbrella above the head of a hastily dressed clergyman wearing a nightcap and carrying his prayer book, Bible, and what looked to be the parish register beneath his arm, down the walkway to the coach. "You've a moment left to change your mind," she told him. "Are you certain this is what you want to do?"

Daniel took a deep breath—as deep as was possible with his ribs tightly bound—then slowly exhaled. "It's hardly the way I envisioned it, but after rousting the bishop from his warm bed, I dare not back out now."

It wasn't the way she'd envisioned her wedding, either. She'd never expected to be married inside a coach instead of a chapel, during a spring downpour, or with a footman and a coachman as attendants. But it was a legal wedding with the groom of her choice, and Miranda seized the moment.

The rain poured from the sky in torrents, pummeling the roof of the coach with such force that the bishop nearly had to shout to be heard when he opened the door of the coach, leaned inside, and greeted Daniel. "Is that you, Your Grace?" The clergyman peered into the interior of the coach.

"Yes, My Lord," Daniel answered.

"Your footman says you have need of me."

"Indeed, I do, Bishop Manwaring."

"How might I be of service?"

"I wish to marry the lady," Daniel announced. "And she has graciously agreed."

"You wish to marry tonight, Your Grace?" the bishop asked.

"Of course," Daniel replied in a conspiratorial tone. "I've waited a long time for her to accept. I'm not about to let her get away again."

The bishop grinned. "Most sensible of you, Your Grace. For in the world in which we live, true love is a rare and precious thing."

Tears welled up in the corners of Miranda's eyes. Daniel could be an ass, but his moments of gallantry made up for it. Her spur-of-the-moment wedding wasn't the stuff of romantic dreams, but the bishop would never know it.

"Won't you come inside out of the weather, Your Grace?" Bishop Manwaring offered, gesturing toward the church.

"Thank you, but no, My Lord, I prefer that you marry us here." Daniel smiled. One of the first things he'd learned when he inherited the title from his father was that men of lower rank almost never questioned a duke's requests, no matter how odd the request might be. "In the coach. If that's agreeable to you," he added as a courtesy. "For the lady and I prefer to avoid the rain and continue our journey in dry comfort."

"Yes, of course, Your Grace," Bishop Manwaring agreed.

"We will, of course, require a special license," Daniel said.

"Have you ever previously applied for a special license, Your Grace?" the bishop asked.

Daniel glanced at Miranda. "No."

"Are there any impediments to the marriage, Your Grace?"

"No," Daniel answered. "And I will send my man of business around with sworn statements at a later date."

The bishop nodded. "As I am empowered to represent His Grace, the Archbishop of Canterbury, here and at his offices in Lambeth Palace and Doctor's Commons, I've everything we need to make the application and issue the license."

"Then climb aboard," Daniel invited, clenching his teeth to keep from groaning at the jolt of pain that shot through him when the vehicle shifted beneath the clergyman's weight.

Miranda smiled nervously and offered her hand to the bishop in greeting as he climbed inside the coach and settled on the opposite seat.

Ned moved to close the door behind the bishop, but the clergyman stopped him. "We'll require two witnesses. I alerted my wife and the curate when your man rang the bell. They're available," he continued. "If you'll go back to the house and tell them we require them."

Ned looked to Miranda for direction.

She nodded.

"I'll fetch them straightaway, miss."

Her footman was as good as his word, and moments later he returned with Lady Manwaring and the curate, who joined them inside the vehicle.

Miranda sat between Daniel and the curate on one seat, while the bishop and Lady Manwaring occupied the other.

Lady Manwaring gave Bishop Manwaring plenty of room as the minister opened his prayer book and began to recite. "Dearly beloved, we are gathered together here in the sight of God, and in the face of these witnesses, to join together this Man and this Woman in holy Matrimony. . . ."

Daniel did his best to concentrate on the bishop's words rather than the pain of his wound, his lightheadedness, and the blood steadily seeping through his bandage, shirt, and waistcoat. He wasn't an overly religious man, but Daniel said a prayer of thanks that the lamps in the coach illuminated enough of the area around the bishop to allow him to read from his prayer book, but left sufficient shadows to conceal the fact that he was injured and bleeding and very intoxicated.

"Daniel, ninth Duke of Sussex, wilt thou have this Woman to thy wedded wife, to live together after God's ordinance in the holy estate of Matrimony? Wilt thou love her, comfort her, honor, and keep her in sickness and in health; and, forsaking all others, keep thee only unto her, so long as ye both shall live?"

Daniel didn't answer, and after waiting longer than usual for the nervous bridegroom to answer, Bishop Manwaring took the liberty of prompting him. After all, a man didn't roust a clergyman out of bed in the wee hours of the morning in order to perform a wedding unless the gentleman truly wanted to get married. "Your Grace, it's time to answer. Wilt thou have this young woman to wife?"

He took his time, but Daniel finally answered in a voice that sounded strong and determined. "Yes."

Miranda and the minister both breathed sighs of relief. He might not mean it. He might not want to marry—and Miranda knew in her heart that he didn't—but he sounded as if he did. She forgave his momentary hesitation. She alone knew how deep into his cups Daniel was, and how weak, and why. She understood how hard it must be for him to ignore his pain and concentrate on what was happening.

Miranda looked over at him and recognized the firm resolve on his face. *He meant it,* she realized. He hadn't wanted to marry, but he was willing to make her his duchess in order to shield her from the scandal he'd unwittingly brought to her door. And Miranda was grateful. She would have gladly endured any amount of scandal to protect Daniel, but she was relieved to know she wouldn't have to. *She* knew he didn't love her. She knew he didn't want to marry her or anyone else. He'd told her so only a short time before he'd suddenly proposed that she marry him.

Miranda was under no illusion about Daniel's feelings for her. She hoped Daniel might eventually fall in love with her, but she realized he might never learn to feel anything more than fondness and admiration for her. But he was giving himself to her before God and witnesses and offering her the opportunity to be a bride instead of a bridesmaid. Successful marriages had been built on much less.

Daniel didn't love her, but he liked her. He didn't trust easily, but he trusted her. And he believed she was a better choice for his duchess than any of the young beauties his mother had tried to foist upon him.

She was going to be his duchess, and he was going to be her husband. For as long as they lived. And, God willing, that would be a very long time. Time enough for Miranda to learn to be the kind of wife Daniel deserved.

"My lady . . ." The bishop looked at Daniel and waited for the duke to supply the name of his intended.

But Daniel hadn't been to enough weddings to know what came next. Miranda, on the other hand, had served as a bridesmaid on more occasions than she cared to count. She'd attended so many weddings and had heard the marriage vows so often she could recite them by heart. She looked at Daniel as she gave the bishop her name. "Miranda, fifth Marquess of St. Germaine."

Bishop Manwaring widened his eyes in surprise as he recognized the name and the title. "Lady Miranda, wilt thou have this Man to thy wedded husband, to live together after God's ordinance in the holy estate of Matrimony? Wilt thou obey him. . . ."

Miranda glanced at the bishop. "I can't promise to obey him," she admitted honestly. "But I promise I will try."

The bishop struggled to keep from laughing. In all the years he'd been married, his wife had never given him the blind obedience she'd promised. And in all the years he'd been performing marriages, he had never had a single young woman admit to doubting her ability to obey her husband. But Bishop Manwaring supposed that was to be expected from a marchioness in her own right. He shook his head. At least His Grace knew what he was getting. "Fair enough. Now, where was I?"

"Wilt thou serve . . ." Miranda prompted.

"Ah, yes," the reverend continued, "wilt thou serve him,

love, honor, and keep him in sickness and in health; and forsaking all others, keep thee only unto him, so long as ye both shall live?"

"I will," Miranda answered solemnly.

Bishop Manwaring turned back to Daniel and asked him to repeat the vows, then did the same to Miranda. And when they'd finished repeating vows and making promises, the minister asked for the ring.

"Have you a ring, Your Grace?"

He didn't—not for Miranda—but he'd worn a gold ring on his right hand since he'd inherited the dukedom. Daniel tugged his gold signet ring off his finger, then looked up at Miranda. "This will have to do for now."

Miranda bit her bottom lip, then gave a slight nod.

"Place the ring on the third finger of her left hand, Your Grace, and repeat after me." Bishop Manwaring waited until Daniel did as he'd instructed. "With this ring I thee wed, with my body I thee worship, and with all my worldly goods I thee endow: in the name of the Father, and of the Son, and of the Holy Ghost. Amen."

Daniel repeated the solemn promise, then slipped the ring bearing his ducal crest onto Miranda's gloved finger.

The ring was heavy, and she automatically closed her fist to keep it from sliding off.

"Those whom God had joined together let no man put asunder," the minister continued. "I now pronounce you husband and wife." He looked at Daniel. "You may kiss your bride, Your Grace."

Miranda kept her fist closed around Daniel's signet ring, clutching it against her heart as she turned her face up to receive his kiss—their first kiss as husband and wife. But Daniel barely brushed the corner of her mouth with his. She gave a little sigh and put away her disappointment. Her wedding barely qualified as a ceremony, and Daniel's brush of her lips barely qualified as a kiss. Both were in perfect accord.

Bishop Manwaring took out his pen and ink, and the

special license with the dispensation from the Archbishop of Canterbury allowing the purchaser to wed at any time or place and issued it to Daniel, ninth Duke of Sussex. The bishop wrote in Miranda's name, and after signing his name with a flourish and affixing his seal of office, he offered the pen to Daniel to sign the parish register.

Daniel made no move to take the pen. "I've no wish to have our marriage made public just yet."

Bishop Manwaring nodded. "I gathered that this was a secret wedding."

"For the moment," Daniel said. "Although we wanted very much to marry, this is not the opportune time to reveal it."

"I see." The reverend looked from the Duke of Sussex to his new duchess. "Rest assured, Your Grace, that the wedding is legal even if it is not recorded. Your special license will bear proof of it. But the church encourages all of its parishioners to record the important events of their lives in as timely a manner as possible."

"How timely?" Miranda asked quietly.

"Before a month has passed."

She looked at Daniel. "We shall do our best to return to sign the register within thirty days, shan't we, Your Grace?"

Daniel gave the bishop a quick nod and reached into his jacket, rummaging through his pockets.

Miranda feared Daniel was reaching for his flask, and was enormously relieved to see him produce his purse. He opened it, shook out several gold and silver coins, and handed them to the bishop. "For the license and your trouble, My Lord."

"You need only pay for the license, Your Grace. You already have my discretion. Your patronage of St. Michael's through the years has always been most generous." He held out his hand, offering to return the coins Daniel had given him.

Daniel frowned. He couldn't think what to do, and he'd

always prided himself on handling awkward situations with more aplomb.

Miranda came to his rescue. "Please, accept it," she told him. "You've done us a very great favor, My Lord, and His Grace and I would like you to use this money wherever it will do the most good, as a way of sharing our good fortune."

"I'd be delighted, Your Grace," Bishop Manwaring said, taking Miranda's hand and patting the back of it. "And may I be the first to wish you happiness on your nuptials?"

Miranda blinked in surprise. *Your Grace.* For better or for worse, she had just become Daniel's duchess.

Chapter 6

"The better part of valor is discretion; in the which better part I have saved my life."

—William Shakespeare, 1564–1616

"Where to, miss . . . ma'am?" Ned asked, returning to the coach after escorting the bishop and Lady Manwaring back to the palace.

"I don't know." Miranda looked down at Daniel's ring on her finger, then slowly slipped it off and turned to hand it to her new husband. "Daniel, where do you want to go now? Daniel?" Miranda leaned closer, and her voice took on an edge of panic when Daniel failed to respond. "Daniel?" Miranda opened the reticule looped around her wrist and dropped Daniel's ducal signet inside for safekeeping, then placed her hands on his shoulders, and gave him a gentle shake.

"Promise . . ." Daniel whispered.

Miranda leaned close to hear him. "Promise what?"

"Me." Daniel closed his eyes once again and gave a heavy sigh.

"Daniel Sussex! Don't you dare die on me!"

"He's not dead, miss," Ned said softly. "He's just passed out."

"Well, fine," Miranda replied a bit more sharply than she intended, now that she knew Daniel hadn't expired on her.

Now that she knew he hadn't made her a widow before she became a wife. Now that she knew he'd passed out from pain, or loss of blood, or too much Scots whisky. Now that she knew Daniel had placed her on the horns of a dilemma and left her to sort out the problem and find a solution. "What am I supposed to do now? We may have exchanged wedding vows, but as long as it's a secret, I've nowhere to take him that doesn't require an explanation except back to his home at Sussex House, and I gave him my word that I wouldn't do that." Leaning close enough to feel his shallow breath, Miranda caressed his cheek with her hand and muttered, "Some wedding this has turned out to be. It would serve you right if I took you home to *my* mother and let you explain all of this. How would you like that, Your Grace?"

Miranda had no intention of doing either, but venting her spleen on him made her feel much better—especially when she knew there wasn't a thing Daniel could do or say about it. She turned to Ned.

"Do you think you could gain entrance and locate the Duke of Avon, or Lords Grantham, Shepherdston, or Barclay, if we returned to Sussex House?"

"Shepherdston's not there."

"Oh?" Miranda didn't bother to hide her surprise. "How did you know that?"

Ned took a deep breath. "Begging your pardon, milady, uh, Your Grace . . ."

"Milady will do fine, Ned," Miranda told him. "You were witness to the ceremony that made me the duchess, but I shall be known as the Marchioness of St. Germaine until His Grace decides otherwise."

"Yes, ma'am." Ned gave a little bow. "After you presented your invitation and entered the house, I overheard one of the duchess's footmen say something about the Marquess of Shepherdston *not* attending even though Her Grace had invited him, and the Marchioness of St. Germaine attending even though Her Grace had not invited her."

Miranda blinked at the stinging indictment. "Do you think you could slip inside Sussex House and find the Duke of Avon or Lords Grantham or Barclay?"

"On any other night, perhaps, but not tonight. Not in this livery." He glanced down at the distinctive St. Germaine livery. "I won't make it past the front door unless I can find another footman willing to exchange livery with me or go in my stead."

"No one can go in your stead," Miranda said firmly. "It has to be you. I don't trust anyone else."

"I'm willing to try if that's what you want, milady."

Miranda chewed her bottom lip. Daniel had asked for her help, and he trusted her to do the right thing by him. Finding a footman willing to exchange livery with Ned could take precious time. Perhaps it was just as well because she wasn't sure Daniel could spare it. She pressed her hand against the front of Daniel's waistcoat. It was saturated with blood, but the fresh flow appeared to have slowed. "I *want* to get His Grace out of the night air and into a warm, soft bed," she said. "Unfortunately, I have no idea where to take him." She sat back against the cushions and worried her bottom lip with her teeth. Where could she take her new husband so that no one would know he was foxed and injured or newly married? Where in London was there such a place? *Of course*. "The house on Curzon Street." She looked at Ned. "Can we get to Curzon Street from here?"

Ned thought for a moment. "We'll have to turn around and make our way through Reeves mews, but we can do it."

Miranda had owned the house on Curzon Street for years, but she hadn't realized she owned it until six months ago, when her solicitor had turned over a box of papers that her father, the late Marquess of St. Germaine, had instructed him to release on the fifth anniversary of his death.

The deed to the house had been among a bundle of deeds to various London rental properties the late marquess had owned.

Reading the papers, Miranda had learned that her father had begun purchasing desirable properties in and around London soon after inheriting the title of Marquess of St. Germaine. Most of the properties had been parts of estates purchased from gentlemen down on their luck. Some he leased back to the original owners for a nominal fee. Others he kept for their income-producing abilities.

Her father's letter explained the significance of the properties and the fact that he'd kept them separate from the other St. Germaine holdings as a form of insurance for Miranda for five years. If she proved to be a good steward of her inheritance and an asset to the title, these properties would insure the growth of her personal wealth. If she proved to be a poor manager of her wealth and title, these properties could be liquidated and used to sustain her position in society in order to protect the entailed St. Germaine lands that could not be sold and could only pass through her to her heir.

The Marquess of St. Germaine had left it to his faithful solicitor to determine whether Miranda should be trusted with the management of the additional properties. And he'd given his solicitor five years in which to observe her.

Fortunately, Miranda had proven to be her father's daughter. She was an excellent businesswoman who saw herself as guardian of the wealth and position she had inherited. When Mr. Thompson, her solicitor, turned the box over to her, Miranda was pleasantly surprised to learn she owned quite a few London properties, including several buildings leased by foreign governments and used as embassies.

She also owned a block of lucrative dockside warehouses, along with several town homes in highly desirable addresses including the villa built by architect John Nash in Regent's Park into which she and her mother were preparing to move, and the town house on Curzon Street.

The house on Curzon Street intrigued Miranda from the start because her father had purchased it to house his mistress—a mistress who had been pensioned off at his death and who had since moved on to another protector.

The fact that he had had a mistress hadn't come as a great surprise to his daughter. It was a common practice among the ton. And Miranda had never doubted the sincerity of her father's affection for her mother, or for herself. The woman he kept on Curzon Street had been a longtime companion whose relationship with the marquess preceded his title and his marriage, and Miranda's father had been unusually forthcoming with her mother about the arrangement before their marriage, and with Miranda in the letter that accompanied the property deeds his solicitor had turned over to her following his death.

And when, after reading her father's letter, Miranda had broached the subject with her mother, Lady St. Germaine had been equally forthcoming in explaining her feelings about her marriage and her late husband's mistress. "I never asked her name," she revealed. "Nor where she lived, because I didn't want to know it. I knew what I needed to know—all I wanted to know. She was much older than I. She was a governess until she married an army officer. He was killed in service to the crown, and she and your father struck up a friendship. They shared common interests. He was very fond of her, but he kept that part of his life separate from the life he shared with me. I wasn't a threat to their friendship, and she wasn't a threat to our marriage." She looked at Miranda. "In truth, I was relieved when I conceived and gave birth to you, for it meant your father and I no longer had to share the marriage bed."

Miranda remembered gasping at her mother's blunt reply, but Lady St. Germaine had overlooked it. "You must remember, my dear, that I was a girl of seven and ten married to a man of two and forty. And while I've been assured that there are delights to be found in the marriage bed, your father and I found it rather awkward and messy and embarrassing. Fortunately, the letters patent of the St. Germaine Marquessate allow the oldest legitimate offspring—male or female—to inherit the title. Your father knew this, of course, and promised that once I conceived and delivered a child, he would seek satisfaction elsewhere and that I might do the same."

Miranda had blurted out the obvious question. "Did you?"

Lady St. Germaine had given her daughter a mysterious smile. "I've enjoyed a flirtation or two over the years, but I prefer to do without the pawing and prodding that accompanies intimate relations." She reached over and patted Miranda's hand. "That's not to say you'll feel the same way about it. I suspect it's quite different with a man your own age and one with whom you're madly, passionately in love."

"You didn't love Papa?"

"I grew to love him very much," Lady St. Germaine answered. "But I was never in love with him—at least not in the way the poets describe. Our marriage was arranged. Your father was forty when he inherited the title from his older brother. As the new marquess, he required a bride of childbearing age. He saw me at Lady Shackleford's musicale and approached my papa. Papa was only a viscount, so he was quite pleased that a marquess had offered for me and overjoyed by the opportunity to add to the family coffers." She smiled. "I, of course, was in love with the idea of becoming a marchioness. It was a good match, and we rubbed along quite well together. And there was never any doubt that your father was quite fond of me or that he adored you. I was very proud to be his wife. I never regretted marrying him or gave him any reason to regret marrying me. When he returned to his lady friend's bed after you were born, he did so with my blessing and my gratitude."

In the house on Curzon Street. Miranda looked at her footman. The house on Curzon Street was closed, and since Miranda had never been there, she had no way of knowing whether they could gain entry without waking the neighborhood, but she was willing to try. "Tell Rupert to reverse direction and make our way to Curzon Street while I try to figure out how to get in."

"That's easy, milady," Ned said with a grin, reaching into his coat pocket and producing a ring of keys. "Yesterday was cleaning day," he replied. "Mr. Hawkins gave me the keys to the house so I could admit the cleaning crew. I neglected to return them."

Miranda shook her head in wonder, amazed that she had been so preoccupied with looking her very best for the duchess's party and preparing for her next encounter with the duchess's son that she'd completely forgotten she'd instructed her man of business to send Ned to attend to the scheduled cleaning of the house. "Thank heavens you did," she said. "Or we would have had to return home to get them, and that would involve more time and more explanations than I'm prepared to make."

"I understand, miss." Ned nodded before turning to relay her instructions to Rupert.

"Oh, and Ned . . ."

"Yes, milady?"

"I'm trusting you and Rupert to keep the events of this evening a secret from everyone—including my mother."

"No need to worry, milady," Ned assured her. "Your secret is safe with us."

"Thank you, Ned."

"You're welcome, milady. I'll alert you when we reach our destination."

Ned was as good as his word. "Curzon Street, my lady," he announced some minutes later, alighting from his perch on the coach as it rolled to a stop at the rear entrance to the house. He opened the coach door and lowered the steps for Miranda, then made his way from the vehicle up the narrow walk to unlock the back door.

"Daniel, wake up. We've arrived." Miranda gave Daniel a gentle nudge.

He groaned his protest.

She nudged a little harder, then reached over and patted his face with her gloved hands. "Daniel, you must wake up. We've arrived at our destination and I cannot carry you into the house."

He opened his eyes and blinked at her, struggling to comprehend. "Not to worry, my sweet, beautiful Miranda. I'll carry you," he said, before falling face-first against her bosom.

"I'll carry him, milady," Ned told her. "If you will slide His Grace onto the floor of the coach so that I might take hold of him, I'll do my best to keep from adding to his discomfort."

"All right," Miranda agreed, shoving Daniel's legs off the opposite seat before tugging on his arm until she'd maneuvered him to the edge of the cushions. Once she got him where she wanted him, Miranda placed her shoulder against his and pushed with all her might.

Sussex rolled off the velvet cushion and landed in a crumpled heap on the floor of the vehicle.

"Very good, milady." Ned leaned into the coach and rearranged Daniel's arms and legs before hefting the duke onto his shoulders in much the same manner the butchers in Market Square hefted sides of beef and pork onto theirs.

Miranda stared transfixed at the sight of the mighty Duke of Sussex hanging upside down across the shoulders of her footman.

"If you would be so kind as to light the way, milady." Ned nodded his head toward the lantern hanging by the door of the coach.

Miranda reached up and unhooked the lantern, then stepped down from the coach and lighted the way as Ned carried Daniel into the house.

Ned provided directions as Miranda made her way

toward the stairs at the center of the house. "There are two guest chambers on the right and two on the left," he said as she left the second-floor landing and headed down the hall.

Although she owned the house, Miranda had never been inside it. But Ned, as head footman, had been inside it many times over the past six months, overseeing the maintenance.

Miranda walked past the guest chambers and headed for the door at the end of the passageway.

Ned gave a slight shake of his head. "That's the main bedchamber," he told her.

"I surmised as much," Miranda replied, opening the door. "My hus . . . His Grace is a duke. And as such, he's entitled to the best bedchamber in the house."

"But, milady, I think the duke would be more comfortable elsewhere. . . ."

"Is there a larger, better bedchamber elsewhere?"

Ned hesitated a moment before replying. "No, milady, it's the most modern and the best-equipped."

"Then he shall have the best." She shrugged her shoulders. "Besides, he's taller and he's indisposed."

"Whatever you say, milady." Ned waited until Miranda lit the bedside lamp, moved a pile of tapestry pillows out of the way, and flipped back the coverlet before depositing the Duke of Sussex on the bed. Ned was as gentle as he could possibly be, but Daniel moaned as he sank into the depths of the soft feather mattresses.

The room was cold, and Miranda shivered involuntarily as she removed Daniel's shoes and set them on the floor beneath the bed. She untied the tapes of his stockings and was about to peel them down his legs when Ned cleared his throat.

"If you'll wait outside, milady, I'll see that His Grace is settled comfortably into bed and build a fire."

Miranda took a step toward the door, then remembered Daniel's wound. Ned had seen the blood on her gown and gloves, and knew the duke was foxed and feverish and that he was sporting injured ribs, but he didn't know the nature of the injury, and although Miranda trusted her footman, she wasn't certain Daniel would approve of Ned knowing that his aching ribs were the result of having been shot. "Build the fire," she instructed. "*I'll* see His Grace is settled comfortably into bed."

Ned arched an eyebrow in disapproval as he walked over to the fireplace and lit the tinder beneath the bed of coals.

"You needn't worry about protecting my delicate sensibilities. We're married." Miranda unbuttoned her gloves, tugged them off, and laid them on the night table alongside her reticule. "And it isn't as if I haven't seen a naked man before," she reminded her footman. "I did help my mother take care of my father."

"Your father was an old man, milady," Ned replied. "His Grace is not."

"What difference does that make?" she demanded. "The anatomy is the same."

Ned stood up and brushed his hands free of dust. "I think it may make a great deal of difference to His Grace."

"Then I shall face that bridge when I come to it," Miranda pronounced, retrieving her reticule from the night table.

"If you're certain, milady."

Miranda drew in a deep breath. "I am. Thank you, Ned. You and Rupert are free to return home and retire for the night."

"But, milady, we cannot leave you here alone," Ned protested.

"I'm not alone," Miranda reminded him. Opening her reticule, she withdrew two gold guineas and handed them to her footman. "For you and Rupert."

"Thank you, miss . . . I mean, ma'am . . . but . . ."

"Don't worry, Ned. His Grace is here." She smiled at her footman, then glanced at the seven-day clock on the mantel and saw that the time had been set and that it was ticking. "Is that the correct time?"

Ned nodded. "I set it myself yesterday."

"Then go home and get some sleep. You've been at my beck and call far too long." He opened his mouth to protest, but Miranda stopped him. "I'll need you later this morning after I've checked the larder and prepared a shopping list."

"I can stay and do that, miss . . ."

"I'm perfectly safe. His Grace is my husband and an absolute gentleman." She shrugged her shoulders. "Besides, he's in no condition to tangle with me. My mother will be worried. I need you to deliver a message to her."

Ned glanced at the bed, realized his mistress was right, and gave her a deferential nod. "Very good, milady."

"When my mother inquires about my absence at breakfast tomorrow, tell her that I decided, on the spur of the moment, to spend time with an old friend." She thought for a moment. "Tell her I rode with my friend and that I sent you and Rupert home to collect enough clothes for a week's stay. It's not uncommon. I've done it before."

Miranda had done it lots of times. She'd spend almost the entire season at Abernathy Manor when Alyssa Carrollton married Griffin Abernathy shortly before he left for the Peninsula three years before. And she'd continued to make frequent visits to Abernathy Manor even after Griffin returned from war a hero and had been elevated to the title of Duke of Avon. She traveled so often that her mother complained that Miranda made a habit of running away from home. "My mother will understand. Have my lady's maid pack the necessary clothing and return here as soon after breakfast as you can. And bring food. His Grace will be hungry when he wakes up. And I'm starving."

"Yes, milady."

"And Ned," Miranda cautioned, "I want you and Rupert to come in a plain coach, without livery and without the grays." The St. Germaine stable was known for its matched gray carriage horses.

"I'll send Rupert back tonight." Her footman lifted his hand to forestall Miranda's protests to the contrary. "His

Grace is ill. You may have need of a carriage to send for a physician."

"You heard His Grace," Miranda reminded him. "No physicians."

"But you may need to send Rupert for help," Ned replied. "And he'll need a vehicle."

"Agreed." Miranda gave in. "You may send Rupert back, but remember that no one must know what happened tonight. No one must know that His Grace and I are here. Absolutely no one."

"You can rely on it, milady."

"Thank you, Ned." She looked him in the eye. "I *am* relying on it. My good name and the duke's depend upon it."

Miranda waited until Ned left the room before she resumed the task of undressing the Duke of Sussex. Miranda smiled at the thought. She had wanted to undress Daniel for years. Now he was her wedded husband, but undressing him this way wasn't quite what she'd had in mind. There was nothing romantic about tugging and pulling and lifting an unconscious man in order to remove his clothing. It was hard, heavy work, and as she tugged his superfine jacket off his shoulders and down his arms, Miranda called herself ten kinds of a fool for dismissing Ned.

Until she'd relieved Daniel of his jacket, untied his elegantly fashioned cravat, removed his black brocade waistcoat, and unfastened the black onyx studs from the front of his shirt, then, pulling his shirt from the waistband of his trousers and peeling it away from his torso and over his head. . . .

She stared transfixed by the sight of his naked chest. Ned was right. There was absolutely no comparison between a man of three score and five years and one of a score and eight.

Miranda had only seen her father's naked torso once, but she remembered it well. Growing up, Miranda had always imagined that her father's shoulders were broad and strong, but she realized that the marquess had benefited greatly from the skills of his tailor. Her father's shoulders were wide, but the muscles were long and weak. His chest was sunken and pale, and his skin felt clammy to the touch. There had been a sprinkling of gray hairs scattered across her father's chest and a ring of them around the flat, pink disks surrounding his nipples. The flesh covering his ribs and abdomen had been soft and doughy, his navel large and deep.

Daniel's naked torso was as different from her father's as night from day. His shoulders were broad and so well-muscled there was no need for padding in the seams of his jacket. His skin was a dark, golden color and appeared to be tanned by the sun, like the flesh of seamen who spent long, hot days amid the ship's rigging, or the flesh of the gypsy men who wore short vests without shirts and who sought permission to camp with their families upon her estates during their journeys across England.

Daniel's muscles rippled and bunched with his every movement, and the hair on his chest was golden brown and formed a neat, compact wedge that spanned the width of his chest and covered his dark, flat nipples. The color contrasted sharply with the strips of snow-white linen encircling his ribs and the square of linen that had been stained red by his blood.

Miranda bit her bottom lip to keep from gasping at her first glimpse of the muscle and flesh covering his ribs and his abdomen. There was nothing soft and doughy about this flesh. Daniel's abdomen was rippled with twin rows of taut muscles, his navel a mere indention bisected by the waistband of his trousers.

His was the body the Greeks and Romans had sculpted, the body of David that Michelangelo had so lovingly freed from the marble encasing it, and Miranda's heart beat a rapid staccato at the sight of it. Except for the bloodied bandage on his side and the strips of linen wrapped tightly about his ribs, Daniel's body was sheer perfection.

She had never seen anything quite as wonderful, had never dreamed that his elegantly tailored clothing had hidden such strength and beauty.

And she had never dreamed that Daniel, bleeding so profusely from a wound in his side, could still find the strength to waltz her out of a ballroom, cross a huge expanse of lawn, stop long enough to carry on a civil conversation with a fellow gentleman, then climb aboard a coach and suffer the jolting ride over the cobblestones to St. Michael's Square and get married before passing out.

Glancing at the shirt she still held gripped in her fist, Miranda saw that the tails of it were stained with his blood in front and on back. She looked at the square of linen covering the wound in his side, then at the buttons at the waistband of his trousers. The buttons beckoned to her like siren songs luring sailors onto treacherous rocks, urging her to slip them from their buttonholes in order that she might satisfy her burning curiosity and explore the flesh hidden beneath the black superfine. But Miranda chose the truest course.

Taking a deep steadying breath, she left the tight binding around his ribs intact, but quickly untied the knots in the bloody bandage and carefully peeled it off the wound.

She couldn't bite back the gasp as she stared at the tear in Daniel's side. Miranda was no expert, but even she could see that Mistress Beekins had done an excellent job of stitching his flesh together. The ball had ripped a jagged gash through the flesh of his side and along his rib cage. Miranda marveled at the other woman's skill, for there was no excess of flesh with which to work, and Mistress Beekins's stitches were uniformly neat and small. Unfortunately, lifting his arm to signal the waltz had spoiled the needlework by pulling a half dozen or so of the long line of stitches out.

A steady trickle of blood oozed through the gap in the pulled stitches, but Miranda was relieved to see that the blood flow had slowed considerably now that Daniel was no longer moving about and exerting himself. He would carry a scar once the wound healed, a scar that would forever mar the perfect display of sinew and flesh covering his torso. But the wound would heal once it was restitched. Unfortunately for Daniel, she would have to do the restitching herself, and Miranda had never exhibited a great talent for needlework.

Gritting her teeth at the thought, she replaced Daniel's bloodied bandage, then lifted the lamp from the table beside the bed and went in search of supplies. Leaving the door to the bedchamber open so she could hear if he cried out for her, Miranda hurried downstairs, retracing her steps, relieved to find that Ned had lit the lamps along the way from the upstairs bedchamber to the passageway that led to the kitchen.

The house was completely furnished and equipped with most of the personal items and amenities one would expect to find in a fashionable household. And since most fashionable households would at one time or another have need of a sickroom, Miranda prayed this one contained the items she needed in order to do the job that must be done.

Her prayers were answered when she located a tapestry sewing basket and a store of linen, including several oilcloth sheets, and, on a shelf in the housekeeper's pantry, a bar of French-milled soap. The linen smelled slightly musty from having been stored, but it was clean and serviceable, and Miranda was profoundly thankful that she wouldn't be reduced to cutting up her silk ball gown or sacrificing her silk undergarments in order to bandage Daniel's wound. Her dress was bloodstained and might be beyond salvaging, but until Ned returned, it was all she had to wear.

The sewing basket contained pins and needles, several pairs of scissors of varying sizes, and cotton, wool, and silk thread. Gathering the basket, the oilcloth sheets, and an armload of linen, Miranda deposited them on a chair near the door, where she could collect them on her way back upstairs, then carefully made her way to the kitchen. She said another prayer of thanks for Alyssa's obsession with gardening and her profound interest in creating healing salves, tinctures, and ointments, and for the fact that she recalled more than she had realized of her friend's teachings. As a result, Miranda knew exactly what she needed to reduce his pain and fever.

She found the jar of dried white willow bark among the assortment of herbs and spices in the spice cabinet in the kitchen. Miranda took a marble mortar and pestle from the shelf beside the spice cabinet, then poured a measure of willow bark into the bowl of the mortar and ground it into a fine powder, using the pestle the way Alyssa had taught her. When she finished reducing the dried bark to powder form, Miranda poured the ground willow bark into a pewter tankard, then filled a copper kettle with water from the kitchen pump. Grabbing an iron trivet from the hearth, Miranda carried the kettle, tankard, and trivet to the chair beside the housekeeper's pantry and placed them alongside the other items.

She made several trips up and down the stairs depositing the supplies she'd collected and two kettles of water, but Daniel was sleeping heavily when Miranda returned to the bedchamber with her last armload of supplies and began making preparations.

Setting the tankard on the mantel and one kettle of water on the tiled hearth, Miranda pushed the fire screen aside and placed the trivet in the fireplace as close to the smoldering coals as possible. She set the kettle atop the trivet to heat, then poured water from the second kettle into the basin on the washstand.

Clearing everything off the bedside table, Miranda draped a tablecloth from her stack of linens over it, and began laying out all the items she thought she might need—needles, thread, soap, the pewter tankard containing the powdered willow bark, and the basin of water.

Miranda spread an oilcloth on one side of the bed, topped it with another sheet, then removed Daniel's bloodied bandage and carefully rolled him onto it. Working quickly, she climbed onto the bed and finished unfolding the oilcloth and the top sheet. It took a mighty effort, but Miranda finally managed to roll Daniel back into place onto the other half of the sheet covering the oilcloth where the lamp provided sufficient light for her to work.

When she had everything in order, Miranda took several folded linen sheets from the stack she'd carried from the pantry and, taking a pair of embroidery scissors out of the sewing basket, sat down on a rocking chair beside the fire. She rocked back and forth as she worked, cutting linen into strips, rolling the strips into bandages, and fashioning larger squares for padding, while she waited for the kettle to boil.

She had torn the first bedsheet into strips and was making larger squares from a second sheet when she realized the kettle was boiling and that it was time to tackle the job at hand. Grabbing one of the folded sheets to use as a mitt, Miranda left the chair, walked over to the fireplace, and retrieved the kettle. Holding the embroidery scissors over the washbasin, she poured boiling water over them. Then she selected a gold needle from a packet and studied the assortment of threads. Silk was best, Alyssa had told her. But Miranda doubted very much whether Daniel would approve of any of the colors of silk from which she had to choose. Still, Miranda threaded the needle with silk thread, then dropped it into the basin of hot water.

"It's important to clean everything with alcohol or boiling water," Miranda recited, remembering Alyssa's insistence that in the case of open wounds or sores, rinsing medical instruments with boiling water or alcohol and washing everything thoroughly with soap and water, including the patient, made all the difference in how patients recovered. Alyssa didn't know how it worked, she only knew it worked, and that was all that mattered. "Always remember the old adage: cleanliness is next to godliness. Especially to people with cuts and open sores." Miranda carefully fished the scissors and the needle and thread out of the water with another pair of scissors and placed them on the tablecloth, then dipped a square of linen in the washbowl and reached for the bar of soap.

She lathered the cloth with soap, wrung out the excess water, and carried it to the bed where Daniel lay sleeping.

Miranda washed the blood from around Daniel's wound and off his stomach, hip, lower back, and the top of his right flank. She tried to work around the waistband of his trousers, tried to ignore the rivulets of blood that had flowed from his wound and disappeared into the mysterious region beneath his trousers, tried slipping her hand and washcloth beneath the front of his garment, but Miranda was nothing if not thorough, and since cleanliness was next to godliness, she had no choice but to slip the buttons from their buttonholes and rid Daniel of the last of his bloodstained evening attire.

Chapter 7

"A sight to dream of, not to tell!"
—*Samuel Taylor Coleridge, 1772–1834*

Seeing Daniel lying on the bed as naked as the day he was born, Miranda revised her earlier opinion of his masculine beauty.

She had been to Rome and to Florence. She had gazed upon the magnificence of Michelangelo's painting on the ceiling of the Sistine Chapel and his depiction of the Pieta. She had visited Florence and seen his statue of David standing in the Piazza Signoria.

That statue was the standard by which she measured all male beauty, and until tonight, when she'd bared Daniel's torso, she had seen nothing to compare with the beauty of the sculptured marble. And if Daniel's face and shoulders and torso equaled the magnificence of those parts of David's anatomy, his lower body far exceeded it.

Now Miranda knew without a doubt that the living, breathing, Daniel, ninth Duke of Sussex, put Michelangelo's David to shame.

She blushed to the roots of her hair as she carefully washed the blood from his body, but she soon overcame her natural reticence in order to satisfy her burning need to do what she had always hoped she might one day have the chance to do—to look upon his body and to touch him, to care for him as a wife and lover would do.

Not like this, of course. Not injured. Not hurt and suffering. But beggars could not be choosers, and Miranda willingly took whatever she could get. If this was the only way she could look upon Daniel and touch him, then she was glad to be of service, glad he trusted her with his secret. So, she took great care in the task, running the warm, soapy cloth over his body, marveling at the way it skimmed over his hard muscles. She didn't touch him where she ached to touch him, except to wipe away the rivulets of dried blood pooled in the thick patch of hair surrounding the most private part of him.

Miranda took full advantage of his injury and his unconscious state to fulfill her heart's desire, and although her conscience pained her for baring his body and greedily soaking in the sight and scent and feel of him while he slept, Miranda decided it was a small price to pay for the privilege.

She dipped the washcloth into the basin, rinsed the blood from it, and wrung it out. She couldn't delay the inevitable much longer. Daniel was as clean and godly as one woman with a washcloth, a bar of soap, and a basin of warm water could make him. And as much as she hated the idea of doing it, his wound still needed stitching. All she lacked was the courage to stab the needle and thread into the bruised and battered flesh around the wound and do what must be done.

Miranda cursed her stupidity in assembling everything she thought she might possibly need from belowstairs and forgetting the liquid courage that might stop her stomach from roiling and her hand from shaking so badly. Ale. Mead. Wine. Sherry. Brandy. Cognac. Whisky. Something. Miranda blew out a breath. She wasn't much of an imbiber, but as far as she knew, she wasn't much of a healer either. And when it came to piercing Daniel's flesh with a needle, she needed all the courage she could get. Suddenly remembering Daniel's pewter flask, Miranda set the washbasin aside and got up to retrieve it from the pocket of his jacket.

Daniel hadn't left more than a swallow or two of whisky in the container, and that was fortunate, for Miranda drank it all. Her eyes watered and she coughed as the potent liquor burned its way from her throat to her belly, but even if the flask had been full, Miranda would have drained it. She capped the flask, returned it to Daniel's coat, and took her place beside the bed, pleased beyond measure to see that her hand had stopped shaking. Seizing the moment, she picked up the needle and thread, took a deep breath, then leaned over Daniel and carefully pushed the needle through his flesh and began to sew.

If he had flinched or groaned or shown any other signs of discomfort, Miranda wouldn't have been able to continue, but Daniel slept through it all as she doggedly repaired the damage he had wrought to Mistress Beekins's neat, uniform stitching. Her stitches weren't quite as neat or uniform as Mistress Beekins's, but Miranda was pleased with the results just the same. She breathed a sigh of relief as she looped the knot in the last stitch and cut the thread. She didn't have a salve or ointment with which to doctor the wound, but Alyssa had once told her that salves and ointments weren't always necessary. So long as the wound was clean and the patient received nourishing food and plenty of sleep, the body would heal itself.

Miranda made a pad from several squares of linen, placed it over the freshly stitched wound, and tied it into place with the long strips of fabric. She unfolded a clean sheet and spread it over Daniel's lower body, then dropped to her knees beside the bed and prayed Alyssa was right.

The avalanche of tears burning her eyes and clogging her throat took her by surprise. She buried her face in the sheet beside Daniel's foot and sobbed. Miranda knew her tears were the result of her fear for Daniel and the hours of tension it had produced. She knew crying was a release of emotions held tightly in check, and Miranda thought it was a measure of just how nervous and tense Daniel could make her, for she couldn't remember the last time she'd hidden her face and wept. But knowing and understanding the reasons behind her flood of tears didn't lessen their volume or their intensity.

Miranda cried until her tears were spent, cried until her head ached, her nose was stuffed, and her eyes gritty and swollen. She cried until her knees ached and her muscles grew stiff from kneeling on the floor, then pushed herself to her feet and began the task of cleaning up the mess she'd made.

She had a long night ahead of her, for she wouldn't rest until she knew Daniel would be all right. Leaning over him, Miranda brushed her hand across his forehead. Perspiration still dotted his brow, his face was flushed, and his skin was hot to the touch. He was still feverish, but whether it was from his wound or the amount of alcohol he'd consumed Miranda couldn't say. Since she refused to wake him from his healing sleep, all she could do was put another kettle of water on to boil and wait.

"Hot."

Miranda opened her eyes and sat up in her chair as Daniel rasped out a single word.

"Here." Miranda reached for the pewter tankard of water and powdered willow bark she'd mixed while he'd slept and moved to the edge of the bed. She sat down beside him, anchoring the sheet into place at his waist, preserving his modesty as Daniel thrashed against the bed linens.

"Hot," Daniel muttered. "Too hot."

"I know," Miranda answered, shifting her position, supporting his head and shoulders as she placed the rim of the tankard against his lips. "But you must stop thrashing about the bed," she told him. "Else you'll tear your stitches once again."

"Burning."

"Drink this," she urged. "It will make you feel better."

"What?"

"Willow bark and water," she told him. "Drink it all down like a good boy and I'll cool you off with a nice sponge bath."

"No willow bark," he complained.

"Yes, willow bark," she insisted. "Alyssa says it's good for you. So drink this and I'll give you a cool, refreshing bath you'll enjoy." She bumped the tankard against his lips once again.

Daniel grimaced and tried to refuse the medicine, but Miranda gave him no choice. Tipping the tankard, she forced him to drink—or to drown.

"Good with the bad, Your Grace," she reminded him. "Dark and light. That's the way life works."

Daniel drained the tankard, then blinked up at her, his surprise at finding her beside him clearly evident. "Miranda?"

"Yes, Miranda." She set the tankard aside and eased Daniel back down on the pillows, then stood up and turned her back to him and crossed to the window. She opened the window a crack to allow the cool night air into the room, then filled the washbasin with tepid water and reached for a clean cloth.

Miranda managed to hide her disappointment when she returned to the bedside and placed the bowl on the table. She dipped the cloth in the water and wrung it out, then firmed her lips together, focused all of her attention on the center of Daniel's chest, and began gently sponging the perspiration from his upper torso. He'd been surprised to see her sitting on the bed beside him. Daniel had clearly expected someone else.

"Miranda?"

She recognized the note of urgency in his voice and looked at his face. It was a grayish green color, and the drops of perspiration on his forehead seemed to have tripled. "I'm here." She took a step toward the head of the bed.

"Sick." Daniel rolled to his side and braced himself on his elbow and forearm, hung his head over the side of the bed, and heaved the contents of his stomach all over Miranda's silk skirts.

"Blast it, Daniel!" Miranda exclaimed as she viewed the mess he had made of her dress. "First you bleed all over me and now this!" The beautiful pale green ball gown her modiste had fashioned to fit her to perfection so Miranda would be certain to catch the Duke of Sussex's eye had caught everything except his eye. She knew he couldn't help it, but that did nothing to change the fact that Daniel had bled upon it and been ill upon it, but hadn't appeared to notice how the style flattered her figure, displaying her bosom and her long legs to perfection, or how the pale green color complimented her auburn hair and made her eyes look green. Her lovely ball gown was ruined, but Miranda barely had time to mourn its destruction. She scrambled to locate the chamberpot as Daniel was ill once again.

Miranda held his head until his retching subsided, then wiped his face and neck with a cool cloth. The stench filling her nostrils nearly overpowered her. Her stomach roiled in protest, and Miranda struggled to keep from disgracing herself as she poured the water from the wash bowl into the chamber pot, then placed the lid on it and slid the pot under the bed.

She helped Daniel lie back against the pillows, then filled the tankard with warm water and offered it to him.

"No more," Daniel gasped.

"It isn't willow bark," she told him. "It's warm water. To rinse your mouth."

Daniel rinsed his mouth and spat in the basin Miranda held for him. The effort it took exhausted him. His teeth began to chatter as he lay back against the pillows. Miranda recovered the chamber pot, lifted the lid, and dumped the water from the basin into the container, covering it with the

lid and pushing it back under the bed. She pulled the single
sheet up to Daniel's chin, then unfolded the coverlet at the
foot of the bed and drew it over Daniel's torso. She tucked
the sheet and coverlet tightly around Daniel's shoulders.

"Cold," he murmured.

Miranda closed the window and crossed over to the fireplace to stir to life the coals she'd banked. One look at
Daniel told her he was suffering fever and chills in equal
measures. His eyes were closed and his teeth were chattering. Miranda's heart went out to him. She knew from her
own personal experience that as soon as he succeeded in getting warm, he'd become too warm, and as soon as he succeeded in cooling off, he'd be chilled to the bone.

Reaching up behind her, Miranda unfastened her dress,
then pushed it down over her hips, allowing it to pool
around her feet. She untied the laces of her short corset,
noting as she did so, that her corset, and the silk chemise
beneath it, were dotted with stains where Daniel's blood
had seeped through the layers of silk. Miranda pulled off
her corset, shrugged out of her chemise, rolled her stockings down her legs, and stepped out of her fine silk drawers, dismayed to find that all of her garments were stained
with vomit and reeked of stale whisky and the remnants of
Daniel's last meal.

Holding her breath, Miranda bent at the waist and bundled her clothes into a tight ball and left them on the floor.
She straightened to her full height, crossed the room, and
opened the door to the massive French armoire. She was
delighted to discover it held an assortment of nightgowns
and undergarments, until she realized that the woman who
had left them behind was half her size. Miranda held up a
delicate lawn nightgown. It was no bigger than a child's
nightdress and had probably been wore by a tiny, small-
boned, delicate sort of creature who made Miranda look
like the female version of Goliath.

Still, Miranda kept searching. It had been her father's

house. Surely, something of his had been left behind. But her search yielded nothing for her to wear.

Daniel's jacket was the least bloody of all his garments, but the cut of his formal evening attire meant that his jacket wouldn't cover any of the essentials. Neither would his waistcoat. His shirt would cover her, but having just shed her own soiled garments, Miranda was in no hurry to replace them with his bloody shirt. But his trousers were salvageable.

Since she needed something to put on to make her way downstairs, Miranda reached for them. She was only two or three inches shorter than Daniel, and because she, as he had phrased it so indelicately, "was no featherweight herself" there was a good chance that she matched him in size as well.

The thought was morbidly depressing, but she was desperate to get out of her dress, and Daniel's trousers offered a solution to her dilemma.

Taking a deep breath, Miranda stepped into Daniel's superfine evening trousers. "If they fit," she vowed, "I'll never eat another morsel as long as I live."

They didn't.

Miranda was torn between delight and consternation. Now she knew that although his trousers made him *appear* slimmer of hip, she *was* slimmer. The trousers that fit Daniel like a second skin gaped at her waist and refused to stay anchored around her hips. Turning toward the bed, Miranda gave in to a childish impulse and stuck her tongue out at Daniel. She might not be a featherweight, but she wasn't a heavyweight either. There wasn't an ounce of extra fat on her. She was exceptionally tall for a woman, and there was no denying that she possessed a generous bosom, but her stomach was flat and her hips, buttocks, and thighs were considerably slimmer than his.

And that left her with nothing to wear, unless . . . She snatched one of the two remaining sheets from the arm of the chair, wrapped it around her body, tied it into place with Daniel's cravat, then draped the tail over her shoulder in toga fashion.

After securing her toga into place, Miranda gathered her clothes and carried them out of the master bedchamber, down the stairs to the scullery.

She left her ruined clothes in a wooden washtub she found in tʰ ᵕcullery because there was nothing she could do to salᵥᵧᵤ them. Miranda possessed a number of domestic skills—more than most ladies of her station—and the fact that she had any domestic talents at all was almost entirely due to her mother and to Alyssa Abernathy. But as far as she knew, neither her mother's nor Alyssa's vast store of domestic knowledge extended as far as the washtub.

These last few hours spent taking care of Daniel had given Miranda a new appreciation for the labor her household servants performed each day in order to make her life more comfortable. She did what she could to make their lives more comfortable, too, but now Miranda realized that she hadn't done enough to compensate her employees for their labor. But that would change as soon as she returned home and resumed her life as the Marchioness of St. Germaine.

If she returned home and resumed her life as the Marchioness of St. Germaine . . . Miranda looked down at her bare left hand. She had exchanged wedding vows with Daniel last night—or rather, early this morning—and become the Duchess of Sussex, but had nothing to show for it except a ruined ball gown and a sleepless night. Not that she'd expected Daniel to have a betrothal or wedding ring in his pocket. But it would be nice to know she had a ring, even if she couldn't wear it. . . .

Leaving the scullery, Miranda hurried back upstairs, stopping long enough to search the armoires in the other bedchambers for clothing. This time, her search yielded results. She discovered a man's brocade robe and a cotton nightshirt embroidered with her father's initials in the room with the dark, oversized, masculine furniture and the floor-to-ceiling shelves filled with books. Her father's room.

She closed the armoire door, dropped the sheet, and pulled the nightshirt over her head. She inhaled deeply, hoping the nightshirt would, by some miracle, retain her father's scent, but the cotton smelled like the cedar wood used to line the armoire. Her father's distinctive bergamot and pine fragrance was long gone—if it had ever been there at all. The nightshirt and the brocade robe looked new—as if they had been ordered from Weston but never worn. The armoires in the other bedrooms were empty of clothing. The only items left in them were spare pillows and quilts.

She glanced down. He might never have worn it, but the nightshirt had been made for her father. Miranda could tell because the hem of the garment reached her knees instead of her calves. During the last years of his life, her father seemed to have shrunk and Miranda seemed to have grown a head taller. She shrugged. Her lower legs were visible, but there was no one to see them except Daniel, and he was asleep.

And Ned.

And Rupert.

Miranda grimaced. She'd forgotten that her footman and driver would be returning in a few hours. She took a deep breath. No matter. Ned and Rupert were entirely loyal to her and would never let on that there was anything untoward in her manner of dress. And it wasn't as if she had any choice. The women's clothing was much too small and far more revealing than her father's nightshirt. The nightshirt was short, but it managed to cover the essentials and was free of blood and gore—so long as she stayed away from the patient asleep in the master bedchamber.

Miranda smiled for the first time in hours. Who in the ton would ever suspect that the always elegantly dressed Duke of Sussex would prove to be such a hazard to her wardrobe? Without ever sharing her bed?

She pursed her lips in thought. Just because he had

never shared her bed didn't mean that she couldn't share his. They were the only two people in the house. And they were legally wed. No harm would be done. Why shouldn't she spend what remained of the night beside him in bed? Why shouldn't she be selfish and snatch her chance to fulfill her heart's desire? For a few hours. While he slept.

What was the harm of holding him in her arms, just once before he awoke and remembered he didn't love her?

Chapter 8

"Her gentle limbs did she undress,
And lay down in her loveliness."
—Samuel Taylor Coleridge, 1772–1834

Her bridegroom talked in his sleep.
Miranda had dreamed of lying beside Daniel in a big comfortable bed for as long as she could remember. She'd dreamed of making love with him, of him holding her in his arms, whispering in the dark, talking to each other, sharing intimate secrets. . . .

Sharing a name.

But Daniel had never seemed to share her cozy vision of domesticity. He had told her once, years before, that no matter how charming the companion or how much he enjoyed the companionship, when it came to sleeping, he preferred to sleep alone.

Miranda had been surprised by his admission and puzzled by his seeming disdain for intimacy. Daniel was a generous man, a friendly man who laughed often and seemed to enjoy the company of women.

Now she understood.

He talked in his sleep. And Daniel didn't trust himself to share a pillow with anyone for a full night, didn't trust himself not to fall asleep because he talked when he slept, recounting his vivid dreams aloud, revealing his deepest thoughts and fears and his darkest secrets.

The way he was doing now.

Miranda didn't know whether to laugh or to cry. She was so tired she thought it very likely that she might do either. Or both. What a wedding night this had turned out to be! Glancing at the clock on the mantel, she realized she had shared nearly forty minutes of blissful slumber beside him before Daniel had awakened her with his feverish raving.

"I must get to London tonight! I've urgent business there."

Propping herself on her elbow, Miranda reached out to touch him. His skin was hot and damp, the sheets around him drenched with sweat—as was the front of her borrowed nightshirt. Miranda plucked at it, self-consciously pulling the sodden pleats away from her chest, wishing her breasts weren't quite so big and prominent, wishing she was small and dainty like most of the other ladies of her acquaintance.

Wishing Daniel would tell her she was beautiful once again. . . .

There was nothing she could do about it now. What was done was done. Marrying Daniel, having Daniel to herself, holding Daniel in her arms for almost an hour, had been the culmination of a lifetime of longings and unspoken dreams, but her wonderful dream had come to an end when her prince charming had awakened her from it by talking in his sleep.

Daniel had been shivering beneath the covers, suffering through a bout of chills, when she returned to the master bedchamber and slipped beneath the sheets to lie beside him, but he was feverish now. "Daniel?"

His eyes were open and he was talking, but Miranda knew he was not awake and that he was not talking to her.

"I thank you for your hospitality, Mistress Beekins, but I cannot stay the night."

Miranda frowned. She ought to wake him to keep him from revealing information she knew he would never reveal in the light of day, but her curiosity and a bit of the old, green-eyed monster got the better of her. Was he dreaming about last night when Mistress Beekins had stitched his wound or some other time? Who was she to Daniel? Was she a kindhearted acquaintance who had tended him in his hour of need as Miranda was doing now, or was she something more? Did he trust Mistress Beekins the way he trusted her?

Trust. Daniel trusted her. Trusted her to keep his secrets. Trusted her to do what she knew was right. By allowing her curiosity to get the best of her, Miranda was in danger of betraying that trust.

"I must return to town," he was saying. "I have a previous engagement in London that requires my presence. I must be there and I must be seen to be there."

"Daniel, wake up," Miranda urged. "You're *in* London."

"Must get to London," Daniel protested. "Mustn't disappoint. Must complete my mission."

"You're in London," she repeated. "And if the previous engagement you mentioned was attending your mother's annual gala, you kept that appointment."

He kicked at the covers. "Lud, but I'm hot!"

Miranda slipped out of bed, walked around to the bedside table. She didn't dare give him any more willow bark, and there was nothing else to give him to soothe his fever, so Miranda filled the washbasin with water and reached for a cloth to cool him down once again. "There now." She placed the damp cloth on his forehead and began to mop the perspiration from his face and neck. "Doesn't this feel better?"

"Micah, have we any more whisky?" He opened his eyes and looked at her, and Miranda had to bite her lip to keep from crying. Or screaming. Daniel dreamed of Mistress Beekins, but he looked at Miranda and called her by a man's name—called her Micah.

She wiped the damp cloth over his neck and throat and left it there while she took hold of his wrist and gently pulled his hand away from the strips of cloth binding his ribs and placed it by his side. She thought he'd resist, but Daniel left his hand where she'd put it, and Miranda picked up the cloth and continued his cooling bath. "I'm sorry, Your Grace," she answered truthfully, "we're out of whisky."

"What of the cargo? Have you delivered it to the address I gave you?"

"Cargo?"

"The cargo we picked up on our journey. Shepherdston is expecting me to deliver it," Daniel answered. "Take the wheel of cheese and the pouches to Shepherdston. He needs the pouches for the meeting at Whitehall tomorrow."

Miranda froze, unable to believe her ears. She'd asked the question out of curiosity and was amazed that he'd answered her. She had heard of people dreaming dreams so vivid they talked in their sleep, but she'd never witnessed it. Until now.

"Shepherdston?" She leaned closer and cradled Daniel's face in her hands. "*Jarrod* Shepherdston?"

Daniel blinked up at her. "Of course. You must deliver the pouches to him without delay."

"What pouches?"

Daniel frowned. "The leather dispatch pouches," he answered succinctly. "He's expecting them tonight."

"But, Daniel, it's late."

"No matter." He winced as he spoke, and Miranda was convinced that his delirium had passed and that he'd awakened. "Merlin requires very little sleep. He'll be up."

"I don't know that I can get there. That stretch of Park Lane has been jammed with vehicles and pedestrians since your mother's midnight buffet began," she replied. "And I've no way to get there. Rupert hasn't returned with the coach. And I cannot pay a call on a gentleman at this time of night. Not dressed like this."

Reaching up, Daniel grabbed a fistful of Miranda's nightshirt and pulled her closer to him, but there wasn't a spark of recognition in his eyes as he looked up at her. "Damn it, man, if you've no vehicle, then walk. And he may be a gentleman, but Shepherdston isn't a snob. He won't give a damn how you're dressed."

Miranda begged to differ. Shepherdston would definitely take an interest in having a marchioness appear upon his doorstep in a man's nightshirt.

"But, Daniel . . ."

"Look, man, you must go!" Daniel was frantic. "We don't have a choice. He's expecting the delivery." He paused to catch his breath. "You must go in my place and deliver the pouches."

"Don't worry, Your Grace," she soothed. "The pouches have been delivered. You're tired and hurt and dreaming."

"With my eyes open?" he demanded. "I don't think so," he protested, his words clipped, his tone of voice regal, sounding exactly like the duke he was despite the fact that he was deeply asleep. "Look, my good man, I require your word of honor that you will call upon Lord Shepherdston and deliver the dispatches immediately."

"But, Your Grace . . ."

"Very well." He pushed her hand and the cool cloth away and sat up in bed. "If I cannot have your word, then I shall deliver the pouches myself."

"No!"

Daniel arched an eyebrow at her as if daring her to contradict him.

"You'll do yourself further injury, Daniel."

"Better I suffer further injury than for the pouches to go undelivered."

Miranda tried to force him to lie back down, but Daniel was as stubborn asleep as he was awake, and he fought to get to his feet. She glanced at the bandage around his ribs and the bandage covering the wound in his side. Afraid that he would manage to undo *her* needlework this time or do further damage to his ribs, Miranda relented. "I'll see that they are delivered."

"I require that you deliver them personally," he corrected.

"All right, Your Grace."

"Have I your solemn word upon it?"

"You have my word, Your Grace."

Daniel exhaled slowly and painfully sank back against the pillows and relaxed. "Your word of honor that you will act in my stead and report to Lord Shepherdston . . ."

"Yes, Your Grace."

"Very good, man," he conceded. "Remember that you have given your word to a duke and that I shall hold you to it." He stared up at her. "What are you waiting for, man? Go!"

"Aye, sir," she replied in quick military fashion. "I shan't disappoint you, sir."

"No," he answered, "I don't expect that you will."

Miranda smiled at that. Even in sleep Daniel did his best to have the last word. And she was no better. When would she stop making promises and giving her word of honor to Daniel Sussex?

Never, Miranda acknowledged. Not as long as he had her heart, and Daniel had had her heart almost from the moment she'd met him. Tonight, he had married her and earned it—along with her loyalty and her word of honor. And she had willingly given it to him while he was asleep and believed her to be a man named Micah who had been sent to help him.

That last thought gave her pause. Daniel had been shot. So what had happened to Micah? Who was he, and more importantly, where was he? Daniel hadn't mentioned him at the duchess's gala. Had he been there? Or had he gone to deliver the leather pouches to the Marquess of Shepherdston?

She pursed her lips in thought. Whatever they held, the leather dispatch pouches were important and obviously on Daniel's mind—so much so that he was dreaming about them, worrying about the completion of his mission and demanding Micah's word of honor that he—that *she*—would see that the leather pouches made it safely into Shepherdston's hands.

Miranda had gleaned enough information from Daniel's feverish ranting to understand that he was engaged in a business venture with Jarrod Shepherdston. Griffin Abernathy and Colin McElreath were also engaged in business ventures with Jarrod Shepherdston. But Griffin, Colin, and Jarrod had been friends since childhood. Miranda didn't find it odd that *they* should be involved in business together. But Daniel hadn't been one of Abernathy's, McElreath's, or Shepherdston's friends or associates growing up. He'd attended Eton instead of the Knightsguild School for Gentlemen, where the other three had received their schooling.

Now that she thought about it, Miranda remembered that Daniel hadn't been close friends with the other three when he'd been halfheartedly pursuing Alyssa Carrollton three years ago, either. He'd been very much the outsider then. So much so that Griffin couldn't remain in the same room with him for long. His close association with the other three men had come after Griffin returned home from the war in the Peninsula, after Daniel had lent his support and had had a hand in helping Colin's new viscountess avoid a nasty scandal.

How was it that Daniel had formed so close an attachment to Griffin and Colin's friend, the Marquess of Shepherdston, within three years that they would venture into business together? And what sort of business was it that would make a sitting duke like Daniel willingly defer to a marquess?

Was it possible that Griffin and Colin didn't know about Daniel's and Shepherdston's joint venture?

Miranda nodded. It was possible. Anything was possible in the world of business, but it wasn't very likely. Abernathy, McElreath, and Shepherdston were as close as brothers— closer than brothers. As far as Miranda knew, they didn't keep secrets from one another. If Daniel was reporting to Shepherdston, it was very likely that the other two friends were not only aware of it but equal partners in the venture.

A venture in which Daniel had managed to get shot.

Miranda found the idea of a partnership among the four men as intriguing as it was unsettling. What venture could attract four of London's most industrious peers of the realm? A great many ventures. But what sort of venture would get them shot?

Snatching Daniel's trousers from the floor once again, she determined to find out. She unbuttoned the buttons, stepped into the superfine breeches, and drew his trousers over her hips once again. She stuffed the tails of her borrowed nightshirt inside the trousers, then grabbed Daniel's cravat and threaded the linen through the top buttonholes, wrapped the length of cloth around her waist, cinched in the waistband, and secured it with a deftly crafted four-in-hand. Her feet were large for a woman's, but Miranda knew they wouldn't fill Daniel's shoes. Retrieving her dancing slippers, Miranda shoved her bare feet into them, tied the ribbons, and shrugged into Daniel's bloodied coat and waistcoat.

Glancing at her reflection in the mirror hanging over the massive chest of drawers, Miranda saw that she made a rather odd-looking gentleman wearing her father's nightshirt and Daniel's jacket, waistcoat, and trousers and using Daniel's cravat as a belt to hold them up. She smiled, certain she'd be the only gentleman on Park Lane wearing a four-in-hand at her waist instead of at her neck and dancing slippers on her feet instead of black leather shoes. Reaching up, she removed the diamond clips from her hair, dropped them on the top of the chest of drawers, then twisted her hair into a tight knot, pinned it into place, and settled Daniel's silk hat atop it.

Miranda took an experimental step and decided she could learn to enjoy not being encumbered by skirts. She could learn to enjoy wearing trousers. So much so that she was seriously considering having a pair tailored for her to wear in the privacy of her home. The servants would be scandalized, of course, and her mother might raise an eyebrow, but they would keep her secret. Trousers suited her. She was tall and long-legged and a marchioness in her own right, equal in rank to any marquess. It was a shame women weren't allowed to wear trousers. What would Daniel think if he saw her dressed like this?

She glanced over her shoulder at the bed. Daniel was sleeping soundly once again, and while Miranda was glad that his tossing and turning had come to an end, she couldn't help wishing she could see his reaction to her unconventional costume. It would prove that while she might not be a featherweight, she wasn't in the Duchess of Devonshire's league either.

The fact that she was taller than most men of her acquaintance might work in her favor during this, the most imprudent undertaking of her life. Miranda shook her head, dislodging Daniel's silk hat in the process. It wasn't enough that she had helped Daniel escape from his mother's party, now she was about to walk through the streets of London at night on what was likely to be a wild goose chase in order to keep her word of honor to Daniel. And if she was lucky and no one looked too closely at her strange attire, she might make it as far as the Marquess of Shepherdston's unscathed.

What would happen afterward was anyone's guess. Because whatever the nature of the venture in which Daniel and Shepherdston were involved, Miranda knew it wasn't for the purpose of increasing their wealth. Daniel, Griffin, and Jarrod had been born with more money than they would ever need, and Colin had fallen in love with and married an heiress, so their venture had to be something more important than the mere making of money.

Miranda knew that Griffin, Duke of Avon, had purchased the Knightsguild School for Gentlemen and was renovating the building and grounds in preparation for a new sort of college and training ground for officers and gentlemen. Griffin's experiences fighting in the Peninsula Campaigns had taught him a great deal about the nature of war and the men who fought it. Bonaparte had not only changed the map of Europe, but he was rapidly changing the way wars were fought and won. There was nothing romantic, chivalrous, or gentlemanly about the Peninsula Campaigns.

War was dirty and brutal and deadly, and Griff was convinced that in order to defeat Bonaparte and the tyrants that would follow him, the British Army had to modernize not only its weaponry but its entire method of operation, and that meant educating its officers. He intended to use Knightsguild as a training center for British officers and their support staffs.

Miranda had heard Griff speak of his plans many times, but she'd never heard Daniel's name mentioned in conjunction with the plans for Knightsguild. In all the time she'd spent with Griff and Alyssa, she'd never heard either one of them breathe a word about Daniel's financial or physical participation in the venture.

And if it wasn't making money or spending money on the renovations at Knightsguild, in what venture were Daniel, Griffin, Colin, and Jarrod engaged?

What sort of venture would attract those four extraordinary men?

Miranda grinned. Not venture, she decided, at last. *Adventure*. What adventure had attracted them? What adventure involved the delivery of cargo and leather dispatch pouches and included gunfire?

Miranda sucked in a breath at her incredible naïveté and at Daniel's reckless, foolhardy, stupid, and endearingly romantic sense of adventure.

Great Mars and Jupiter! What was she waiting for? Her new husband was a smuggler—and she was about to join the adventure and become an accomplice in order to make certain that Daniel had completed his mission.

Chapter 9

"The day shall not be up so soon as I,
To try the fair adventure of to-morrow."
—William Shakespeare, 1564–1616
King John

She was a fool.

A fool married to a smuggler. A fool who'd forgotten about the rain when she'd hurried out of the house on Curzon Street and begun her mission. Now she was standing in the shadows beneath the eaves of Viscount Walcott's town house, hidden against the branches of a massive early blooming lilac bush, staring across the street at the Marquess of Shepherdston's house and shivering inside the shoulders of Daniel's jacket. She'd forgotten about the rain when she'd slipped out of the Curzon Street house and made her way to Park Lane, and now she was wet, cold, and miserable. Daniel's hat offered protection from a vertical downpour, but it provided no protection from the horizontal rain, or the wind that had been blowing rain in her face ever since she'd embarked on this foolhardy mission. Her borrowed costume was soaked, and for the first time in her life, Miranda could truly say she no longer had a thing to wear.

The brocade robe she'd found in the armoire in her

father's room was the only dry garment left at Curzon Street that would fit her or Daniel, and Miranda had been saving it for him. Now she was going to be reduced to donning her sheet toga and going barefooted until Ned returned with fresh garments for her. Miranda frowned. Daniel, at least, would have the brocade robe and dry shoes. Everything she'd worn tonight was ruined, including her green silk dancing slippers.

In fact, the only good to come from the cold, soaking rain was that it had washed the blood from Daniel's clothing and dispersed the crowds that had filled Park Lane and made the street impassable only hours earlier. Miranda listened as the Tower clock struck the hour. Three quarters of an hour past three in the morning, and the streets were all but deserted—except for the hooded figure hurriedly making its way to the Marquess of Shepherdston's front door. . . .

Miranda squinted through the rain and brushed the raindrops from her eyelashes with the back of her hand in a futile attempt to get a better look at Shepherdston's early-morning visitor.

Was it Micah?

She had never seen the man. How would she know if it were he? Miranda took a step closer and bit back an unladylike curse as a stream of cold rainwater rolled off the brim of her borrowed hat and down the back collar of her shirt. Miranda watched as Shepherdston's visitor glanced over his shoulder, then put his head down and increased his pace, hurrying down the walk the way a woman would do. According to Daniel, the Marquess of Shepherdston was expecting Micah. But there was something decidedly female about the visitor. . . .

Shepherdston's caller should be a man, but what gentleman would wear a hooded cloak? And what lady in her right mind would travel about town alone in this weather and at this time of morning? Miranda grimaced. Except herself, of course. But then, she'd never claimed to be in her right mind where Daniel was concerned. Why else would she be dressed as a man and standing in the rain in the wee hours of the morning, hoping for the opportunity to pay a call on the Marquess of Shepherdston?

Miranda scrutinized the caller, following his movement, watching as a gust of wind caught the hem of the visitor's outer garment and lifted it, revealing a delicate white lawn nightgown and a glimpse of a bare leg wearing a black slipper much like her green ones. Miranda widened her eyes in amazement. What gentleman indeed?

Good heavens, but she'd managed to make it to the Marquess of Shepherdston's town house in time to witness another young lady's arrival. Miranda almost smiled at the irony. There were, it seemed, two young ladies roaming the streets of Mayfair in the downpour, both intent on calling upon the Marquess of Shepherdston and both attired in scandalous and unconventional costumes—one in a night-dress and one in gentleman's dress. One intent on business and the other apparently intent on pleasure.

Miranda nearly cried out in frustration. If she'd arrived a few minutes earlier or the other woman had arrived a few moments later or had been turned away at the front door, Miranda might have gained an audience with Lord Shepherdston. But that was out of the question now. The front door had opened, the female caller had been admitted inside, and the Marquess of Shepherdston was suddenly otherwise engaged.

Miranda firmed her lips into a thin line and tasted the bitter taste of disappointment. She had failed. Her journey had been for naught. She was no closer to finding out whether Micah had delivered the pouches, or in what sort of smuggling ventures Daniel and the Marquess of Shepherdston were involved, than she had been before she left Curzon Street.

And Miranda needed answers. Smuggling was a crime

punishable by imprisonment or death. Daniel might require protection, but she couldn't protect him as long as she remained ignorant of his activities.

And he couldn't protect her if she had knowledge of his activities.

The thought came to her unbidden, but once in her mind, it refused to leave. Daniel professed to trust her, yet he hadn't breathed a word about smuggling when he'd told her he'd been shot or mentioned returning from the coast in time to attend his mother's party. Yet that's what he must have done, otherwise he would have spent the night with Mistress Beekins as she'd invited him to do. Was he keeping her in ignorance of his illegal activities in order to protect her from the consequences should he be caught? Or had he insisted on marrying her in order to protect them both?

Either way, he'd done what he had to do in order to protect her. Thank heavens she'd thought to remove the special license from Daniel's jacket and place it beneath the cardboard bottom of her reticule for safekeeping. If she hadn't, the proof of her wedding—the proof they might both have to produce—would be a mass of wet parchment and illegible black ink.

Pulling Daniel's jacket tighter about her, Miranda shoved her cold hands into the pockets and retreated into the shadows of the lilac bush once again. She watched Shepherdston's caller enter the mansion, waited until the front door closed behind her, then turned and began the long walk back to Curzon Street, wondering all the while what she would say to Daniel, how she would explain her failure to complete the mission.

Provided, of course, that Daniel remembered the mission. . . . Provided that Daniel remembered what he'd demanded of her. . . . Or that he'd married her. . . .

Not that it mattered, Miranda decided, clamping down on her bottom lip to keep her teeth from chattering. She couldn't blame Daniel for her current discomfort. He'd made her promise that she'd pay a call on the marquess, but she was to blame for her own state of affairs. She had, after all, willingly taken instructions and given her solemn oath to a man who'd been asleep at the time.

It would serve her right if she caught her death of cold. Of all the reckless, foolhardy, stupid things to do, Miranda had chosen this one. Not only chosen it but leaped at the opportunity to pursue it. Why? Because Daniel had asked her. Because Daniel needed her. Because she had married him for better or for worse and Miranda wanted to do everything in her power to help him.

Miranda took a deep breath and slowly released it. And she'd kept her word. She'd gone to Shepherdston's house. Unfortunately, she wasn't the only lady paying the marquess a call. Miranda shrugged her shoulders. She was bold, but not bold enough to present herself at Shepherdston's door and interrupt his tryst.

Shepherdston was entitled to a romantic rendezvous. He was, after all, a handsome bachelor with a presumably normal, healthy appetite for the opposite sex. He was entitled to companionship and entitled to keep his rendezvous and the identity of his partner a secret if he chose to do so. He had suffered enough notoriety to last a lifetime. He deserved whatever happiness he could find.

Miranda wouldn't intrude. She had a companion of her own back on Curzon Street—her husband, Daniel, ninth Duke of Sussex. Miranda thrilled at the thought. Daniel was hers at last—or at least until he recovered.

She wanted to believe that he would always be hers and that he had meant every word of his wedding vows, but she couldn't count on it. Daniel had a way of dashing her hopes and disappointing her. Miranda hoped that wouldn't be the case this time, but the fact that their wedding had to remain a secret troubled her.

Daniel had married her tonight, but would he remember it in the morning? She was his bride, but she didn't know if he would ever truly allow her to be his wife.

All she knew for sure was that she still had a few hours to spend alone with him before Ned returned, and Miranda intended to make the most of her opportunity.

Squaring her shoulders, Miranda trudged through the rain back to the house on Curzon Street and slipped quietly through the back door. She hurried up the stairs to the room that had been her father's, stopping long enough to collect the sheet she'd used as a toga before returning to the master bedchamber and Daniel.

He had kicked the covers off once again, and his skin was hot to the touch. Miranda's heart caught in her throat when he opened his eyes and looked up at her. She waited for him to say something as she placed her hand on his forehead, but he showed no signs of recognition. She slowly released the breath she'd been holding.

He was feverish again. Miranda didn't think he was as hot as before, but she couldn't be sure. She'd spent the better part of an hour in the cold rain. She was chilled to the bone and her hands were freezing.

They made a good pair. He needed the touch of her cool skin, and she needed the heat of his.

Miranda removed Daniel's hat, unpinned her hair, shed her wet garments, and slipped, naked, into bed beside him. She snuggled against his uninjured side, absorbing the excess heat from his body, inhaling the scent of him—a unique blend of Daniel, lime, exotic spices, and a slightly excessive amount of Scots whisky.

Miranda was familiar with the lime and spice cologne custom mixed for him by Taylor's of Old Bond Street. Daniel had worn that fragrance for as long as she could remember. She had caught a faint whiff of it when she'd donned his waistcoat and jacket, but the fragrance had been overshadowed by the metallic smell of his blood. The rain had washed the blood and the scent of Daniel's cologne from the fabric. But she now was surrounded by it once again, and the added cachet was the feel of his skin and the not unpleasant aroma of Scots whisky surrounding him. An unconventional blend of fragrances to be sure, but a blend she found strangely comforting and appealing.

Pressing her body as closely as possible against him, Miranda closed her eyes and fell into a deep, dreamless, exhausted sleep.

Chapter 10

"A few honest men are better than numbers."
—*Oliver Cromwell, 1599–1658*

"What do you mean he's late?" Colin, Viscount Grantham, demanded of Griffin, first Duke of Avon, who announced that the Marquess of Shepherdston had sent a note saying he'd been delayed. "Jarrod is never late."

"Shepherdston sends his apologies," Griffin elaborated. "He's been detained and will be late."

The Free Fellows were meeting in their customary meeting room at White's on Thursday morning following the Duchess of Sussex's annual gala. The room was set with enough coffee, spirits, and cigars for six men: the three original Free Fellows—Griffin, Colin, and Jarrod—and the three newest ones—Daniel, Duke of Sussex, Jonathan Manners, the Earl of Barclay, and Alexander, the Marquess of Courtland.

Barclay had settled onto a chair near the fire. Courtland sat at one end of the massive leather sofa, and Griffin sat on the other end. Colin was sprawled on his favorite large chair beside the drinks table, but Shepherdston's habitual place was empty.

Griff cupped his hand around his ear, exaggerating the motion as the casement clock chimed the half hour. "There is always a first time. And today is Jarrod's. He's late."

"He's not the only one." Colin glanced around. The Duke of Sussex's favorite chair opposite Barclay's was also empty. "Where's His Grace? Hasn't he returned from the coast yet?"

"I saw him last night at his mother's gala, so he must have returned late yesterday," Griff offered. "I didn't get the opportunity to speak with him in the crush of people there, but I saw him."

"So did I," Barclay added.

"Then where is he?" Colin asked.

Courtland shrugged his shoulders, then leaned forward to pour himself a cup of coffee from the silver coffee service on the low table. "I was at the duchess's ball last night, but I arrived later in the evening. I didn't see Daniel."

"Sussex knows we're meeting this morning," Colin said. "And he knows he's supposed to brief us on the progress of his mission. It isn't like him not to be here."

"Shepherdston is late and Sussex is missing," Barclay added. "It's a most unusual morning already."

Although they'd originally begun as a secret group of schoolboys, the members had put their secret league to work against Bonaparte, working very closely with the Foreign Office and the War Office.

The secret work that Colin and Jarrod and Sussex did came under the auspices of a staff of graduates of the Royal Military College and Lieutenant Colonel Colquhoun Grant. While Grant gathered battlefield information on the Peninsula, Jarrod, Colin, and Sussex gathered information on a much larger field of battle, and all of it was analyzed, enciphered, deciphered, and included in the constant flow of military dispatches overseen by Griffin's father, the Earl of Weymouth.

When Griffin became a national hero, the Prince Regent and Prime Minister had asked that he retire from active duty in his cavalry regiment, and he'd agreed. But retirement from the regiment hadn't kept him from engaging the enemy.

Griffin and Jarrod and Sussex occupied higher positions in society and were subject to more social obligations and more scrutiny than the other Free Fellows. They were limited, in many ways, to planning, arranging, and financing the clandestine war against Bonaparte, but they were still very much a part of it.

While Griffin had been publicly honored for his service to his country, the Free Fellows League and each member's connection to it remained secret to all but a handful of close associates. Griff, Jarrod, and Sussex engaged in the occasional secret smuggling holiday, but Colin, as a relatively unimportant and poor viscount, had been the primary foot soldier in the field, and therefore the Free Fellow most at risk.

But that had all changed when Colin had married an heiress. With two of the original Free Fellows married, more help was needed. Jarrod and Colin had recruited Sussex while Griffin was serving with his cavalry regiment on the Peninsula. And in turn, Griffin and Jarrod and Sussex had approached Barclay and Courtland while Colin was on his honeymoon.

The number of close associates had expanded slightly with the addition of Sussex and the two newest candidates for admission into the Free Fellows League, Jonathan Manners, the eleventh Earl of Barclay, and Alexander, second Marquess of Courtland, but Jarrod, Griffin, and Colin were satisfied that their secret was safe and that the associates close to Sussex, Barclay, and Courtland were entirely trustworthy.

As the newest members of the League, Barclay and Courtland had gradually assumed Colin's role as primary foot soldiers in their clandestine war with their French counterparts. And Sussex and Jarrod had undertaken more smuggling missions so the married members of the League could stay close to London to fulfill social and business obligations and to spend more time with their wives.

Sussex had spent the past two days on a smuggling

mission to France, but had been scheduled to return in time to attend his mother's annual gala ball.

Jarrod had sent word that he would be late, but they had heard nothing from Sussex, which was unprecedented and very troubling.

"You're certain you saw Daniel at the duchess's party last night?" Colin asked Griffin.

"I'm quite certain," Griff answered.

"But you said there was a huge crush." Colin began to pace back and forth in Jarrod's customary pattern.

"There was." Griff looked at Colin and frowned. "Which is why I didn't catch a glimpse of you and Gillian all evening."

"You didn't catch a glimpse of us all evening because Gillian and I weren't there," Colin replied.

"You didn't go?" Griff was astonished.

"We weren't invited," Colin answered.

"What do you mean you weren't invited?" Courtland and Barclay demanded in unison.

"I'm only a viscount."

"So?" Barclay demanded. "There were a dozen viscounts and viscountesses at the party."

"Tons of them," Griffin added. "A great many with lesser titles than yours. You have one of the oldest and most revered titles in Scotland. Granthams and McElreaths have held titles from the time of Macbeth."

"Aye," Colin agreed in a thick burr. "But they were Scottish titles, and, present company excluded, when have the English ever been impressed by Scottish titles?" He shrugged his shoulders. "Besides, everyone knows there's no money behind my title."

"That may have been true once," Griff reminded him, "but it's no longer the case. Your hard work and your marriage to Gillian put a great deal of money behind the title. You're worth a bloody fortune, Colin." Griff ran his fingers through his hair. Colin had married Gillian Davies, the daughter of Baron Carter Davies, a silk and linen merchant who owned a fleet of ships and dozens of lucrative trade routes all over the world. Gillian's father had become one of the richest men in England and been rewarded with the title of baron for services to the crown, but he and his wife and daughter had yet to be fully accepted by some members of the ton. "Of course piles of money don't mean a thing to the dowager Duchess of Sussex, who is, and has always been, a terrible snob. But don't let it bother you. You're in excellent company, you know. She and my mother don't particularly get on." He smiled. "Apparently the duchess had set her cap for the duke *and* my father. She married the duke, but she never forgave my father for not offering for her. And you know my mother—" He glanced over at Colin and grinned. "She has no use for anyone who dislikes my father."

Colin knew Griff's parents quite well, and anyone who knew them knew that Lord and Lady Weymouth's marriage had been a true love match. Colin also knew that if there was anyone Lady Weymouth loved more than her husband, it was Griffin, her only child.

"And," Griff continued, "Her Grace hasn't quite gotten over the fact that Alyssa chose me instead of Daniel. The duchess only invited Alyssa and me because I'm the hero of Fuentes de Oñoro, and because His Highness elevated me to the rank of duke." He stared at his friend, trying to read between the lines. "And you know that if Daniel had realized his mother had omitted your name from the guest list, he would have rectified the error."

"Of course he would have," Colin agreed. "But it didn't matter. I'd much rather spend a quiet evening at home with Gillian than fight my way through the crush of people at Sussex House. And although she missed getting all decked out in her finery, Gillian didn't mind staying home either." Once upon a time, Colin would have felt slighted by the duchess's snub, but things had changed after he married Gillian. Now he no longer needed the ton's approval, and Colin truly didn't feel the duchess's slight. His only regret was that he knew Daniel would be embarrassed to learn that his mother had slighted one of his friends. But he and Gillian were about to celebrate their first wedding anniversary, and they enjoyed each other's company far too much to worry about missing the social event of the year. "If there's anything she despises, it's the snobbery of the duchess's set."

"Daniel and I are the ones who need consoling." Griff raised his hands in a sign of surrender. "Count yourself fortunate that your mother-in-law isn't a part of the Duchess of Sussex's set, like mine is." He shrugged. "Alyssa and I would rather have stayed home like you and Gillian, and you know Daniel would rather avoid all the fuss, but . . . It's worse for him. The duchess is his mother. There is no escape for him."

Colin nodded. "I can't imagine returning from a mission and having to face that."

"It's the same for me," Jonathan said gloomily. "The Duchess of Sussex is my aunt, and Aunt Lavinia would never forgive me for missing her party, either. And if my aunt is unhappy, my mother is unhappy. Unfortunately, those two sisters are as alike as peas in a pod, and they're both capable of making my life miserable."

The Free Fellows had all become as close as brothers, but only Sussex and Manners were related. Their mothers were sisters. Daniel's mother had married a duke. Jonathan's mother had married the younger son of an earl. Daniel and Jonathan jokingly called themselves *distant* cousins because until he'd unexpectedly inherited his paternal uncle's title, Daniel's mother had done her best to keep distance between the two boys by limiting her son's contact with his much poorer cousin. The duchess had made certain that Jonathan and Daniel had gone to different schools. Jonathan had been sent to Knightsguild with Griffin, Colin, and Jarrod, and Daniel had followed in his father's footsteps and gone to Eton.

Fortunately for Jonathan, Daniel had sought his companionship whenever possible and had generously rewarded Jonathan for information about the Free Fellows League. Jonathan had slept in the cot next to Jarrod's and had often overheard bits of information about the mysterious League and the three boys who had formed it and patterned it after King Arthur and his Knights of the Round Table. He eagerly shared his information with Daniel, and Daniel had supplied him with coins and trinkets in return. The cousins had thrilled to the exploits of the Free Fellows League, and both boys had aspired to join it.

It had taken years, but Sussex and Barclay had finally been granted membership and earned their secret code names. Shepherdston was Merlin. Avon was Lancelot. Grantham was Galahad. Sussex was Arthur. Barclay had become Bedivere, and Courtland had become Tristram.

"I shudder to think about it," Alex added.

"So do I," Colin said. "I've made more crossings than I care to count, and I know that even if everything went smoothly, a trip to the coast of France and back in two days is a hardship."

"Daniel would have had to have ridden like the hounds of hell were on his heels in order to make it to his mother's party on time. And it's not as if he could beg off. He's the duke. It's his house, and what's more, he actually lives there." Griff's smile grew into a broad grin. "Think about it. He probably had to fight his way through the crowd of coaches to get down the drive to the house. No doubt he overslept."

"I did no such thing."

Four Free Fellows turned at the sound of the protest to find Jarrod standing in the doorway.

"Shepherdston!" they greeted him.

"My tardiness had nothing to do with oversleeping," Jarrod continued in a sharp tone. "I am only a quarter of an hour late, despite the fact that I've been up all night."

"We were talking about Sussex oversleeping," Colin said. He walked over to the silver coffeepot, poured a steaming cup of the brew, and carried it over to Jarrod. "Not your going without." He thrust the cup in Jarrod's hand. "Drink this. You look like hell."

It was true. Jarrod's brown eyes were bloodshot, and there were dark circles beneath them. "Thanks," he said, gratefully accepting the cup of coffee Colin handed him.

"What did you do, Shepherdston? Put in an appearance at Aunt Lavinia's ball last night, then go home and work on dispatches?" Barclay inquired.

Jarrod shook his head. "Unlike the rest of you, I declined my invitation." He met Colin's gaze and smiled. "How was Her Grace's party? Did you and your lovely viscountess have a good time?"

"We had a very nice time," Colin told him. "But not at Sussex House."

Jarrod frowned. "You didn't go?"

"Colin and Gillian stayed home," Griff answered to spare Colin another explanation.

"Why?" Jarrod demanded. "Was Gillian ill?"

"No," Colin assured him. "She's fine."

"Then why the devil didn't you take her to the duchess's party? Gillian would have loved it. It's the biggest ball of the season, and the most exclusive."

"Too exclusive," Colin answered.

Jarrod frowned.

"Colin and Gillian didn't receive their invitations in time to attend," Griff explained diplomatically.

"Why the devil not?" Jarrod glanced toward Sussex's customary seat.

Jonathan intercepted his glance. "You know the duchess."

"Yes," Jarrod sighed. "I know the duchess. That's why I declined. She only invites me to her celebrations because I'm unmarried and available to partner the eligible young ladies."

"She invites you because you're considered unattainable," Alex Courtland corrected. "And she would like to be the one to snag you."

"She's a lovely lady and quite well-preserved for her age." Jarrod pretended not to understand. "But she's still a bit too old and too tyrannical for my taste. She outranks me, and she would never let me forget it."

Courtland choked on his coffee at the idea of the dowager Duchess of Sussex sharing a bed with anyone—much less Shepherdston. As far as he was concerned, Daniel's conception was the second miracle birth.

Jarrod glanced at Colin and couldn't resist baiting him a bit. "Once upon a time, you and I were both considered unattainable. Apparently she's decided to punish you for going and getting yourself leg-shackled last season without her help or approval, else you'd have received your invitation this season."

Colin chuckled. "Give me my leg shackles any day." He looked at Griff, the only other married Free Fellow, for confirmation. "I prefer marriage to Gillian over the Duchess of Sussex's invitations any time."

"And I prefer to remain unmarried." Jarrod winked at Barclay and Courtland. "Unlike these two who, no doubt, accepted her invitation and ventured into dangerous territory last evening." He took a drink of coffee, then looked at the others. "So I stayed home and spent most of the night deciphering."

"Any new information?" Colin asked.

"I don't know. Unfortunately, I was interrupted before I completed the deciphering." Jarrod didn't offer any explanations for the interruption, and the others didn't ask for one.

Griff raised his hands in a sign of surrender. "I thought the War Office requested the dispatches be delivered this morning," Griff ventured.

"They did." Jarrod turned to Colin. "Do you think Gillian would mind . . . ?"

Shortly after his marriage, Colin had accidentally discovered that his bride was extremely proficient at solving anagrams, all sorts of word puzzles, and deciphering French code. Gillian's talent had come as a most pleasant surprise. Colin was a proficient code breaker, but Gillian was exceptional. Colin trusted her talent as much as he trusted her.

"She'd be disappointed if you didn't ask," Colin confided.

It was true. Colin's wife didn't know the history of the Free Fellows League or all of the work it did, but she knew he and his friends were part of it and that continuing their secret work was vital to the war effort. Gillian's gift for numbers and her uncanny ability to break code had made her the Free Fellows League's secret weapon, and she was delighted to have the opportunity to contribute to the fight against Bonaparte. And they all knew that she would die before she would betray her husband or any member of the League.

Jarrod reached inside his jacket, removed the key to his desk drawer, and handed it to Colin. "The dispatches are locked in the top drawer of my desk. I'd be obliged if you'd get them and take them to your viscountess. Tell Henderson I sent you."

Colin nodded and pocketed the key.

"I'll stop by your house on my way to my meeting with Scovell at Whitehall later this morning and pick them up," Jarrod continued. "Now, where's Sussex?" He glanced around. "I want to know why he didn't invite Colin and Gillian to his mother's party, and I want to hear his report on his mission."

"Our sentiments exactly," Griff told him.

Jarrod frowned.

"But, as you can see, Daniel isn't here yet," Courtland added. "We spent the past quarter hour waiting for both of you."

"I apologize for being late," Jarrod said. "But something unexpected came up, and it couldn't be helped. And I did send word to His Grace," he nodded toward Griff, "that I had been unavoidably detained. I take it that Sussex didn't send word."

Griff shook his head. He and Sussex were the highest-ranking Free Fellows, but Jarrod was the leader of the group, and the two dukes deferred to his leadership. "Not yet."

"You haven't seen him?"

"Not since last night," Griff explained. "And I only saw him briefly from across the room last night. By the time I made it through the crush to where I'd seen him standing, he was gone." He turned to Jonathan. "Barclay saw him, too."

"So he made it back safely." Jarrod heaved a sigh of relief. He hated sending the sitting Duke of Sussex on secret missions, because there would be hell to pay and a million questions to answer if anything happened to him.

"Didn't you see him when he delivered the dispatch pouches?" Barclay asked.

Jarrod shook his head. "Henderson accepted the pouches in my stead." Although Jarrod preferred to accept the dispatches himself, that wasn't always possible, and Henderson, his butler, was entrusted with the duty. The Free Fellows delivered the pouches to Jarrod as soon after returning from a mission as they could, to allow as much time as possible for the deciphering before Jarrod turned the information over to men at Whitehall, so it wasn't unusual for Jarrod to get the dispatches before he met with the Free Fellow who'd collected them. He looked at his colleagues. "I assumed Sussex arrived home safely because I received the dispatches, but I'd prefer confirmation from Sussex himself or one of you."

Griff nodded. "We know he made it back to town. So, you can rest easily on that account."

"Then where is he?" Jarrod asked, pinning each of them with a look.

"Unless he escorted a lady home from the party and decided to stay overnight or simply overslept, we've no idea," Barclay answered.

"We need to get an idea," Jarrod told them. "I've a very full schedule this morning, with personal matters that demand my immediate attention and meetings at the War Office in a few hours with men who require the most accurate and current information we can give them on the French movements along the coast." He finished his coffee and set the empty cup in its saucer on the silver tray. "Let's see if we can find our errant King Arthur before eleven of the clock this morning. There's no point in meeting without him."

"Where do you suggest we begin?" Courtland asked.

"Anywhere but Madam Theodora's," Jarrod replied.

Puzzled, Barclay asked, "Why not?"

Madam Theodora's was the Free Fellows' preferred house of pleasure. If Sussex were with a woman, they would most likely find him at Madam Theo's—unless he'd made a private arrangement with a lady of the ton. . . . And if that were the case, he could be anywhere in London.

"Because that's where I'm going to look," Jarrod answered. "I'll see you all here at the usual time this afternoon."

"Well," Colin drawled as Jarrod left the room. "Merlin's personal matter must be urgent." He looked at the others. "You heard him. It's time we discovered what's become of our King Arthur."

Chapter 11

"Whatever this is that I am, it is a little flesh and breath, and the ruling part."

—*Marcus Aurelius, A.D. 121–180*

*D*aniel awoke to a piercing light penetrating his eyelids. He opened his eyes a fraction. Sunlight streamed in the window, bathing the ceiling and the walls of the room where he lay listening to the pounding beat of a thousand angry, discordant drummers echoing inside his head in a pink and white light. He blinked against the bright light and found that even that slight movement sent daggers flying into his brain.

Squeezing his eyes shut, Daniel attempted to shield them with his forearm, only to discover that raising his arm was impossible.

His left shoulder and arm were pressed against the mattress, held in place by a heavy weight, and the tingling pins-and-needles sensation in that part of his body told him the circulation had been constricted for quite some time. Restoring the circulation to his left arm and shoulder would be agony, so Daniel attempted to shield his eyes with his right arm instead. But using his right arm was more painful than moving his left. He aborted the attempt as the movement ignited a firestorm of aggravated nerve endings along his side that made his breath catch in his throat and brought involuntary tears to his eyes.

A flash flood of anxiety coursed through him at the knowledge that both of his arms had been rendered useless. Ignoring a nauseating jolt of pain, Daniel raised his head an inch or so from the pillow, glanced down and realized the weight pinning his left arm and shoulder to the bed was caused by the head nestled upon his shoulder and the long slender arm draped across his stomach.

Daniel wondered, for a brief moment, if the French coast watch or the British Navy frigate had succeeded in blowing the *Mademoiselle* out of the water, if he was lying beneath what remained of one or more of his crew. For the last thing he remembered was exhorting the crew of the *Mademoiselle* to row for all they were worth in an effort to avoid the rifle balls coming at them from English and French sides of the Channel.

But the arm lying across his stomach was slim and pale and appeared more female than male. Daniel hazarded another glance. The effort cost him, but he had his answer. He sank back against the pillow, secure in the knowledge that the head on his shoulder and the arm draped across his body were decidedly female and still attached to their owner.

He blew out a breath he'd been holding and gingerly moved his head from side to side. Several strands of soft hair caught in the stubble on his chin, and the fresh, clean scent of spring rain and some sort of fragrant flower filled his nostrils. . . .

Some sort of fragrant, *familiar* flower . . . Not roses. Not lilies. Not violets. Blast it! He owned the finest gardens in London, perhaps in all of England, gardens he opened to the public on Sunday afternoons during the season so everyone could enjoy them, yet Daniel couldn't put a name to the scent. Not hyacinths or geraniums . . .

He closed his eyes, breathed in the scent, and concentrated on matching the name to the aroma. Something else . . . Something soft and romantic . . . Something that brought back memories . . .

Lilacs. She smelled of spring rain and lilacs. Daniel struggled to recall which young lady of his acquaintance wore the essence of lilacs and spring rain. But he couldn't recall anyone who wore that particular combination of fragrances.

Not that it mattered at the moment. Putting a name and a face to the scent of the body molded against his paled in comparison to the pleasure of waking up to it. He tried to recall the last time he'd done so and frowned.

Had it been that long since the girl at Oxford? The barmaid in the Red Lion tavern. What was her name? Helen? Ellen? He struggled to remember, and the pain in his head increased tenfold. *Arden.* That was it. Arden. How could he have forgotten pretty little Arden with the soft brown eyes and the equally soft bosom? He had spent many a boisterous night with Arden and made love with the sunlight pouring though the narrow window in her room.

Opening his eyes once again, Daniel squinted against the light, peering through his eyelashes at a white-and-gold Rococo ceiling decorated with a multitude of fat plaster cherubs staring down at him, and at the shockingly pink satin floral paper covering the walls.

Where the devil was he?

Not at home. Surely. For none of the bedrooms in any of his residences had such gaudy ceilings. Several of his houses, including Sussex House, had frescoed ceilings, but those ceilings, painted by masters, tended to depict tastefully bucolic scenes of blue skies, fluffy white clouds, and the occasional biblical morality tale.

And not the Red Lion. If he had, for some unknown, nostalgic reason, traveled the tortuous path back to his university days to pay a call on Arden, he was in the wrong room. And the wrong tavern. The Red Lion was a dark, half-timbered structure, and Arden's room had been a dark, low-ceiled room with a single, narrow window. And she'd never smelled of lilacs. Arden had smelled of bread and ale and sex. And while there had been any number of women since Oxford and Arden, Daniel couldn't recall spending an entire night with any of them, couldn't recall waking up to them in the morning light. Couldn't recall any who smelled of spring lilacs.

Nor did he remember any of Madam Theo's rooms being quite so pink. Not that he'd visited all of them, but the rooms he'd occupied at Madam Theo's exclusive house of pleasure at Number Forty-seven Portman Square in London had been more subdued, less blatantly *feminine*.

Of course it was possible that Madam Theo had redecorated since his last visit, but Daniel didn't think so. He turned his head ever so slightly, wincing as the roar caused by the rustle of his head against the pillow resounded in his brain. Madam Theo's taste was quiet and understated, and there was nothing quiet or understated in a room where the bed was made up with a pink silk coverlet, shockingly pink sheets, and pillow slips bordered in gold thread.

The only thing of which he was certain was that he was lying in a woman's bed and in a woman's room. But which woman's room? He turned his head ever so slightly in the opposite direction and came face to face with a tapestry cherub. Where the devil was he? Because there was no doubt that he wasn't at home. Or that the woman lying beside him, whoever she was, had a passion for pillows, fat, baby-faced cherubs, and all things pink.

Passion.

Daniel became aware of the twin points of her breasts pressing again his upper arm, became aware of the length of her molded against his left side, the triangle of soft hair pressed against his flank, and long limbs intimately entwined with his, and instantly regretted his choice of words. *Passion.*

His eyes burned, his head pounded, his right side ached, his limbs trembled in agony, and his mouth and throat were as dry as a desert, but the portion of his anatomy that made him uniquely male sprang to attention, tenting the garish pink sheet in an impressive display of unadulterated lust.

For the woman lying beside him.

Who was she? Which of Madam Theo's young women had agreed to provide him with a few hours of pleasurable oblivion in exchange for a significant amount of gold and silver? Daniel lifted his head once more in an effort to put a face and a name on the body cuddled against him, but all he could see was a mass of auburn hair.

Daniel scowled. *Auburn* hair. None of the women he favored at Madam Theo's had auburn hair. He made it a point never to choose women with hair that color because auburn-colored hair reminded him of . . .

Bloody hell! The oath exploded inside his head as a kaleidoscope of memories came flooding back. The harrowing journey across the Channel. Waking up in the Beekins' cottage. The agonizing journey from Dover to London. Sneaking into Sussex House and awaiting his mother's gala. Arriving late so he wouldn't have to help his mother receive her guests . . . Avoiding the crowd of partygoers . . . Waiting for . . .

Daniel gritted his teeth. Hell's bells! The only woman he knew who arrived at most any gathering swathed in various shades of pink was the mother of . . .

He didn't remember everything that had happened. . . . But he thought he remembered most of it. . . . And the last thing he remembered was holding on to . . .

Miranda.

Daniel buried his nose in her hair. *Miranda.* She used to wear ginger and lilies. When had she switched to lilacs and spring rain? Why had she switched when her other fragrance suited her so well that he could never smell a lily without thinking of her?

Miranda wasn't given to making idle threats, and Daniel wouldn't be a bit surprised to learn he was sharing a roof with the dowager marchioness. Unlike her daughter, the dowager Lady St. Germaine had displayed a taste for pink in all its incarnations on numerous occasions. This bed-chamber looked like the sort of room of which the dowager marchioness would approve, and if that was the case, Miranda had a great deal for which to answer.

"Miranda." Daniel didn't realize he'd spoken aloud until her name came out as a painful croak, barely recognizable as his voice.

The woman on his shoulder slept on.

Daniel tried again, louder this time. "Miranda."

She stretched like a cat, languorously extending her arm, across his lower abdomen, brushing the part of his anatomy tenting the pink sheet, pressing her lower body into his side as she did so.

Daniel sucked in a breath and was immediately grateful for the bands of cloth wrapped around his ribs.

"Hmm?"

"Are we in your mother's house?"

Miranda smothered a yawn, propped herself on her elbow, and shoved her hair out of her eyes. "What?"

Daniel bit back a groan as the circulation returned to his arm and shoulder with a vengeance. "Is your mother in residence?"

The sheet slipped off her shoulders, giving Daniel an unrestricted view of her naked breasts as Miranda reacted, bolting upright in bed, and blinking in confusion. "Here?"

Daniel's mouth went dry as he stared at Miranda's unfettered breasts. They were, quite simply, the most spectacular pair of breasts he'd ever seen. Pear-shaped, ivory-toned, and pink-tipped. Big enough to fill his hands, but not weighty enough to droop. He'd known that Miranda was well endowed. The fashions of the day, with their revealing décolletage, made it impossible not to notice her impressive display, but Daniel hadn't realized how much her revealing bodices concealed, or quite how blessed Miranda was—until now.

He didn't answer, and Miranda squeaked her dismay as she followed Daniel's gaze and realized she was as bare breasted as an Amazon warrior and that he had taken full advantage of the view. Blushing to the roots of her hair, she yanked the sheet to her chest and tucked it around her. "Daniel, did you say my mother is here?" she repeated, frantically searching the covers for hairpins. Was it possible that Ned had returned to Curzon Street with the dowager Marchioness of St. Germaine?

"I assumed that must be the case," he answered. "You tell me."

"How can I?" Miranda asked. "When I just woke up?"

"As did I," he told her.

Miranda frowned, clearly puzzled by their conversation. "Then why would you assume my mother is here?"

"You threatened to take me home to your mother," he reminded her. "I didn't believe you would do it—until I woke up here with you."

She glared at him as understanding dawned. "You believe I brought you home to Mother?"

Daniel managed a slight nod. "It's what you threatened to do."

"I thought you trusted me." Miranda sounded hurt.

"I did. I do."

"You have a fine way of showing it, Your Grace," she said.

"What was I to think?" he demanded, appealing to her logic. "It's the last thing I remember clearly."

"The last thing . . ." she sputtered.

"Yes." He squeezed his eyes shut, then opened them once again. He remembered parts of the previous evening, but he couldn't tell what had happened from what he'd dreamed. "Everything else is fuzzy."

"You don't remember anything I said after that?"

Daniel frowned. "Bits and pieces. But nothing clearly." Something about a wheel of cheese. St. Michael's Church. And Miranda looking quite fetching in a nightshirt and trousers.

Miranda sighed. "Of course you don't. How silly of me to

think otherwise. Why would you automatically believe the best of me, when I've given you every reason to believe the worst?"

Her sarcastic rebuke stung. Daniel did his best to ignore the pounding in his head and the pain in his side as he struggled to push himself up against the pillows. Praying he wouldn't do himself further harm, Miranda watched as he finally managed to sit up, but didn't offer to help. "What would you believe if you awoke and found yourself sharing a bed with a person 'who'd threatened to force a meeting with her mother on you?" He leaned against the headboard.

"I *did* wake up and find myself sharing a bed with a *person* who forced a meeting with *his* mother on me," Miranda pointed out.

"I caught you before you entered the receiving line," Daniel replied defensively. "You didn't have to meet her face to face."

"The point is that you invited me to your mother's gala knowing she didn't want me there."

"You didn't have to accept my invitation."

"Lucky for you I did," Miranda retorted. "Where would you be if I hadn't?"

Chapter 12

"Oaths are but words, and words but wind."
—Samuel Butler, 1612–1680

"*Where am I now?*" he asked. "*Because this certainly isn't my bedchamber.*"

"Nor mine," Miranda replied.

"Then whose?" Daniel winced when he raised his voice and quickly lowered it a notch. "Look around you. We're swimming in a veritable sea of pink. Who but your mother would have a room this color?"

"*Your* mother, for all I know," Miranda retorted. "And heaven knows the clothes left in the armoire would fit the duchess."

Daniel widened his eyes in a show of alarm. "You don't know where we are either?"

Miranda was tempted to let him labor under that misconception, but decided on a different course to see if Daniel recalled more of the previous evening than he realized. "Of course I know where we are. We're in a house on Curzon Street that my father purchased as a home for his mistress. This room appears to have been hers."

"Curzon Street?" Daniel was genuinely puzzled. "What are we doing sharing a bed in a house on Curzon Street?"

Daniel was aware that certain sections of Curzon Street

were dedicated to exclusive houses of pleasure as well as a number of private clubs catering to the more jaded members of society—all set among rows of houses gentlemen of the ton leased or purchased for their mistresses. He was surprised that Miranda knew about her father's mistress and the purpose of the house, even if Miranda didn't seem to be.

"What couples who share a bed usually do, Daniel."

"How? Why?"

Miranda arched an eyebrow at him. "Why not? Since you know how?"

Daniel looked her in the eyes and realized for the first time that she looked as tired as he felt. There were dark circles beneath her eyes and worry lines at the corners of her mouth. "I understand why I'd want to share a bed with you, Miranda. Any man with half an eye would leap at the chance to do that. What I don't understand is how it came about."

Miranda took a deep breath and told him the truth. "Would you believe that you were so foxed you insisted upon calling at St. Michael's Palace and summoning the bishop from his bed in order to preserve my reputation and to prevent my mother from having to prevail upon you to do so?"

Daniel blanched. Miranda watched as the small amount of color he'd had in his face leeched out. "No, I wouldn't believe it." He couldn't believe he'd go so far as to suggest marriage to Miranda or anyone else, no matter how foxed he was.

"You should," Miranda said softly.

The aching in Daniel's head told him she was right. "I proposed?"

Miranda nodded.

Daniel gave a little laugh. "You mean to tell me that if I had secured a special license, we'd be married by now?"

"I suppose that depends," Miranda told him.

"On what?"

"On whether or not I'd accept." She stared into Daniel's bloodshot eyes. He didn't remember.

"Then I needn't worry." He rubbed his temple in a vain attempt to alleviate the pain building there, then raked his fingers through his hair. "You would never accept a proposal under those conditions." He met her unflinching gaze. "Would you?"

He didn't remember. He honestly didn't remember.

It shouldn't come as a shock. Miranda had known Daniel was extremely intoxicated. She'd warned him that he was acting rashly and that she was afraid he wouldn't remember his actions in the morning. Or worse, remember and regret. The fact that her prediction had come to pass, the fact that he didn't recall summoning Bishop Manwaring or participating in the ceremony, shouldn't shock or hurt her. But it did.

A few short hours earlier, Daniel had promised to love, honor, and cherish her. Keeping his vows was written into the ceremony. Remembering them was not.

"Miranda?" Daniel made no effort to hide the concern in his voice. "You wouldn't accept a proposal under those circumstances, would you?"

"And bind myself to you on a whim?" She pretended an outrage she didn't feel. "For better or worse as long as we both shall live?" She looked him in the eye and said what he wanted to hear, said what he expected her to say. "You must be joking."

Daniel exhaled. "Then it wouldn't have mattered if I'd secured a special license?"

The look on his face spoke volumes. Miranda wondered how she was going to bear the pain of knowing he found the idea of marrying her so repugnant. "You did secure one."

"I don't believe it." Daniel pinched the bridge of his nose. "I purchased a special license and took you to St. Michael's Square?"

Miranda took a deep breath and willed herself not to cry as she met Daniel's gaze. "That's right, Your Grace," she answered softly.

"I don't remember any of it."

Miranda looked him in the eye, read the expression on his face, and determined to salvage what she could of her pride by setting his mind to rest. "It happened, Your Grace, but you fell asleep in the carriage before you could repeat your vows, thereby narrowly escaping a leg-shackling to me."

Daniel's body sagged with relief. "*That* explains why I've no memory of a wedding ceremony, how I came to be here, or how we came to be sharing a bed."

The amount of whisky he'd consumed explained why he had no memory of repeating marriage vows or of being carried to this room, but Miranda refrained from pointing it out. He wouldn't believe it anyway. Because he didn't want to believe it.

"How did I get here?"

"Ned and I brought you. . . ."

"Ned?"

"My footman," she reminded him. "You were bleeding quite badly, and I didn't know where else to take you." Miranda reached for the brocade robe lying at the foot of the bed, slipped it on over her sheet, then rolled gracefully off the mattress and onto the floor. She had to get away before she made a complete fool of herself.

"Where are you going?"

"Nature calls, Your Grace." Miranda smiled brightly. Too brightly. And ruthlessly held back the tears threatening to overtake her, but her voice barely wavered. "For me and no doubt for you as well." Walking around to the foot of the bed, Miranda bent over and pulled the chamber pot from beneath the bed, then handed it to Daniel.

Daniel blinked in surprise. "I may require assistance," he told her. "Will you send a footman in to help me?"

"Would that I could, Your Grace, but I'm afraid you'll have to make do without one—or wait until I return to help you."

"What?" He was truly astonished.

"There's no one here but us, Your Grace."

"Ned?" Daniel glanced down at the pink sheet. He was as naked beneath it as she had been.

Surely, Miranda hadn't . . .

"Ned carried you up here, put you on the bed, and helped me remove your coat and boots before I sent him home." She answered his unspoken query. "Under the circumstances, I thought the fewer people who knew the nature and the gravity of your wound, the better."

Daniel turned his attention to the fresh bandage covering the wound in his side, then back to Miranda. The bleeding had stopped, and although the wound ached like the devil and his head felt as if it would explode, he didn't feel feverish. "Who tended it?"

"I did." Miranda shrugged her shoulders. "My needlework isn't as neat as your Mistress Beekins's, but I managed to stop the bleeding and disinfect the wound."

"You sewed me up again?"

"Yes. But I've never stitched a person before, so you'll most likely carry a scar to remind you of your narrow escape from—" She looked at him. "You told me you'd been shot, but you didn't tell me how it came about."

"It came about when the man on the other end of the pistol pulled the trigger."

Miranda felt her heart skip a beat. "Would that man happen to be a certain Mistress Beekins's husband?"

"Mistress Beekins's . . ." Daniel frowned.

"You talk in your sleep, Your Grace."

Apparently not enough, if Miranda thought . . . The woman was old enough to be his mother and married to boot. . . . "I don't dally with other men's wives, Lady Miranda."

"I'm delighted to hear it," she retorted. "But you *were* shot, Your Grace."

Daniel made a face at her.

"Please, tell me you weren't dueling over a point of honor."

"I wasn't."

She blinked at him, all wide-eyed innocence. "Over some other woman then?"

The corners of Daniel's mouth turned up in a small smile. "Fishing?"

"How does one manage to get shot while fishing?"

"I didn't," he replied.

"You said . . ." Miranda began.

Daniel cut her off. "I said you were fishing. For answers."

"You aren't going to tell me, are you?" She asked the question, but Miranda already knew the answer.

"I don't think so," he replied.

"Do you think that's fair?" she demanded, knowing she sounded like a petulant child but unable to keep from asking. "After everything I did for you last night?"

He slowly turned his head from side to side. "No. But fairness has nothing to do with it. We have a history together. I cherish our friendship, Miranda, and I appreciate the help you've given me." He paused to take a breath. "Indeed, I don't know what I would have done without your help, but accepting your help doesn't obligate me to share every facet of my life with you. Or mean I want you to share every facet of your life with me." He glanced down at the sheet covering him and offered her his most charming smile to take the sting out of his words. "I've few secrets left. And a man's entitled to keep a bit of an air of mystery about him."

Miranda fought to keep from doubling over at the pain he inflicted so thoughtlessly, fought to keep from retaliating in kind, but failed. "I'll remember that the next time your body's wracked with chills or you're burning up with fever. I'll remind myself that I'm under no obligation to share my body heat or anything else with you."

"Share your body heat . . ." He'd experienced his share of childhood bumps and bruises and endured the aftereffects of too much drink on more occasions than he cared to remember, but Daniel had never been ill. He hadn't suffered more than the occasional head cold since he was a child. He found the idea that he'd endured fever and chills without knowing it remarkable. "I've never suffered from fever or chills."

"You did last evening." She ran a hand over her hair in an effort to smooth the tangles and blushed. "Off and on throughout the night. I dosed you with willow bark and did everything I knew to do to ease your discomfort, but . . ."

He lifted his eyebrow in query. "Willow bark doesn't agree with me." As a treatment for a hangover or anything else.

"Would that I had known that before you spewed it all over me," Miranda answered wryly, recalling the damage he'd inflicted on her green silk dress.

Daniel softened his voice. "You must be exhausted."

She shrugged her shoulders once again and focused her attention on the pink rug to keep from seeing the look in his eyes. "Yes, well . . . I slept a bit."

"With me?"

"One does what one must to help a friend," she replied awkwardly.

"I suppose so," he agreed, "but sharing your body heat . . ." He wrinkled his brow in thought. "You've gone above and beyond the bounds of friendship, Miranda."

"Like you said before, Your Grace, I only did what any other wi . . . friend . . . would do."

Daniel thought about his friends. Would Jarrod or Colin or Griff or Jonathan or Alex have crawled beneath the covers while he was suffering chills and shared their body heat with him? It was possible. But only if his life or theirs had been in danger. . . . A man would lay down his life for his friends, but . . . "A female friend, perhaps," Daniel replied. "I'm not so sure about the male ones." He ran his fingers through his hair, then flashed Miranda a wicked smile. "At any rate, waking up to find a female friend sharing her body heat is a pleasure. Waking up to find a male friend doing the same doesn't bear contemplating. . . ." He shuddered at the possibility. "At any rate, I don't know how to thank you."

"There's no need to thank me, Your Grace. As you pointed out so eloquently, our friendship doesn't obligate you to me in any way." Miranda turned and hurried out the door before she made a bigger fool of herself by bursting into tears.

Daniel realized he'd hurt her the moment the words left her mouth. "Miranda . . ." he began, trying to stop her, trying to make amends.

But it was too late.

The room was empty.

He was alone. Talking to himself.

Chapter 13

*"It was a dream of perfect bliss,
Too beautiful to last."*
—Thomas Haynes Bayly, 1797–1839

*H*er eyes were red and swollen when she returned to the bedchamber. And although she'd splashed cool water on her face in the kitchen, where she'd retreated to make her ablutions, there was no disguising the fact that she'd spent the better part of half an hour sobbing.

She didn't know why she always allowed him to get beneath her skin. But she did, and it had taken less than a day for marriage to Daniel to turn her into a veritable watering pot.

In all fairness, Miranda knew that she wouldn't have shed a single tear had Daniel remembered taking the vows that had made her his duchess—or if he'd seemed the least bit happy by the prospect. But nothing was further from the truth.

Daniel was horrified by the very idea.

What should be the happiest day of her life was turning into a nightmare. Ned hadn't returned, and neither had Rupert. She was tired and hungry and disappointed, and she hadn't anything to wear. She had married a man who didn't want a wife. And compounded her mistake by lying to him, telling Daniel what he wanted to hear, telling him that he'd fallen asleep before the bishop could marry them instead of telling him the truth.

Miranda had no one to blame for her tears but herself. She had known Daniel was in no condition to marry her or to remember it afterward. She had taken advantage of his moment of weakness. But how could she deny herself the thing she wanted most when it was within her grasp? How could she refuse his proposal? When Daniel had insisted on marrying her then and there?

And now that it was done, how long could she pretend she'd never said "I do"?

Taking a deep, calming breath, Miranda knocked once, then opened the bedroom door to find Daniel standing by the casement window overlooking Curzon Street with the coverlet from the bed wrapped around him and tucked beneath his arms.

He turned to face her as she entered.

"What are you doing out of bed?"

"Answering the call of nature was easier on my feet."

Miranda looked at the open window, then at Daniel, and back again. "You didn't."

"Of course not," he assured her. "I know better than to use a front window."

She relaxed.

Daniel couldn't resist. "I used the chamber pot and the side window."

Miranda glanced at the side window that overlooked the narrow lane between her house and the one beside it, and at the chamber pot sitting on the floor at the foot of the bed, its porcelain lid firmly in place. She didn't know whether to believe him or not.

Until he gave her a wicked smile.

"You're in luck, milady, for this happens to be a very modern house. There's a bath through that door." He pointed toward a door that Miranda had supposed led to a sitting room. Ned had neglected to mention that the master bedchamber connected to a bath, and Miranda hadn't thought to look. "With a Bramah toilet, sink, and bath, complete with hot and cold taps." He shrugged his shoulders. "But the water coming out of both taps is cold." He turned suddenly, leaned out the front window, and whistled to someone down below. "Up here."

"Daniel!" Miranda's heart beat a rapid tattoo. "Someone might recognize you."

"Wearing a pink toga and morning whiskers?" he asked, rubbing his hand over the whiskers that had appeared on his face overnight. "Not likely."

"I recognize you," Miranda shot back. "And there may be other residents of Curzon Street who will. Especially if you fall out of the window and onto the street below." She frowned as he leaned a bit farther out the window. "What on earth are you doing?"

He glanced over his shoulder at Miranda as if the sight of a half-naked duke leaning out an upper story window was a common occurrence. "Ordering breakfast."

Miranda was clearly surprised. "Breakfast?"

Daniel nodded. "I'm hungry. It seems like days since I've eaten." He paused. "I missed the milkmaids and the bakers, but the pieman's down below. Didn't you hear him?"

"No, I didn't." She glanced at the clock on the mantel. It was nearly half past seven. The St. Germaine town house sat in the middle of the block on Upper Brook Street, behind Park Lane, and the dairy maids generally reached the streets surrounding it at seven, followed by the bakers, piemen, and fruit vendors around eight o'clock in the morning. Miranda supposed it took them a bit longer to reach Curzon Street. Still, she hadn't heard the noise outside the house because she'd been crying in the kitchen.

"Well," Daniel drawled, "would you like a pie?"

Miranda nodded.

Daniel held out four fingers. "Two apple and two cherry." He turned back to Miranda. "Have we anything to drink? Tea? Coffee?" He shuddered. "Lemonade?"

"I don't think so," she answered. "And at any rate, I don't know how to brew coffee or tea or make lemonade."

"Tsk, tsk." Daniel made a clucking sound with his tongue. "I'm a duke," he reminded her, "and I know how to brew tea and coffee. And you, a mere marchioness . . . I thought all women of lesser title knew how to brew tea and coffee."

"We know how to *pour* tea and coffee," she corrected. "And how to ask suitors to fetch lemonade. We employ servants who brew it."

"Not at the moment." Daniel turned to the window and ordered three coffees from the pieman—two strong and black and the other with cream and sugar. "And luckily, since we're in London, we won't have to wait for servants to come and do it. All we need are a few pennies . . ."

Miranda took the hint. Collecting her reticule from the drawer of the night table, she reached inside for a shilling and handed it to Daniel.

"Thanks." Daniel took the shilling and flipped it out the window to the pieman. "He's leaving the basket on the front steps. I'll go down and collect it," he said, as he turned to Miranda. "It is Thursday, isn't it?"

"Yes."

"Then I'd better hurry. I've an important meeting at eight." Glancing around for his clothes, Daniel discovered his jacket, waistcoat, and trousers lying in a heap in a puddle on the bedroom rug along with what looked to be a gentleman's nightshirt and a pair of mint green dancing slippers.

Puzzled by the fact that Miranda's green dancing slippers were beneath the pile of wet garments he identified as mostly belonging to him, Daniel bent at the waist to retrieve them. But the morning's exertion caught up with him. His knees went weak as his legs refused to support his weight. He became lightheaded, and his face lost all color. Clutching the green ribbons in his fist, Daniel grabbed for the window ledge, missed, and fell to his knees.

"Daniel!" Miranda caught him as he hit the floor.

He offered her the ribbons and the ruined slippers attached to them. "These are yours, I believe."

Miranda tossed the slippers aside.

"You may need those," Daniel informed her in a weak voice. "To go downstairs and collect our breakfast from the front steps." He looked up at her. "I'd be a gentleman and go, but my garments are all wet. And at any road, I don't believe I could manage just yet." He looked at her, amazement etched on his features. "Suddenly I'm as weak as a kitten."

"It's no wonder," she said. "You lost a lot of blood last night, and you haven't had time or the nourishment to regain your strength." She noticed the beads of perspiration forming on his upper lip and placed her palm against his forehead.

His fever had returned.

And it was his own fault, Miranda thought uncharitably. The stubborn man hadn't stayed in bed but had insisted on opening the window and ordering breakfast.

"I bled on your ball gown," Daniel suddenly remembered.

"No matter," Miranda told him. "I've plenty of other dresses."

"You don't seem to be wearing one," he commented dryly.

"I'm not going anywhere," she said. "And neither are you."

"My meeting is very important," he told her. "I must be there."

"Important enough to risk having someone discover you're injured?" she asked. "Because that's what you'll be doing if you try to go there. And even if you had the strength to manage, I cannot see you walking into your meeting wearing a pink bed sheet and bandages, and that's all I have to offer until Ned returns."

"When will that be?"

Miranda shrugged. "I've no idea," she admitted. "He should have already returned, but he's obviously been detained. Most likely my mother needed Ned and the coach for errands."

"Most likely," Daniel grumbled, unhappy with the state of affairs.

"I could find a runner who could send a note around to your valet at Sussex House requesting a full change of clothing," she suggested.

"No!" Daniel protested. "My valet would insist on bringing it himself, and if Malden learned of my injury, there would be no keeping it quiet. The news would be in every ton household within minutes."

"What?"

"It's true," Daniel affirmed. "I've learned over the years that Malden cannot keep a secret. It's simply not in his nature."

Miranda was alarmed at that admission. A man in Daniel's position needed a valet he could trust implicitly. Especially since Daniel talked in his sleep. "Why do you keep him?"

"He's an excellent valet, and he's been with me since I left the university," Daniel replied. "What grounds should I give to dismiss him? The fact that he cannot be trusted to keep a secret? He told me that when I hired him. I can't dismiss him for it now simply because it's sometimes inconvenient."

"Make a list of what you need and I'll send Ned to your tailor's on Bond Street."

"Ned isn't here," Daniel pointed out. "And even if he were, I doubt he could secure a suit of clothing for me in time for my meeting."

The Free Fellows League meeting was important, but not important enough to risk having Jarrod find out he'd been shot. The information Daniel had to offer on French and Spanish troop movements was almost identical to the information Jonathan had brought back on the previous mission. The French and Spanish were massing their troops for a battle, and although Salamanca appeared to be the most likely place, no one could say for sure if that was the destination. All anyone knew for certain at the moment was that Wellington was retreating from Burgos by way of Venta del Pozo and heading toward the area where the French and the Spanish troops were gathering.

The only other thing Daniel knew for certain was that even if he were able to do so, there was no way he would walk into White's wearing bandages and a pink toga for any reason. "My clothes are wet," he said, "and yours are . . ."

"Ruined," she replied.

"That's a shame," he said. "I liked the dress you wore last night. The one that matched those shoes." He frowned. "I thought the style and the color were most becoming."

So much so that he'd bled all over it and then been ill upon it.

"I'll have Madam Racine make up another one just like it," Miranda promised. "And send you the bill. Now, let me help you back into bed." She gripped him around the waist, half-lifting, half-pulling him to his feet, and supporting his weight as she walked him back to the bed.

He tried to help her by carrying as much of his weight as possible, but Daniel was as weak as a newborn babe, and Miranda bore the brunt of it. "You may be hungry, but you aren't in any danger of starving to death right away," she said with a groan. "You weigh just as much this morning as you did last night."

"A ton and a half if I remember correctly."

If he remembered correctly. Miranda wondered how he could remember the inconsequential parts of the previous evening and not recall the most important few minutes of it. How could he remember that she had accused him of weighing a ton and a half as she had half-carried him across the lawn and not remember exchanging wedding vows with her? Using a bit more force than necessary, Miranda boosted Daniel into the mattress.

Daniel was a man accustomed to giving orders and accustomed to having servants at his beck and call twenty-four hours a day, but he wasn't accustomed to having anyone *care* for him the way Miranda seemed determined to do.

Daniel hated succumbing to weakness and relying on Miranda's help for the most basic of necessities, but he was only a man—a man who had been shot, lost a great deal of blood, and drunk a great deal of whisky the previous evening to mute the pain. He was only a man, who hurt like the very devil, and Daniel heaved a grateful sigh as Miranda shoved him back into bed—where he no doubt belonged for a while longer. "Thanks, Miranda." He let go of the coverlet he'd wrapped around his waist and slipped between the sheets. "You're the only woman I know strong enough to . . ."

Miranda held up her hand. "Please, Your Grace, don't thank me or pay me any more compliments. I don't think I can stand it." She pulled the pink sheet up over him, then plumped the pillows at his head, arranging them so he could sit up and lean against them.

He stared up at her face, saw her red, puffy eyes, and realized that Miranda had been crying. "I'm sorry."

"For what?"

"Making you cry."

"You didn't," she said.

"Someone did."

Miranda glared at him. "I don't want to discuss it. And if you insist on pursuing this line of conversation or in paying me any more compliments, I'll help myself to the pies and coffee you purchased with my shilling and let you do without."

"Miranda, you wouldn't . . ."

"Yes, Daniel, I would."

He flashed her one of his devastating smiles. "You're a very remarkable woman."

Miranda's heart seemed to skip a beat when he smiled at her like that, when he looked at her with that look of sincerity in his dark blue eyes. . . . "That sounded suspiciously like a compliment, Your Grace."

"It was."

She slowly shook her head and clucked her tongue. "And I thought you were hungry. . . ."

He studied the expression on her face and was convinced she was about to do as she'd promised.

When would he learn that Miranda St. Germaine wasn't like other women? She was different. And that's what he liked about her. She was strong and straightforward and intelligent and honest and dependable. She didn't play girlish games, didn't pretend to be what she wasn't, and she didn't expect him to pretend to be what he wasn't. He had been born male and a marquess. She had been born female and a countess. He'd inherited a dukedom. She'd inherited a marquessate. And none of that made any difference to her.

Miranda St. Germaine was one of a handful of people he knew who wasn't intimidated or impressed by his title or his wealth. She didn't defer to him simply because he outranked her. She looked him in the eye and spoke her mind, acting as if they were equals. Daniel had forgotten how much he liked that about her, forgotten that while her green eyes, auburn hair, and long legs had been the first thing he'd noticed about her, he'd been enchanted by the person inside the beautiful exterior. He kept forgetting that Miranda rarely made idle threats. "Ah, Miranda, have a heart. . . ." His stomach rumbled, protesting its emptiness.

She arched an eyebrow at him. "I had one once," she reminded him. "I gave it to you. You broke it."

"I was young and foolish," he said. "I'm older now."

"Are you suggesting I give you another chance, Your Grace?"

"The compliment I gave you was genuine."

She grinned, showing her perfect white teeth. "Yes, I believe it was. And since I've heard it said that the way to a man's heart is through his stomach, you would do well to remember that so long as you are dependent upon me for care and sustenance, the way to this marchioness's heart is through genuine adoration."

Daniel thought for a moment. "How long do you intend to keep me dependent upon you for care and sustenance?"

Miranda shrugged her shoulders. "That depends upon how rapidly you mend, Your Grace."

"In that event . . ." Daniel's blue eyes sparkled with mirth despite his fever. "Do you prefer verbal or physical genuine adoration?"

For once, Miranda's quick wit failed her.

Daniel pressed his advantage. "Or a combination of both?"

"Why don't I go collect our breakfast so you can find out?" Miranda asked suggestively.

Chapter 14

"A man says what he knows,
A woman says what will please."
—Jean Jacques Rousseau, 1712–1778

Miranda was as good as her word.
    She made her way down the stairs to the front steps, where she collected the basket with the fruit pies and the coffee and carried them inside the house to the kitchen. Miranda set the basket on a worktable, walked over to the butler's pantry, and gathered everything she needed for a breakfast tray—a large tray, napkins, serviceable china and flatware, and a small china pot for the coffee—then returned to the kitchen table.

    She emptied the basket, took the two plates she'd brought from the butler's pantry, and placed an apple and a cherry pie on each one. She poured coffee from the pieman's metal pot into a small china one, added two cups and two saucers, two spoons and two forks, and two linen napkins, then set everything on the tray. She poured a dollop of cream into one cup, added a lump of sugar from the two lumps the pieman had sold them, then carefully arranged everything on the tray and covered it with a clean linen cloth.

    With the breakfast tray arranged to her satisfaction, Miranda carried it up to the stairs to Daniel.

"I expected to dine out of a vendor's basket and pewter mugs." Daniel rubbed his hands together in anticipation and looked up at her as Miranda set the tray across his lap and lifted the cloth.

"There were no pewter mugs in the pieman's basket," Miranda informed him. "Only cheap tin ones."

"These are much nicer," Daniel agreed, waving his hand through the air above the tray, indicating the table set with linen napkins and china, before reaching for the small pot of coffee.

"Allow me." Miranda bent over the tray. "I cannot brew it, but I excel at pouring it from pot to cup."

"Be my guest."

She did just that, filling his cup to the rim with the steaming brew without clinking the spout against the rim of the cup or spilling a drop of the precious liquid.

"You're a very talented pourer, milady," Daniel said, lifting his cup from its saucer and taking his first sip of coffee.

"That's just one of my many talents," Miranda replied, placing the small coffee pot back on the tray before sliding a plate of fruit pies close enough for Daniel to reach. "Wait until you see the others."

"I like what I see already," he admitted.

"Then I'm sure you'll be most impressed with my needlework." She grinned at him. "I'll need to check your wound after we break our fast."

Daniel groaned.

"Eat," she advised, when she realized he was politely waiting for her to pull up a chair and join him. "I know you're hungry. You needn't wait for me."

He didn't.

He devoured two pies—an apple and a cherry—and drank his first cup of coffee in the time it took her to pull up a chair, sit down, and spread her napkin on her lap.

Daniel was eyeing a third pie when Miranda reached for her cup of coffee and the apple pie. "Help yourself to the cherry one," she offered.

"I bought it for you."

"One pie is more than enough for me." She looked up at him. "I generally make do with tea and toast in the morning," she said, savoring the last bite of apple pie. "And I'm not overly fond of cherries. I prefer apple. Besides, I had a light repast before I left for the party last night. You apparently did not."

Daniel frowned as his stomach rumbled once again. "My last meal was Tuesday evening."

Miranda took another swallow of coffee, then set her cup down on its saucer. She lifted the remaining cherry pie and offered it to Daniel. "Take it. Please."

"Cherry is my favorite." Daniel didn't hesitate a second time. He lifted the cherry pie from the plate, swallowed it in three bites, and licked the cherry filling from his fingers.

She stared at his mouth, mesmerized by the sight. Miranda couldn't remember the last time she'd seen an adult enjoy a fruit pie more. He reminded her of a child tasting a sweet for the first time.

Suddenly self-conscious, Daniel met Miranda's intense stare. "Has my nose doubled in length? Or have I suddenly sprouted horns?"

She shook her head. "You've cherry filling on your face."

"Where?"

"There." She gestured toward the left side of his mouth.

He swiped at it just as Miranda reached over and captured a bit of the filling caught in the corner of his mouth on the tip of her finger and offered it to him. "You missed this," she told him.

"Thanks."

When Daniel licked the cherry filling off her finger, Miranda shivered from her head to her toes, warmth suffusing her body. She marveled at the effect. If the mere swipe of his tongue against her finger could produce such a reaction, imagine what his kiss could do to her. Miranda shivered again in anticipation. She reached for her coffee and rattled the cup in its saucer.

Daniel looked over and gave her a knowing smile. "You taste as good as you look, Miranda."

She blushed, glanced down at the brocade robe she was wearing, then automatically reached up to push her hair off her face and smooth it back into place. "I'm a mess."

Daniel finished his cup of coffee and placed his empty dishes on the tray. "I rather like you looking a bit mussed in the morning," he told her.

"That's nice to know," she said. "Because until Ned returns, this is all I have to wear."

"The robe is most becoming, and seeing you this way is not nearly as daunting as having you perfectly turned out and so sharp-tongued all the time."

His comment gave her pause, and Miranda frowned. "Is that how you regard me? Daunting and sharp-tongued?"

"I regard you as perfect and sharp-tongued," he replied. "Whenever we're together."

Miranda sought refuge in her coffee. It was cold. But she lifted the cup and drank it anyway. "I don't mean to be sharp-tongued or perfect." She looked at him over the silver rim of the cup. "I try not to be—especially when I'm around you—but we seem to bring out the worst in each another."

The look Daniel gave her was tender and knowing. "Is that what you think it is?"

Miranda set her cup down once again and nodded. "We simply rub each other the wrong way no matter how hard we try not to or how much we wish it were otherwise."

"I think our problem is just the opposite, Miranda," Daniel said.

"I don't understand." She studied the expression on his face, searching for the meaning behind his words. The opposite of rubbing each other the wrong way was rubbing each other the right way, and she and Daniel had never been in harmony. . . .

"We didn't rub each other the wrong way when I first paid a call upon you," he said. "Nor on the other times we spent together during our courtship."

"No," she agreed, "I don't suppose we did. But our courtship only lasted a few weeks. . . ."

"What about the weeks we spent at Abernathy Manor keeping Alyssa company while Griff was away at war?" he asked. "We got along famously then."

They had. And it had given Miranda hope for the future, but Daniel had withdrawn once again, and they had gradually resumed their old adversarial relationship.

"We got along beautifully," Miranda replied. "But we couldn't sustain it. One day everything was wonderful and the next day, you were gone. That was three years ago, Daniel, and except for the disaster that is your mother's annual gala, we've hardly spoken."

"We could have sustained it," he disagreed. "If we had wanted to. If *I* had wanted to. Why do you think I left Abernathy Manor?"

Miranda shrugged her shoulders. "I've been asking myself that question for three years."

"Then it's time you had your answer," Daniel replied.

"Which is?"

"I left because you and I were getting along too well," Daniel admitted. "Because I was afraid I might come to enjoy your company too much."

"You left because you *enjoy* my company?" Miranda was having a difficult time comprehending the fact that Daniel had sacrificed her companionship because he liked her.

Daniel nodded. "I left because the fact is that we don't rub each other the wrong way. Quite the contrary. We rub each other the right way. We don't scratch and claw because we dislike one another, we do it because we like each other too much. It's called sexual attraction, and it's a prelude to mating. We're fighting our attraction to one another."

"The question is why?" Miranda asked.

"I think you're fighting it because I hurt you once and you're afraid I'll do it again."

Miranda blinked.

"I'm fighting it because I don't want to be encumbered

with the responsibility of a wife in addition to everything else for which I'm responsible," Daniel paused. "And more than that, I fight my attraction to you because I don't want to hurt you again."

Too late. Miranda inhaled sharply at the pain, but Daniel didn't seem to notice.

"When I marry, it must be for the good of the Duchy of Sussex."

"You consider me a poor choice for the Duchy of Sussex?"

Daniel shook his head. "It isn't that simple." He pinned her with his gaze, willing her to understand why he felt the way he felt. "My primary duty is to continue the Sussex line, and I need a duchess who is willing to take on the responsibility of bearing my children and of providing for the people whose survival depends upon me. It's a job to which she must devote a lifetime."

"I understand duty and responsibility quite well, Your Grace," Miranda reminded him. "For I hold an ancient and honorable title of my own. Like you, I must see to the welfare of the people who rely upon the St. Germaine holdings for their livelihoods."

"Then you should understand why I must choose with my head instead of with my . . ." Daniel frowned. He'd almost said his heart, but he wasn't completely convinced he was thinking with his heart rather than his head and was fairly certain that it was another more insistent part of his anatomy. "I'm a duke and the title affords me great wealth and opportunities of which other men can only dream, but it also means that duty to the title comes before personal desires. A duke must hold a part of himself in reserve. He must practice restraint and never indulge himself over-much." He could hear his father's voice repeating the tenets that had been such a large part of his childhood lessons. "A duke has few friends and fewer peers. He cannot wear his heart upon his sleeve or put his wishes above the needs of his people. He cannot shirk his duty or burden anyone else with it. The responsibilities come with the title and they must never be parceled out to others. The duty is his alone."

"Did your father teach you those things?"

Daniel nodded. "It was the code by which he lived. The code by which all the dukes of Sussex have lived."

"You're describing a very lonely life, Your Grace," Miranda murmured.

"It *is* a lonely life." Daniel shoved his hair off his forehead. "I wouldn't wish it upon anyone." He heaved a sigh. "A duke is always set apart from everyone else. Even Griffin is having a difficult time adjusting to the added pressure of being a duke."

"Griffin has Alyssa to help him."

"My father had my mother," Daniel replied. "And although I know you'll find it difficult to believe, she was a great source of strength for him."

Miranda wrinkled her brow. He was right. It was difficult for her to believe the duchess had been a source of strength for anyone, but . . .

"My mother was the daughter of a viscount, and she's always been very conscious of the fact that she married well beyond her position in society. She devoted herself to the running of Sussex House and maintaining our position in society. She did everything she could to assist my father in his efforts to increase and preserve our holdings, but the weight of the responsibility drove him to an early grave." Daniel briefly bowed his head, then met her gaze. "My father was the strongest man I've ever known. He died reviewing account books at his desk in his study at Sussex House at the age of five and thirty. One day he was strong and healthy and full of life, and the next afternoon, he complained of eyestrain and a headache while deciphering the account books, then suddenly slumped over his desk and died." Daniel took a deep breath. "My mother was five years his junior when she became a widow and assumed the daunting task of raising a son and protecting my inheritance until I came of age. Fulfilling her obligations and living up to the promises she made when she married my father has made her the woman you see today." He pulled a face. "And I can't imagine asking a woman with a title and grand estates of her own over which to worry to give up dreams and a large part of herself in order to become what my mother has become. I can't imagine subjecting any woman to the constant scrutiny of the ton and the public— much less a woman for whom I might have deep feelings. I don't want her to have to put away her girlish dreams or to sacrifice her original obligations in order to fulfill the obligations of a duchess."

"Everyone puts away their childish dreams and makes sacrifices for the ones they love, Daniel. That's part of growing up, part of life."

"I don't want the people about whom I care to have to make sacrifices simply because they wish to share my life. I was born to this position," he said simply. "I'm a duke. I didn't ask to be one, but like you, I had no choice. Still, I never believed I would have to assume the title." Daniel closed his eyes. "I adored my father. We were both early risers."

Miranda gave him a smug, knowing smile.

"You may not be able to tell it from your experience this morning, but I am generally quite an early riser," he protested. "And when I was a little boy my father used to sneak up to the nursery, remove me from Nanny's supervision, and carry me on his shoulders to the front of the house. Long before Cook had the ovens in the kitchen hot, Father would open a window and we'd call down to the street vendors ordering whatever took our fancy for breakfast."

"Like cherry pies."

"Cherry was always my favorite," Daniel said. "We ate cherry pies from the street vendors nearly every day of the season when we were in London. It was our secret, and it made me feel special to have my father's undivided attention for a while." He wiped the sheen of perspiration from his brow with the back of his hand. "I never had his attention at Haversham House or any of our other houses because there were too many other people who demanded it. The only time I ever really spent with my father was at home in London early in the mornings, when we'd order milk from the dairymaids and hot cherry pies from the pieman.

"I was only three and ten when he died."

"I'm sorry." Miranda and Daniel had moved in the same circles of society since they were children, but he'd been sent away to school when he was seven, and Miranda had been educated at home. She knew a lot of his history but not all of it.

"And I've been responsible for hundreds of people since that day. Suddenly, everyone looked to me for answers instead of to my father or my mother. Suddenly, everyone depended upon me." He exhaled. "And although my father had done his best to prepare me, I wasn't prepared." He gave a little snort of derision. "What boy that age is? Suddenly, I employed hundreds of people whose livelihoods and in some cases, their very lives depended upon how well I did my duty. And now that I'm a man grown, I find myself in the rather odd position of admitting that I haven't rushed to the altar for the simple reason that I don't wish to assume responsibility for anyone else. I'm not ready to put away all my childish dreams or ask anyone else to do so."

Especially a freethinker like Miranda. He admired her strong, independent spirit and rebellious streak, and hated the idea of watching her change, hated the thought of watching Miranda reinvent herself as the Duchess of Sussex or anyone else. Daniel wanted her to stay just the way she was. He liked the fact that she stood straight and tall and looked men in the eyes, liked the fact that she considered herself an equal, even if most men—including the peers who sat in the House of Lords—did not. He applauded the fact that Miranda petitioned the Crown for the right to occupy her seat in the House of Lords every year at the opening of Parliament, even though she knew she would never be allowed to take her seat among her peers. But she petitioned the Crown all the same and had done so ever since she'd inherited her father's title. Daniel admired her for refusing to remain in the background. And he wished he could be more like her.

He was haunted by the thought of dying the way his father had died. Of being overwhelmed by the business of running the estates, of dying before he had ever truly lived.

"I still have dreams," Daniel told her, "and goals to accomplish before I'm required to forfeit my wild ambitions in order to settle down and produce an heir to succeed me." *So that I can die prematurely while working at the same desk where my father died.*

He wanted to tell Miranda the whole truth, but the truth sounded juvenile and childish—even to his own ears. The truth was that he was enjoying being a Free Fellow, enjoying the cloak-and-dagger work, the adventure that was so different from his day-to-day life as the Duke of Sussex. "Despite what my mother wants or hopes or thinks, I have no intention of marrying for at least"—he paused to calculate—"another twenty years."

"You were ready to marry Alyssa Carrollton three years ago," she pointed out.

"I was *willing* to consider marriage to Alyssa in order to get my mother to stop pushing her candidates for duchess at me."

"Three years ago you were willing to marry, but now, you won't consider it for at least another twenty years?"

"That's right," he said. "Because three years ago, I made a bargain with my mother that I would offer marriage to the girl of her choosing, provided the girl agreed to have me. Alyssa, as you well know, had the good sense to reject me wholeheartedly."

"You pretended to pursue her," Miranda realized, "but secretly, you were glad she rejected you."

"Glad isn't the word for it," he admitted. "I was thrilled

beyond belief." He looked at Miranda to gauge her reaction, well aware that he was talking about her closest friend.

She scowled. "Yet you continued to play the role of determined suitor after she married Griffin."

"I had good reasons for doing so," he explained. "After all, I am a duke. And Griff was only a viscount. I had a reputation to protect."

Miranda smiled. "You didn't give a fig about your reputation. You simply wanted to make Griffin jealous enough to claim his wife."

Daniel refrained from answering. Making Griffin jealous had been a result of his continued pursuit of Alyssa, but it hadn't been the principal reason behind it. He'd extended his pursuit of Alyssa in order to pass Colin and Jarrod's test. Passing their test had been Daniel's entrée into the Free Fellows League.

"You took a very big chance," Miranda said. "Your plan might have misfired and Alyssa might have chosen you."

He raised his eyebrows and looked at Miranda. "Not likely. She was far too sensible to want to be molded into society's idea of what a duchess should be."

"There's always a chance you might find someone who would be happy to take on the daunting task of becoming the Duchess of Sussex. A lot can change in twenty years." She folded her hands in her lap and looked down at them. In twenty years, she'd be too old to provide an heir to carry on the St. Germaine line or a ducal one. "For the better."

Daniel nodded. "Or I may have even more responsibility in twenty years than I do now."

He wasn't being completely honest with Miranda or himself. Daniel knew that the war with France would be over long before twenty years passed. There might be other wars to fight, but the current Free Fellows would most likely be retired from active service, and there would be nothing to keep him from marrying and having a family. Nothing except the fact that Daniel dreaded the day he would look in his son's eyes and realize that *he* was the only thing keeping his son from fulfilling his destiny. Because as long as the ninth duke drew breath, the tenth duke would be forced to bide his time and wait in the wings.

And the realization would start when his son became old enough to think for himself, old enough to figure things out and see the chinks in his father's armor. Daniel had been seven when his father had begun to push him away and withdraw. His father had delighted in his company until Daniel had gone away to Eton. Daniel had continued to delight in his father's company, but the eighth duke had grown colder and seemed determined to avoid Daniel, until the distance between them widened into a gulf that had increased with every birthday.

There was no question that the eighth Duke of Sussex had loved his young son, but for some unknown reason, he hadn't been quite as enamored of the adolescent who would one day take his place.

Daniel didn't understand why his father had changed. He only knew that he had. And Daniel never wanted to do the same to his own son.

"That is generally how it works, Your Grace," Miranda reminded him. "The older we get, the more responsibilities we have. Until the day we hand our responsibilities and our titles to our heirs. Hopefully, those heirs will be the children we've borne and reared and prepared for the job ahead of them."

"It's not going to work that way for me," he protested.

"Planning to live forever, are we?" She looked him in the eye. "Because if that's your ambition, Your Grace, you'd best stay away from men who point firearms at you."

"I don't intend to live forever," Daniel replied.

"From the looks of you, I'd say that was obvious." Miranda lowered her gaze to the strips of bandages binding his ribs.

He didn't appreciate the devil's advocate role she'd assumed. "What's your point, Miranda?"

"My point is that in twenty years, you'll be two score

and eight, older than my father was when I was born. He was two score and four," Miranda said. "He didn't inherit the title until he was forty, so he was compelled to marry a much younger wife. Just as you will have to do in order to get an heir."

Daniel frowned. He could barely tolerate the young society misses intent on capturing a lofty title now. How would he manage in twenty years? Daniel had settled on twenty as the number of years because it sounded a long way off, but he hadn't considered that the passage of time would change him physically or affect the way he chose his duchess. He was foolish not to have realized that the passage of time changed everything. He wouldn't stay young forever, and neither would Miranda.

Ignoring Daniel's mighty scowl, Miranda continued her story. "My father grew to love my mother, but they had almost nothing in common. And although my mother was fond of my father and respected him very much, she married him to please her parents, not because she loved him." She met Daniel's gaze. "My mother was ten and seven, and Father was over twice her age. So, they agreed that he wouldn't trouble my mother with his conjugal visits once she had conceived and borne an heir. My mother did her duty when she conceived and gave birth to me. And because my father kept his word, he knew I would be his only child and his heir. But I was a female who hadn't a prayer of surviving and prospering in a man's world unless I learned to think and act the way a man would think and act. My father barely lived long enough to see me reach my majority." She met Daniel's gaze. "I certainly wouldn't wish his way of life on you, Your Grace."

"What way of life would you wish on me?" he asked.

"A long, happy, and healthy one," she replied. "Surrounded by the people you love and the people who love you—with a wife and children who love you."

Daniel recognized the sincerity in her eyes and tried to lighten the atmosphere. "With the way I feel at the moment, there is always the possibility that I won't be here in twenty years."

Miranda nodded, then reached out to press her palm against his forehead. "There is that."

"What?" Daniel sounded alarmed.

"You may die reviewing the account books at your desk in the study at Sussex House at the age of five and thirty like your father. Or you may succumb to this fever," she reminded him. "Your Mistress Beekins may not have gotten everything out of your wound. Or you may have damaged something when you pulled the stitches loose. Or I may have done something wrong or forgotten to do something when I restitched the wound. You could die from infection in this wound despite my best efforts to insure that you do not."

"What do you intend?" Daniel was wary of the look in Miranda's eyes.

"I intend"—she paused for effect—"to have my way. So, lie back and let me look at your injury."

Chapter 15

"Thank me no thankings, nor proud me no prouds."
—William Shakespeare, 1564–1616
Romeo and Juliet

"*Pastel thread?*" Daniel watched Miranda remove the bandage from his side to reveal a long S-shaped gash, two or three inches of which were stitched in sky-blue thread. "You sewed me up with pastel thread?" Thank God Malden couldn't see that!

She bit her bottom lip at the sight of his injury. The area around the gunshot wound was bruised, and the bruise had turned from dark red to an angry blue-and-purple color. Miranda untied the bandage and removed it, immensely relieved to find the linen clean and fresh. The ugly gash was about five inches long and marked a line from his ribs to his abdomen. The neat blue stitching she'd done on him had held, and although the wound was an angry pink color, there was no sign of infection.

"Be glad I sewed you up at all," Miranda defended her actions and her choice of thread. "And be thankful that I found silk, because according to Alyssa, it works best." She gave him a quelling look. "Or would you rather have had pink?"

"You couldn't match Mistress Beekins's serviceable black? Don't they make silk thread in black?"

"I'm sure they do, Your Grace," Miranda snapped, "but

beggars cannot be choosers. I was only able to find one sewing basket in this house, and it contained a limited supply of silk thread." She turned away and picked up the bar of soap she'd used the night before and a clean cloth, and dipped them into the basin she'd filled with water from the bathing room tap. "I chose blue because it matches your blood, and because I thought you would rather have blue silk stitches than stitches the color of this room." She wet and soaped the cloth, then wrung out the excess water and pressed it against Daniel's side.

He sucked in a breath. "Blast it, Miranda! That's cold!"

"As cold as your heart, Your Grace?" Miranda asked in a sickly sweet tone of voice. "Could mere water be that cold?"

Daniel blinked. "I've no idea what you mean."

"Then allow me to make it clear for you, Your Grace," Miranda continued, diligently bathing the wound, pleased to see that her blue stitches had held and that while there had been a bit of drainage, the bleeding had stopped. "Might it be possible that you've become so spoiled by your lofty title that you have no consideration for lesser beings?"

"Might it have been possible for you to set the basin near the fire to warm the water?" he inquired just as sweetly. "Because your ill-tempered accusation couldn't be further from the truth." He winced as Miranda scrubbed a bit harder with the soapy cloth than was necessary.

"You couldn't prove it by me." Miranda looked down at him. "'You sewed me up with pastel thread?'" she repeated, mimicking his tone. "'You couldn't match Mistress Beekins's serviceable black? Don't they make silk thread in black?' Do you have any idea how hard it was for me to sew you up at all? Do you have any idea how difficult it was for me to push a needle and thread—any color thread—through your flesh? I had to borrow your liquid courage and finish off what was left in your flask to keep my hands from shaking. And the entire time I was stitching your wound in sky-blue silk, I prayed I wasn't doing you further harm. . . . Wondering if you were going to live or die . . ." Miranda began to cry and angrily wiped at her tears with the back of her hand. "Are you so spoiled and arrogant that you've forgotten other people have feelings? Or have you simply forgotten that *I* have feelings? Feelings you seem to enjoy trampling?" She looked at him and shook her head. "The devil take you, Daniel! Have you, after all these years, finally become your mother's son? And if so, what in Hades do you want from me?"

Daniel was momentarily stunned by Miranda's outburst. They had been getting along so well, and then he'd gone and spoiled it with an uncharacteristic blunder. What did it matter what color his stitches were, so long as she had repaired the damage? Daniel clamped his jaw shut. But seeing sky-blue stitches in his side had come as a surprise.

Had he finally become his mother's son? Was he guilty of being callous and insensitive to the feelings of others? He didn't think so.

But he was guilty of being insensitive to Miranda's feelings.

He'd made her cry. Twice in one day. And Miranda never resorted to tears, never resorted to the weapon women had used against men since the beginning of time. Miranda fought back with wit and words and wisdom. She didn't cry. At least, Daniel had never known her to cry.

Until today.

Of course, he'd never asked the sort of favors from her that he had last night or this morning. He had never depended upon her to stitch his wound or to sit with him during the night or keep him safe and warm. But Daniel knew that everyone had a breaking point, and Miranda had apparently reached hers.

And no wonder.

Not only had he trampled her feelings, but he had asked more of her than he had ever asked of anyone. Daniel grimaced. He hadn't asked. He'd demanded. He'd ambushed her and demanded that she put her reputation and her emotions at risk by doing his bidding without regard for her feelings or for the consequences.

Blister it! He couldn't remember all the details of the previous evening, but he remembered this morning. Daniel was ashamed of himself. Miranda was right. He had thought the worst of her instead of the best. He had been demanding and ungracious and ungrateful. He wanted to blame it on his massive headache, but Daniel knew that he had, much to his chagrin, finally become his mother's son!

He'd expected Miranda to do the near impossible. And she'd done it. He shuddered. Miranda had kept him from bleeding to death, and he'd thanked her by criticizing the color of the thread she'd used. She'd been the best friend for whom any man could ask, and he'd treated her shabbily.

Daniel closed his eyes. He'd thanked Mistress Beekins for her care and had gone so far as to show his gratitude by giving her money. He hadn't been nearly as gracious to Miranda, and her task had been more difficult. Daniel had tried to thank her, of course, but his attempts had been so awkward and condescending that Miranda had threatened him with bodily harm if he complimented or thanked her again.

Mistress Beekins was a common woman with a husband and grown sons engaged in a very dangerous enterprise. Mistress Beekins was a midwife and a healer, accustomed to performing menial labor and tending the sick and wounded.

Miranda was a lady, a peer of the realm, an unmarried woman who had been born into a position that enabled her to have servants who took care of her every need. The only menial task Miranda had ever performed was weeding flowerbeds and cutting the blossoms. And she only performed those when she felt like gardening.

And now she was bathing him, cleansing the wound she'd sewn up, and assisting him with the most intimate of tasks. Daniel shuddered. The thought of pushing a needle and thread through *her* tender flesh sent cold shivers down his spine. And although he was not intimately acquainted with Miranda's body, Daniel was intimately acquainted with the *female* body.

As far as he knew, Miranda had never seen a naked man, much less bathed one.

She had dried her tears and composed herself by the time Daniel opened his eyes and reached up to take hold of her hand. "I owe you an apology, Miranda."

"I accept."

Daniel had expected her to make him grovel a bit. "Don't you want to hear it?"

"Not particularly."

"Why not?" he demanded.

"Because you're not very good at them," she answered.

"What makes you think that?" Daniel asked, genuinely curious.

"You're a duke, Daniel."

"So?"

"You're out of practice, because no one ever expects a duke to apologize or allows you to do so."

Miranda spoke the truth as she saw it, and Daniel rewarded her honesty with a smile. He was out of practice among most members of the ton for exactly the reasons Miranda mentioned. His friends in the Free Fellows and Miranda were the exception. "No one expects an unmarried lady to do what you're doing either."

"Which is?"

"Bathe a naked man."

Miranda gave him a mysterious smile.

Daniel was intrigued in spite of himself. "You haven't have you?"

"Haven't what?" She looked at him from beneath her eyelashes in a way that could only be called coy.

It was the first time Daniel had ever seen Miranda behave in such a manner. Flirtation had never been her forte. "Seen a naked man before?"

"How impolite of you to ask, Your Grace." Miranda ran

the bathing cloth over Daniel's torso, rinsed off the soap, then dried him with a length of toweling.

Daniel smiled once again. He was beginning to read her state of mind. Her use of his style was telling. Miranda only called him, "Your Grace," when she was angry or upset with him. "Impolite or not, I'm asking, milady."

"As a matter of fact, I have."

Daniel pursed his lips in thought. The Marchioness of St. Germaine was full of surprises today. "I don't believe you."

"It's true."

"Whom?" His blue eyes sparkled with mischief. "What man caught your fancy? Come now," he coaxed, "you can tell me. Was it the gallant Patrick Hollister with whom you danced this evening, or . . ."

"Last evening," Miranda corrected.

"Last evening," he amended. "Or was it Linton? Carville? Nash? Or the Austrian archduke?"

Daniel had seen her dancing with Lord Hollister, but Miranda gasped in surprise when he named the others. They were the gentlemen who'd seen her at Almack's last season and attempted to court her. She hadn't seriously considered any of them because she wanted Daniel. And she hadn't realized Daniel had been paying such close attention. "What do you know about those gentlemen?"

"I know Hollister is a good man who would make you a good husband," he answered truthfully. "I know that Linton and Nash are fortune hunters, and that Carville's very well set but has rather interesting alliances. The Austrian archduke is, well—" He paused, trying to find fault with the young, handsome archduke. "*Austrian*. And not at all suitable for you."

"I vow that if your opinion of me gets any higher, I shall die from the lack of atmosphere."

"I'm only trying to look out for you."

"Do you take me for a complete ninny?" she demanded. "I know Lord Hollister is a good man. I was friends with

Clea, his late wife. And I know Linton and Nash are for-tune hunters. *Everyone* knows they're fortune hunters. To you and to other members of the ton, I may appear desper-ate to marry, but I refused their persistent offers to court me. I'm not desperate enough to consider marriage with gentlemen who don't give a fig about my family heritage, or me—gentlemen who would marry a Jersey cow if she came with a lofty title and a healthy fortune." She glared at Daniel. "Do you really believe I would marry someone who would go through my fortune and leave me to fend for myself? Or that I would ever leave England to marry an archduke, no matter how attractive or wealthy? And what makes you think that I don't know that Lord Carville prefers young men?"

Daniel widened his eyes in surprise. "You allowed him to pay court to you."

"I allowed him to pay a call," Miranda corrected, "to state his business. He proposed generous terms for a suit-able marriage arrangement. I refused."

Daniel was momentarily stunned. "Carville proposed?"

"Yes, Daniel, Carville proposed to me last season." She pinned him with an unwavering gaze. "Is that so surpris-ing? You proposed to me last night."

"I was drunk last night," he defended.

"Lord Carville was sober last season," Miranda told him. "But I refused him just the same."

Daniel reached up and raked his fingers through his hair. "I had no idea that you were aware of Carville's pro-clivity. It's a very well kept secret." It was such a well kept secret that had he thought Miranda was serious about mar-rying the man, Daniel would have been forced to warn her about Carville's mating habits himself.

"Pooh!" she exclaimed. "My footman warned me about Lord Carville, and that was *before* Carville propositioned him. I may not understand exactly how two men . . ." She let that thought trail away. She didn't understand exactly how a man and a woman made love either. "But I know there are men who prefer other men, but who require a wife and an heir all the same.

"And while I appreciate the offer, I don't need you to keep my secret, Your Grace, for you have more than enough to worry about in keeping your own." Miranda's cheeks flushed with color when she realized she hadn't meant to go quite that far. She consoled herself by answering Daniel's question. "And to answer your question: I helped bathe my father during his last illness."

"Your father?" Daniel showed his discomfort at the physical comparison. "The only nude male body you've ever seen was your father's?"

"Except for paintings and statues and yours." She looked at him from beneath her lashes once again.

"Your father was an old man, Miranda," he said. "I am not."

"Ned said as much when he helped me undress you."

"Oh?" He glanced around.

"Yes," she confirmed. "And he told me you wouldn't appreciate the comparison to my father, but I assured him that as far as I was concerned, one naked male is very much like another."

Daniel laughed, a rich full-bodied laugh that made his ribs hurt like the very devil. "Only a woman of your *vast* experience," he emphasized the word, "could make such a patently ridiculous statement. That's like saying all horses are black in the dark."

She folded a clean square of bandage, then leaned over him to tie it in place.

Daniel gaped as the lapels of her brocade robe opened wide enough to give him an unhampered view of her truly spectacular bosom.

"Aren't they, Your Grace?"

Magnificent. Superlative. Gorgeous. Tempting. "Aren't they what?" It took Daniel a moment to comprehend her question.

"All horses black in the dark."

Daniel reached up, without warning, tangled his fingers in Miranda's hair, gently pulled her face to his, and kissed her.

The first touch of his lips on hers was tentative, like the soft touch of a moth's wings. He kissed her gently, lightly, allowing Miranda time to become accustomed to the taste and touch of him. Then he slowly moved his mouth over hers, nibbling at the corners of her mouth, tasting and testing the texture of her lips before gently coaxing them to part.

And like a moth drawn to a candle flame, Miranda succumbed to the lure of Daniel.

He swept his tongue past her lips, inside the warm, sweet recesses of her mouth, inhaling her breath as he did so, taking his time persuading her to grant him further liberties.

Miranda gave a soft sigh of surrender, leaned closer, and did as he willed, tentatively meeting his questing tongue with her own. Her breath quickened and her heart began a rapid tattoo as she explored the interior of his mouth and urged him to continue his exploration of hers.

She felt the blood rushing through her body as he stopped exploring the interior of her mouth long enough to nibble at her lips once again, tracing the texture of them with a light brush of his mouth, warming her in places she'd never realized could become so feverish.

Her legs began to quake, and Miranda thought her knees would buckle from the force of the white-hot emotion flowing through her. He urged her closer as he deepened his kiss. His tongue delved deep into the lush sweetness of her mouth, and she mirrored his actions as he plundered the depths, then retreated into politeness, before plundering again.

Daniel loosened his hold on Miranda's hair, sliding his hand out of her hair, down the line of her jaw, beneath her heavy tresses, where he cupped the nape of her neck while he tenderly massaged her earlobe with the pad of his thumb.

Miranda had never felt anything so soothing or so exhilarating. He tasted of cherries and coffee and a flavor that could only be Daniel. And suddenly Miranda developed an immense craving for cherries and coffee a la Daniel.

She'd been kissed before, but never like this. She had no idea kissing could be so extraordinarily wonderful. The only other kisses she'd ever received had been mere brushes of lips upon her gloved fingers, or wrists, or a slight brush of lips against her face or eyelids. The closest Daniel had ever come to kissing her had been the brush of his lips against the corner of her mouth that had sealed their wedding vows the night before. And that slight touch of his lips against her flesh couldn't begin to compare with this.

No wonder mothers warned their daughters against allowing gentlemen to kiss them full on the lips. No wonder girls fell from grace every season. Running off with dancing masters and army officers, eloping to Scotland or sailing off to ports unknown. If other men kissed half as well as Daniel, if other girls felt half of what she was feeling, it was a wonder there were any maidens left in England.

He swept her mouth with his tongue again, and Miranda moaned her pleasure.

Daniel heard her soft moan, and somewhere in the midst of kissing her, he forgot she was inexperienced. He blazed a path with the palm of his hand from the soft curls at the nape of her neck, over her shoulder, down her arm, and inside the open lapels of her robe. Gently cupping the soft underside of her breast, Daniel skimmed his fingers over her supple flesh, caressing one rosy-tipped crest with the pad of his thumb before turning his attention to the rosy tip of her other breast and massaging it.

Her breasts plumped, the tips hardened into insistent little points, clamoring for more attention, and the jolt of electricity that went through her body at the boldness of his kiss settled in the region between her thighs causing an unremitting ache for something she couldn't name—something she suspected Daniel would have no trouble recognizing or supplying.

Miranda shivered involuntarily as Daniel tugged at the sash of her brocade robe, then slipped it off her shoulders and down her arms, baring her body from the waist up.

He kissed her once more, then gently urged her to take a step backward so he could get a good look at her.

"Are you certain, Your Grace?" she murmured against his lips.

"Very certain." His voice was deep and rough. "Unlike you, my lovely marchioness, I know better than to believe the dark makes all horses black."

Miranda stepped back and pushed the robe over her hips, allowing it to fall in a puddle at her feet.

"Miranda?" Daniel's voice rose as he studied her tall, statuesque, and flawless body from the tip of her shining auburn head, over her beautiful breasts, past her flat stomach and the curve of her slim hips, to the auburn triangle at the juncture of her long shapely legs.

"It's only fair that you get a look at my naked body, Your Grace." Miranda amazed herself with her boldness. "After all, I've gotten a very good look at yours. You might say I've made quite a study of it."

"And?"

"You're incomparable," she said softly. "The dark doesn't make all horses black, it only makes it harder to see their true colors."

"And you're having trouble discerning my true color?" He phrased it as a question, but Daniel already knew the answer. He saw it in the troubled expression on Miranda's face, recognized the blaze of newly awakened desire and the confusion it brought.

She nodded. "My head warns me to be wary, but my heart encourages me to give you whatever you want from me." She looked him in the eye. "What do you want from me, Daniel?"

"At this moment, I want nothing more than to be the

man who introduces you to the delights of lovemaking," he answered.

"Because you want me or because you want to make love to me?"

Daniel sucked in a breath as the question sliced through his viscera. He knew what she wanted to hear. He could say the words and have her. But Miranda was honest and straightforward, and he couldn't be anything less with her.

"I want to make love to you."

"I'm sorry," she whispered, bending to pick up the robe she'd dropped on the floor. "But I'm saving myself for my husband."

With that, Miranda turned and walked to the door before she made a huge fool of herself by confessing her love for him and producing their marriage lines, before she gave him the chance to hurt her once again.

Daniel had finally kissed her like a lover, and Miranda walked away while her shaky legs were still able to support her.

Chapter 16

"Prudence and love are not made for each other;
As love waxes, prudence wanes."
—François, Duc de La Rochefoucauld, 1613–1680

She was still fretting over what she should do next when Ned arrived that afternoon with baskets of provisions, a travel trunk full of clothes for Miranda, a handful of mail, and her most recent invitations—along with profuse apologies for his tardy return.

"I'm so sorry, milady," he said as soon as Miranda opened the back door to admit him. "I gave Lady St. Germaine your message when I delivered her breakfast tray this morning. Rupert and I intended to leave as soon as my breakfast chores were complete, but when your mother learned that you'd decided to visit friends, *she* decided to pay calls and do some shopping." Ned appeared a bit chagrined. "Rupert drove, and I accompanied her." He exhaled. "I believe we paid a call on every establishment on Bond Street."

"I understand." Better than anyone. Miranda knew that her mother could be quite formidable when she set her mind to do something. And the dowager Lady St. Germaine loved to shop.

Ned looked at Miranda and realized that she was naked except for a brocade robe. "I came as soon as I could, but it's quite clear that I've come at an inopportune time. Please forgive me for interrupting your honeymoon, my lady."

Realizing Ned had been misled by her dress or lack thereof, Miranda looked down at her robe and blushed. "You didn't interrupt my honeymoon," she told him.

Her mode of dress said otherwise and Ned couldn't help but stare at her. Either Lady Miranda had just come from the bath or something was amiss.

"His Grace is still not quite the pink." Miranda lifted her chin a notch higher and straightened to her full height. "And his memory of last night's events is rather faulty. Especially the visit to St. Michael's Square."

"Heavy drink has been known to affect a man's memory, miss," Ned commiserated.

"I suppose it has," Miranda agreed. "Perhaps, he'll remember when he wakes."

"Perhaps."

Miranda closed her eyes for a minute, then opened them again. "I've no one to blame but myself. I knew better than to marry him when he was so foxed. But, I . . ."

"His Grace was most insistent, miss," Ned reminded her. "He didn't give you much choice."

"I know," Miranda admitted, "but that's no excuse. I knew what I was doing, even if he did not. And I'll not have him think I persuaded him to marry me for my own purposes. So, until His Grace remembers—we'll pretend it never happened."

"And if he never remembers?" Ned asked the question Miranda had been asking herself.

"We'll pretend it never happened."

"I beg your pardon, my lady, but you won't be able to pretend it never happened forever," her footman said. "Lady Manwaring and the curate were witnesses, and Rupert and I were there as well. We heard the bishop say the marriage should be recorded in the parish register within thirty days. Someone is bound to find out about it."

"Not if we don't tell them," Miranda insisted. "Who in the ton is going to request the St. Michael's parish register? In the meantime, we'll go on as we always have."

"Will that be possible, miss?"

"Of course it's possible," Miranda replied with a great deal more bravado than she felt. "Why shouldn't it be?"

Ned cleared his throat and turned his gaze to the marble floor before meeting her gaze. "I beg your pardon again, milady, but you've nothing on but a man's robe. I would never have left you alone with him if I had known this would happen. . . ." he replied.

"Nothing happened," she reminded him.

"Then why aren't you wearing your dress?"

Miranda made a face. "His Grace was violently ill upon it." She looked at Ned. "I couldn't wear it after that, or the garments that go under it, so I bundled them up and left them in a laundry tub in the scullery."

Ned's relief was palpable. He and Lady Miranda were much the same age and had known each other all their lives. Ned's father was the head gamekeeper at Blackstone Abbey, the St. Germaine county seat in Northamptonshire. Ned and Lady Miranda had played together and built a solid friendship as children. And when he'd arrived in London to serve the family, when he was seven and ten, he'd immediately resumed the role of Miranda's friend and confidant. They were more than mistress and footman— they were lifelong friends, and Miranda trusted him implicitly. Ned and Crawford, the butler, were the rocks upon which she and her mother relied so heavily.

"There's an armoire full of ladies' clothing in the master bedchamber," Miranda told him. "But none of them fit me." She plucked at the fabric of her robe. "This and a gentleman's nightshirt were the only clothes I could wear. And the nightshirt got wet." Miranda saw no point in revealing how the nightshirt got wet. "So I was reduced to wearing this and a toga made from a bedsheet."

"And His Grace?"

"He'll need clothes, too." Miranda didn't elaborate.

"From his valet at Sussex House or from his tailor on Bond Street?"

"Bond Street." Miranda knew Ned was entirely trustworthy, but Daniel hadn't given her leave to tell Ned of his injury or to have Ned reveal that information to His Grace's valet. "Buy buff breeches, a white linen shirt." She looked at Ned. "You know the style I like best with collar and cuffs instead of ruffles." She tapped her bottom lip with her index fingers. "Stockings, drawers, neck linens, a razor and strop, hair brushes. Whatever a gentleman needs. I'll give you enough money to pay for the purchases. And be very discreet, Ned. Neither His Grace's tailor nor his valet can know about this."

"Of course, miss." Ned nodded. "Malden, His Grace's valet, is known belowstairs in all the fashionable households as having a loose tongue."

"Boots," Miranda remembered suddenly. "His Grace was wearing shoes last night. He'll need boots for buff breeches."

Ned gave his mistress a smile. "No need to fret, miss. I know His Grace's bootblack. I'll take care of it."

"I'll leave it to you, then," Miranda assured him.

Ned nodded, then turned and began unpacking the baskets.

The aromas coming from a wicker picnic hamper were heavenly. Miranda's mouth began to water. "What did you bring us?"

"Yorkshire pudding and fresh vegetables with cake for dessert."

"Bless you," Miranda told him.

"I took the liberty of bringing your mail and your invitations." Ned finished unpacking the food hampers, then reached for Miranda's mail and handed it to her. "And I instructed Pinder to pack clothes enough for a week's stay in the country."

Miranda glanced at the handful of invitations she'd

received that bore today's date. She knew her lady's maid well enough to know that Pinder wouldn't have thought to pack a ball gown suitable for Lady Garrison's party in Richmond. Not for a week in the country. Simple day dresses, an evening gown or two, and perhaps a riding habit would be the extent of her wardrobe for the week. Miranda waved the invitations like a fan. "I suppose I should tend to these." She frowned. "I was rather looking forward to Lady Garrison's party tonight, but since my mother believes I'm in the country and I haven't anything suitable to wear, I suppose I should sent my regrets."

"I could send Rupert to Upper Brook Street to fetch you a ball gown if you truly wish to attend Lady Garrison's party," Ned offered.

Miranda was tempted. "And leave my husband alone on our honeymoon? It simply isn't done." She gave Ned a mischievous smile. "But since no one knows I *have* a husband or that I'm on my honeymoon, perhaps I should attend . . ."

"I think you should send your regrets to Lady Garrison and worry about the other invitations tomorrow," Ned told her. "I'll deliver them on my way home. Rupert will be up shortly with your trunk. Where shall I have him take it?"

"The bedroom that connects to the master bedchamber will be fine," Miranda replied.

"Very good, miss."

"Thank you, Ned."

"Don't mention it, miss. You attend to your toilette and your correspondence," he told her, "while I dish up the food."

"Please prepare a plate of food for His Grace," she instructed, "but could you wait a bit before dishing up mine?"

"Certainly, milady."

"And could you heat some water for me?"

Ned nodded. "Yes, of course, milady."

"I would like a bath," Miranda explained. "And the water coming out of the tap is cold."

"I'll fire up the burner beneath the water reservoir in the attic," he volunteered. "It should warm it in no time."

c—>

Miranda knocked on the bedroom door and waited until Daniel bade her enter.

"I was afraid you wouldn't come back," Daniel admitted when Miranda opened the door.

"I wasn't sure I would either," she replied. "But you are the Duke of Sussex, and I can't allow a royal duke to starve to death in my house."

"Even if he deserves to?" Daniel asked.

"Even so," she answered, turning to collect the tray she'd set on the floor outside the door. "I brought you something to eat."

Daniel recognized an olive branch when he saw one. He grabbed it and held it close to his heart. "The food smells delicious. What is it?"

"Yorkshire pudding, vegetables, and cake for dessert."

He arched an eyebrow and pretended to be skeptical. "Magically conjured up by a woman who confessed to being unable to brew tea or coffee?"

"Or lemonade," Miranda reminded him. "Don't forget the lemonade." She placed the tray over his lap and removed the covers from the plate of pudding and vegetables, and from over the dessert plate containing a slice of chocolate cake. "Ned arrived with some provisions."

Daniel smoothed the pink sheets and the spread covering him, pushed himself up against the pillows at his back, then lifted his knife and fork. "Any clothes?"

"For me," she told him. "Not for you. At least not until he pays a call on your tailor."

"I ordered several sets of clothing about a month ago," Daniel said. "They should be ready. I took the liberty of writing a note for Ned to give to Weston." He nodded toward the secretary and the folded piece of white stationery lying on top of it. The note had taken him nearly an hour to write and had all but exhausted the last of his strength. Daniel had been amazed that he'd managed to make it from bed to writing desk and back again. "I thought about having Ned take my shirt or my waistcoat, but they are probably stained and stiff with my blood, and since my tailor and my valet gossip, my tailor doesn't need to see that."

Miranda didn't meet his gaze. "With a note from you, Ned shouldn't have any trouble collecting your new clothes from the tailor."

"I signed and sanded the note, but it isn't sealed," he continued between bites of Yorkshire pudding. "I seem to have lost my signet ring." Daniel put down his knife and fork and stretched out his right hand. A pale strip of skin outlined the place where his gold ring had been.

"You didn't lose it, Your Grace." Miranda walked over to the bedside table and opened the reticule she'd left sitting there. "You gave it to me last night." She removed the ring from her purse and held it out for him to see. "For safekeeping."

That surprised him. The only time he ever removed his signet ring was when he practiced boxing at Gentleman Jim's, and then it was locked in his safe in Sussex House. He never willingly parted with it otherwise. She offered him the ring. Daniel brushed her fingers with his as he took it from her. The slight touch sent a jolt of awareness rushing through him. "Thank you, Miranda," he said, sliding the ring into place. "I'm grateful."

She turned and headed for the bedroom door. "You're welcome, Your Grace."

"You aren't leaving?"

"Yes, I am," Miranda answered.

Daniel frowned. "Aren't you hungry?"

"Very," she admitted, "but I'll eat later. Right now, I'd rather have a bath."

"No doubt," Daniel agreed.

It hadn't escaped his notice that while Miranda had

bathed him several times, she had been forced to go without. He focused his gaze on a spot to the left of Miranda's left shoulder in a vain attempt to pretend he hadn't been affected by the kiss they'd shared or by a barrage of mental images of Miranda in the bath. He fought to keep his body under control while his mind conjured up images of water droplets rolling down the slopes of her breasts, or down the curve of her spine.

And Daniel wasn't relegated to using his imagination when picturing her naked body, for after kissing him senseless, Miranda had gifted him with a spectacular view of it.

"I'd like you to come back," he said softly. "After your bath. I'd like to keep you company while you eat your dinner."

"I don't know that that's a good idea, Daniel," she said.

"Why not?"

"Because I want to kiss you again," she answered truthfully. "And I want you to kiss me again." She bit her bottom lip. "Because I want more than kisses. I want to be a wife, and the one thing you don't want to be is a husband, so . . ."

He nodded. "So, you were right to walk away this morning. Things were close to getting out of hand. And as much as I enjoyed kissing you—and I did enjoy it, very much—I was afraid I was in danger of taking what should be reserved for your husband. . . ."

"Daniel," she began trying to explain. "You don't understand. . . ."

"Perhaps I don't understand the desire to be permanently tied to someone else," he conceded. "But I understand the desire for temporary companionship, and I want you to come back."

Miranda hesitated. He didn't understand anything.

Because she hadn't been able to tell him the truth.

"Please."

He didn't understand anything—except that she had a terrible weakness for him. "We'll see."

"I won't touch you," he promised.

Miranda didn't appreciate his promise or find the prospect that he might live up to it the least bit appealing. On the contrary. She rather thought that kissing might present a solution to their problem.

Daniel continued. "I've been staring at these pink walls all day and I'd appreciate the company."

She frowned.

"Miranda . . ."

She had already promised to love, honor, and cherish the dolt. She didn't know if she had anything left to give. "We'll see. I can't promise anything more."

Chapter 17

*"Have you not heard
When a man marries, dies, or turns Hindoo,
His best friends hear no more of him?"*
                    —Percy Bysshe Shelley, 1792–1822

"*A*ny word from Daniel?" Jarrod asked without preamble as soon as Griff, Colin, Jonathan, and Alex settled into their customary places in the private room at White's.

"Nobody has seen him since his mother's gala last night," Colin answered.

"And no one has heard a word from him or about him," Griffin added.

"I made discreet inquiries all day," Alex, Marquess of Courtland, the youngest and newest member of the League, reported. "I went everywhere I could think of, and I agree that if anyone has seen him since last night, they're keeping very quiet about it."

Jonathan nodded. "If I hadn't seen him at the party last night, I would swear he hadn't made it back from France."

"He can't have disappeared without someone seeing him." Jarrod emptied his coffee cup, placed it on its saucer, set both of them on a side table, stood up, then began to pace the perimeter of the room. "Someone saw something."

Colin hooked the leg of a leather ottoman with the toe of

his boot and pulled it out of Jarrod's path. He pushed the ottoman closer to Griff, allowing more room so Jarrod might circle the room without having to go around obstacles. "I agree," Colin replied. "Someone has to have seen him, but so far we've had no success in locating that someone."

"I asked Henderson how the dispatches were delivered last evening," Jarrod told them. "And who delivered them."

"And?" Colin prompted.

"Henderson informed me that Sussex didn't deliver the dispatches, that he sent someone in his stead."

"Travers?" Jonathan mentioned the name of the Duke of Sussex's secretary.

"No." Jarrod hated to disappoint Sussex's cousin, but they were concerned with facts, not sentiment. "Henderson had never seen the fellow before, but he knew the code phrase. He repeated it to Henderson and handed over the leather pouch and the round of cheese Sussex chose as his signature, then returned to his coach."

"The duke's coach?" Alex asked.

"No." Jarrod shook his head. "He arrived alone and in an unmarked coach."

"What about the dispatches?" Colin asked.

"They were sealed. They showed no signs of tampering, and the information they contained appears to be genuine."

"And Henderson was certain that the messenger repeated the correct phrase and delivered a round of French cheese?" Griff asked the question no one else wanted to ask, then looked at Jarrod for confirmation.

The Free Fellow entrusted with the dispatches usually delivered them to Jarrod or to Henderson, but there were times when that wasn't possible, and the Free Fellows had devised a code for each mission whereby anyone sent in their stead was required to relay a specific message and deliver a specific item. The messages and the items were decided upon at the planning of each mission and given to Henderson, who accepted pouches in Jarrod's absence.

"Henderson was worried that he might have gotten the

message wrong," Jarrod told them. "But he repeated it to me, and he was correct. The message was the message we settled upon before the mission, and a round of cheese was the item Sussex chose to present as proof that the message was from him."

"What was Henderson's impression?" Colin asked. Before he and Gillian married, Colin and Jarrod had shared Jarrod's town house. Colin knew that Henderson was the very soul of discretion and believed wholeheartedly in the work of the Free Fellows League. He also knew that Henderson was a first-rate judge of character.

"Henderson doesn't believe His Grace would ever willingly miss a meeting."

Griff nodded. "We're all in accord, and we're all concerned."

"I was concerned enough to pay a call upon Sussex House this afternoon," Jonathan volunteered. "Daniel wasn't there, and the dowager duchess hasn't seen him since last evening either, but that's not unusual, since her apartments are in the opposite wing."

"Did she sound concerned?" Griff shifted his weight on the sofa, then propped his right leg on the ottoman Colin had removed from Jarrod's path. Leaning forward, he reached down to massage his thigh in an effort to relieve the ache from the saber cut he'd taken across his hip and thigh during the battle of Fuentes de Oñoro. It had been two years since his injury, but the wound still pained him when he stood for long periods of time or when he danced, and he'd spent a good portion of the previous evening dancing with his wife at the Duchess of Sussex's ball.

"She didn't sound so much concerned as annoyed," Jonathan told them. "Aunt Lavinia was quite exasperated with him for failing to stand with her to greet their guests. She was convinced that Daniel deliberately avoided her last night because he was angry at her for failing to include Lady St. Germaine on the guest list." He glanced at Colin. "It seems that Aunt Lavinia always omits Miranda St. Germaine's name from the gala guest list, and that Daniel has made a habit of sending her a separate invitation—much to Aunt Lavinia's chagrin."

"Miranda's wasn't the only name the duchess omitted from the guest list," Jarrod reminded them. "Why didn't she include Colin and Gillian? And why didn't Sussex send separate invitations to everyone his mother had failed to invite?" Jarrod demanded, pacing harder and faster, equally annoyed that Daniel had managed to include the Marchioness of St. Germaine on his mother's guest list, yet neglected to add Colin and Gillian to the list. "When did Sussex add the marchioness's name to the list?"

"I'm sorry," Jonathan apologized for his aunt and his cousin. "I don't have an answer for that. Aunt Lavinia didn't mention Grantham or his viscountess. But she was quite upset at having the Marchioness of St. Germaine appear at the front door with the invitation Daniel had sent her."

Griff drummed his fingers on the arm of the sofa in a show of agitation. "I'm afraid that doesn't bode well for the future," he muttered. Lady Miranda St. Germaine was his wife's closest friend and had served as Alyssa's maid of honor at their wedding. Miranda was a frequent guest at Griff and Alyssa's Park Lane house, and at Abernathy Manor, their country house in Northamptonshire. Griff was privy to a good many of Miranda's aspirations regarding the Duke of Sussex, whether he wanted to be or not, because Alyssa thought Sussex and Miranda were a perfect match and was determined to see Miranda become the next duchess.

"Maybe not." Jonathan grinned. "Because this battle of wills over Miranda has been going on for quite some time. Daniel sends the marchioness an invitation every year and adds her name to the final guest list. The dispute has become so heated of late that my aunt refuses to tell Daniel when the invitations go out or allow him to see the final guest list. Last night she gave the staff strict orders that Miranda was not to be allowed entrance to Sussex House unless she was accompanied by the Prince Regent. Aunt Lavinia was furious because Miranda got past both footmen and Weldon, the butler, by waving the invitation Daniel sent her."

"That's outrageous!" Courtland exclaimed. "Lady St. Germaine has never done anything to warrant having the duchess bar her from the house."

"Except threaten her," Griff said softly.

"Miranda threatened Aunt Lavinia?" Jonathan couldn't contain a small satisfied smile. "I would have paid money to see that."

"Then open your eyes, Barclay," Colin said. "Because as long as Miranda St. Germaine remains unattached, she's a threat to the duchess."

Jonathan widened his eyes, and his smile as understanding dawned. "I assumed Daniel's infatuation with Miranda was over and done with years ago."

"So does everyone else," Jarrod said. "Except Her Grace, the Duchess of Sussex . . ."

"Who is afraid of losing her influence over society and over her son if she's consigned to the lesser role of dowager duchess," Colin added.

"Her Grace is already the dowager duchess," Courtland reminded them.

"That's true," Griff agreed. "But her position as mistress of Sussex House and everything else Sussex owns is secure because Daniel is not married."

"But Aunt Lavinia's been pushing young ladies in Daniel's direction for years," Jonathan pointed out.

"She pushes a new crop of young ladies in Sussex's direction every season, knowing he isn't going to pay them an iota of attention. She knows he isn't interested in girls fresh from the schoolroom," Colin explained. "Sussex likes a challenge, and there's no challenge in having young ladies and their mamas clamoring for him to court them. He's bored to tears by the whole thing and hasn't noticed anyone in years. . . ."

"Except Alyssa," Griff added, reminding them all that

he had almost lost his wife to Sussex when Sussex's mother and Alyssa's mother, who were fast friends, had planned to unite their families with a marriage between their offspring. But Griff and Alyssa had ruined the plan when they had chosen each other. "Not that I can fault the man's taste in the least."

"Alyssa was the exception," Jarrod reminded him. "And you know it. You must admit, in all fairness, that there were several extenuating circumstances to Sussex's pursuit of Alyssa."

"I know that *now*," Griff agreed. "But I didn't know it or appreciate it at the time."

It had taken him a while to get over his jealousy of Sussex and to forgive the man for seeing Alyssa's potential as a duchess, but he'd finally managed. He genuinely liked Sussex as a man, and as a friend and fellow Free Fellow, and Griff truly admired the way he carried the burden of his position in society—a position to which Daniel had been born but had been thrust upon Griff, and to which he was still learning to adjust.

"Barclay, you're his cousin," Jarrod said. "You've known Daniel longer than any of us. So tell us, how many ladies, other than Griff 's duchess, have captured and held Sussex's attention for longer than a night or two?"

"I can only recall one since he left university," Jonathan answered.

"And the lady's name is . . ." Colin prompted.

"Miranda, Marchioness St. Germaine."

Jarrod turned to Griffin. "Have you seen Miranda since the party last night?"

Griff frowned. "No. She and her mother were supposed to accompany us to Sussex House, but Miranda suggested we meet there so Lord and Lady Tressingham and my parents could ride with us."

"It sounds as if Lady Miranda knew she might be turned away at the front door and wanted to spare you and herself a bit of embarrassment," Alex observed.

Colin nodded in agreement. "Did you see Miranda or her mother there?"

Griff shook his head. "No."

"I didn't see her either," Jonathan added, "but I know Miranda was there because Aunt Lavinia was furious with Daniel for inviting her and furious with Miranda for not being more like her mother and having the good manners to stay away from where she wasn't invited."

"Lady St. Germaine didn't attend?" Jarrod stopped pacing.

Jonathan shook his head. "No."

Jarrod met Colin's gaze and they both looked at Griff. "Did Alyssa mention anything about Miranda leaving town?"

"No."

"They're together." Jarrod grinned. "For whatever reason, Sussex and Miranda are together."

Colin hesitated. "Maybe."

Jarrod glared at Colin.

But Colin wasn't deterred. "Sussex and Miranda *may* be together, but it's just as likely that they aren't."

"Nobody has seen either one of them," Jarrod insisted.

"Nobody we've *talked* to has seen either one of them," Colin reminded him. "But that doesn't mean they've headed to Scotland or that they're sharing an address. Things are rarely what they seem—especially in our line of work."

"Grantham's right," Courtland said. "We can't assume anything. We're just going to have to keep looking until we hear from Sussex."

Griff glanced at Jarrod. "They're right."

"I know," Jarrod conceded, "but I'd rather believe that Sussex and Miranda are otherwise engaged than the alternative. . . ."

"Because the alternative is that Daniel may be in trouble." Colin gave voice to their fears. "We may not want to think about it, but we'll be remiss in our duty if we don't. We're engaged in a desperate and dangerous business, and we all know there are French agents here in London. . . ."

"And if any of them suspected Daniel might be involved in a little clandestine smuggling . . ." Jonathan picked up the direction of Colin's thoughts.

"The crush at the Duchess of Sussex's party would have been the perfect place to set a trap for him. No one would have noticed anything unusual in all that crowd," Courtland said. He shuddered, remembering how close one French agent had come to penetrating the League not so very long ago.

"I was hoping Sussex would walk in tonight with a reasonable explanation for his absence this morning," Jarrod admitted.

"We were all hoping that would happen," Jonathan said.

"Then I suppose we're all in agreement that his continued absence and the information we've gathered today means we'll need to do a bit of reconnoitering among the ton tonight," Jarrod said.

"Agreed," replied all the Free Fellows in unison.

"Luckily we all dressed the part." Jarrod spread his hands wide to indicate his own formal evening dress, then nodded at the other Free Fellows, who were all wearing evening clothes, knowing luck hadn't played any part in the way they were dressed. They'd each seen the course of action independently and then come together to confer as a unified league.

Courtland grimaced. "I'm escorting my mother to the opera. Where are the rest of you going?"

"Lady Cleveland's," Jonathan replied.

"Colin and Gillian and Alyssa and I are going to my sister-in-law's ball," Griff said.

"So am I," Jarrod volunteered.

"What?" Griffin was stunned.

"I'm going to Lady Garrison's ball."

"I'm sure my sister-in-law will be delighted," Griff said. "And I'm not trying to discourage you from attending, but are you certain that's what you want to do?"

"Quite sure," Jarrod pronounced. "Since Lady Garrison was kind enough to extend the invitation, I think it's time I accepted."

"Every hostess in London invites you to her parties," Griff reminded him. "And unless our League business requires it or it's one of Alyssa's gatherings, you rarely attend any of them."

"I'm making an exception for Lady Garrison," Jarrod replied.

"A major exception," Griff said. "And what I want to know is why?"

Jarrod smiled. "Let's just say that it's time I stayed on your duchess's good side by accepting her sister's invitation."

Colin glanced skyward and shook his head at Jarrod's patently transparent prevarication. "Let's just say that it probably has something to do with the wager entered into the betting books this afternoon."

Although Colin rarely wagered except with his closest friends, his father was an inveterate gambler and Colin had made it a matter of habit to check the betting books at White's in the morning and in the afternoon almost every day to see if his father had wagered on anything recorded on the pages.

"Damnation!" Jarrod swore. "He certainly didn't waste any time recording it. I only had coffee with him this morning."

"It was on the books by early afternoon," Colin told him.

"Has anyone else taken the wager?"

"Of course," Colin answered. "A wager that large is bound to attract attention."

"Your father's?" Jarrod asked.

"Thankfully no," Colin replied, refilling his coffee cup and taking a sip of the brew. "But there are several others who can't afford to lose that amount."

"Who?" Jarrod demanded.

"Carville, Jackson, Munford, and several others."

"For or against?"

"Those I mentioned are betting on you," Colin told him. "The others are wagering against it."

"I haven't looked at the books lately," Jonathan said. "So tell us, who wagered what?"

"Yes." Courtland was fairly chomping at the bit for details. "Who did what?"

"Lord Dunbridge recorded a wager he made with Jarrod," Colin answered.

"Dunbridge?" Griff scowled. Dunbridge wasn't one of their contemporaries. And as far as he knew, Jarrod was barely acquainted with the man and didn't like what he knew of him. "What sort of wager do you have with Lord Dunbridge?"

"A thousand-pound wager," Colin answered.

"Jupiter!" Barclay exclaimed.

"Must be a sure thing," Courtland added.

"Far from it, I'd say," Colin replied. "Lord Dunbridge wagered a thousand pounds that he would marry a certain young lady at the end of the season."

"At least he had the good manners not to mention her by name," Jarrod said.

"Oh, but he did," Colin told him. "*I* had the good manners not to mention her by name, but Dunbridge wrote it out for all to see."

"I don't believe it!" Jarrod was outraged at that breach of etiquette. One might mention a mistress or a widow or a woman of dubious character in wagers of this nature, but never an unmarried young lady of good family.

"Believe it," Colin said. "It's there in plain English." He stood up, then walked to the bell and summoned a footman to bring the current betting book.

The footman returned moments later with the book in hand. Colin handed it to Jarrod.

The entry page was dated with the day's date, time, and year. Several gentlemen had scrawled their names beneath the wager, recording wagers of their own on the outcome, including the three gentlemen Colin mentioned, all of whom were betting on Jarrod.

Jarrod read the recorded wager aloud. "I, Reginald Blanchard, fourth Viscount Dunbridge, do record this wager of one thousand pounds with Jarrod, fifth Marquess of Shepherdston: I wager that Miss Sarah Eckersley and I shall be married by His Grace, the Archbishop of Canterbury, at Westminster Abbey at season's end. Lord Shepherdston wagers that I shan't marry Miss Eckersley at season's end or at any other time. The cash to be paid at the outcome." Jarrod finished reading the entry and raked his fingers through his hair. "Bloody hell!"

"What on earth possessed you to wager a thousand pounds on Lord Dunbridge's proposed nuptials?" Griff was astonished by the amount and by Jarrod's uncharacteristic behavior.

"I'm acquainted with the young lady he hopes to marry."

"And?" Griff prompted.

Colin snapped his fingers. "Eckersley. Wasn't that the name of the young woman you danced with at Esme Harralson's ball last season? The night I met Gillian?"

Jarrod didn't answer.

Colin frowned. "Jarrod?"

"Yes," Jarrod ground out. "And I can guarantee Dunbridge won't win his wager. Because I won't allow it."

"How?" Jonathan inquired.

"I'm escorting her and her aunt to Lady Garrison's tonight," Jarrod said.

As if the outcome was already assured.

The other Free Fellows looked at one another. First they would find their missing colleague, then they would get to the bottom of Jarrod's wager.

Chapter 18

"Persuasion hung upon his lips."
—Laurence Sterne, 1713–1768
Tristram Shandy

*M*iranda returned to the master bedchamber wearing a dark blue dress with a square décolletage that showed off her neck and shoulders and created a frame for her bosom. Daniel noticed that her skin was still a little pink and damp in places from her bath, and that she had piled her hair atop her head, confining it in a tight knot, but loose tendrils had escaped to curl around her face. She looked as lovely as Daniel had ever seen her look, and she smelled incredible.

He sighed and shifted his weight from one hip to the other before grabbing a pillow and placing it in his lap, doing everything in his power to keep from tenting the pink bedsheets with his erection once again.

He'd spent the past three quarters of an hour listening to the sound of water splashing in the bath, and his imagination had run wild. He recognized the sound of water running off her as she rose from the bathwater. He imagined Miranda stepping out of the water and bending at the waist to dry her feet before running the towel up her shapely legs, over the soft skin of her stomach and between her thighs. He imagined droplets of bathwater clinging to her downy auburn triangle like the diamonds that had sparkled in her hair last night. And Daniel imagined tiny droplets of moisture secreted in her navel, decorating the slopes of her breasts and hiding in the valley between them.

"Enjoy your bath?" he asked.

"Very much," she answered.

"Have you eaten yet?"

She nodded. "I ate in the kitchen and kept Ned company while I waited for the water to heat."

"You seem rather close to your footman," he ventured.

"I am," Miranda told him. "We're the same age. He grew up at Blackstone Abbey, our country house, and when we were in residence there, my father arranged for Ned to accompany me wherever I went. We became friends when we were small, and our friendship endures to this day."

"I see." Daniel glanced down at his plate. "I hoped you would reconsider and decide to keep me company while you ate." He tried to keep the note of disappointment out of his voice and failed.

"I made a list of errands for Ned to run and sent him on his way to your tailor on Bond Street."

"Then I shouldn't complain at being left alone."

"No, you shouldn't, Your Grace, for I brought you something." Miranda turned around, then bent and picked up a marble chessboard set with carved marble chessmen.

"A chessboard?" He leaned forward to get a closer look at the marble board and the exquisitely carved black and white marble pieces occupying the matching squares.

"Yes," she said. "I saw it in the library downstairs."

"You brought me a chessboard?" Daniel couldn't hide his surprise at Miranda's thoughtful gesture. She'd left the bedchamber with no promises and returned with a gift for him. "May I?"

"Of course." She walked over and set the chessboard on top of the coverlet.

"Thank you, Miranda." Daniel held up a pack of playing cards. "I found these in the drawer of the bedside table."

"Oh, well . . ." She turned to leave. "If you've got those, you don't need me. You've plenty of games to keep you busy."

"As it happens, I'm heartily sick of my own company, and of solitaire." Daniel spoke the truth, for all he'd done since Miranda had left him alone was eat, sleep, play card games, and listen to Miranda bathe. He patted the coverlet. "Shall we?"

Miranda accepted his challenge and climbed onto the bed beside him. She settled the chessboard between them. He was so close she could feel the heat of his body, and her heart quickened its pace. "All right."

Miranda glanced at the pillow in his lap. Daniel followed her gaze.

"That's a nice thought," he said bluntly. "But I doubt I could perform, and even if I could, I have the feeling we'd both be disappointed."

Miranda stared at him, astonished that he'd admit such a thing. "Then I'd rather play chess."

Daniel nodded. "Ivory or black?"

"Black," she answered. "I should warn you, Daniel, I'm an excellent chess player."

"Then you're the opponent for whom I'm looking."

Miranda's face lit up at his challenge, but Daniel didn't see it. He had his attention turned to the chessboard, carefully aligning the ivory pieces on the proper squares. "Ready?" Daniel looked over at her.

Miranda nodded.

He opened with his king's pawn, then smiled at her. "Your move."

She countered with a black pawn, and the game began.

Miranda hadn't lied. She played an excellent game of chess, but Daniel was better. He beat her handily in a matter of minutes, but she challenged him to a rematch. He quickly and efficiently checkmated her a second time.

"You might be a gentleman and allow me to win,"

Miranda protested when she lost again. "At least one game."

"I've never read that in the rules of etiquette." Daniel smiled at her move, then moved his ivory pawn into play. "Or in the rules of chess."

"If it isn't there, it should be," Miranda said, advancing her pawn as they started a new game. "I don't mind losing a game now and then," she told him, "because that's the only way to improve my play, but I heartily object to losing every game."

"How will you improve your play if I let you win?" he asked, countering her move by taking her pawn en passant.

Miranda groaned. "I won't," she admitted. "But it will make me feel better. And it will make you feel better, too, because it's ungentlemanly to beat a lady."

"I agree."

"So you'll let me win the next game?"

"Not at all."

"But you said . . ."

"I agree that it's ungentlemanly of a man to beat a lady. Physically. I don't agree that it's ungentlemanly of me to win at chess." Daniel stared at her over the chessboard as she placed another piece into a precarious position. "Who taught you to play?"

"My father."

"You're very good," Daniel complimented her. "But you take too many chances."

"In your opinion," Miranda said, moving her knight into position. "And I find that observation ironic coming from you."

Daniel studied the board. "Why?" He moved his bishop.

"Do you see any bandages on my person?"

Daniel leaned forward and leered at the front of her dress in a manner no gentleman should ever do unless invited. "No bandages."

"Daniel!"

He raised his eyebrows in an expression of pure innocence. "You issued the invitation."

"So I did." Miranda imitated his wide-eyed look.
"Check."

Daniel looked down at her move, then back at her.
"Damnation." She'd distracted him long enough to put his
king in jeopardy.

She smiled at him.

He returned her smile. So that was how she intended to
play. "Your eyes are blue," he said softly, truly surprised by
his discovery. "I always thought they were green."

"They change colors," she replied, watching as he managed to save his king.

He arched an eyebrow in query.

"When I wear green my eyes appear to be green and
when I wear blue, they look blue." Miranda made her next
move. "Check."

"Extraordinary." He didn't look at the board. There was
no need. He couldn't go anywhere.

"Mate," Miranda added, doing her best not to grin.

Reaching over, Daniel grabbed a spare pillow and passed
it to her. "Get comfortable. We may be here a while," he
said as he reset the board for another game.

She took his advice, bunching the pillow beneath her and
adjusting her skirts so she could stretch out on the coverlet.

"No fair," Daniel decried when her new position placed
her bosom into prominence and wreaked havoc with his
concentration.

"All's fair . . ." she began.

"In love and war?" he prompted, completing the quote.

"I was going to say 'in chess,'" Miranda told him.

"Chess is a form of warfare, Miranda," Daniel reminded
her.

"So is love, Your Grace."

Hours later, he opened another game by advancing his
king's pawn.

Miranda recognized the opening gambit and quickly countered it.

Daniel shifted his weight on the bed, resting his back and his aching ribs by relaxing against the pillows. He countered Miranda's move, then smothered a yawn.

"Is it the company?" Miranda spoke for the first time in half an hour as she advanced another chess piece. "Or my strategy?"

He glanced over her head to the clock on the mantel across the room. "I think it's the hour."

Miranda followed his gaze to the clock. It was nearly three in the morning. She started to get up, but Daniel stopped her.

He moved a rook. "Not until we finish the game."

"That could take hours," she said, advancing a bishop.

"It won't." He smiled at her. "Check."

"Blast it!" Miranda swore, looking at the board, trying to find the solution. "I hate losing."

"Might I make a suggestion?" he offered.

"No."

"So be it," he drawled.

"All right," she gave in. "What's the solution?"

He chuckled and Miranda noticed the strong line of his lean jaw, the dimple on the side of his mouth, and the way the network of fine lines at the corners of his eyes crinkled. "I'm not giving you the solution. The object of this game is to win. I intend to."

"You asked if you could make a suggestion." She tried to pout and failed.

"My suggestion is that you pay attention to the game," he replied. "You're off somewhere woolgathering."

Miranda looked down at the chessboard, smiled a dreamy sort of smile, recognized the solution, and quickly moved her king out of danger.

He gave her a look of approval. "So, tell me, my lady," he said softly, "what's all this woolgathering about? Where would you be if you hadn't been sitting here playing chess with an invalid all evening?"

She looked up from the chessboard to see if he was baiting her or if his question was genuine. "I'd be lying on satin cushions in the prow of a punt with my hair down around me, trailing my hand in the water, wearing nothing but sunshine, rose petals, and a smile, while my strong, handsome companion poles me around a lake."

Daniel's body reacted to the mental picture she drew in typical male fashion. He shifted his position to accommodate the sudden increase of blood flow to his nether region and reached for another cherubic-faced tapestry pillow. He turned the pillow face down in his lap and said the first thing that came into his head. "A lake?"

"Of course, a lake." She chuckled. "I've never heard of anyone punting on bodies of water other than ponds, lakes, or rivers—except, perhaps, bayous and estuaries. But I think a lake would be best."

"For whom? You or the strong, handsome companion poling you around it?"

"For me, of course," she answered. "It is my fantasy, after all."

"It would have to be, to have someone poling you around a lake in the sunshine like that." He looked over at her. "And while you're fantasizing, my lady, you might wish to make it a private lake. That isn't the sort of thing that can be managed in Hyde Park on a midsummer's afternoon."

She looked at him from beneath the cover of her lashes.

"Don't look at me," he warned.

"You do enjoy a private lake at Haversham House," she teased.

"I *don't* enjoy punting on it."

She sighed. "Oh well, the lake at Regent's Park should do nicely. It's private."

"It won't be when Nash finishes building villas around it." He looked at Miranda. She refused to be dissuaded once she'd made up her mind to do something. "You do know about the villas John Nash is building around Regent's Park?"

"Of course I know about them," she replied. "One of them is mine. Or rather it will be as soon as he completes construction on it."

"What's wrong with your town house on Upper Brook Street?"

"Nothing, but Papa invested quite a bit in the Regent's Park project, and I think I'd enjoy living there, where it's far enough from town to be rustic, but not so far as to be inconvenient."

Daniel gave a thoughtful nod. "Well, find yourself a strong, handsome companion and some rose petals and you're all set."

"That may present a problem," she said. "Because none of the men of my acquaintance have ever offered to take me punting. Although it's quite romantic and just the thing to do on a midsummer's day, poling a punt around a lake requires a bit of exertion, and all the men I know reserve that romantic endeavor for featherweight ladies under six feet tall." She moistened her lips with the tip of her tongue. "Of course, that's only a fantasy. The truth is that if I hadn't been here playing chess, I would have been at Lady Garrison's party in Richmond." She paused. "I had intended to go with Alyssa and Griff, and I was looking forward to it." She exhaled. "Of course, it would be breaking up by now, and everyone would be leaving or preparing to leave. What about you?" she asked. "If you hadn't been injured and forced to spend your evening playing chess with me, what would you have been doing?"

He thought for a moment. "I'd probably be spending a quiet evening at home." Resting up for his next mission.

Miranda lifted her eyebrow in a show of disbelief.

"Or I'd be at Lady Garrison's party dancing with you."

Or on the Channel smuggling. She thought it, but she couldn't bring herself to say it.

"I'm sorry you missed your party."

"There will be other parties." She straightened her back, then stretched out her legs, taking great care not to jostle the chessboard. "And if the truth be known, I'd rather be here playing chess with you than anywhere else in the world."

"Careful, Lady Miranda," he cautioned. "You're in danger."

She looked down at the chessboard.

"Checkmate," Daniel said, before shoving the board out of the way and closing the distance between them.

He covered her mouth with his, and Miranda yielded to temptation, parting her lips, allowing him to deepen the kiss. He complied, moving his lips on hers, kissing her harder, then softer, then harder once more, testing her response, slipping his tongue past her teeth, exploring the sweet hot interior of her mouth with practiced finesse.

Daniel kissed her as if his life depended upon it, leisurely stroking the inside of her mouth in a provocative imitation of the mating dance, while Miranda followed his lead, moving her lips on his and returning his kiss.

What she lacked in experience, she made up for in natural ability and enthusiasm. And her newfound talent delighted him. Daniel made love to her mouth, sharing his store of knowledge, offering her the advantage of his greater expertise as he patiently taught her everything he'd ever learned about kissing.

Miranda absorbed his knowledge as she absorbed the feel of his lips on hers. She eagerly accepted his kisses and returned them in full measure, as she advanced from being a novice in the art of kissing, to becoming an intermediate and ultimately a virtuoso, in a matter of minutes. Mimicking the action of his tongue, Miranda took what he gave her, and succeeded in adapting the motions into a technique all her own.

The pleasure he felt while kissing her shook Daniel to his core. She took his breath away, and with it went all vestiges of his precious self-control.

He grew rock hard beneath the pink sheets. The blood

pounded in his head, and his body trembled with the force of the passion that rolled over him, urging him to pull her closer so he could experience the exquisite pleasure of settling himself against her and surrounding himself with her warmth and softness.

Forcing himself to slow down, Daniel pulled his mouth away from hers as her soft sigh of surrender registered in his brain, reminding him that despite her extraordinary talent for kissing, she had never lain with a man.

He rolled away.

"Daniel?" Miranda rolled with him and placed her hand on his shoulder.

He felt her cool palm on his back and heard his name on her lips, but the sound seemed to come from a distance as he battled for control. He sucked in a breath as the tightening in his loins hit him like a punch to the belly. Damnation! Looking at her had the power to make him ache. Daniel struggled to tamp down his raging desire. His muscles were taut, his member rigid and insistent, and his control was stretched almost to the breaking point.

Miranda pressed her face against his back and wrapped her arms around his shoulders. Inhaling the clean pear and vanilla scent of her, Daniel closed his eyes. An image of Miranda lying naked on a cushion of satin pillows in the prow of a punt popped into his brain.

He did his best to blot out the image as she placed a kiss on his bare back. But he trembled beneath her touch. Miranda was dangerous. Dangerous to his peace of mind. And far more potent than the whisky he'd consumed the night before.

Because he wanted her with a passion that astounded him. He wanted to lie naked, buried to the hilt, between Miranda's thighs. But first, he wanted to touch her and taste her and make her writhe with the force of the pleasure he gave her. He wanted to explore her depth, feel her pulse around him, and to spill himself deep enough to make a miracle take root.

And then he wanted to do it again.

He wanted to fall asleep in her arms and wake up to the morning light holding her in his.

Reaching up, Daniel took hold of her wrist and brought it to his lips, where he planted a kiss on the vein where her pulse beat a strong, steady tattoo. "Go, Miranda," he whispered. "Go before it's too late."

"I can't," she whispered. "Because it's already too late."

Chapter 19

"Marriage has many pains, but celibacy has no pleasures."
—*Samuel Johnson, 1709–1784*

Miranda rolled off the bed and stood beside it. She thought for a moment, then reached up, unbuttoned her dress, and let it fall to the floor. Her undergarments followed, and Miranda felt a moment of panic as Daniel turned and looked up at her.

She thought he was going to change his mind. She thought that his willpower was stronger than his desire for her. She needn't have worried. He moved over on the bed so she'd be against his uninjured side, flipped the covers back out of the way, and invited her to join him.

"I won't make you any promises," he said.

"I don't remember asking for any," she retorted.

"Are you sure this is what you want?" he asked, allowing her another opportunity to change her mind.

Miranda nodded. "Are you?"

Daniel gave her a dazzling smile. "At this moment, I want to make love to you more than I want to breathe."

"Then shut up and do it."

He patted the mattress. "Won't you come in?"

Miranda slipped between the sheets and Daniel enfolded her into his arms.

"I'm not sure what to do," she admitted, staring into his face, meeting his gaze. "Where to begin . . ."

Daniel traced the contour of her bottom lip with the tip of his finger. "I generally start with kisses." He followed his words with action, lightly covering her lips with his, teasing and tempting her to relax. "Why don't we try a few kisses and see where they lead?"

"Lie back against the pillows," Miranda suggested.

Daniel arched an eyebrow in query.

"And let me kiss you," she finished, gently pushing him back against the pillows, leaning over to kiss him. "You're quite good at it already. *I* need to practice." She smiled a naughty little smile. "Besides, you're an injured man. You need your rest."

"Practice all you like." Daniel followed her suggestion and made himself comfortable against the pillows while Miranda leaned over him and experimented with a wide variety of kissing techniques designed to drive him out of his mind.

Daniel groaned his pleasure against her mouth as Miranda knelt above him. He felt the brush of her bare breasts against his chest and shuddered with the effort it took to keep from rolling her onto her back and burying himself inside her, or to keep from framing her hips with his hands and guiding her down until she settled herself upon his hard length.

For all her experimentation, she was, as far as he knew, still very much a virgin who deserved tender consideration and gentlemanly restraint.

But Miranda was pushing him to the limits of his endurance. She nibbled his bottom lip, sucking it into her mouth before slowly releasing it in order to lave it with the tip of her tongue.

"Miranda." He breathed her name.

She cradled his face between her hands. "Do you want me, Daniel?"

"Very much," he answered.

"Then take what you want," she offered. "But don't make love to me as the Duke of Sussex. Make love to me as Daniel Sussex. Without holding back. Without restraint."

For a moment, he thought she'd read his mind, but Daniel looked into her eyes, recognized the emotion shining in them, and realized Miranda was offering him an incredible gift of herself. He tangled his fingers in her hair, pulled her closer, and kissed her with a passion he hadn't realized he possessed.

His desire for her seemed to engulf him until she was all he could see or hear, taste, touch, or smell. The scent of the soap she'd used in the bath enticed him to explore all her tiny nooks and crannies and learn all her secret places. He combed his fingers through her hair, over her shoulders, down her back, along the curve of her spine, to her hips.

The soft caress of his fingers on her skin sent shivers coursing through her, and Miranda warmed to his touch. When he placed his hands on her hips and guided her toward him, there was no holding back.

She followed, carefully straddling his lean hips, balking only when he urged her to move up his torso instead of down. "This can't be right. . . ." Miranda frowned down at him.

He laughed. "There are no rules, Miranda. No restraint. No holding back. We can do whatever gives us pleasure. And this will give us both great pleasure."

She hesitated, still unsure. "If you're certain . . ."

"I'm certain," he said. "For I'm the man who has wanted to do this with you almost from the day I met you. Trust me." Moving his hands from her hips, Daniel cupped her bottom and pulled her toward him, up his chest until his hot breath caressed the tight curls at the juncture of her thighs and her bottom rested against the front of his shoulders. He skimmed his hands over her thighs, spreading her legs a bit wider, pressing her forward, tilting her pelvis and adjusting the angle so that he might lie back amongst the pillows—as she'd suggested—and pleasure them both.

And the first touch of his tongue against that most intimate part of her was electric. It touched every nerve ending in her body and set her pulse to beating so rapidly that Miranda feared she might explode in a fantastic burst of flame. Her body melted against him, seeking release, and Daniel was merciless in providing it.

Miranda, who had always prided herself on her independent spirit, was astonished to discover that she was more than willing to relinquish her independence and become a willing slave to her desires.

Daniel bathed the spot where her pulse throbbed with his tongue. He licked the hard little nub hidden beneath her soft folds and felt the effect of it as Miranda began to move against him and his name escaped her lips as a high-pitched keen. "Daniel . . ."

Arching her back, Miranda filled the bedroom with incoherent, little sounds—soft sighs, guttural groans, and sharp, high-pitched squeals of pleasure—she made without knowing she did so. She squirmed in his arms, moving steadily closer to the source of her pleasure, and whimpered as Daniel blew his warm breath on her damp curls and ignited little currents of electricity that raced through her body.

He chuckled deep in his throat, thrilled with Miranda's response, heady with the powerful sensations swirling around them and with the incredible realization that she enjoyed his touch as much as he enjoyed touching her.

And his need to touch her, his desire to touch all of her, to taste the sweet hot essence of her, to bury his length inside her warmth and to feel the heat of her surrounding him as he throbbed and pulsed within grew so strong that Daniel knew it was the reason he'd been born. He had been born to capture her lips and swallow her cries as they careened toward the heavens on an intimate journey where two became one. He'd been born to introduce her to the world of passion and desire, where a man and a woman learned to give and to take, to advance and retreat, to pleasure and be pleasured in the dance of life.

"Daniel," Miranda gasped his name again as she pressed herself against his incredibly talented mouth. There were no words to describe the shockingly delicious and forbidden sensations she felt as Daniel performed the intimate act, working his magic until she was one big, quivering mass of sensation.

Daniel's familiarity with all the secret places on her body should have scandalized her, but Miranda was thrilled by his knowledge, enthralled by his experience, and grateful beyond belief for his genuine desire to give pleasure. She vibrated with passion as Daniel stroked and probed with such infinite tenderness and such agonizing care that she couldn't think of being scandalized. How could she be shocked and angry at a man who gave her such incredible bliss?

"Please," she murmured, squirming as desire—hot and thick and dangerous—surged through her, filling her body with urgent longings she couldn't name but which all came from the place Daniel graced with his magnificent attention.

Daniel deepened his caress, consciously applying every lesson he'd ever learned from the women who had shared his bed, as he feverishly worked his magic on Miranda. She was teetering on the edge of the precipice, desperately close to finding satisfaction, and he ached to join her in blissful release, but he ignored the painful throbbing of his member and concentrated on pushing Miranda over the edge.

Miranda sighed, and then shuddered deeply as her fragile control shattered and she gave herself up to the extraordinary pleasure that rushed through her, satisfying every ache, every longing—except the need for more.

Gripping the bedpost, she opened her eyes moments later, and looked down at him with an expression of sheer joy on her face.

Daniel's heart seemed to catch in his throat, and he was humbled by the emotion he saw in her eyes.

Miranda blushed. "You were magnificent," she

whispered, still awestruck by the magnitude of the feelings coursing through her.

"*You* were magnificent," Daniel corrected. "Now, come down here and let me hold you."

Her arms and legs felt limp and lifeless, but Miranda gave him a brilliant smile that spoke of deep satisfaction as she climbed over him, then lay beside him, her body pressed against him, her legs intertwined with his. Reaching up, she placed her palms on both sides of face. "Thank you," she said simply, as she pulled his face down to meet her lips.

"It was an honor," he whispered seconds before he captured her mouth with his and she tasted herself on his lips.

"Hmm," Miranda murmured, stretching languidly, like a cat.

"Good?" he asked, pulling away from her mouth to kiss the tip of her nose.

"Better than good, but I must admit that lovemaking appears to be rather one-sided." Miranda opened her eyes and gazed at him.

"How so?"

"You've done all the work," she answered. "I've done nothing except hold onto the bedposts and revel in the most exquisite feeling of bliss and satisfaction I've ever felt." She cradled his face in her hands, feeling with her hands the rough texture of his two days' growth of whiskers, which she'd felt against her inner thighs minutes earlier. "But in my experience, men are generally selfish creatures. And although you seem to enjoy it, I don't understand what you get out of it."

"The joy of watching you," he answered. "The pleasure of knowing that I've given you bliss the likes of which you've never known and that you allowed me to do it."

"What lady wouldn't want to experience such pleasure?" Miranda asked.

"You would be surprised at the number of gentlemen and ladies who have no idea such pleasure is possible and would be repulsed by the very idea. . . ."

Miranda shook her head. Apparently her parents had been among that number. What else could explain why her mother had told her lovemaking was embarrassing and uncomfortable? "We are acquainted with a great many ignorant and foolish ladies and gentlemen. Fortunately, you are not one of them." The smile she gave him was positively wicked.

"And neither are you, milady." Daniel cupped one of her breasts, then moved close enough to lick the tip of it.

She sucked in a breath. "I can't help wondering where you came by such knowledge. . . ."

"The way most enlightened gentlemen do," he said. "I had a generous and marvelously uninhibited teacher for whom I am eternally grateful."

"So am I," Miranda replied. "I don't quite understand how I could lose my virginity by doing what we did, but . . ."

Daniel laughed. "Miranda, my sweet, what we did is one of the ways a gentleman can pleasure a lady without taking her virginity."

"Oh." She looked at him and Daniel recognized the disappointment on her face. "Well, of course. How stupid of me. You're a gentleman. I should have realized you would know how to be intimate without . . . It's just that I thought you wanted to make love to . . . It's just that I thought . . ." She struggled to find the right word. *"Otherwise."*

"I *am* making love to you," Daniel told her. "There are as many ways to make love as there are couples doing it. Women generally take a bit longer to find satisfaction than men. What I did to you, what we just shared, is usually a prelude to the other ways of making love that result in the loss of your virginity and the possibility of a child. . . ."

"There's . . ."

He read her mind. "More," he promised. "In fact, it's only the beginning. Because, while I should know better . . ." He took a deep breath. "I am going to make love to you in as many ways as I possibly can. In as many ways as you'll allow. . . . God help me, but I fully intend to dispose of your virginity. Now. Tonight." He looked her in the eyes so there would be no misunderstanding. "Unfortunately, that's the part of lovemaking that may be uncomfortable for you and incredibly pleasurable for me." He made a face at her. "And the part selfish men generally enjoy most."

"I knew it was too good to be true," Miranda replied in a slightly disappointed tone of voice. "I knew there had to be discomfort somewhere."

"Not for you," he said, brushing her lips with a tender kiss. "Not if I can help it. I may be selfish in other ways, but you'll find I'm a very generous lover."

"Prove it," she challenged.

"I thought I already had," he replied. "With your prelude to lovemaking."

Miranda looped her arms around his neck and pulled him down for another passionate kiss. "Prove it again with the finale," she ordered. "And start by licking my breast again."

Daniel's body tightened with each word. He sucked in a breath and held it as the male part of him grew rigid and insistent, staining the sheets with the beads of moisture that appeared each time he thought about what was to follow.

Miranda smiled, then cupped her breast and offered it to him.

Daniel's blood rushed downward. The throbbing in his groin increased with each beat of his heart. Aching to sheathe himself in her warmth and end the exquisite torment, he accommodated her request, rolling her onto her back before lifting himself to cover her.

Settling between her legs, Daniel pressed himself against her. His male member nestled against her mound, cushioned by the soft curls covering it as he lavished attention on her breasts.

Reaching up, Miranda trailed her fingers up and down his spine, over the strips of cloth that bound his ribs and the bandage that covered his wound, then over his firm, muscular buttocks, down the tops of his thighs, and around to the front, where she brushed her fingers against him.

Momentarily forgetting about her breasts, Daniel sat back on his heels and groaned aloud as his hard jutting length surged up to greet her.

Miranda chuckled at his reaction. She wrapped her fingers around him, marveling at the feel of iron encased in velvet as she moved her hand up and down, testing the effect.

But Daniel put a quick end to her experiment by gripping her wrist and guiding her hand safely out of reach. He leaned forward, lifted her hips, and slipped inside her.

His entry was smooth and painless. Daniel bit his bottom lip to keep from groaning aloud as he gently pushed forward until he reached the bit of tissue barring his way.

"Why are you stopping?" Miranda squirmed against the pressure building inside her.

"Sssh," he soothed, placing a gentle kiss on her eyelid and then on the corner of her mouth. "Lie still for a moment. We're in no hurry. There's no need to rush."

But there was. Filled by a sense of urgency she couldn't name, Miranda moved against him.

"Don't . . ." He tried to warn her, but Miranda pulled him to her and Daniel pushed past the barrier to sheath his full length inside her.

The tearing pain lasted only a heartbeat or two, but it was enough to give Miranda pause.

"That hurt," she murmured against his ear, seconds before biting down on his lobe.

Daniel yelped.

"Now, we're even," she told him.

He smiled down at her. And then he kissed her with all the pent-up passion and frustration and longing he felt. He kissed her until her breasts heaved with exertion, until her bones seemed to turn to jelly, until all she could do was cling to him, returning his kisses as she fervently gave herself up to the rhythm as old as time.

He set the pace, and Miranda followed, matching his

movements thrust for thrust. She held on to him, reveling in the weight and feel of him as he filled her again and again, gifting her with himself in a way she'd never dreamed possible.

Tears of joy trickled from the corners of her eyes, ran down her cheeks, and disappeared into the silk of her hair as she felt the first tremors flow through her.

Surrendering to the emotions swirling inside her, Miranda gave voice to the passion building inside her as Daniel rocked her to him and exploded inside her. *"I love you, Daniel."*

"I think I've lost the hearing in one ear," he whispered, brushing his lips against her cheek, burying his fingers in her hair, tasting the saltiness of the tears on her face. "You might have warned me that you were a screamer."

"How could I?" she asked. "When I've never been one until now?"

He lifted his head and looked down at her face. God, but she was beautiful. Daniel shuddered as a rush of emotion raced through him. He should have spoken words of love instead of words of passion.

I love you, Daniel.

She had said the words loud enough for him to hear. He smiled. She'd *screamed* the words loud enough for the neighbors to hear. He should have done the same.

He should have cherished her and treated her more tenderly instead of using her to slake his raging desire. She deserved a better introduction to passion than the one he'd just given her. And he'd see that she got it.

Just as soon as he recovered from this one.

Chapter 20

"*Every one complains of a poor memory, no one of a weak judgment.*"

—*François, Duc de La Rochefoucauld, 1613–1680*

Miranda awoke with a start to the sound of a coach driving up. She pushed the hair out of her eyes and looked around. The bedroom drapes were open and the room was filled with sunshine. She looked at the clock. It was a few minutes past nine in the morning and Daniel was still fast asleep.

She covered a yawn with her hand, then rolled out of bed and pulled on her undergarments and dress. The marble chessboard was lying on the carpet surrounded by toppled chessmen. She righted the chessboard and began collecting the pieces along with the handful of hairpins scattered on the floor. Miranda stepped into her slippers and quietly opened the door and walked down the hall, where she made her way to the bath so as not to disturb Daniel.

She finished her toilette and was anchoring the last of her hairpins in place when she entered the kitchen to find Ned already inside, surrounded by more baskets of provisions and several brown-paper-wrapped packages bearing the name of Daniel's tailor.

"I came as soon as I could!" he exclaimed, breathless with excitement. "I thought His Grace would want to know about it. The news is all over town. And in the morning papers."

"His mother?" Miranda demanded. "Has something happened to his mother?" She didn't care much for the dowager duchess and she knew the dowager duchess despised her, but Daniel loved his mother, and to her credit, Miranda's first thought was for her.

"No, milady."

"Our marriage? Has news of it leaked out?"

"Not that I'm aware, milady," Ned answered.

"Then what is it?"

"It's the Marquess of Shepherdston," Ned announced. "He fought a duel this morning."

"Against whom?" Miranda held her breath, praying she wouldn't hear the name Micah.

"Lord Dunbridge."

Miranda frowned. "Lord *Reginald* Dunbridge?"

"The same."

"Shepherdston isn't . . . ?"

Ned shook his head and continued feverishly unpacking the things he'd purchased.

"Injured?"

"No."

"Thank goodness," she breathed. "Why in the world would Shepherdston duel with a dandy like Dunbridge?"

Ned set out cups and saucers, spoons, small plates and napkins, then reached into a basket and brought out a metal container of hot coffee and a bag from Gunter's, the confectioner's on Berkeley Square. "I heard it when I stopped by the Cocoa Tree Coffeehouse to purchase the coffee." He took a cup and saucer from the shelf above the worktable, unscrewed the top from the metal container, and poured Miranda a cup. He set her cup of coffee in front of her, then filled a plate with an assortment of pastries and handed it to her along with her napkin. "It began with a wager recorded in the betting books at White's. Lord Dunbridge wagered a thousand pounds that he would wed a certain young lady in a ceremony conducted by the Archbishop of Canterbury, in Westminster Abbey, at season's end. Lord Shepherdston wagered Dunbridge wouldn't marry the lady at season's end or at any other time."

The image of the young woman in the dark cloak and the nightgown furtively hurrying through the rain to the Marquess of Shepherdston's town house two nights before popped into her brain. "Thank goodness Lord Dunbridge didn't mention the young lady by name or her reputation would be ruined." She didn't know how she knew it, but Miranda was convinced that the girl she'd seen the other night and the girl of the thousand-pound wager were one and the same.

"Oh, but he did."

A gentleman of breeding did not include the name of a lady of good family in any wager recorded in the betting books at White's. He might include initials, but never the names. "Tell me the lady in question is a widow or someone's mistress."

"Apparently, she's a young unmarried lady of good family," Ned told her. "At any road, the dispute came to a head last night at Lady Garrison's party." He offered her the *Morning Chronicle*. "Here, read it for yourself."

Miranda took it and saw that Ned had already folded it to the third-page "Ton Tidbits" column. She groaned as she read the column. "Oh, good gracious! Lady Garrison is the Duchess of Avon's sister, and Alyssa and Griff were attending the party last night. I was supposed to go with them." Lifting her cup, Miranda took a sip of coffee.

"Be glad you didn't," Ned said. "Be glad you weren't there to witness it, because I heard it got rather ugly."

"I'm very glad I wasn't there." Miranda wouldn't trade what had happened to her the previous evening for all the tea in China. "I regret Lord Shepherdston felt compelled to challenge a fool like Dunbridge."

"Lord Shepherdston didn't issue the challenge," Ned corrected. "Lord Dunbridge did. I heard he slapped

Shepherdston across the face with his glove when Shepherdston refused to allow him to dance with the young lady at the heart of the wager."

"Dunbridge is a fool," Miranda pronounced, biting into a pastry.

"On that, everyone in town agrees," Ned confirmed. "And a ruined fool now that he failed to show up for the duel he demanded."

"Did he send word of his refusal?"

"No one knows. He simply failed to show up at the dueling oak. But I heard it mentioned that he was in attendance at a certain house of pleasure and that he was drinking heavily."

"No doubt trying to find the courage to face the marquess."

Ned nodded in agreement as he finished setting the breakfast tray with coffee and pastries for Daniel. "At any rate, rumors and gossip are flying all over town, and I thought His Grace should know."

"You were right," Miranda confirmed. "He's feeling much better today. So well that I suspect he will have need of some clothes."

He lifted one of the large brown-paper-wrapped packages. "They're here. I collected two suits of clothing for His Grace at his tailor's, and the other items you asked me to get." He produced a basket full of men's toiletries.

He unwrapped the brown paper so Miranda could inspect the buff breeches, white shirt, waistcoat, coat, and neck linen.

Miranda nodded her approval.

"Shall I take them up to His Grace?"

Miranda shook her head. "I'll take them. You can follow with the tray." She looked around the kitchen. "Boots. Did you get His Grace a pair of boots?"

Ned frowned mightily. "I wasn't able to accomplish that task. I couldn't get to His Grace's bootblack this morning without alerting the staff at Sussex House."

"No matter," she offered. "His Grace can wear his evening

shoes. I know you weren't hired to be a cook and house-keeper, lady's maid, valet, or errand boy, but I am deeply grateful to you for assuming these roles."

Ned grinned at her. "It all becomes a part and parcel of my training, milady. One day, I hope to be elevated to the position of your personal secretary or butler."

Miranda returned his grin. "And so you shall." She swallowed her last bite of pastry, wiped her hands on her napkin, and reached for Daniel's clothes, the newspaper, and the basket of toiletries.

Ned hefted the breakfast tray and followed her up the stairs.

"Leave the tray outside the door," Miranda instructed when they reached the bedroom. "And tell Rupert to have the coach ready."

Ned sent her a questioning glance.

"If I know His Grace, he's going to want to find out what happened at the duel this morning, and he'll go straight to the Marquess of Shepherdston or one of his friends for answers."

❧

"Daniel?" Miranda leaned over the bed and touched him on the shoulder. "Wake up. It's morning."

He bolted upright, then let out a yelp of pain as the sore muscles along his ribs protested. He blinked in confusion, then gave her a devastatingly beautiful smile as images from the night and the morning came flooding back. "Good morning."

His greeting resembled the rumble of a large cat, and his smile did funny things to her heartstrings. She stared at the bed, blushing at the memory of all they had done there and all they had shared.

"I'm sorry to wake you, but Ned arrived with your clothes, and, well . . ." she hesitated. "We knew you'd want to know."

"Know what?" The cobwebs of sleep dissipated, and Daniel was instantly awake. He looked at the clock on the mantel, read the time, and turned to face her. "I slept that long?"

She nodded. "You were tired."

"I was nothing of the sort," Daniel protested. "I was *exhausted* by a certain insatiable auburn-haired beauty who screams like a banshee when she . . ." He broke off and gave her a lopsided grin. The words she'd screamed hung between them. Four little words he'd left unanswered. *I love you, Daniel.* He ought to answer them now. This morning. But he couldn't bring himself, in the sober light of day, to say the words he'd always managed to avoid. Not after a night of extraordinary lovemaking. With Miranda. Not when she knew him so well. Not when he feared they would sound like a sop to his conscience. Better to say them later when he'd had more time to come to terms with the fact that he was in love with Miranda. That he'd always been in love with Miranda. Daniel drew in a painful breath. Better to yell the words in the heat of passion when there was less chance of her doubting his sincerity. "Who would have thought that a nice little marchioness like you could be so incredibly demanding in bed? Or so incredibly giving?"

She looked down at the floor and noticed that a wayward chess piece—a bishop—lay half hidden by the bed linen. She'd told him she loved him and he couldn't say the same.

Daniel reached out and lifted her chin with the tip of his index finger. "Have I thanked you yet for the best night of my life?"

She shook her head. "But then, I haven't thanked you, either."

He leaned forward and gave her a good morning kiss. "Strange, isn't it?" Daniel asked after kissing her thoroughly.

"What?"

"Waking up with you like this. No longer at cross

purposes." He shook his head as if to clear it. "I haven't spent an entire night with a woman since I left the university. I never spend the night with a woman sharing my pillow, and I've done it twice with you in as many days." He met her gaze. "I wonder what that means."

"Maybe it means you know I can be trusted to keep your secrets," she suggested.

"Maybe it does," he agreed, reaching for her hand to pull her back into bed. "Or maybe it means I simply enjoy sharing a bed with you."

Miranda reluctantly pulled away. "Would that we could . . ."

"We can." He gave her a wicked grin. "Quite thoroughly. And in the full light of morning."

She took a deep breath, then slowly exhaled. "Not *this* morning."

"Why not?"

"Because there were a great many strange goings-on in town last night while we were otherwise engaged—not the least of which was a certain Lord Dunbridge challenging the Marquess of Shepherdston to a duel at Lady Garrison's last night." She spread his clothes across the foot of the bed.

"What?" He sat up and swung his feet over the side of the bed. "How do you know that?"

"Ned heard all about it at the Cocoa Tree this morning." Miranda turned around and left the room to retrieve his breakfast tray. When she returned, she filled his cup with coffee and handed it to him, then set the tray with the coffeepot and plate of pastries on the bedside table and related everything Ned had told her in the kitchen. "It's in this morning's papers if you want to read it." She waved the copy of the "Ton Tidbits" at him.

"You read it to me while I dress." Daniel took a deep swallow of his coffee, wolfed down a pastry, then set his cup aside. Ignoring the stockinette drawers, he stood up and reached for the new pair of tightly knitted stockings and the new pair of buff breeches she'd laid out for him.

Miranda read: " 'What's to become of Miss Sarah Eckersley, who was seen at Lady Garrison's elegant gala last evening in the company of the elusive Marquess of Shepherdston? Has she been taken off the market? No one can say for sure, but Miss Eckersley proved to be the bone of contention last evening when Lord Dunbridge, a devoted follower of the Prince Regent's close friend, Mr. George Brummell, challenged Lord Shepherdston to a duel. Are wedding bells in the Marquess of Shepherdston's future? Has the perennial bachelor marquess finally succumbed to the lure of orange blossoms? Can a rustic rector's daughter take him off the market? No one seems to know for sure. . . . But we will surely find out soon. . . .' "

Miranda finished reading and watched as Daniel pulled on his stockings, then stepped into his breeches. She watched as he pulled the buff breeches up his long legs and over his hips and buttocks, where they molded to him like a second skin. He buttoned two buttons, then reached for his lawn shirt. "No drawers?" Miranda asked.

"Not in these." Daniel gave her a lascivious wink. "There's no room." He lifted his shirt and attempted to pull it over his head. But the wound in his side and the binding around his ribs made it impossible. He sat down on the edge of the bed. "Do you mind?"

"Of course not." She laid the newspaper aside and walked over to help him with his shirt. Once they managed to settle the garment in place, Daniel stood up to tuck the tails of it into the waistband of his breeches and button the remaining buttons.

He slipped on his waistcoat and glanced around for the tall boots that should have completed his ensemble.

She opened the drawer in the bedside table so he could collect his personal items from the ones she'd stored there. "Ned wasn't able to locate a pair of boots, but here are your other belongings."

"No matter," he answered. "I know where to get a pair of boots."

Miranda left the drawer open and stepped back. Inside it were his purse, his pocket watch and chain, the pewter flask, and her reticule and fan.

Daniel reached in to gather his things. "The reticule and the fan are yours, I believe," he said with a smile as he retrieved his coin purse and tucked it into the inside pocket of his waistcoat. He removed his watch, wound it, and checked the time against the time on the mantel clock before fastening the chain to his waistcoat and pocketing the timepiece. Turning away from the open drawer, Daniel grabbed a hairbrush and a toothbrush and cleaning powder from the basket of toiletries she'd brought and walked toward the bathing room.

"What shall I do with this?" She waved the flask at him.

Daniel turned. "Inside coat pocket."

"It's empty," she offered.

"I know where to get more," he said, as he opened the door to the bathing room.

"You seem to know a great many things this morning," she teased.

"I'm a man of knowledge, milady, who wishes to specialize in discovering all there is to know about you." He blew her a kiss from the doorway.

"You already know more than anyone else," she reminded him.

"Doesn't matter," he replied. "For I've a burning desire to add to my store of knowledge." He leered at her, waggling his eyebrows to make her smile.

Miranda laughed as he disappeared into the bathing room, then picked his coat up off the foot of the bed and slipped the flask into the inner pocket. She was about to close the table drawer when she spied her reticule and remembered what it contained. Taking a deep breath, she opened the drawstrings of the mint green reticule, withdrew the folded sheet of paper from beneath the cardboard bottom, and tucked it inside the coat pocket beside the flask, then impulsively retrieved the bishop from beneath the bedcovers and dropped it into his pocket as well.

She bit her bottom lip. He was leaving. Without telling her how he felt about her. And she was giving him the only proof of what they'd done to take with him. Once he discovered it, he could keep it or destroy it as he chose. She blinked back a tear and wiped her cheek with the back of her hand as Daniel returned, moments later, from the bathing room with freshly brushed hair and clean teeth. He ran his hand over his cheeks and chin, gauging the length of his whiskers. He ought to shave, but he couldn't take the time.

Miranda looked at the whiskers shadowing his jaw and was reminded of the pink abrasions he'd unwittingly left on her stomach and thighs.

Daniel read her thoughts. "I promise to shave next time."

"Is there going to be a next time?"

"If you want one."

"I do." Miranda nearly cringed when she said the words that were eerily close to the words she'd uttered to seal the vows she'd exchanged with Daniel two nights ago. Vows he still didn't seem to recall.

He leaned down to kiss her. "Tell me, my sweet marchioness, what happened to the notion of saving yourself for your husband?"

She almost told him the truth, but Miranda was afraid of spoiling the tender moment. "I decided that saving myself for a man who may or may not take me to wife was foolish. I've decided it's far better to give myself to a man who isn't interested in sharing my fortune or my future— only my bed."

Daniel looked fierce. "So long as I'm that man."

Miranda's smile was as mysterious as it was seductive.

"I may not be able to see you for a few days," Daniel told her. "But make no mistake about it, I intend to see you again. Soon."

"I'll look forward to it."

Her politely distant response puzzled him. "Miranda?"

"Go." She reached up and caressed his cheek with the

palm of her hand, then turned her back to him to keep from crying.

Daniel started through the door, but stopped when Miranda called his name.

"And, Daniel . . ."

He glanced over his shoulder. "Yes?"

"It was so nice having you shower me with genuine adoration that I should hate to have it end abruptly. Please, be careful."

He smiled. "Not to worry."

"I won't worry," she told him. "So long as you come home without any more holes in you."

Her words gave him pause. *Home. As long as you come home . . .* Suddenly home wasn't Sussex House but wherever Miranda was. "I *am* coming back."

She turned to face him. "Take care of yourself."

Daniel nodded, then walked out of the bedroom, down the stairs, and out the front door to the street in his stocking feet. He climbed into the coach Rupert had at the ready, and propped his feet on the opposite bench.

Reaching up to pull the curtain at the window, Daniel saw a coach roll to a stop at the house across the street. The coach looked familiar. He stared at the man exiting the house across the street and blinked in recognition, then quickly dropped the curtain and called out to Rupert with the address he needed. "Take me to Albany."

Chapter 21

"One finds many companions for food and drink,
But in a serious business a man's companions are few."

—Theognis, c. 545 B.C.

"Where the devil have you been?" Jonathan, eleventh Earl of Barclay, greeted his cousin, Daniel, as soon as he walked through the door of Barclay's Albany apartments. "We've been looking everywhere for you."

"It's good to see you too, Jonathan." Daniel shook hands with his cousin and let out a groan when Jonathan clapped him about the shoulder.

"You had us worried."

Daniel smiled. "I had a bit of trouble on my return from France."

"I surmised as much," Jonathan told him. "You need to shave, and you look as if you haven't slept in days." He looked down at Daniel's feet. "And where the devil are your boots?"

"At Sussex House," Daniel answered, "and since I've no intention of returning there for a while, I need to borrow a pair of yours."

"Sit down." Jonathan gestured toward a leather chair. "I'll get you a pair."

Daniel sank down on the chair and put his feet up on the

matching ottoman while Jonathan disappeared into his bedroom and returned with a pair of tall boots. One of the nice things about having a cousin the same age and weight and approximate height was that he knew Jonathan's boots would fit.

Jonathan set the pair of boots on the floor beside Daniel and grinned.

Daniel looked up at him. "Thanks."

Jonathan shrugged. "It's rather nice to be able to loan you something for a change."

"That's good to know," Daniel drawled. "Because I also need a place to stay." He lifted one boot and leaned forward to pull it on, only to be brought up short by the stiffness in his back.

"Leave 'em off for a while," Jonathan advised. "So long as you're staying, I'll help you put them on later." He studied Daniel. "Aunt Lavinia was right. You have been avoiding her."

Daniel nodded. "Quite right. I've been avoiding Mother, Weldon, Travers, Malden, and everyone else at Sussex House." He looked at his cousin. "Especially Mother and Malden."

Jonathan sent him a questioning look.

"I'm avoiding Mother because I don't want her to ask questions I can't answer, and I'm avoiding my valet because he cannot keep a secret and I can't hide this one from him."

"Why? What happened?" Jonathan asked. "I caught sight of you at the Gala, but Aunt Lavinia pressed me into substituting for you in the receiving line, and by the time I got through, you'd disappeared."

"I got hit by a rifle ball during the Channel crossing."

"Bloody hell!" Jonathan swore. "Going or coming?"

"Coming back."

"How badly? Are you all right? Was anyone else injured?" Jonathan was instantly concerned not just for his cousin but for the crew. He worked with the brave crew to smuggle men and supplies across the Channel as often as Daniel did and knew that most of the men Colin and Jarrod had recruited hailed from the villages of Pymley and Coldswater, not far from the Dover coast.

"Shavers caught one through the flesh of the arm and Pepper's got a new part in his hair, but I got the worst of it," Daniel said. "The ball cut a groove through my side and cracked a rib or two, but it missed the vital organs." He smiled. "I'll live. But I wasn't as certain of it at the party the other night."

Jonathan exhaled. "I can't believe you made the journey at all. It must have hurt like the very devil."

Daniel shook his head. "Mistress Beekins stitched me up, bound my ribs, handed me a flask full of Scots whisky, then sent her son, Micah, along with a large jug of the stuff with me to London." He flashed his grin at his cousin. "My wound barely pained me at all once I had that much whisky in me. But because I had that much whisky in me, I had Micah memorize the phrase and sent him to Shepherdston's house with the dispatch pouches and the round of cheese. Did he get them?"

"He got them. Gillian decoded them and Jarrod has reported the findings to the men at Whitehall." He grinned at Daniel. "Job well done."

"Except for getting shot." Daniel thought for a moment. "And something bothers me about that. There was something odd. Something I can't quite put my finger on."

"Give it time," Jonathan advised. "You'll come up with the answer." He shook his head in amazement. "I know you hold your spirits well, but to drink all the way from Dover to town . . ."

"I had to," Daniel replied. "It was the only way I could endure the trip."

"Good God, Daniel, why didn't you just stay the night with the Beekinses?"

"And miss making an appearance at the Duchess of

Sussex's annual gala?" He threw a glance at his cousin. "Would you?"

Jonathan shook his head. "And she's only my aunt. Not my mother." He smiled at Daniel. "But by the time you arrived at your mother's party, you must have been drunk."

"As the proverbial lord," Daniel replied. "I've never had so much whisky in my life." He gave a little laugh. "I still have an aching head and gaps in my memory."

"No wonder you found it necessary to avoid your mother." Jonathan whistled through his teeth. "She'd have known you were foxed the minute she saw you."

"Which is why I left you to stand by Mother in the receiving line," Daniel admitted. "Still, I could have avoided her and muddled through, but I accidentally tore Mistress Beekins's stitches open and started bleeding. With no way to hide that, I was forced to prevail upon Miranda to waltz me out of there. Fast."

"Miranda?" Jonathan was only partly surprised. "St. Germaine?"

"She's the only Miranda I know."

"So, you've been staying with Miranda for the past two days?"

Daniel glanced up at Jonathan's clock. "Until a half hour ago."

Jonathan chuckled. "Courtland owes me ten pounds. I wagered you'd be with Miranda and Courtland wagered that you were holed up in a house somewhere."

"Split the difference," Daniel advised, "because you're both right. And tell me you didn't record that particular wager in the betting books at White's."

"Like that dunderhead Dunbridge?" Jonathan scoffed. "I've got better sense and better manners." He glanced at Daniel to make certain Daniel had gotten the joke. Until he'd inherited the late Earl of Barclay's title, Jonathan had been known as Johnny Manners. "I'm a gentleman. Dunbridge is a cad masquerading as a gentleman."

"Cad or not, he's certainly caused Jarrod a great deal of trouble."

"That's the truth."

"How is Shepherdston, by the way?" Daniel asked.

Jonathan glanced at the casement clock. "I'm sure he's fine. He's either getting married or on his wedding trip by now."

"What?" Daniel was stunned. "Shepherdston?"

"You said you saw the paper, Daniel. Shepherdston's nothing if not a true gentleman. What did you expect him to do?"

"Exactly what he's doing," Daniel replied. "It's just such a shock. When I left, he was a confirmed bachelor, and I've only been gone a few days!"

"I'm told that sometimes it happens like that."

"Marriages forced by scandal?"

Jonathan smiled. "Those too. But I was talking about people falling in love."

"Shepherdston's in love with Miss Eckersley?"

"Head over heels," Jonathan confirmed. "He's known her forever, and it's taken him this long to realize he's in love with her." He looked at his cousin to see if Daniel could handle another shock. "And that's not all."

Daniel prepared himself for the worst. Whatever the worst was.

"Lord Rob got married this morning."

Hearing Lord Robert Mayhew, Jarrod's godfather, had gotten married after fifteen years as a widower came as an even greater shock to Daniel. Daniel had no idea Lord Rob had ever contemplated remarriage. "To whom?"

"Lady Henrietta Dunbridge."

"Dunbridge?" Daniel vaguely recalled being introduced to a lovely widow several years Lord Rob's junior who had accompanied a young lady making her presentation into society some three or four seasons ago. "There was a Lady Dunbridge. But I believe she was some relation to the current Lord Dunbridge."

Jonathan nodded. "His aunt by marriage."

"Lord Rob married Reggie Dunbridge's aunt?"

Jonathan smiled. "She also happens to be Miss Sarah Eckersley's maternal aunt. She was born Miss Henrietta Helford. She became Lady Calvin Dunbridge upon her marriage, but she and her husband were later estranged, and he insisted that she not be styled with his given name, so on her rare occasions in London, she became known as Lady *Henrietta* Dunbridge."

"You're joking!"

"Not at all," Jonathan answered. "Imagine, several days ago, Jarrod had no family except the Free Fellows League and Lord Rob. And today, in addition to Lord Rob and us, he's getting an aunt by marriage and a bride."

Daniel began to laugh. He'd only been gone a few days, and the world as he knew it had been turned on its ear. Everything had changed. He couldn't have been more surprised if Jonathan had told him the dowager duchess had gotten married. "So, Johnny Manners," Daniel drawled, "tell me everything that's happened since I left for my trip to the coast. And start with the duel I read about in this morning's papers." Daniel took his feet off the leather ottoman, stretched his legs, then propped them up again.

"Despite what you read in the papers," Jonathan explained, "there was no duel. Jarrod, Griff, and Colin waited at the dueling oak for over an hour past the appointed time, but Dunbridge didn't appear."

"So I heard."

Jonathan arched an eyebrow in query.

"Miranda's footman heard it at the Cocoa Tree when he stopped for coffee this morning. He told us that nobody knows why Dunbridge made it a point to challenge Jarrod, then failed to appear."

Jonathan snorted. "Somebody knows."

"That's exactly what I thought when he told me," Daniel said. "And that's exactly why I came to you."

"Well, it's one story you won't be reading in the

papers." Jonathan glanced disapprovingly at a copy of the *Morning Chronicle* on the table beside his favorite chair.

"I knew it!" Daniel crowed.

"Knew what?" Jonathan tried to look innocent and failed.

Daniel recognized the look on his cousin's face. "I knew you wouldn't allow your hero to face a duel alone, and since you weren't with Shepherdston, Avon, or Grantham at the dueling oak, I knew you had to, behind Dunbridge's failure to appear."

Jarrod Shepherdston had been Jonathan's hero since Jonathan had occupied the cot beside Jarrod's at Knights-guild. Back then, Jonathan Manners had been a lonely and frightened boy of seven. He'd whined incessantly and cried for his nanny nearly every night. The other boys at Knights-guild had made him their whipping boy, but Jarrod Shep-herdston and the other Free Fellows had gone out of their way to be kind to him and to protect him as best they could—if only, Jarrod had confessed when they'd invited Jonathan to join the Free Fellows League a year ago, to bring an end to Manners' whining and crying.

Jonathan had grown into a strong, fine, principled man, who stood shoulder to shoulder with Jarrod and Colin and was only slightly shorter than Griffin and Daniel. He had never forgotten the kindness Shepherdston and the others had shown him and had been thrilled to finally be asked to take his place beside them in the League. Daniel knew that Jonathan would do almost anything in the world for Jarrod Shepherdston, including deliberately hindering his enemy.

"So, Johnny, what did you do?"

Jonathan stood up and gestured for Daniel to do the same. "Step into my bedchamber and I'll show you."

Daniel followed Barclay into his bedchamber and dis-covered that nearly every surface in the room was covered with men's clothing of every description. The floor, the bed, the chairs, the tables, even the top of Jonathan's mas-sive armoire was covered in clothes.

Jonathan plucked a garment from the pile. "It's a shame you didn't come to borrow a waistcoat," he said, tossing it to Daniel. "I've a few dozen of those to spare."

Daniel caught the waistcoat. "As if I were desperate enough to borrow anything as gaudy as this." He stared at the bold green and purple pattern, then tossed it back to Jonathan.

"Well, there are plenty of other garments from which to choose," Jonathan continued. "As you can see, we've enough men's clothing here to open a haberdashery."

"Only if one's tastes run along dandyish lines."

Jonathan quirked an eyebrow. "In any other town, I'd say that might present a problem. But not in London."

"Unfortunately, I have to agree," Daniel replied, eyeing the room with a mixture of disgust and awe. "It looks as if you helped yourself to Lord Dunbridge's wardrobe."

"So I did," Jonathan confirmed.

"It must have taken you a while to collect all this." He swept his arm through the air.

"It took us hours." Jonathan tossed Dunbridge's waistcoat back onto the bed and motioned Daniel out of the bedroom, back into the main sitting room. Closing the bedroom door to keep from having to look at the mess, he followed him.

Daniel walked over and helped himself to coffee from the urn on the buffet, then turned and offered to refill Jonathan's cup.

"Yes, thank you." Jonathan handed Daniel his empty cup and saucer. "There are pastries from Gunter's in the box by the urn. I picked them up this morning. I just got the coffee before you arrived, and I haven't cut the string on the pastry box yet. Bring those, too, if you don't mind," Jonathan instructed, before adding, "Your Grace."

Daniel brought Jonathan his coffee and the box of pastries, then made a second trip to the buffet to get his own coffee. He settled back onto his chair, set his cup and saucer on the table beside it, then reached for a pastry and propped his feet back up on the ottoman. He took a bite of a cherry tart.

"You were saying it took you and someone else hours to collect Dunbridge's garments. Who was the someone?"

"Alex Courtland."

Chapter 22

"People are not always what they seem."
—Gotthold Ephraim Lessing, 1729–1797

"*Of course.*" *Daniel grinned.* "*Who else but Courtland* would agree to help you with something like this?"

"Thank God he did," Jonathan said. "Else I'd still be picking up clothes from Dunbridge's lawn."

"Surely you didn't take all of his clothes?"

"How else were we going to be certain he wouldn't appear at the dueling oak at the appointed time?" He grinned at his cousin. "And even then, we couldn't be sure he wouldn't go buck naked. Courtland wanted to tie him up, but I thought it better just to leave him as he was and with nothing to wear."

"Imagine that," Daniel said. "A dandy with nothing to wear."

"Right," Jonathan agreed. "The joke was on him. But Courtland and I didn't count on the man having so many clothes. We were picking up clothes until the small hours of the morning as it was. I swear Dunbridge must have a thousand neck cloths and handkerchiefs."

"I can't believe you took his neck cloths and his handkerchiefs."

"You saw it for yourself."

And he wouldn't have believed it otherwise. But Daniel

had seen the mountain of linen on Jonathan's floor. "Did you leave him with anything?"

"One pair of brief drawers," Jonathan answered. "And that was only because I dropped them when we were shoving everything into the coach and neither one of us wanted to bend and pick them up."

"I'm impressed by your complete and thorough ruthlessness." Daniel laughed. "And curious as to how you and Courtland managed to get into Dunbridge's house and abscond with his clothes?"

"His butler let us in."

"Dunbridge's butler let you in to steal his clothes?" Daniel bit back a smile. "It appears the man has more enemies than he knows."

"I'm sure there are a few hundred people in town who hate him for his taste in clothes alone. But in all fairness to his butler, the man let us in because he thought we were doing his employer a favor by bringing him home."

"From where?"

"Madam Theodora's," Jonathan answered, helping himself to a cream puff. "He was at Madam Theo's after the ball last night boasting about his upcoming duel with Shepherdston."

"And?" Daniel prompted.

Jonathan grinned. "I thought Madam Theodora was going to faint. I know she's fond of Jarrod, but she must be even fonder of him than we thought, because she turned as pale as a ghost."

"Maybe she's fond of Lord Dunbridge," Daniel suggested, playing the devil's advocate.

"She doesn't give a fig about the current one," Jonathan said. "But she apparently adored the previous one. It seems Madam Theo's house originally belonged to the previous Lord Dunbridge, who happened to be the late husband of Lord Rob's bride."

Daniel recalled the name. "Lord Calvin Dunbridge."

Jonathan nodded. "There's a history there I'm not privy

to, but suffice it to say that Madam Theo has some attach-ment to Miss Eckersley and to Lady Dunbridge and is very protective of both of them. Any road, Madam Theo recov-ered from her shock or fright or whatever it was soon enough. She called the girls together in the parlor and told them that as long as Lord Dunbridge remained in the house, the night's entertainment and drinks were free. It must have cost her a bloody fortune, because the house was bursting at the seams all night long." He shook his head. "It was quite a party."

Daniel stared at Barclay's pallor and red eyes and agreed. "I don't doubt it a bit."

"As you can imagine, no one wanted him to leave. Every time he attempted to go, someone pulled him back inside and handed him a drink. He put up a good argument for a while. Kept telling everyone that he had to go home and prepare for his duel, but it was hard to say no to all his well-wishers." Jonathan paused to polish off his cream puff before resuming his story. "When he finally passed out, in the arms of the new redhead, Mina, Madam Theo came to me and asked me to assist her in removing him. I sent for Courtland and asked him to assist me." He smiled a wicked smile. "Together we hauled him down the back stairs of Madam Theo's, shoved him into my coach, and took him to his town house."

"Where his butler let you in."

"Right. We didn't have any trouble there because Dun-bridge's butler was glad to have us there to help his master up the stairs." Lifting his cup and saucer, Jonathan took a long swallow. "And once we gained entrance, it was a sim-ple matter of dismissing the butler and carrying Dunbridge up the stairs to his bed." He smiled at the memory. "I have to say it was the best adventure I've had since university days that didn't involve smuggling."

"I don't even know the fellow and I would have paid money to see you and Courtland carrying him up the stairs." Daniel smiled.

"Especially when we were none too steady on our feet, either." Jonathan threw back his head and laughed. "We had to have been drunk to do what we did, and I have to say it was a first for me." He looked at Daniel. "I hope he's the last drunken lord I ever have to strip naked." He shuddered in mock horror. "Carrying him up the stairs was hard enough. But getting his clothes off him while he was asleep was worse. I swear it felt as if he weighed a ton, and it was all dead weight. . . ."

Good heavens, Daniel, you weigh a ton.

Miranda's complaint came back to haunt him so clearly that he could almost believe she was standing beside him. *I take it back, Daniel. You weigh a ton and a half.*

"Tossing his clothes out the window and picking them up, though it took a while, was easy in comparison."

"I'd say you and Miranda St. Germaine have a lot in common."

"She stole your boots?"

"She waltzed me out of Sussex House and practically carried me across the lawn on her own." He gazed at Jonathan over the rim of his coffee cup. "If I remember correctly, she accused me of weighing a ton and a half. I still can't believe she managed it."

"Miranda's a big girl," Jonathan reminded him.

Daniel knew Jonathan wasn't intentionally belittling Miranda. He knew Jonathan hadn't meant his comment to be hurtful, but it stung. And Daniel realized, suddenly, how Miranda felt when he'd repeatedly reminded her that she was no featherweight. "She's a tall girl," Daniel corrected. "And I'm an even taller, heavier man. Getting me out of my clothes while I was unconscious and stitching me up must have been a Herculean task."

Jonathan's shock showed on his face. "Miranda took care of you?"

"Yes." Daniel drank the last of his coffee, placed the cup on the saucer and set them on the table.

"Alone?"

"Yes."

"Where was her mother?" Jonathan asked. "And what about the footman? Where was he?"

"I suppose Lady St. Germaine is in residence at Upper Brook Street. Miranda and I were not," Daniel admitted.

"Where were you?"

"For her sake, I'd rather not say."

"And the footman?" Jonathan asked again.

"He didn't stay. He brought provisions, did chores, and ran errands. He's been with Miranda for years and is entirely devoted to her."

"I hope you're right, or else you may find yourself the topic of that"—Jonathan pointed to the newspaper lying on the table—"in the morning. Daniel, what the devil were you thinking to compromise her like that? And what the devil was she thinking to allow it? Miranda St. Germaine isn't just a lady, she holds a title in her own right. You've been attracted to Miranda for a long time now, but I can't believe you were so careless. Are you looking to ruin her? Are you looking to cause a scandal?"

Daniel shook his head. He hadn't deliberately set out to compromise her. It had just happened that way. "No one knows I was there except Miranda and her footman and driver, and they're completely trustworthy."

"Are you certain?"

"Absolutely."

"No one else saw you there?"

"Perhaps a street vendor." There was no perhaps about it and Daniel knew it. But the odds on the pieman recognizing him as the Duke of Sussex were very slim.

Jonathan groaned. "And no one other than Miranda, her footman, and her driver saw you go in." He looked at Daniel for confirmation.

"As far as I know," he answered. "I was unconscious at the time."

Jonathan asked one last question. "What about coming out?"

"Thunderation!" He looked at his cousin. "Send word to Colin and Griff and Courtland. Tell them we'll meet them at White's."

"Impossible today," Jonathan said. "Jarrod assigned us tasks before he left for his wedding and honeymoon. Griffin is meeting with the men at Whitehall about the need for a permanent training facility for ciphers, and that may take the rest of the afternoon." He related the details of dispatches Colin's wife had deciphered, the plot they'd uncovered to kill Wellington and prominent members of the English government—including them. "There's a leak in the government somewhere, and Colin and his lady are trying to decipher the rest of the code in order to find it. And Courtland is preparing to make the next smuggling run to France. We're to meet and brief Jarrod as soon as he returns from his honeymoon."

"When will that be?"

"A few days. He's scheduled to sail to Spain to brief Grant and Scovell at week's end. And to warn Wellington in person."

Daniel thought for a moment. "Are we certain the leak is in the government?"

"We can't be absolutely certain," Jonathan replied. "But if it isn't there, where else can it be?" He looked at Daniel. "It's not one of us. We're collecting the information and bringing it back to Shepherdston. Scovell and Grant are gathering information on the Peninsula and sending it to Lord Weymouth. Weymouth and Shepherdston share information."

"We provide information to Lord Weymouth and to the men at Whitehall and Abchurch Lane. Lord Weymouth provides information to us and to the men at Whitehall and Abchurch Lane. But we work independently of the government, and we're not the only ones collecting information," Daniel reminded him, as the seed of an idea took root. "What about the couriers Scovell sends to Lord Weymouth? Are they reporting the same things we're discovering?"

Jonathan shook his head. "For the most part. But the information Colin and Gillian have deciphered has proven to be much more accurate than the information the men in Abchurch Lane have produced."

"Even after Lady Grantham furnished Abchurch Lane with a corrected cipher sheet?"

"Even so," Jonathan answered. "They've missed things Gillian found."

"Like troop movements?" Daniel asked, knowing that Lieutenant Colquhoun Grant's staff was privy to that information before they were. Grant was in Spain. He had first-hand knowledge. The Free Fellows' information came from a broader network of spies they'd recruited in London and Edinburgh, in France, on the Peninsula, and from the dispatches they received from Grant.

"And a plot to kill Wellington and us because Abchurch Lane's primary source of information is the dispatches Grant's couriers deliver to Lord Weymouth, and Lord Weymouth . . ." Jonathan broke off.

"Reports to Lord Bathurst," Daniel concluded. "Who would Lord Bathurst trust to collect the dispatches from Weymouth? Who would Weymouth trust to deliver them? And do either Lord Weymouth's or Lord Bathurst's names appear on the list of intended victims?"

"Lord Bathurst's does."

Daniel took a deep breath. "I need to talk to Colin, Griffin, and Weymouth. Colin first," he instructed. "Then Griffin and Weymouth at the same time."

"Why?"

"I think I may have stumbled upon the possible leak in the government."

"Jarrod will want to know as well," Jonathan reminded him.

Daniel smiled. "No need to interrupt the man's wedding trip unless my suspicions are correct, and I won't know if they're correct until I speak with Lord Weymouth."

"Shall I send a note around later this afternoon?"

Remembering his hasty exit from Curzon Street, Daniel shook his head. "I think tomorrow before breakfast will be soon enough." He looked his cousin in the eye. "I delivered the latest dispatches—or rather, Micah did, on my instructions. Colin and Gillian have deciphered them, and Jarrod's already given the men at Abchurch Lane the results. Until Courtland makes the next run, there's nothing else for the leak to discover."

Frowning suddenly, Daniel stood up and walked to the window in his stocking feet. *Micah.* A piece of a dream came flooding back. Daniel suddenly remembered grabbing Micah by the front of his nightshirt. *"Damn it, man, if you've no vehicle then walk. And he may be a gentleman, but Shepherdston isn't a snob. He won't give a damn how you're dressed."* Except Micah hadn't been wearing a nightshirt when they'd left the coast. Or when they'd reached London. But there had been a nightshirt just like it lying in a puddle on the floor at Curzon Street. . . . Atop a pair of wet dancing slippers. Green to match the ball gown Miranda had been wearing.

Daniel squeezed his eyes shut. He had talked in his sleep and accidentally sent Miranda to Shepherdston's on a mission.

She'd never breathed a word of it.

All he could do was hope that she'd made it to Shepherdston's and back unseen. He opened his eyes and looked at Jonathan. "If there's any damage, I'm afraid it's already been done."

Chapter 23

"Love and scandal are the best sweeteners of tea."
— Henry Fielding, 1707–1754

"*Have you seen this?*" The dowager Duchess of Sussex demanded of her butler, Weldon, as she opened the *Morning Chronicle* the following morning, turned it to the third page, and read the latest "Ton Tidbits" column.

"Yes, Your Grace, the article caught my eye while I was ironing it." Part of Weldon's responsibility as butler was to iron the newspapers and set the ink before the dowager duchess or her son handled them.

" 'Has the long-standing feud between the Duke of Sussex and the Marchioness of St. Germaine finally come to an end? How else to explain the elusive duke's early-morning departure from a house owned by the marchioness at Number Eight Curzon Street? The duke, who hasn't been seen since he waltzed with the marchioness at his mother's gala ball on Wednesday evening, appeared quite satisfied, despite his extreme state of dishabille, when he was seen exiting the house after spending two nights cozily ensconced in the home in which the marchioness was staying. The Marchioness St. Germaine left the house later in the afternoon for whereabouts unknown. Will the ton's most frequent bridesmaid finally become a bride? Or has the marchioness, a peeress in her own right, decided to forgo the ceremony in favor of an illicit honeymoon? Will the duke present his mother, the dowager duchess, with a by-blow and a mistress, or a wife and an heir?' " After reading the column aloud, the dowager duchess carefully folded the newspaper so the column was visible, then set her toast and chocolate aside, threw back the covers on her bed, and swung her feet onto the floor.

"What do you make of it?"

Weldon averted his gaze as the duchess uncovered her limbs. "I don't know what to make of it, ma'am," Weldon told her.

"Do you think it possible that his association with Lady Miranda has progressed to that level?"

"I have no idea, madam, as I haven't seen His Grace since the night of the party."

She looked at the butler she'd relied upon for nearly thirty years to run her household and to speak the truth. "Send someone to His Grace's apartments and tell His Grace I wish to speak to him immediately."

"His Grace has been away from his apartments for nearly a week, ma'am."

"Then order my carriage brought around posthaste."

"May I ask where Her Grace wishes to go?"

"Wherever my son is." She glanced at the newspaper. "Which was apparently Number Eight Curzon Street, but is now most likely Number Fifteen Upper Brook Street."

❦

"The Duchess of Sussex is here to see you, milady." Crawford, the St. Germaine butler, announced the unfashionably early morning caller.

"My," the dowager Marchioness of St. Germaine drawled, "how nice of the duchess to come calling." She glanced at her daughter, took note of her red and swollen eyes, and knew that Miranda had spent the hours since her arrival at Upper Brook Street the previous afternoon and the time they sat down to breakfast, sobbing into her pillow. "And what a happy coincidence that you've returned from your visit to the country in time for the duchess to call upon you."

Miranda had planned to tell her mother the truth about her whereabouts when she returned to the house on Upper Brook Street, but the *Morning Chronicle* had beaten her to it, and the dowager marchioness was still smarting from it. "Perhaps she decided to call upon you to apologize in person for omitting your name from her invitation and guest list," her mother continued.

Miranda smiled at her mother's sarcasm. "As you well know, the dowager duchess and I have a long, varied history. She's come because she's seen the article in this morning's paper."

"It was rather eye-opening," Lady St. Germaine acknowledged. "For a parent to read such news and to know it's being read and shared with the rest of the city over breakfast. I don't suppose she enjoyed being one of the last to know."

"Mother . . ."

"Of course, she might have come calling because she's interested in property you own on Number Eight Curzon Street . . ." Lady St. Germaine speculated.

Miranda bit back a smile. There was no love lost between the dowager duchess and the dowager marchioness. "Or both."

"Shall I come with you to greet her, my dear?" Lady St. Germaine asked.

"Can you keep a civil tongue?" Miranda shot her mother a quelling glance.

"With the woman who gave my child the cut direct and continues to snub her at every turn?" Lady St. Germaine asked. "Are you joking?"

"Then, no, you may not accompany me in greeting her." Miranda pushed her chair back from the breakfast table and stood up. "I have enough trouble with the duchess . . ."

"*Dowager* duchess," Lady St. Germaine corrected.

"*Dowager* duchess," Miranda continued, "without your compounding it." She turned to Crawford. "Where is Her Grace?"

"In the Blue Salon, my lady."

"Thank you, Crawford," Miranda smoothed her hair and brushed imaginary wrinkles from her skirts, straightened her shoulders, and pulled herself up to her full height. "Please bring a tray of refreshments to the Blue Salon."

"That's a very nice touch," Lady St. Germaine added, approving. "And Crawford."

"Yes, ma'am?"

"See if you can find a nice fast-acting poison to go in Her Grace's beverage."

"Mother!" Miranda protested.

"All right," the dowager marchioness said. "A nice agonizingly slow-acting poison." She looked at her daughter. "While the duchess cannot die fast enough to suit me, it might be a pleasure to watch her expire slowly."

"Mother, you may not like Her Grace, but she is Daniel's mother. . . ."

"And isn't it remarkable that His Grace has been able to overcome such a hardship?"

"You don't mean that."

"I most certainly do," Lady St. Germaine informed her daughter.

Miranda shook her head as she followed Crawford out of the breakfast room, down the hall to the Blue Salon.

Bracing herself for an attack, Miranda curtseyed to the dowager duchess as she entered the room.

"What is the meaning of this?" the dowager duchess demanded, waving the newspaper bearing the "Ton Tidbits" at Miranda as soon as she rose from her curtsey.

"I believe the meaning is quite clear, Your Grace." Miranda pretended a nonchalance she didn't feel. "Someone has set out to ruin my good name and reputation. And they are using your son as a means to accomplish it." She looked at the duchess. "May I offer you a cup of coffee or chocolate, Your Grace, before we continue this confrontation?"

The duchess frowned, forgetting a lifetime of admonitions not to frown in order to avoid premature wrinkling of the brow. She hadn't expected the young marchioness to politely offer refreshments, or to have eyes that were bloodshot and swollen red from crying or a nose that was only slightly less red. "I did not come for coffee or chocolate," she replied, refusing Miranda's offer of refreshments. "I came for answers. Do you deny spending two days and nights with my son?"

"I don't deny it, Your Grace, or confirm it."

"Do not play word games with me," the dowager duchess snapped. "I came for the truth, and I shall have it."

"I do not give credence to an article written by an anonymous columnist." Miranda stood her ground. "And neither should you."

"Do not presume to tell me what I should or should not do."

"Or what, Your Grace?" Miranda demanded. "You'll put me in my place by giving me the cut direct? Or by snubbing me? Or slandering me? Will you seek to punish me by failing to invite me to your parties?" She smiled at the dowager duchess. "You've already done that. What more can you do to me?"

"I can keep you from seeing my son," Her Grace replied coldly.

Miranda arched an eyebrow. "Can you?"

"Inform my son that I wish to speak with him straightaway." The duchess glanced around the room as if waiting for Daniel to appear.

"Your son is not here," Miranda answered truthfully.

"Then where is he?"

"I don't know."

The dowager duchess looked Miranda in the eye in an attempt to take her measure. "I don't believe you."

"Believe me or not, Your Grace," Miranda told her. "It's the truth."

The duchess snorted in contempt. "You think if you wait long enough my son will marry you, but I shall never allow you to usurp my role as the Duchess of Sussex."

"Your son is fully grown, Your Grace. He doesn't require your permission to marry anyone. And I have never had any desire to usurp your role as the Duchess of Sussex."

The duchess scoffed. "Of course you do. Every young girl wishes to marry a duke and become a duchess. Who wouldn't want to live in Sussex House and have the best of everything?" She sighed. "I know I did."

"Perhaps you're mistaken in assuming everyone is like you, Your Grace. I was born a peeress," Miranda reminded her. "I may desire a husband, but I do not have to purchase my title or secure a fortune. I have grown up with the knowledge that my responsibilities and duties are equal to those of any male marquess. I've no need for a loftier position in society."

The dowager duchess firmed her lips into a thin line. "I knew your father. I liked him very much. But I don't much care for your mother and I have never liked or approved of you, Miranda."

"I am well aware of that, Your Grace."

"You are too strong-willed to make a suitable duchess. My son should have a young, adoring, biddable girl for his consort. The type of girl who won't question and challenge him at every turn. Or make too many unnecessary demands. He needs a wife who will gladly provide him with an heir and a spare and not ask for too much in return."

Miranda smiled at the dowager duchess. "Are you seeking a suitable bride for Daniel or a biddable daughter-in-law for yourself? Because His Grace prefers ladies who do challenge him."

"I have a duty to see that my son marries and sires the next Duke of Sussex," the duchess replied. "And while my son thinks he prefers women who challenge him, he would soon discover that having such a wife means having a wife who would delight in telling him what to do and managing his life for him."

"A job that's been reserved exclusively for you, Your Grace."

The dowager duchess inhaled sharply and sputtered, "How dare you?"

"I dare because I love your son. But unlike you, I believe that your son deserves far better than the sort of beautiful but useless wife you would provide for him." She returned the dowager duchess's stare, refusing to back down from it. "You think choosing a young, biddable bride for him will keep him close to you, but the truth is that you will drive him further away. Your son is well aware of his duty to his name. He won't shirk it. He loves you, Your Grace, and wishes to please you, but he despises your machinations. He is a man born to a lofty title who recognizes his responsibility and his duty to the people who depend upon him for their livelihoods. He believes in making the world a better place for them, and he deserves the sort of wife who will stand at his side and help him shoulder his responsibilities and accomplish his goals, not one who would unwittingly add to his burdens every day. You chose wisely, Your Grace, when you attempted to match him with Alyssa Carrollton, but . . ."

"I thought so too," Her Grace admitted, "but he thought otherwise. Since Alyssa, I've done my best to choose a different sort of girl, but he shows no interest at all in pursuing them."

Miranda smiled at the duchess's confusion. "Then perhaps, ma'am, your purpose would best be served if you would allow your son to do his own choosing."

The duchess met Miranda's gaze, and for once they were in accord. "If only he would."

Miranda saw the sheen of tears in the older woman's eyes and knew that despite everything, the duchess loved her son. And that gave them a common bond. "He will,

Your Grace," Miranda assured her gently. "But he must be allowed to do so in his own good time."

The dowager Duchess of Sussex nodded as she turned to go. "You understand that this changes nothing between us, Miranda."

Miranda exhaled. "I understand, Your Grace."

The dowager duchess glanced back over her shoulder. "You also understand that I am not at all pleased at the prospect of becoming a grandmother at my age. I'm much too young."

"Your Grace . . ." Miranda began, staring down at the toes of her slippers.

"Unless, of course, my grandchild is born into a legal union. And is female."

Miranda looked up and met the duchess's gaze.

"Boys grow up to break their mothers' hearts."

⌇

At Albany, the Earl of Barclay walked, fully clothed, into the guest room where Daniel had spent the night and found his cousin moving stiffly, and struggling to shave. He hung a fresh shirt and neck cloth on a wooden valet stand, then took the razor from Daniel's hand and finished shaving him. "Colin sent word that we should join him for breakfast at home, and Griff and his father will meet us and Alex at White's later in the morning."

Daniel rinsed the soap from his face, then reached for a towel. "Thanks."

"You'd do the same for me," Jonathan shrugged. He studied the strips of cloth binding Daniel's ribs, testing the tightness of them before adding, "Now, let's have a look at what's under that bandage on your side."

Daniel would have protested, but Jonathan had already untied the cloth holding the padding over it. "Nice color."

Daniel looked down at the large green, yellow, and dark

purplish bruise surrounding his wound. "The bruise or the wound?"

"The stitches," Jonathan chuckled. "Your injury is literally black and blue."

"Miranda used silk," Daniel defended, "because according to Griff's wife, it's the best thread for sewing up flesh."

"Alyssa would know." Jonathan acknowledged the Duchess of Avon's talent for healing.

"Blue and pink were the only colors from which she had to choose."

"Blue suits you much better than pink," Jonathan teased, tracing the outline of the wound with his finger, checking for signs of infection or fever. "I'm impressed," he said. "Miranda has a talent for needlework."

Daniel reached for the borrowed shirt while Jonathan rewrapped the wound and secured it. Holding it up, he eyed it skeptically. "One of yours or one of Lord Dunbridge's?"

Jonathan watched Daniel's attempt to slip it on and lent assistance. "As if Dunbridge would wear a shirt as conservative as that one. Of course it's one of mine." He smiled at Daniel. "But you might take note of the fact that beggars shouldn't be choosers, Your Grace."

"So I've heard." He was thoughtful for a moment, recalling a similar conversation a few days ago. *Don't they make silk thread in black?* he had asked. *I'm sure they do, Your Grace,* Miranda had snapped, *but beggars cannot be choosers.* "But as it happens, I was exercising a bit of caution," he teased. "Think what might happen if Dunbridge or one of his contemporaries were to recognize his shirt. . . ." He grinned at Jonathan. "I might be accused of having participated in the theft of them. The scandal would be enormous. And I've my reputation to consider."

"There is someone else's reputation you might want to consider as well." Jonathan held out the newspaper.

Daniel took it and saw that it was folded to the "Ton Tidbits" column. He quickly scanned the article, then sat down hard on a chair. "Damnation! Miranda." Daniel glanced over at Jonathan. "Damage?"

Jonathan knew what his cousin was asking. "I wish I could say I'd snagged one of the first papers off the press. But by now," he glanced at the clock, "everyone who reads the *Chronicle* will have seen it." He met Daniel's gaze. "You should go to her."

"I will," Daniel promised. *I will.* He frowned. Those two words sounded eerily familiar. As if he had spoken them to someone else quite recently. "How much time do I have before the meeting with Colin?" He hastily fashioned his neck-cloth into a neat four-in-hand and slipped his arms into his coat as Jonathan acted as his valet and held it open for him.

"Not enough," Jonathan admitted. "But Colin will understand if you're a few minutes late."

"Go to his house," Daniel instructed. "And tell him I'll be there as soon as I can, then collect Alex and go on to the club. I'll follow with Colin."

"All right," Jonathan agreed. "Should I tell them anything? Or should I wait for you?"

"Wait for me," Daniel instructed, leaning over to reach for the boots Jonathan had loaned him and groaning as the empty pewter flask dug into a tender spot on his ribs. "It will be better if I disclose my theory when we're all present." He put his hand into his pocket to retrieve it and discovered a folded sheet of vellum and what felt like a chess piece. He pulled them out along with the flask. Laying the pewter flask and the chess piece aside, Daniel unfolded the vellum and recognized it immediately.

It was a special license to marry, complete with names and signatures. His name and his scrawled signature. Miranda's name and her signature. As well as the names of and signatures of Bishop Manwaring, Lady Manwaring, and Curate Linley. He stared at it, stunned, yet strangely relieved and satisfied, as the memories of their hasty wedding in the carriage came flooding back.

Daniel picked up the bishop and held it in his hand. He

knew what it meant. He had used it to checkmate her king in their final game of chess, right before he'd shoved the board out of the way, toppled the pieces, and kissed her as if his life depended on it. Kissed her as if he would never let her go.

The bishop was her way of telling him that she'd made the last move.

I love you, Daniel.

The words popped into his mind.

She had offered him her heart with those four words, and he, fool that he was, had pretended not to notice. But she had known they were legally wed and she hadn't said a word or shed a tear when she'd watched him walk away.

Apparently, Miranda loved him enough to let him go.

"I didn't believe her." He shook his head. "She told me the truth and I didn't believe her."

"Who? What?" Jonathan asked.

"Miranda," Daniel answered, extending the sheet of vellum and showing it to Jonathan. "My wife."

Chapter 24

"Love sought is good, but given unsought is better."
—William Shakespeare, 1564–1616

"I've come to see Miranda," Daniel announced unceremoniously as Crawford, the St. Germaine's butler, showed him into the Blue Salon where Miranda's mother, Lady Frederick St. Germaine, was waiting.

"I'm afraid she isn't here, Your Grace." Lady St. Germaine curtseyed.

Daniel raised an eyebrow at that. It was still early and he'd gone to the house on Curzon Street before he'd called upon Upper Brook Street. The Curzon Street house was locked and deserted.

"You just missed her," Lady St. Germaine was saying. "Miranda left shortly after your mother departed."

Her statement caught Daniel off guard. "My mother came here?"

Lady St. Germaine snorted. "We were, unfortunately, graced with the dowager duchess's presence while we were taking breakfast. She was none too happy to be here. And we were less than pleased at having our breakfast interrupted in order to open our doors to her." She looked up at Daniel. "Whatever did you do to put her into such a fine fettle?"

"I think you know what I did, ma'am." Daniel blushed. "Or rather, what we—Miranda and I—did."

"My daughter didn't volunteer details," Lady St. Germaine told him. "All I know of the matter is what I read in this morning's paper."

"Then I've some explaining to do." He smiled at his mother-in-law. "And I'll be happy to do just that as soon as Miranda joins us."

"Would that she could, Your Grace," Miranda's mother murmured, "but as I said before, Miranda is not here."

"Have you any idea where I might find her?"

"She mentioned something several days ago about staying with friends in the country."

"I see," Daniel nodded. "And these friends must be very good friends to leave town in the midst of the season with a woman whose good name has been besmirched by a scandal sheet this very morning."

"As the besmircher of her good name, I'm sure Your Grace knows more about that than I."

He laughed. "I now know from whom my wife gets her sharp tongue."

"And I now know from whom Your Grace has obtained his exquisite manners. . . ." Her words drifted off and the marchioness looked up at Daniel. "Did you say *wife*?"

"I did." He tugged his signet ring off his finger and pressed it into Lady St. Germaine's hand, carefully closing her fist around it. "Please give this to my wife when you see her, and remind her that it is hers for safekeeping until I can do better. Ask her to be ready to join me when I call for her later this afternoon so that we might conclude our business at St. Michael's and discuss our future."

"I would be most happy to, Your Grace." Lady St. Germaine smiled broadly.

"Daniel," he corrected, leaning down to whisper close to her ear. "What sort of ring do you think Miranda would like?" he asked conspiratorially. "Diamonds? Emeralds? Sapphires? Rubies?"

"An old one," Lady St. Germaine told him, recalling that the betrothal ring of the Duchesses of Sussex was a large, beautifully set square-cut emerald surrounded by diamonds dating back to the time of Charles II. The dowager duchess had never worn it. She'd preferred a large diamond surrounded by dozens of smaller diamonds, but she'd delighted in showing the emerald off and in owning it.

"What a coincidence!" Daniel laughed once again. "For I happen to be in possession of a large quantity of old family jewelry I think she'll love."

"The dowager duchess isn't going to like parting with her jewelry," Lady St. Germaine warned.

"My mother understands duty and tradition. And the dowager Duchesses of Sussex know that relinquishing the Sussex family jewels is part of their duty. It's traditionally done upon the announcement of the impending marriage of the sitting duke or his heir, but since Miranda and I wed without announcing it, my mother will relinquish the jewelry as soon as I inform her of my nuptials."

"Learning you've married my daughter should send her into raptures," Lady St. Germaine remarked dryly.

Daniel cracked a smile. "It should," he said. "She's been trying to marry me off for the past three years." He looked at his new mother-in-law. "Besides, she'll retain her title as dowager duchess and keep all of her considerable fortune in personal jewelry."

"That's small consolation for the fortune she'll be losing."

"But she'll have the daughter-in-law she's always wanted." He leaned over unexpectedly and kissed Miranda's mother on the cheek, before turning to exit the Blue Salon. "And I'll have the wife I love. Trust me," he said. "Everything will turn out fine."

Miranda stood at her bedroom window and watched him leave. It broke her heart, but she loved Daniel enough to let him go. She had known for years that he didn't want to be married, and she had no right to hold him to his vows.

Especially when she knew he didn't remember making them.

"That is the last time I lie to your husband for you, Miranda," her mother said from the open doorway.

"What?" Miranda turned to look at her mother.

"I said that if you wish to hide from your husband, you will have to find some other way to put him off your trail," Lady St. Germaine repeated. "I won't be used in this way again."

"My hus—" Miranda sputtered. "Mother, he's not—"

"Yes, he is," Lady St. Germaine contradicted.

"How did you find out?"

"I got it from the horse's mouth. Daniel told me." Her mother pinned her with a glance. "Sorry I missed the wedding. I would have been there had I been invited. Of course, I'm only your mother and your only living relative."

Miranda shook her head. "How could he tell you about it? He didn't remember it."

"He does now." Lady St. Germaine walked over to the window, took hold of her daughter's hand, and pressed the Duke of Sussex's signet ring into it. "He asked me to give you this for safekeeping until he can do better."

Miranda opened her fist and stared at the ring, then closed her fingers around it and pressed it to her heart. "He remembered."

"He did indeed," Lady St. Germaine confirmed. "He also asked that you be ready when he arrives to pick you up later this afternoon in order that you may conclude your business at St. Michael's."

Miranda exhaled the breath she hadn't known she was holding. Concluding business at St. Michael's could only mean that he intended to record the marriage. "What should I do?" Miranda turned to her mother.

Lady St. Germaine's heart skipped a beat. Miranda hadn't asked her advice in years. Not since she'd inherited her father's title. "I suggest you bathe and put on your prettiest dress so you'll be ready when he arrives. . . ."

She glanced at her daughter. "Unless you wish to continue avoiding him and pretending your marriage never happened."

Miranda shook her head. "No, of course not."

"The green merino day dress Madam Racine made for you is nice," Lady St. Germaine murmured. "If I were you, I'd wear that."

"Thank God you're all right." Colin greeted Daniel an hour or so later than scheduled, as his butler, Britton, showed him into the study at Number Twenty-seven Park Lane. "It's good to see you, Daniel. We were beginning to get concerned."

"I apologize," Daniel told him, surrendering his hat and gloves to the butler. "For the delay."

"Not to worry," Colin said. "Barclay explained that you were running behind schedule this morning, so Gilly and I took advantage of it and lingered over breakfast."

Daniel looked around for Colin's wife, Gillian, and for his cousin.

"Gillian's in the room next door working on the cipher codes. Barclay stayed for a cup of coffee, then left for the club," Colin said. "We thought it best we continue with our normal routine."

"I suggested meeting with you at your home because I needed you *and* Lady Grantham to confirm separate discoveries I've made and suspicions I've had. Beginning with my mission to France."

Colin ran his fingers through his hair and frowned. "What sort of trouble did you have in the Channel?"

"An English frigate and the coast watch at Calais," Daniel explained. "We were caught between the two when they started firing at each other."

Colin was silent a moment longer. "An English frigate engaged the coast watch at Calais?" He'd been making smuggling runs to and from Calais for nearly three years, and he'd never known any British ship to fire upon the French coast watch for any reason. It didn't make sense. An English frigate patrolling the English side of the Channel couldn't hit moving targets on the French coast. "The foot coast watch? Are you sure they weren't shooting at you?"

"Positive," Daniel replied. "The coast watch fired at us and one or two of the balls hit the boat, but the frigate never saw us."

"So no one was hurt?"

Daniel made a face. "We suffered two minor injuries and one slightly more serious one."

"How serious?"

"The rifle ball passed through my right side and bounced off my ribs."

"*Your* ribs?" Colin's Scottish burr grew more pronounced with his agitation.

"Aye," Daniel replied. "My ribs. I was shot in the back as we rowed toward shore."

"In the back?" Colin was surprised. "But that would mean that . . ."

"I was shot by someone on the *English* side of the Channel. Presumably someone on the frigate."

"An English frigate firing upon the coast watch shouldn't have been firing down at the water."

"Exactly," Daniel said.

"Could they have been providing cover for you?"

"It's possible," Daniel speculated, "but they would have had to have known we were there in order to provide cover, and the fog was so thick the frigate nearly rammed us before we could get out of the way, yet it gave no indication that it knew we were there."

"And if it knew you were there, why didn't they shoot you or arrest you for smuggling?" Colin thought for a moment. "As far as I know, we didn't alert the Royal Navy to ask for cover. But someone either knew you were there . . . or expected you to be." He looked at Daniel. "Did you catch sight of the name of the frigate?"

"I didn't," Daniel admitted. "One of the crew might have."

Colin frowned again. "Without the name of the frigate, we have no way of knowing if they knew you were there."

"I may have a way," Daniel said.

"How?"

"A list of all the officers serving on frigates patrolling those waters should provide the answer."

"You've someone in particular in mind, haven't you?" Colin asked.

"What I have at the moment is only a suspicion," Daniel offered, walking rather stiffly over to the window and opening the drapes to look down at the street below, where a familiar carriage was parked on the opposite side of the street.

"A suspicion?"

Daniel nodded. "Would you ask Lady Grantham to join us?"

"Aye. Of course." Colin crossed the room and opened the door that connected the library to the study. "Gilly? His Grace would like to speak to you if you don't mind." He stepped back to allow his wife to enter the room, and Gillian walked in.

Colin's wife possessed a quiet beauty, and quick intelligence radiated from her like rays of sunshine. She adored her husband and it showed.

"Good morning, Your Grace," she greeted Daniel. "How can I be of service?"

"Good morning, Lady Grantham." Daniel left the window and walked over to take her hand and raise her from her curtsey. He smiled at her. "I've a question or two about the work you've been doing."

Gillian nodded.

"Have you noticed any gaps in the missives you've deciphered? Any letters or messages out of sequence? Any parts that haven't made sense?" Daniel asked.

"No," Gillian answered. "Every letter I've deciphered has made perfect sense in relation to the other letters I've deciphered. As far as I can tell, nothing has been missing."

"And I'm correct in assuming that you provided the men in Abchurch Lane with the latest corrected cipher tables?" Daniel inquired.

"Yes. Why?"

"It occurred to me that Abchurch Lane has missed vital bits of information they shouldn't have missed."

"I've thought that, too," Gillian told him.

Colin nodded in agreement.

"Some of the work I've done seemed far too easy," she continued, "and yet the other ciphers missed it. I know I've a talent for this, but I've wondered how I could be so accurate and they could make such big mistakes."

"What if the men in Abchurch Lane only received the complete information when we supplied it?" Daniel posed the question that had been troubling him.

"I don't understand," Colin admitted.

"What if the information you and Gillian decipher and give to Shepherdston are the only complete ciphers they receive?" Daniel repeated his theory.

"That's highly unlikely," Colin replied, "since the men in Abchurch Lane receive information from the front lines and from couriers in the field."

"Do they?" Daniel asked. "What if they only get bits and pieces of seemingly unrelated information?"

"How?" Colin demanded.

"Couriers. At least one, perhaps more, who withhold information."

"For what purpose?" Gillian asked.

"I'm not sure," Daniel told them. "It could be for personal gain or monetary reasons, but I suspect it may be political." He walked back over to the window and looked out. The coach was still there, parked where he knew it would be until he left for his next destination. He motioned for Colin and Gillian to come to the window. "Recognize that coach?"

Colin shook his head. "Do you?"

"Yes," he answered. "It appears to be following me."

"Are you certain?"

"I've only been a few places since I returned, and I don't believe it's a coincidence that I've seen this coach everywhere I've been." Daniel took a breath. "I saw this coach parked outside Albany yesterday afternoon, Curzon Street yesterday morning, Park Lane the night of my mother's party."

And it was parked on Park Lane once again. Colin thought Daniel was right but felt compelled to point out, "The night of your mother's party, you could have seen every coach in town."

Daniel looked him in the eye. "Except yours."

Colin shrugged his shoulders.

"Barclay informed me that my mother neglected to invite you and Gillian." Daniel looked embarrassed. "I'm sorry I didn't catch the oversight in time to correct it."

"That's all right, Daniel. Gillian and I understood that the omission was the duchess's, not yours."

"It won't happen again. I promise you that." He looked at Gillian, then extended his hand and offered it to Colin.

Colin grasped it firmly and shook it in friendship. "Apology accepted."

"Thank you."

Colin released his hand, and Daniel moved to sit down on a leather chair near the fire. A pretty embroidered pillow in a Scottish thistle design rested in the seat.

"If there's nothing more you require of me, Your Grace, I'll return to work on the ciphers," Gillian said.

Daniel pushed himself to his feet, took Gillian's hand, and brought it to his lips. "I'm deeply grateful for your help, Lady Grantham."

"I'm thrilled to be able to help." Gillian lifted her face for her husband's kiss, then quietly returned to her work in the room next door.

Daniel settled gingerly onto the seat of the chair he'd just vacated.

"Does your injury pain you much?" Colin asked. "I can offer you some whisky."

"I'm a bit stiff, but that's mostly due to the bindings around my ribs." Daniel smiled. "I thank you but I've had as much whisky as I can stand for a while." He related the story of his journey from the coast to London. "I saw that coach at the docks at Dover as well."

"You're certain?" Colin flushed red. "I don't doubt that you thought you saw it, but you admit you were quite drunk."

"I saw it before I became so intoxicated," Daniel explained. "Before I reached London. Before my wound began to hurt like the very devil. Before it kept me confined to bed for a couple of days. . . ." He stared down at the side table near his chair, where a copy of the *Morning Chronicle* lay folded to the "Ton Tidbits" column. Turning to Colin, he said, "I see you read the *Chronicle* this morning and know to whose bed I was confined."

"So it's true." Colin frowned mightily.

"It's true," Daniel confirmed. "But not in the way you think."

"I've a vivid imagination, Your Grace, and a good idea of human nature. I know what I'd be doing if I were confined to bed with a beautiful young woman if injury permitted."

"Injury permitted," Daniel replied.

"And now her reputation is ruined." Colin was especially touchy where ladies' reputations were concerned, for he had had to marry his beloved Gillian under exceptional circumstances in order to save hers. "How are you going to make amends to Lady St. Germaine?"

"Making amends with Lady St. Germaine isn't necessary," Daniel said. "Making up with her will be."

Colin lifted his eyebrow in query.

"I married her *before* we shared a bed," he explained. "Which is, I believe, the preferred method. Unfortunately,

I was quite intoxicated when I did so and had no memory of it until this morning." He gave Colin a halfhearted smile. "Hence the making up."

Colin slapped him on the back, congratulating him. "There must be something in the air. You, Jarrod, and Lord Rob within a week of one another. I can't believe it."

"I'm having trouble believing it myself," he admitted.

"Imagine how Miranda must be feeling after that article in the paper this morning," Colin reminded him.

"And a visit from my mother." He shuddered but finally managed a small smile. "I'd like to think she's fighting mad about it. At least I hope that's the case. But I'm afraid she's retreated to lick her wounds."

"That doesn't sound like Miranda."

"No, it doesn't," Daniel agreed. "But I tried to see her this morning when I discovered our marriage license in my coat pocket, and she wouldn't see me. She had her mother tell me she wasn't at home."

He still couldn't quite comprehend the fact that after all these years of taunting and teasing him, of offering herself and of challenging him, Miranda had let him go after one night in his bed. And had returned the only piece of proof she had that she was, in fact, the new Duchess of Sussex.

Why would she decide to set him free now? After working so hard to get him? He couldn't make sense of it. Why would she let him walk away without a word?

Because love sought is good, but given unsought is better. Shakespeare's quote lodged itself in his brain and refused to leave it. Miranda had sought his love for as long as he could remember and had despaired of ever having it. She had always been there for him, waiting for him to claim her steadfast and loyal heart. She had become his bride to protect him from the consequences of his actions, only to discover that he had no memory of the deed. And she had sent him on his way without telling him, in order to prove that she had no intentions of binding him to her if he would rather be somewhere else.

Daniel closed his eyes and saw her face, heard her sharp-tongued replies, felt the surge of energy she gave him, the spark of desire that ignited whenever they were together. Miranda. He had always had Miranda. And he had always managed to disappoint her.

He looked up at Colin. "I think Miranda is afraid I'm going to let her down."

"Are you?"

"No." He smiled. "For once, I am going to exceed the Marchioness of St. Germaine's wildest expectations."

Chapter 25

"There are truths which are not for all men, nor for all times."

—Voltaire, 1694–1778

Daniel exited Colin and Gillian's house some twenty minutes later, crossed the street, and called out to the driver. "Driver, have you a passenger?"

The driver doffed his hat and shook his head. "No, sir."

"Are you waiting for someone?"

"No, sir."

"Are you for hire?"

The driver shook his head once again. "No, sir. I'm a private coach."

"Then, may I ask why you're following me?"

"I'm not following you, sir."

Daniel lifted an eyebrow at that falsehood. "Interesting, since I seem to run into you at every turn. . . ."

"Perhaps you've mistaken my coach for someone else's," the driver suggested.

"Perhaps," Daniel allowed, gesturing for the driver to lean down. "What is your name?"

"Yates, sir."

"Well, Yates, am I to assume that as a private coach, you are in someone's employ?"

"Yes, sir."

"Might I have the name of your employer?"

"I'm not at liberty to say, sir," the driver replied.

Daniel paused. "I'm the Duke of Sussex," he told him, "and there's fifty pounds in it for you if you'll be so kind as to return to your employer and stop shadowing me."

"Yes, Your Grace," the driver answered as Daniel peeled off the pound notes and handed them up to him.

"Be off with you, then," Daniel instructed. "And don't let me catch sight of you or your coach again."

"I can't promise that, Your Grace," the driver protested. "I work for a living, driving my employer to and from. We're sure to cross your path now and again, as you gentlemen all frequent the same establishments."

Daniel nodded. "I see your point, Yates."

"I knew you would, Your Grace."

"So, let's amend my earlier advice to don't let me catch sight of you or your *empty* coach again."

The driver groaned.

"I never forget a face," Daniel warned, "or a vehicle. If I see you or your coach anywhere near me, you'd best have your employer inside it or there will be dire consequences for you, Mr. Yates. Do you understand me?"

"Yes, sir, Your Grace." The driver doffed his cap.

"Good," Daniel pronounced. "Here's another ten for your trouble." He handed Yates another pound note, then waved him on his way.

Daniel watched as the coach Yates was driving rounded the corner, then climbed into his own vehicle and waited for Colin to join him before heading to his appointment with Griffin and Lord Weymouth at White's.

"I see you lost your shadow," Colin commented as he climbed aboard.

"Indeed," Daniel acknowledged.

Colin was curious. "Mind if I ask how you managed?"

"I paid the driver to go away."

"That simple?"

"One of the advantages of being a duke is that I can pay most coach drivers to do my bidding—whether their employers like it or not."

"Will he return?" Colin asked.

Daniel looked at Colin, then shook his head. "Not without his employer. I saw to that."

The Free Fellows League minus Jarrod but with the addition of Lord Weymouth assembled in their usual meeting room at White's.

Griffin, Lord Weymouth, and Alex Courtland expressed relief at finding Daniel relatively unharmed. And after ordering coffee and drinks, they and the other Free Fellows—Jonathan and Colin—sat down to business.

"I asked you to meet us here," Daniel was saying, "after Barclay informed me this morning of the problem within our network. When he explained the nature of the problem, I realized, quite by accident, that I may have discovered the source of it. But before I continue, I must ask if we are all in agreement that there is a leak in our network that threatens our identities and the work we do?"

"Yes," the Free Fellows answered in unison.

Daniel nodded. "I had to be sure because I've no wish to put forth a theory that would result in our accusing a man unjustly. After Barclay and I spoke, I paid a call on Lord Grantham to discuss the result of my most recent mission. I shared my concerns with Colin, and he informed me that he and his w—" He glanced at Lord Weymouth and decided to use discretion where Gillian was concerned. The deciphering Gillian did had provided invaluable information to the government, but there were men in government who would never accept that such critical information came from a woman, so Daniel thought it best to omit that bit of information until he discovered how Weymouth felt about it. "*Colleague* had concerns of their own. Their concerns were identical to my own and have confirmed my suspicion."

"What suspicion?" Lord Weymouth asked.

"My suspicion that the information Lord Grantham and his colleague have been deciphering and the information the men in Abchurch Lane have been deciphering are not the same."

"Impossible!" Lord Weymouth was stunned. "All ciphered messages come to me. I make a copy of each message that crosses my desk. I give the originals to Lord Shepherdston to give to his ciphers, and I give the copies to Lord Bathhurst's courier to present to the men in Abchurch Lane. The messages are always identical, for I copy them myself."

That was the answer Daniel had hoped to get, but he had to be sure. "No one else copies them for you? Or helps you copy them?"

"Do you take me for a fool, Your Grace?" Lord Weymouth shot to his feet and began to pace in a manner very similar to Jarrod's. "I copy each message myself, and they do not leave my person until I give them to Lord Shepherdston and to Lord Bathhurst's representative."

"Not to Lord Bathhurst directly?" Griffin asked.

His father shook his head. "I'd prefer that, of course, but unfortunately, Lord Bathhurst does not. And as he is my superior in the War Office . . ."

"If the messages do not leave your person until you give them to Shepherdston and to Lord Bathhurst's representative, how do we explain the discrepancies in them?" Daniel asked.

"What discrepancies?" Lord Weymouth demanded. "I'm not aware of any discrepancies."

Daniel turned to Griffin. "He doesn't know about the list?"

Griff shook his head. "I haven't had the opportunity to tell him yet."

"What list?" Weymouth demanded.

"Colin, you're the one who deciphered the message." Griffin looked over at Colin. "Tell Father what you discovered."

Colin quickly relayed the details of the dispatches he and Gillian had deciphered about the plot to assassinate Wellington and other prominent members of the English government—including them.

"Good lord!" Weymouth exclaimed. "Even Bathhurst's name is on the list and his primary job was to assemble the men in Abchurch Lane and to collect their reports and present the information to the Prime Minister."

"Is Lord Bathhurst privy to our comings and goings?" Colin asked.

"He knows the approximate dates of your arrivals," Lord Weymouth told them. "Because he receives status reports and copies of the dispatches. He doesn't know who you are or whether you act alone or as a group, and neither he nor I know exactly when one of you leaves." He looked at each man in turn. "*I* didn't know who you were until now. Shepherdston is very protective. He's never volunteered the information and I've never required it. I trust Shepherdston to have the best men possible." He looked up and smiled. "And I'm happy to confirm that he does."

"If the only time the dispatches leave your possession is to go into Jarrod's and Lord Bathhurst's hands, we've found the source of the problem," Jonathan concluded. "Since Jarrod is above reproach and the dispatches he has deciphered are extremely accurate, the only reason for the other deciphered messages not to be accurate is if the ciphers are making mistakes or not receiving the complete dispatches."

"And since Colin and his colleague have provided the men in Abchurch Lane with the latest cipher tables, there should be no mistakes in the deciphering," the Marquess of Courtland continued.

"So the other ciphers aren't getting the complete dispatches." Colin ran his fingers through his hair. "Because

Lord Bathhurst's representative is withholding information."

"And Lord Bathhurst's representative is?" Daniel prompted.

"His private secretary, Lord Espy," Lord Weymouth confirmed.

"Espy!" Alex Courtland gasped. "Are you certain?"

"I wasn't," Daniel answered. "But now I'm almost positive. It certainly supports my theory."

"What theory?" Lord Weymouth asked.

"The theory that you're about to be blamed for the failure of our intelligence and for the assassination attempts—whether successful or unsuccessful—of some of our most prominent members of government, including your political rival and immediate superior, Lord Bathhurst." Daniel sat down on his favorite leather chair and poured himself a cup of coffee from the silver pot on the tray at his elbow.

"Me?" Lord Weymouth was incredulous.

Daniel took a sip of coffee and nodded.

"Why?" Griffin demanded, propping his aching leg on the closest ottoman.

"Politics," Lord Weymouth answered softly. "Lord Bathhurst and I have been political rivals for years. Unfortunately, the Prime Minister dislikes Lord Bathhurst and enjoys playing us off one another. Bathhurst is my superior at the War Office, but I have the ear of the Prime Minister and the Prince Regent. Successes credited to me reflect badly on Lord Bathhurst, and successes credited to him are often the result of my efforts. I report to Bathhurst, so the work I do behind the scenes makes him look very good, but he doesn't like the fact that I am the force behind a great deal of his success. He undermines me every chance he gets in a game of political cat and mouse that does none of us any good. Unfortunately, what looks bad for me can be made to look very good for Lord Bathhurst because he's able to change facts and shift the blame onto my shoulders."

Griffin looked at his father. "Fortunately, you have very broad shoulders."

"But if anything goes wrong with the intelligence we've collected or any of the men on the list we intercepted become victims of assassination or attempted assassination, your father must ultimately accept the blame," Daniel added.

"And resign my post." Griffin's father closed his eyes and released a long, slow breath.

"Tell me this, Lord Weymouth," Colin began, "would you happen to know if Lord Espy has a brother in the Navy?"

"Two, I think." Lord Weymouth pinched the bridge of his nose between his thumb and index finger. "One assigned to a ship out of Barbados and the other commands the HMS *Colchester,* a frigate that patrols—"

"The Dover coast," Jonathan finished.

"Yes." Lord Weymouth turned to look at Barclay. "Is that significant?"

"Very significant," Daniel answered, relating the events that had transpired since he had left on his last mission—except, of course, his hasty wedding and the two days he'd spent with Miranda in the house on Curzon Street.

When he finished telling his tale, Lord Weymouth and the Free Fellows League devised a trap to catch a rat. Each of the Free Fellows had a role to play, but Daniel assumed the lion's share of the trap because he was the man Espy had spent the past few days following.

They planned to spring it as soon as Jarrod returned from his wedding trip and began preparations for his meetings with Wellington, Scovell, and Grant.

In the meantime, there was a personal matter to which Daniel needed to attend.

Miranda.

He'd hoped to escape the meeting without revealing his plans for the remainder of the afternoon, but Griff had read the morning paper and demanded to know Daniel's intentions toward Miranda St. Germaine.

"What about Miranda?" Griff asked.

"What *about* Miranda?" Daniel answered.

"Alyssa and I are very fond of her," Griffin told him. "I'll take great exception with you if Alyssa and I are called upon to help pick up the pieces of Miranda's shattered heart."

"You need not concern yourself with Miranda's heart," Daniel said. "For it's still intact. I've no intention of shattering it, now or ever."

"You never intend to hurt her," Griff reminded him. "But you do."

"Not this time," Daniel swore. "Miranda became my duchess the night of my mother's gala." He faced his colleagues and told them the truth. "I married Miranda in order to protect us both. To protect her from the guilty knowledge of my injury and to protect the League and all of us in it from those that might try to force Miranda to bear witness against me should I be caught smuggling."

"Why would you think that necessary?" Alex wondered.

"Because Lord Espy saw me leave the party with her," Daniel explained. "I was very foxed, but something about Espy's demeanor struck me as odd. And I was afraid Miranda's reputation would suffer because he saw us alone together."

"Her reputation *has* suffered because of it," Lord Weymouth pointed out. "Everyone in town who reads the *Chronicle* already assumes she's your mistress or that you are her lover." He looked at Daniel. "And those who don't read the paper will have heard the gossip and assume the same. And you know what will happen. Miranda will be ostracized by polite society unless you protect her. And the only way you can protect her is to reveal your marriage as soon as possible."

"So everyone can speculate whether or not she's with child," Daniel finished.

"Everyone's already speculating," Jonathan reminded him. "Only they're speculating whether the child will be a bastard or a marquess."

"I'm picking Miranda up as soon as we conclude this meeting." Daniel revealed his plans for the afternoon, not because he wanted to but because his friends were as concerned about his bride and her reputation as he was, and the least he could do was to ease their minds. "We're going to St. Michael's to sign the parish register."

"Have you a ring?" Colin asked, knowing that in the haste to get married, important details like a ring for the bride were often overlooked.

"Not in my possession."

"Might I recommend Dalrymple's Jewelers?" Lord Weymouth suggested.

"I appreciate your suggestion," Daniel told him, "because I've seen Dalrymple's exquisite work, but I think Miranda might prefer a family piece."

Griffin and Lord Weymouth frowned simultaneously. It was well known among the Free Fellows that the Abernathy family betrothal ring that had belonged to Lord Weymouth's grandmother and Griffin's great-grandmother was a forty-carat canary diamond with matching rows of lesser diamonds surrounding it. It was worth a fortune, but Griff disparagingly referred to it as the bird's egg. The current Lady Weymouth had preferred something a good deal less gaudy, and her son, Griffin, had shared her opinion and purchased a gorgeous ring from Dalrymple's when he'd proposed to Alyssa.

"I thought I'd give Miranda the Sussex Emerald and the band to match it," Daniel said upon seeing father and son's expressions.

Griff nodded approvingly. "She'll love it. The bird's egg can't hold a candle to the Sussex Emerald. There's nothing gaudy about it. It's big and bold, but simple and elegant. It will suit Miranda perfectly."

Lord Weymouth and the other Free Fellows agreed.

"Anything else?" Daniel couldn't keep humor out of his voice when he realized his friends were assisting him in making the most important decisions of his life.

"Speak to Aunt Lavinia first," Jonathan advised. "It might be best to clear the way and move her into the dowager house before you take Miranda to Sussex House and present her as your duchess."

Chapter 26

"Change everything, except your loves."
—Voltaire, 1694–1778

Daniel took his cousin's advice and paid a call on his mother.

He entered her sitting room and greeted her without preamble as soon as Weldon announced him.

"Mother, I've come to collect the Sussex Emerald and the accompanying pieces, and to let you know that I'm meeting Miranda St. Germaine"—he looked at the clock on the mantel—"in a little less than an hour."

"Good afternoon, Daniel," she said, ignoring his abrupt announcement. "What a pleasant surprise."

"I know you saw the item in the *Chronicle* this morning, and I know that you've already paid Miranda a call, so if you would be so kind as to retrieve the ring from your safe, I would be most grateful."

"So," the duchess heaved a sigh as she looked up at her son. "It's finally come to this. My son, the Duke of Sussex, intends to offer marriage to a young woman in order to avoid scandal. . . ."

"I don't intend anything of the kind," Daniel contradicted.

"Then what do you call it?" For the second time that day, the duchess forgot her years of training otherwise and indulged a frown.

"I call it presenting Miranda with the wedding and betrothal rings I should have given her when I married her. Three nights ago after your gala."

"What?"

"The gossipmonger writing for the *Chronicle* has his facts all wrong." Daniel smiled at his mother. "Miranda and I were married *before* we honeymooned at her house on Curzon Street."

"How could you . . ." she began.

"By special license," he replied. "It's all quite legal. Bishop Manwaring married us at St. Michael's."

"That's ridiculous! I saw the girl this morning, and she didn't so much as hint at being married to you. In fact, she did quite the opposite."

Daniel narrowed his gaze. "The girl has a name, madam. It's Miranda, and when you speak it, do so with kindness. For she deserves no less. Especially from you."

"If she were your wife . . ."

"She *is* my wife."

The duchess glanced at her son. "If she is your wife, why didn't she say so?"

"And endure having you call her a liar?"

"All she had to do to prove me wrong was show me the marriage lines," the duchess insisted.

"She couldn't prove it," he said. "Because she gave me the only proof we have, to keep or destroy as I will."

"That was rather stupid of her." The duchess was surprised. She'd always believed Miranda was smarter than that. Smart enough and ruthless enough to set her cap for a duke and not to settle for anything less. The duchess didn't see it as fortune hunting so much as fortune saving, for Miranda was extremely wealthy in her own right and had been besieged by men looking to secure that fortune for their own from the day she inherited. The duchess knew Miranda was infatuated with Daniel, but she'd believed it was because Daniel was one of the only young, handsome, marriageable men in London who outranked her and were strong enough and rich enough to stand up to her. Not to mention tall enough. Daniel, the Marquess of Shepherdston, and the Austrian archduke who had chased her the previous season were the only three such men the duchess could name. Miranda's choices for a husband were limited by her position in society. For the Marchioness St. Germaine, marriage to anyone other than another marquess or a duke would be marrying beneath her, and although the duchess hated to admit it, she admired the girl for not being foolish enough to give a lesser-ranking husband control of her fortune. "She should have kept the marriage lines to force your hand in case you decided not to acknowledge the marriage." She looked at Daniel. "I would have."

Daniel swore, then raked his fingers through his hair and gave his mother a pitying look. "That's the difference between you and Miranda. Miranda doesn't have to prove anything. To you or to anyone else. You would use everything in your power to make me stay. She loves me enough not to. She set me free and allowed me to choose."

"And you chose her."

"Yes, I did," Daniel said. "And I'm fortunate that she chose me as well. We chose each other long before either of us realized it."

"This hasty, clandestine marriage will have everyone in the ton counting on his or her fingers to see if she presents you with an heir," his mother warned.

"Let them count," Daniel told her. "It makes no difference. Miranda was an innocent until I took her to bed. And I took her to bed *after* we spoke our vows. If she presents me with a child, I'll be the happiest man on earth. Whether it's nine months or nine years from now, I'll welcome my daughter or son with open arms and give thanks for the miracle. And I'll expect you to do the same."

The duchess stared at him open-mouthed. "You love her."

"Of course I love her," Daniel said simply. "I've always loved her."

"And she loves you," the duchess continued. "Enough to want you to have the kind of wife who would be an asset to you and make you happy. She told me so this morning."

"That's what I want for her as well," he said. "And I pray that I will be that kind of husband." He stared down at his mother, meeting her gaze with an almost identical one of his own. "You've loved me and protected me all of my life, Maman. Don't stand in my way now. I don't care how you do it, but please, find it in your heart to welcome Miranda and wish us happy."

The duchess got up from her chair and rang the bell for Weldon.

The butler must have been waiting close by, for he hurried into the sitting room immediately.

"Weldon, we're about to welcome a new duchess into the family," the dowager duchess announced when her butler entered. "Please bring us the Sussex family jewel box. His Grace requires the emerald."

Weldon returned minutes later with the heavy oak cask that contained a fortune in priceless jewels handed down through the years, and handed it to Daniel along with the key.

Daniel opened the box, then looked at his mother. "I don't want your personal jewelry," he said. "Only the family pieces."

"That cask only contains family pieces," she told him. "My personal jewels are kept in a separate one." She peeked around Daniel to make sure everything was in order. "The Sussex Emerald is in a box beneath the third tray of rings."

Daniel lifted the trays of rings and set them aside, then removed a small black velvet box from the compartment beneath it. He opened it to reveal the magnificent emerald ring and its matching band.

"Thank you for these, Maman." He studied the flawless emerald betrothal ring for a moment, then closed the box and slipped it into his coat pocket.

"No need to thank me, son. The rings were never mine.

They always belonged to you." She managed a smile. "They'll suit the new duchess much better than they ever suited me."

"Then I thank you for taking very good care of them for her." He leaned down to kiss his mother on the forehead, then straightened and started toward the door.

The duchess's eyes sparkled with unshed tears. "Daniel?"

The note in her tone of voice stopped him. "Yes?"

"I'll make arrangements to move out of Sussex House and into the dowager house."

"There's no need, Mother. I don't intend to push you out of Sussex House. If we choose to live here, Miranda will simply move into my wing. You may remain in your apartments for the rest of your natural life."

"Tell me you aren't going to invite Marianna St. Germaine to move in with us from Upper Brook Street," the duchess pleaded dramatically.

He smiled. His mother was nothing if not predictable. "I hadn't considered it. But it might be nice for my children to have both their grandmothers in residence. . . ."

Weldon coughed.

"And Sussex House is certainly big enough for all of us," Daniel continued. "It was good of you to suggest it, Maman. Lady St. Germaine is welcome to a set of apartments or an entire wing of the house if she wants it. And the two of you need never see each other. Except at meal times. Or when you cross paths in the nursery."

"I've no intention of becoming a grandmother or sharing grandchildren with Marianna," the duchess informed him. "I'm too young."

"You've nothing to say in the matter," Daniel told her. "It's up to Miranda and me to decide. And make no mistake, Maman, I intend to fill this old house with the sounds of love, and laughter, and children." He gazed at his mother. "And I hope you'll choose to be a part of it."

"Daniel . . ."

"Think about it." He kissed her again, this time on her

cheek. "I love you, Maman. And I love Miranda. You are both duchesses of Sussex, and you are both my family."

❦

Miranda was waiting for him in the Blue Salon when Daniel's coach rolled up in front of her town house on Upper Brook Street. She held her hands tightly clenched in her lap, partly out of nerves at seeing him again and partly to keep from losing the signet ring she'd returned to the third finger of her left hand.

She'd changed dresses four times before finally settling on the green merino with the black velvet trim her mother had suggested. Miranda knew she should have looked her best, for the green color did wonderful things for her creamy ivory complexion and auburn hair, but not even a morning spent beneath an avalanche of cold cucumber compresses could compensate for her swollen red eyes or her matching red nose. She glanced up at the oval mirror hanging above the mantel and grimaced. She looked exactly like what she was—a beautifully dressed woman who'd spent the night crying into her pillow.

"His Grace, the Duke of Sussex, milady."

Miranda stood up as Crawford announced him. The sight of Daniel in his buff breeches, lawn shirt, brocade waistcoat, dark blue coat, and tall boots nearly took her breath away.

"Good afternoon, Miranda."

The sound of his deep voice sent shivers up and down her spine. "Good afternoon, Daniel."

"You look beautiful," he said suddenly.

Miranda blushed. "Thank you." She reached up and touched the corner of her eye in a self-conscious gesture that drew attention to the area she'd been desperately trying to hide. "So do you."

Her compliment took him by surprise. "With you in your green plumage and me in my dark blue, we must resemble a proud peacock and his mate."

"I hope not." Miranda giggled. "For pea hens are rather drab little birds."

"Not to the peacock," Daniel reminded her. "And there could never be anything drab about you, Miranda. Everything about you sparkles." He offered her his arm. "Shall we?"

Miranda hesitated a brief moment before placing her hand in the bend of his elbow. "Where are we going?" she asked. "Because my mother said . . ."

He read the uncertainty in her eyes. "Your mother was correct. We've an appointment to meet Bishop Manwaring at St. Michael's in a quarter of an hour. If we don't hurry we'll be late." He escorted her out of the Blue Salon, through the entryway, out the front door, and down the steps to the coach.

"I don't understand."

Daniel couldn't keep from smiling. "We're to sign the parish register, remember?" He handed her into the coach, then climbed in behind her and settled himself on the seat beside her instead of on the opposite one.

"Of course I remember," she told him. "I didn't think *you* remembered. You didn't give any sign of it yesterday morning. . . ." She winced as her head bounced against the velvet squab when the coach lurched into the busy afternoon traffic.

"To my very great shame, I didn't remember yesterday morning or the day before that." He leaned closer and brushed the black velvet-trimmed brim of her bonnet with his lips. "I remembered *this* morning. Although how I could forget making you my duchess is beyond my comprehension."

"Why should it be?" she asked. "When you made it quite clear that you didn't want a duchess." She turned so she could look at him. "You don't have to do this."

He frowned. "Do what?"

"This." Miranda waved her arm and nearly hit him in

the face with his signet ring. "It's quite obvious that you read the article in this morning's paper and rushed to my side to rescue me and save my reputation. But I assure you it isn't necessary."

"I beg to differ," he drawled, "for it's very necessary."

"To protect me?" she asked. "Or you?"

Daniel lifted an eyebrow in query.

Miranda took a deep breath and slowly expelled it. "You didn't have to marry me to ensure that your secret was safe. I would have kept it without the bonds of marriage."

"Secret?" Daniel repeated the word as if he'd never heard it before.

"I know about your smuggling, Your Grace. I know that you command a group of men who cross the Channel and slip into France at regular intervals, and I know that you return with precious cargo and leather dispatch pouches that you deliver to the Marquess of Shepherdston."

Daniel sat back against the seat of the coach and smiled at her, waiting for her to continue.

"You talk in your sleep."

"I know," he said softly. "That's why . . ."

"Why you don't trust yourself to spend an entire night with a woman, isn't it?"

He nodded.

"And now you're blaming yourself because you're afraid you've betrayed yourself and your colleagues, and that your weakness has put them and your enterprise in jeopardy. But you needn't worry," Miranda told him. "Because you aren't alone. Other people talk in their sleep."

"Name one."

"Griffin," Miranda announced. "Alyssa says Griffin has suffered nightmares since he returned from the Peninsula and often talks in his sleep because of them."

"Griffin endured a year of horrors we can't begin to imagine. I'd be surprised if he didn't suffer from nightmares or talk in his sleep. But until I was injured, I had never endured hardship of any kind. There's no reason for me not to rest easily at night. But . . ." He shrugged his shoulders. "I'm as bad as my valet. Apparently I cannot be trusted with a secret either." He met her gaze. "What did I say?"

"You called me Micah," she told him. "And you sent me to Lord Shepherdston's house to deliver leather dispatch pouches."

Daniel nodded, remembering the glimpse he'd caught of Miranda in trousers and a nightshirt, and the pile of wet clothing lying in the floor of the master bedchamber of the house on Curzon Street. Men's clothing. His clothing. Except for a nightshirt and a pair of ruined mint-green satin dancing slippers. Clothing that had never reappeared. "You went to Shepherdston's. You put on my clothes, and you made your way from Curzon Street to Shepherdston's house on Park Lane in a downpour to deliver the leather pouches." He frowned. "But there weren't any leather pouches because Micah had already delivered them."

Miranda nodded.

"Good god, Miranda, anything could have happened to you." Daniel raked his fingers through his hair. "If something had happened to you . . ." He looked at her. "Why would you do such a thing? You didn't know Micah. Or the significance of what you were doing. Or the danger you might be facing."

"I did it because you asked me to," she replied simply. "Because you threatened to get out of bed and go to Shepherdston's if I didn't, and I couldn't allow you to do yourself further harm." Her hands were folded primly in her lap, and Miranda lowered her gaze and stared at them as she twisted Daniel's signet around and around her finger. "I don't know what I would have done if I'd seen Lord Shepherdston. Or how I would have explained. But Lord Shepherdston was entertaining an early-morning guest, so I returned to Curzon Street to take care of you."

Daniel was suddenly quite proud of the fact that he'd had the good sense to fall in love with Miranda. For who and what she was. A peeress in her own right who didn't need to marry a title or secure a fortune, but who had made no secret of the fact that all she had ever wanted was to be his wife.

"Miranda." Her name was as soft and as fervent as prayer upon his lips as Daniel reached over, untied the black bow beneath her chin, removed her bonnet, and tossed it onto the opposite seat, before he leaned over to kiss her.

"You don't have to marry me," she reminded him as soon as he stopped kissing her long enough for her to speak. "I shall always keep your secrets safe." She stared into Daniel's blue eyes. "I would die before I'd betray you."

"I don't want you to die for me," he said softly. "I want you to live with me for the next fifty or sixty years so I can die a happy man."

"Daniel?" She almost didn't dare to hope.

"Hell and damnation, but you're going to make me say it, aren't you?"

Miranda nodded. "And I'd rather you didn't say it with a curse upon your lips."

"How about with the taste of you upon my lips?" Daniel asked, moments before he kissed her again. "I love you, Miranda," he whispered when he pulled his lips from hers.

"Since when?" she demanded.

"The easier question would be: when haven't I loved you?" He turned on the seat as the coach rolled into St. Michael's Square, took Miranda's face in his hands, and looked her in the eye. "I can't remember a day since I met you that I didn't find something to love about you. Your face. Your figure. Your honesty. Your directness. Your sharp tongue and quick wit. Your intelligence. Your compassion. Your dignity. Your loyalty. Your friendship. Your love."

"You loved me yet you didn't want to marry me?"

"I didn't want to marry anyone *except* you," he told her. "But I was young and I wanted to wait a bit." He pursed his lips in thought. "I still had dreams I wanted to pursue and adventures to experience. I wanted to have more to offer the world than a big house and a magnificent garden." He smiled. "I wanted to be more."

"A smuggler?"

He nodded. "With a cargo far more valuable than brandy and lace."

Miranda grasped his meaning. "Oh, good heavens!" she exclaimed. "You're a . . ."

Daniel silenced her with a kiss. And kept her silent with kisses until the temperature in the coach reached an unbearable level and he had to fight to keep from stripping off both their clothes and making love to her in the center of St. Michael's Square.

"Shall we make it official and restore your good name?" he asked, as she lay in his arms. "Or would you like to reconsider?"

"I would delight in having my good name restored by making it official," she told him.

Daniel quickly helped her put her clothes to rights. He handed her her bonnet and opened the door.

Miranda settled her bonnet on her head, tied the bow under her chin, then placed her hand on his arm and allowed Daniel to accompany her into the church, where Bishop Manwaring was waiting with the parish registry.

Daniel signed his name with a flourish, then watched as Miranda did the same before shaking hands with the bishop.

"I'm afraid I need my signet back, my sweet," Daniel whispered, reaching down to slide it off her finger and onto his before he unbuttoned her glove and tugged it off.

"You gave it to me," she murmured in protest. "For safe-keeping until you could do better."

"Why don't we make a trade?" Reaching into his coat pocket, he pulled out a small box. "Because I believe these will fit you much better." He opened the box to reveal the Sussex Emerald and a gold band.

Miranda gasped. "Oh, Daniel . . ." Tears sparkled in her eyes as she beheld his gift. If she'd doubted that he would ever claim her, she could lay those doubts to rest, for once she wore the Sussex Emerald in public, everyone would know that she was Daniel's chosen bride.

He lifted the rings out of the box and slipped them onto Miranda's finger. "With this ring, I thee wed."

Miranda extended her hand to admire the way her betrothal ring and its matching wedding band complimented her hand. "I don't know what to say."

He laughed. "Miranda St. Germaine at a loss for words? I don't believe it!"

"Miranda Sussex," she corrected, quickly finding her tongue. "And extraordinary wedding rings will do that to a girl." She looked up at him. "I don't know how to thank you."

"I do," Daniel said, leaning close to suggest several ways she might want to express her gratitude. "Why don't we go home so you can show me?"

C~~~

But home presented a problem.

Neither of them wanted to return to Upper Brook Street or to Sussex House. Curzon Street was no longer a secret haven, and Haversham House, the place they both longed to be, was too far away from town to be practical.

Clarendon's Hotel offered an immediate solution, but it wasn't the solution they wanted.

Daniel helped Miranda back into the coach, climbed in beside her, and paused when his driver asked, "Where to, Your Grace?"

"Where to?" Daniel repeated the question. "Aye, there's the rub. For I'm a man of many houses with not one private bed to call his own."

"Not to worry," she said, reaching over to caress his face with her hand. "For you've married a woman of considerable property." Turning, she called out to the driver: "Regent's Park Lake."

Chapter 27

*"Let those love now who never loved before;
Let those who always loved, now love the more."*
—Thomas Parnell, 1679–1718

*T*he villa John Nash was building for Miranda at Regent's Park was nearly completed and already partially furnished. It was so near to completion that the locks had already been installed on the doors and windows. And Miranda had come away from Upper Brook Street without a key.

Fortunately, Daniel was better prepared. Reaching down, he withdrew a knife from his boot and set to work on the lock on the conservatory door. It yielded to the pressure of his blade within minutes.

"I would carry you over the threshold," Daniel said, as he pushed the conservatory door open and ushered Miranda inside. "But I don't think my ribs will allow it." He closed the door behind him, relocked it, and glanced around at the room. "Please tell me there's a bed."

"There is." She took him by the hand. "In a room up one flight of stairs, where the doors open onto a balcony overlooking the lake."

Daniel groaned at the mention of stairs, but Miranda gave him a look that promised she would make climbing them worth his while, and he happily followed her lead,

allowing her to pull him up the flight of stairs to the bedroom with the balcony overlooking the lake.

Where a large bed awaited him.

Miranda led him to it, then turned and unfastened her
dress, pushing it off her shoulders, over her hips, and down
her long legs, allowing it to puddle on the floor at her feet.
She dispensed with her undergarments, untied her stockings, and stepped out of her green slippers. And stood before Daniel in all her naked glory.

He had seen women who were more beautiful than she
was, had courted them and shared their beds, but he had
never seen a woman he wanted more than he wanted Miranda. She was his equal. His match. The part of him he
hadn't known was missing until she had taken him inside her
and made him her own.

Standing a few feet away from him, Miranda moistened
her dry lips and stood quietly waiting for him to make a
move.

Daniel stood in the center of the room at the foot of the
bed and continued his study of her. He leaned against the
footboard, barely daring to breathe as he waited to see what
she would do next.

Realizing suddenly that they were playing a chess game
of sorts where he was encouraging her to be the aggressor,
Miranda looked him in the eyes.

Daniel fought for control. He narrowed his gaze until a
furrow formed between his eyebrows and he was practically scowling. But Miranda wasn't fooled or intimidated
by his apparent disregard. She stalked him like a tiger
stalking her prey, smiling as a muscle in his jaw began to
pulse. She moved closer, then lifted her arms, looped them
over his head and brushed her breasts against his shirtfront.

Daniel abandoned all thought of maintaining control.
He opened his arms in welcome and Miranda settled into
them—a peeress in her own right and now his duchess, as
naked as the day she was born.

The sight of her nearly took his breath away. Daniel

bent his head to kiss her and Miranda met him halfway.

"I apologize for keeping you waiting all morning, milady," he murmured. "But there was business to which I had to attend."

"Smuggling plans, no doubt." She licked the seam of his lips.

"No doubt," he agreed, running his hands up her ribs before filling them with the weight of her breasts. He nibbled at her lips, then trailed a line of kisses from her mouth down her chin and neck to the tops of her breasts, finally ending his journey by suckling first one and then the other of her perfectly fashioned globes, dropping down onto his knees in front of her in order to do so.

"I missed you." He surprised himself with the admission. "I found myself thinking about you at the oddest times."

"That's good," she said, sliding her fingers through his thick dark hair, pressing his face against her stomach. "Because I missed you, too. And I found myself thinking of you at the oddest times, wondering if you'd come back or if my declaration of love would frighten you away."

"I'm not that easily frightened, Your Grace," he teased. "Honored, perhaps. Humbled, surely. But frightened of a shy, retiring little thing like you?"

"I'm pleased to hear it," she answered. "Because I intend to exhibit a great deal more shy and retiring behavior in your presence."

"Go ahead," he encouraged. "I dare you." Reaching behind her, Daniel cupped her buttocks and pulled her closer. He tilted his head and teased the tiny kernel of pleasure hidden beneath the silky auburn curls of her woman's triangle with the tip of his tongue. "A lady of impeccable manners and taste," he drawled. "I like that in a duchess."

Tasting and teasing her with his mouth and tongue, Daniel worked his magic until she screamed his name in pleasurable release. He held her close as he got to his feet, pressing her against him as he gently lowered her onto the bed, then retreated far enough away to divest himself of his garments.

Miranda watched as he bared his body, then slowly parted her legs in invitation as Daniel joined her on the bed, settling against her and sighing with pleasure as he carefully sheathed himself inside her.

He pressed his lips against the curve of her neck and focused on the feel of their exquisite joining. She was warm and wet and welcoming, and he was rock hard and consumed with wanting. Theirs was a perfect fit and Daniel stroked her with a passionate urgency that bespoke his great need of her. Miranda answered him stroke for stroke, giving as much as she took, and begging for more.

They made sweet passionate love throughout the long hours of the afternoon and far into the night, and when at last he collapsed on the pillow beside her and closed his eyes, Daniel knew he need never fear revealing his secrets, for they were safe with her—as safe as the part of him she cradled within her. And Daniel knew, without a doubt, that he was forever changed by her touch because Miranda had captured his heart and soul with her essence.

Daniel knew with unshakable certainty that even should he live to be a thousand years old, he would never love anyone or anything as much as he loved Miranda.

He whispered in her ear, but the words came out as a soft, satisfied murmur too low for her to hear.

She slept undisturbed.

Daniel kissed the top of her head, fanning her hair with his breath as he held her cradled against his side, and dreamed the dreams of the future.

The early-morning light had begun to fill the sky when Miranda opened her eyes. She reached for Daniel and knew a moment of panic when she realized he was gone.

She threw back the covers, got to her feet, and hurried to the balcony door. Pushing the door open, she scanned the balcony, hoping to find him there.

But Daniel wasn't on the balcony.

He was below it, standing on the bank of the lake, staring at the small punt bobbing on the surface of the dark water.

Wrapping herself in a sheet, Miranda left the bedroom and hurried outside to join him.

He jumped when she touched him on the shoulder, and when he turned to look at her, Miranda saw that his face bore a decidedly greenish cast. "Daniel, what are you doing out here? Are you ill?"

"I've a confession to make," he said, trying desperately to smile.

"I spoiled your surprise?"

He shook his head. "Don't paint me with the brush of romance just yet," he warned. "Because I'm not at all certain I can live up to it."

She gave him what she hoped was a come-hither look. "We've got a boat, a lake, and you and me. All we need are sunshine, satin pillows, and some rose petals, and my fantasy's complete."

"Not quite," he replied.

"Why not?"

"I hate boats."

Miranda blinked in confusion.

"I hate boats," Daniel continued, "all boats. Every boat. Any boat. From the smallest rowboat to the royal yacht."

"That's unfortunate in your chosen occupation," she commiserated, "for smugglers generally use boats as their primary form of transportation."

"I know," he reminded her. "And the last time I was in one, I got shot."

"I see." Miranda thought for a moment. "Can you swim?"

"Of course." He sounded a little affronted at having her discover another of his weaknesses.

"You'd be surprised at the number of people who can't," she told him, stepping over the pole Daniel had left lying on the bank. "Sailors and smugglers included."

"Known many sailors and smugglers have you?"

"Two sailors," she replied. "Neither of whom could swim. And one smuggler who could. Splendid fellow. Unfortunately, his smuggling career is likely to be of brief duration since *he* doesn't like boats." She picked up the pole and placed it inside the boat. "Not that I'd mind, of course, for I rather like the idea of having him home."

He exhaled. "I'll be leaving in a few days."

"On business?" she asked.

"In a manner of speaking."

"This?" Miranda stared at the boat.

"Yes."

"The last time you went out like that, you got shot."

He smiled. "Yes, I know."

"But . . ."

"There's work to be done, Miranda, and a war to be won, and I have a part in winning it." It was the closest Daniel could come to telling her the truth about the Free Fellows League.

"I see." Lifting the hem of her sheet to keep from dragging it in the water, Miranda walked over to the boat, waded into the water, and climbed aboard. She doubled the sheet, spread it in the bottom of the boat, and lay down upon it. "Tell me, Your Grace, what is it about this boat you don't like?"

"The motion," he admitted. "The rocking."

"It isn't rocking now," she said.

"It will be," he countered. "As soon as it leaves the bank for open water."

"How did you make it on your last smuggling run?" she asked.

"I didn't think about the boat or the water, I only thought about the important job I had to do."

Miranda smiled a cat-that-ate-the-cream sort of smile

and crooked her finger at him. "I've a most important job for you to do, Your Grace. . . ."

He ached all over. His ribs. His wound. His sunburned skin.

But poling Miranda around the lake had proved excellent therapy for him. He had been so busy making love to his wife that by the time they reached the opposite shore, he'd forgotten all about the sick feeling he usually felt when the boat began rocking side to side.

And just when he feared his sick feeling had returned, Miranda had returned the favor and made love to him in several rather inventive ways.

He would never look at the little boat, or any boat, the same way again. Miranda had turned the tables on him, by showing him that there was pleasure to be found even in the thing he feared most. Just as she was showing him that marriage to her could be an endless source of pleasure. Teaching him to enjoy marriage instead of fear it.

In return, he had very nearly brought her fantasy to life. Next time he would have the satin pillows and the rose petals to go along with the sunshine, for he'd quickly learned that the floor of a boat was hell on the knees.

He smiled at her. "You're going to regret this tomorrow, milady."

Miranda laughed her throaty laugh and trailed her hand in the water. "Impossible."

"You're a bit too pink in a few very interesting places," Daniel observed as he poled them toward the bank where they'd begun several hours earlier.

"So are you," she reminded him. "But your clothes cover it up. Whereas I've only a sheet and I'm lying on it."

"In your fantasy, the poling was easier," he said, gasping for breath as he pushed the boat across the water.

"That's true," she admitted, sitting up and rolling to her

knees. The boat tipped precariously, then righted itself as Miranda made her way to the stern and climbed up beside him.

"What are you doing?" His voice rose a fraction.

"My turn to pole," she replied, reaching for it. "Your turn to rest."

Daniel hesitated, but the allure of having a six-foot-tall naked woman pole him across the lake was too tempting to ignore. He inched his way to the prow as he exchanged places with his bride, then lay back and enjoyed the view as Miranda pushed them home.

Chapter 28

"The first step is the hardest."
—Marie de Vichy-Chamrond, 1697–1780

Daniel paid another call on his mother, the dowager duchess, four days later. She greeted him as he entered her sitting room.

"Good morning, Daniel."

"Mother," Daniel bowed. "I haven't a great deal of time. I'm going away on business and I'm leaving within the hour."

"It seems to me that you're making a habit of that lately," she said. "No trouble in paradise, I hope."

"Of course not," he replied. "But my business demands that Miranda and I be apart for a few days. . . ."

"What brings you to see me so bright and early?"

"I wanted to see you before I left, and to ask a favor."

The duchess raised one elegant eyebrow at that. "Twice in one week. What have I done to deserve this distinction?"

"You're my mother," he replied, handing her a thick goatskin folder full of legal documents. "I've brought you copies of my personal papers. You'll find them quite in order. If anything should happen to me, I'd like you to see that my wishes are carried out."

"What do you mean, if anything happens to you?" She stared at him. "You are my only son and the Duke of Sussex, nothing had better happen to you."

"The business I'm about is very serious and very important. I hope to return in a few days' time none the worse for wear, but I cannot guarantee that that will be the case. I've left instructions for you on the first page of that letter." He gestured toward an envelope. "And I'd appreciate it if you would begin work on that project right away." Daniel smiled down at her. "It's for Miranda."

He watched as his mother scanned the letter of instructions. "Miranda has copies of every legal document here except my letter to you. Everything has been made current in order to reflect my change in marital status—including my will." He looked at his mother. "I would be most grateful if you would use whatever you need to make this possible."

"Daniel, I'm not sure this is appropriate. . . ."

"It's most appropriate," he said. "You've had time to consider the consequences of continuing the current state of affairs. And to decide whether or not you're willing to try another path."

"I'm willing," his mother said softly. "And I must admit I was surprised that you allowed it to go on as long as it did."

"You're my mother," Daniel answered. "Miranda is the love of my life. I don't want to have to choose between you. Or to have members of the ton take sides. You've treated her abominably, Maman, and now it's time for you to start making amends."

Recalling her conversation with Miranda a few days earlier, the dowager duchess attempted to circumvent the instructions Daniel had given her. "Miranda and I have already reached an understanding."

"I'm pleased to hear it," he told her. "But I expect you to do this for me all the same."

The dowager duchess's concern showed on her lovely face for the first time in years. "Everything sounds so final." She looked into her son's eyes. "You are planning to return, aren't you?"

"Of course I am. I'll send word as soon as I know when."

"This is a great deal to accomplish in such a short amount of time," she complained.

"You can manage it. You're the dowager Duchess of Sussex. You took on the Gas-Light and Coke Company and had gaslights installed where they said it couldn't be done in time for your gala. You can accomplish anything."

She gave him her most devastating smile. "When you put it like that, I suppose you're right."

"I know I am." Daniel leaned down to kiss his mother on the cheek. "Take care. I'll see you when I return." Turning, he headed toward the door.

"Daniel?"

"Yes?"

"I thought I might surprise your bride by redecorating your wing of the house in a manner more suitable for a duke and his duchess."

"That's very nice of you, Maman," he said. "Redecorate if you like, but you needn't go to the trouble on our account. Miranda and I have decided to live in Miranda's villa in Regent's Park."

"But Sussex House has always been the primary residence of the Dukes of Sussex," she protested.

"Sussex House is your home, Maman. You've lived here thirty years."

"But . . ."

"And Upper Brook Street, as the traditional residence of the Marquesses of St. Germaine, is Lady St. Germaine's home," he reminded her. "Marriage to me made Miranda the Duchess of Sussex, but she's the fifth Marquess of St. Germaine by birth. You and Miranda and I could live here at Sussex House. Or Lady St. Germaine, Miranda, and I could live at Upper Brook Street. But we cannot do both. And since we don't want to live in your house or in Lady St. Germaine's house, Miranda and I have decided to make the villa in Regent's Park *our* home."

"Then I suppose it would be all right if I sent along a few things? Paintings, pieces of furniture, the cask of Sussex jewelry, a few objects d'art, and the like . . ."

"It would." Daniel looked at his mother. "But I'm sure Miranda would appreciate it more if you invited her here so that she might *choose* the things she'd like for our new home from among these things. Excluding your apartments, of course."

"Did she like the emerald?"

"Very much."

"I suppose I could invite her for refreshments and a tour of the attics and the storerooms."

"The *house,* the attics, and the storeroom," Daniel said firmly. "She is the new duchess, after all, and should be allowed to choose whatever she wants from her husband's home. As the dowager duchess, I should think that you would understand that and be prepared to be quite magnanimous."

"All right."

"Have I your word of honor that you'll follow my instructions and invite Miranda and her mother for refreshments and a tour of the house, the attics, and the storeroom this afternoon?"

She nodded.

"I would appreciate hearing the words."

"You have my word of honor that I will follow your instructions and invite Miranda and her mother for refreshments and a tour of the house, the attics, and the storeroom." She studied his resolute expression, then gave in. "I'll send a note around right away."

"Thank you, *Maman.*" He kissed her cheek one last time, said his good-bye, and left.

❧

Leaving Miranda had proven much harder.
She hadn't cried when he left, but her eyes had

shimmered with unshed tears and she'd tried her best to hide the quaver in her voice and the fact that she was wearing his trousers beneath her dress. But he'd run his hands up under her skirts and discovered them.

Daniel arched an eyebrow. "New style, milady?"

"Take me with you," she'd pleaded.

"I can't," he answered, shoving her skirts higher so he could see the trousers she had on. "Mine, I suppose?"

Miranda frowned. "Yes, of course."

He cupped her round buttocks, then smoothed his hand over the taut fabric. "I seem to recall that you look quite fetching in these." He grinned. "What's the occasion?"

She let out an exasperated sigh. "You know the occasion. I'm going with you."

He shook his head. "Would that you could, my love, but I'm afraid you won't be modeling your costume for me on this trip."

"Please, Daniel," she said. "I can't bear the thought of you in a boat out on the Channel alone."

"I won't be alone," he said.

"But you'll be in a boat. How will I know if you're all right?"

"I'll be all right because I have you to come home to." He pressed her against him, then kissed the tip of her nose, marveling at the way she fit him so perfectly. "And a little while from now, you'll be receiving a note from my mother inviting you to join her for refreshments at Sussex House, where you'll have the opportunity to choose furnishings for our new house. I'd like it very much if you'd accept her invitation."

"But, Daniel . . ."

"Don't worry, if all goes well, I'll be home by tomorrow evening," he told her.

"I can't help but worry," she admitted. "I know what went wrong last time."

"I'll be fine. Please go to Sussex House and let my mother begin making amends for her behavior."

Seeing the look in his eyes, Miranda capitulated. "All right."

"That's my duchess," Daniel approved, lingering over his kiss, putting all the passion he felt into bidding his wife good-bye.

❦

The Free Fellows League waited until Jarrod returned from his honeymoon to bait the trap.

Jarrod had boarded one of Lord Davies's merchant ships and crossed the Channel bound for Spain under cover of darkness some hours before. Alex, second Marquess of Courtland, had gone with him, boarding the boat in London earlier in the day. Courtland's mission was to take much-needed provisions to their network of couriers and spies scattered along the Peninsula while Jarrod conferred with Wellington and his staff.

Daniel and his group of smugglers were the decoys, for their precious cargo was Micah Beekins, a few cases of brandy taken from Daniel's own cellar, and a leather dispatch pouch full of counterfeit dispatches Colin and Gillian had spent two days constructing.

The dispatches, when deciphered, would condemn the person presenting them, and the Free Fellows had decided to use them as a safeguard should things go awry and allow the rat to slip through their trap.

Lord Weymouth had played his part by relaying tiny bits of information in conversation with his superior in the War Office. Leather dispatches were due to arrive on the evening tide at Dover, along with one of the secret men who carried the dispatches.

Jonathan, playing the part of a naval officer assigned to the coast watch, was ready to board the HMS *Colchester* to thwart the rat's escape by water. And Colin and Griffin remained behind in London to follow him. All the way to the coast if necessary.

Everyone had a role to play. Even Rupert and Ned. For Daniel had instructed them to watch over Miranda and keep her safe when he'd taken her back to Upper Brook Street to stay with her mother and kissed her good-bye.

"I don't think he's coming, Danny Boy," Billy Beekins murmured from his position at the back of the boat.

"He's coming," Daniel answered with complete conviction. They'd been sitting in the boat for hours, hugging the coastline, waiting for a signal from Jonathan to tell them that the frigate and a coach were coming.

"There it is!" Shavers whispered. "There's Johnny Boy's signal."

Daniel looked to his left and saw that his cousin had given the signal. "Shove out." He instructed the crew to row out a few hundred yards in order to time their arrival to coincide with that of the coach.

"How're you holding out, Danny?" The boatswain's mate asked. "Your injury paining you?"

Daniel put his shoulder to the oar. "It's burning like bloody hell," he admitted. "But I'll make it."

"Aye, lad, you will." Billy Beekins smiled a gap-toothed smile. "You're not nearly as peckish-looking this trip. You've lost your greenish cast."

Daniel grinned. "I've come to appreciate boats," he answered truthfully. "And the things a man can accomplish in them."

"That's the spirit, lad. Now, buck up, for the party's about to begin."

"Ride in," Daniel said quietly, lifting his oar and locking it into place as the others did the same, allowing the skiff to ride the tide to shore.

They clamored out of the boat and into the surf, beaching the craft before unloading the French brandy, the leather dispatch pouches, and Micah.

"I'll take that."

Daniel turned to find Lord Espy exiting a coach that Daniel knew all too well, pointing a gun at Pepper, who stood holding a case of brandy.

"Have you a sudden taste for brandy, Lord Espy?" Daniel asked. "Or has your cellar run dry?"

"Consider it payment," Espy said. "For the commander of the frigate. He likes fine brandy."

"Would that be your brother? Commander Selwin Espy?"

"Touché, Your Grace."

Daniel nodded to Pepper. "Give the man the case of brandy with my compliments."

"You are a gentleman, Your Grace." Lord Espy gestured with the gun. "Over here."

Pepper carried the case of brandy to a spot in front of Espy's coach and put it down.

"Now I'll take the rest of it," Espy directed.

"Greedy, my lord? Or merely thirsty?" Daniel taunted.

"A little greed is a virtue, Your Grace. And a great thirst for the finer things in life is likewise." He brandished the weapon. And Daniel signaled to Pepper to unload all the brandy and give it to Lord Espy. "Now the rest."

"I'm afraid that's all there is," Daniel told him.

"Not the brandy," Espy said. "I want the spy and the dispatches."

"We're not carrying spies." Daniel met Espy's gaze without flinching. "And what makes you think I would turn one over to you if we were?"

"I have something you want."

"Have you?"

"Yes, indeed," Espy elaborated. "That is how this game is played. I have something you want. You have something I want. The gentlemanly thing to do is make an exchange." Espy kept his weapon trained on Daniel as he backed up a step, reached into the coach, and pulled Miranda out, and twisted her arm behind her back. "May I congratulate you on your nuptials, Your Grace?"

"Hello, Daniel." Her voice was a tiny bit wobbly, but she kept her head high, refusing to show fear.

"And here I thought Lady Miranda was merely your lover," Lord Espy said. "Imagine my surprise and delight when I learned she was your new bride."

Daniel thought his heart might stop at the sight of her. He'd planned everything to the utmost, but the sight of Espy holding his wife by the arm while brandishing a weapon gave him chills. But he had a part to play. He looked Miranda up and down. "Has he hurt you?"

"No."

"Then may I say that you look as fetching in that dress as you did in the one earlier?" She had dispensed with his trousers and changed dresses. He smiled at her. "New frock?"

She nodded. "Your mother invited me to Sussex House for refreshments. I thought I should look my best. . . ."

Daniel's heart skipped another beat. "Is my mother . . . ?"

"I'm a gentleman," Espy informed him. "I would never hurt your mother."

"Yet you manhandle my wife," Daniel growled.

"Only as a matter of business," Espy said. "Your wife was leaving Sussex House as I arrived."

Miranda glared at Espy. "Did you know that he and the duchess were keeping company?"

"I knew she had a *gentleman* friend," Daniel admitted. "I didn't know her taste in them was so deplorable."

"You should stay home more," Espy told him. "Then you'd know what is going on beneath your nose. You would know that I've been paying court to Her Grace for several weeks now. She is still a very lovely woman and a most generous *companion*."

Daniel thought he might be ill at the thought of the *companionship* Espy and his mother had shared.

"At any rate, your wife made the mistake of exiting Sussex House and calling for her coach immediately after her driver recognized mine." Lord Espy shrugged his shoulders. "Unfortunately, I was in the process of rendering her footman unconscious when she saw me."

"I didn't see Rupert," Miranda told Daniel. "But Lord Espy swung his walking stick at Ned and hit him upon the side of the head, then left him lying on the street."

"I was in a bit of a hurry. There was no time to waste," Espy continued. "Your bride proved to be quite a handful. Naturally, I had no choice but to bring her along on the journey. Especially after she tried to emasculate me with her knee."

"My men?" Daniel queried.

"Your driver is tied up inside your coach," Espy replied. "And when we departed, your footman was still lying in the street." He tightened his grip on Miranda's arm.

She gasped as the pain shot up her arm, then kicked at Espy through her skirts. "You blackguard!"

"Enough!" Espy let go of Miranda's arm long enough to grab hold of her waist, anchoring his arm around her from behind, waving his weapon around before calmly pointing it at her. "Give me what I want and I'll give you what you want. Hurry," he advised, staring at Daniel. "The clock is ticking."

"Very well," Daniel said calmly. "Give me my wife and I'll give you the dispatches." He reached back and Micah placed the leather pouches in his hand.

"And the spy," Espy insisted, licking the drops of perspiration that beaded on his upper lip. "I need them both."

"For what reason?"

"For money, of course," Espy spat. "There are those who have more than enough, like you, Your Grace. And there are those who never have enough. . . ."

"Like you."

Espy nodded. "So I devised a way to get more of it."

"In lieu of marrying my mother?"

Lord Espy chuckled. "You know the duchess. She

would never marry a man of lower rank, no matter how good he is in bed."

"So you decided on espionage and ransom," Daniel guessed.

"Of course," Espy crowed. "And a spy in the hand is worth a great deal more than dispatches to the French. Give him to me!"

"Miranda," Daniel spoke softly. "Do you know that I love you?"

"Yes," she breathed.

"Do you trust me never to do anything that might jeopardize your life?"

"Without question."

"Then pick up your feet. Now!"

Miranda did as he instructed, lifting her feet from the ground in the same instant that Daniel flung the leather pouches at Espy's head and sprinted toward him. Espy fired his weapon as Daniel knocked him to the ground. Miranda fell back, landing in the soft sand beside the leather pouches.

"Is everyone all right?" Daniel asked, gingerly rolling to his knees to watch as Micah, Billy Beekins, Pepper, Shavers, Colin, and Griff surrounded Espy and jerked him to his feet.

"We're fine," Micah called. "His shot hit the water."

"Miranda?" he gasped.

"I'm all right." She reached out and touched him on the shoulder.

"Thank God," he breathed. "My head knew the danger was minimal, but my heart . . ."

"Your heart?" she prompted.

"My heart was in my throat," he whispered. "I thought I might die of loving you." He closed his eyes and keeled over on the beach.

"Daniel? Daniel!" She shook him. "Are you shot?"

"No," he groaned. "But I'm afraid I've destroyed your needlework."

"Lean on me," she ordered as she attempted to lift him and fell to her knees. "You still weight a ton."

Daniel yelped. "You're no featherweight yourself. Thank God."

"Allow us."

Miranda looked up as Colin and Griffin helped Daniel to his feet.

"Now you know what we do for an evening's entertainment away from home and hearth," Griff said with a wink.

Colin nodded. "And we'd appreciate it if you'd keep all this excitement to yourself, Your Grace." He smiled at her. "No need to worry our lovely wives." Colin put an arm around Daniel's waist, and together he and Griffin boosted him into the coach.

"Indeed," Miranda replied. "I'll have nightmares just thinking about it, but your secrets are safe with me."

"Well done, Your Grace." Micah offered his hand.

"Thank you."

"I'm Micah Beekins," he told her as he helped her into the coach, then climbed up beside her. "Not to worry, ma'am. We'll take Danny Boy . . . I mean . . . His Grace . . . to my mother. She knows just what to do. She's done it afore and she'll have him stitched up again in no time."

Chapter 29

"Kiss till the cow comes home."
—*Francis Beaumont, c. 1584–1616,*
and John Fletcher, 1579–1625

"*The morning post has arrived, Your Grace.*"

"Thank you, Ned." Miranda lifted the letter from the silver tray he offered to her and placed it on her lap.

"It's Beckham, ma'am."

Miranda looked up from the newspaper she was reading. "Pardon?"

"It's Beckham, ma'am," Ned insisted. "Now that I'm a butler, you should call me by my surname, Beckham."

"I'll try, Ne . . . Beckham," she promised, as Daniel walked into the room and placed a kiss on her neck.

"Problems with the help?" he teased.

Miranda nodded. "Now that he's recovered from his wound and been promoted to butler, Ned insists on being called Beckham." She looked over at her husband. "I've known him all my life and I've always called him Ned." She sighed. "Beckham is going to take some getting used to."

"You elevated him to the position of butler, Your Grace," Daniel reminded her. "And that entitles him to be called by his surname." He leaned over her shoulder. "Anything newsworthy in the *Chronicle*?"

She shook her head. "I keep waiting for the 'Ton Tidbits' column to recant their earlier article about us."

"No luck?" he asked.

"Not yet."

"No matter. We can always bring suit against them." Daniel stared at the cream-colored heavy vellum envelope in Miranda's lap. "What's that?"

"Morning post."

"Aren't you going to open it?"

Miranda folded the newspaper and laid it aside, then reached for the envelope in her lap and flipped it over. "That's odd."

"What is?" Daniel had to bite the inside of his mouth to keep from grinning like a jackanapes.

She frowned. "It's from your mother."

"Well, open it," he urged, "and see what she wants."

Miranda ripped open the envelope and read: " 'Her Grace, the dowager Duchess of Sussex, requests the honor of your presence at the wedding of her son, His Grace Daniel Edward Arthur, Ninth Duke of Sussex, to the Most Noble Miranda Margaret, Fifth Marquess of St. Germaine on Wednesday, 30th June at nine o'clock in the morning at St. Michael's Church, St. Michael's Square, London. Gala breakfast to follow at Sussex House.' " Puzzled, Miranda looked up at her husband. "She's inviting us to our wedding."

Daniel shook his head. "The invitation was addressed to you," he said. "She's inviting *you* to the wedding she's hosting for us."

"She wants us to get married again?"

Daniel leaned down and kissed her on the lips. "She wants to make amends by publicly inviting you to her second gala celebration of the season."

Tears formed in Miranda's eyes. "She doesn't have to do that."

"Yes, she does."

"Thirtieth of June?" Miranda squeaked. "That's barely a fortnight away. What should I wear?"

Daniel laughed. "Strange that you should ask that particular question." He leaned down and picked up a dress box from Madam Racine's and handed it to her. "For I seem to recall owing you a ball gown fit for a queen."

Miranda untied the bow on the box, removed the wrapping, and gasped at the cream-colored dress inside it.

She lifted it out of the box and held it up.

It *was* a dress fit for a queen, made from yards of silk and lace and embroidered with hundreds of pearls and diamonds.

"I almost ordered a green one identical to the one you wore to our first wedding," he admitted. "But I decided that only something extraordinary would do."

"Oh, Daniel . . ."

When she said his name like that, something inside him melted, then thrilled with pride. "Marry me again, Miranda," he said softly. "So I might have the opportunity to repeat my vows before all of London and let everyone know how happy and honored I am to be the man with whom you walk down the aisle. Because I love you and I want everyone to know that I'm the luckiest husband in all the world to have you for a wife." He kissed her then, a kiss that was long and hot and sweet and full of the promise of tomorrow.

"I love you, Daniel," she whispered. "And I'll be happy and honored to marry you as often as you like. Because I'm yours. Truly and forever."

Epilogue

"It is good news, worthy of all acceptation!
And yet not too good to be true."

—Matthew Henry, 1662–1714

From the *"Ton Tidbits"* column of Wednesday, 30th June 1813:

> The editors and publishers of the Morning Chronicle are pleased to offer to Their Graces, the Duke and Duchess of Sussex, our most humble apologies for an earlier column suggesting Their Graces committed acts of impropriety in a house on Curzon Street earlier in the season.
>
> According to the parish register of St. Michael's Church, the Duke and Duchess of Sussex were married by special license in a ceremony performed by Bishop Manwaring immediately prior to their sojourn on Curzon Street, where they spent the first two nights of their honeymoon.
>
> The editors and publishers of the Morning Chronicle *deeply regret the unfortunate error and extend our sincere felicitations to the happy couple.*

Official Charter of the
Free Fellows League

On this, the seventh day of January in the year of Our Lord 1814, we, the sons and heirs to the oldest and most esteemed titles and finest families of England and Scotland, do amend the original charter of our own Free Fellows League.

The Free Fellows League is dedicated to the proposition that sons and heirs to great titles and fortunes, who are duty-bound to marry in order to beget future sons and heirs, should be allowed to avoid the inevitable leg-shackling to a female until we find the love of our lives, for England's and Scotland's greatest heroes deserve no less than the love of extraordinary females.

As active and equal members of the Free Fellows League, we agree that:

1) We shall only agree to marry when we've no other choice, or when we're old enough, or when we know in our hearts that it's the right thing to do.

2) We shall no longer require our fellow Free Fellows to pay the sum of five hundred pounds sterling to each of us upon the occasion of a marriage before reaching our thirtieth year. We shall not refuse the sum should our fellow Free Fellows choose to follow established tradition and offer it, but we shall not expect or require it.

3) We shall reserve the right to never darken the doors of any establishments that cater to 'Marriage Mart' mamas or

their desperate daughters unless forced to do so. Nor shall we frequent the homes of any relatives, friends, or acquaintances that seek to match us up with prospective brides, unless we want to do so.

4) When compelled to marry, we agree that we shall only marry women we love or women we hope to love or women we pray will one day love us.

5) We shall never feel encumbered by the sentiment known as love or succumb to female wiles unless we choose to do so because love is a gift, not an encumbrance, and the females who hold us enthralled are wives who love us to distraction and are dearly loved in return.

6) We shall sacrifice ourselves on the altar of duty at every opportunity in every way we can, in order to give and receive pleasure and to beget our heirs and pray that we always find great satisfaction in doing so.

7) We shall install our wives in our hearts and keep them there and by our sides in our country houses, in London, or wherever our journeys take us.

8) We shall drink and ride and hunt, and consort with our boon companions whenever we are pleased to do so, and then eagerly return home to our wives and families with smiles on our faces.

9) We shall not dictate to the wives who have given us their hearts, but shall love, cherish, and respect them and do everything in our power to share our work and our lives with them. Furthermore, we shall take care not to put our feet upon tables and sofas and the seats of chairs, or allow our hounds to

sit upon the furnishings and roam our houses at will, if such behavior causes our spouses distress.

10) We shall give our loyalty and our undying friendship to England and Scotland and our brothers and fellow members of the Free Fellows League, and equal loyalty to the wives and families we love and who love us in return.

Signed (in blood) and sealed by:

Griffin Abernathy, 1st Duke of Avon and 1st Marquess of Abbingdon, aged thirty years and two months. Happily married since May 1810.

Colin McElreath, 27th Viscount Grantham, aged thirty years and five months, eldest son and their apparent to the 9th Earl of McElreath. Happily married since June 1812.

Jarrod, 5th Marquess of Shepherdston, 22nd Earl of Westmore, aged thirty-one years and three months. Happily married since May 1813.

Daniel, 9th Duke of Sussex, aged eight and twenty years and eight months. Happily married since May 1813.

Jonathan Manners, 11th Earl of Barclay, aged eight and twenty years and ten months.

Alexander, 2nd Marquess of Courtland, aged six and twenty years and one month.

Continue reading for a special preview of
Nicole Byrd's next novel

GILDING THE LADY

Coming in August 2005 from Berkley Sensation!

Prologue

The face . . .

It was the face that haunted her nightmares—but here, in clear daylight, distinct amid the crowd.

Clarissa Fallon drew a deep, disbelieving breath. It couldn't be. A moment ago she had been happily engrossed in the street scene, inhaling the aromas of savory meat and pastry that drifted from a street vendor's cart, as his call of "Hot meat pies!" rose above the clatter of horses' hooves and carriage wheels. She had paused on the sidewalk to relish the sparkle of sunlight off the polished panes of shop windows and admired enticing wares like a new bonnet trimmed with yellow roses, a pair of elegant ecru kid gloves, or a flowing swathe of crimson silk draped artfully across a stand . . .

And Clarissa herself was free, at last, to consider such once-unheard of luxuries, free to lift her head to meet the eyes of the ladies and gentlemen strolling along the walkway. Free . . .

And then she'd caught sight of the once-familiar face, and fear pierced her like a thorn hidden amid a nosegay of roses.

Her brother had promised that Clarissa would be safe now. He'd said . . . But the face was here, and it was turning—at any moment, those dark bulging eyes would meet Clarissa's horrified gaze, and then—

Clarissa jerked her head aside and plunged away from

the specter which had appeared so abruptly out of the cheer-
ful melee. She pushed her way past two chatting women and
ran as if the devil himself waited to snare her soul.

Behind her, someone called, "Miss Clarissa, wait!"

Ignoring the cry, Clarissa plunged ahead. Her heart beat
so loudly, the blood pounding in her ears, that she could
hear nothing else. Even the noise of the busy London street
faded, and she was lost in her worst nightmare.

She ran.

Chapter 1

*D*ominic Shay, seventh earl of Whitby, sipped a glass
of port. His head was lowered, and he didn't seem to
notice when Timothy Galston paused, standing just to the
side of the comfortable club chair.

"Whitby!"

Timothy had practiced his tone of righteous indignation
carefully in the privacy of his own rooms, and he was annoyed to observe the other man ignore his greeting. They
were old acquaintances, and there was no reason for the
slight prickle of unease that the earl always seemed to pro-
voke in the younger man, but there it was. Timothy almost
had second thoughts about his rehearsed speech, wishing
for a moment he could just slip away, but dash it all, the girl
was his cousin.

He cleared his throat and said, more loudly, "Whitby,
I'm speaking to you!"

And the earl lifted his face, his perfect features set in an
expression of arctic disinterest, his deep brown eyes so
dark that they could make one shiver. "Oh, hello, Galston.
Have some wine; the butler has just uncorked a quite toler-
able bottle."

Timothy waved away such a minor consideration. No,
perhaps not minor, but he could not be distracted until he'd
aired his grievance.

"How could you do it? Why shoot down a girl in her first

Season, who needs all the advantage she can muster, what with those freckles and the habit she has of smirking—" He paused. No, no, he was getting off the track. "I mean, she's a perfectly nice girl, with only a moderate dowry to recommend her, and you had no call to say that she dances like an African giraffe who's drunk too much homebrew. The girl can't help being tall, you know!"

The earl frowned, but it seemed more in puzzlement than in anger. "Of whom are we speaking, Galston? Some new infatuation of yours?"

Timothy shook his head. "No, dammit. But she's my cousin, and she deserves better. You dashed her chance of a good Season with one careless *bon mot,* and you don't even recall? Miss Emmaline Mawper, that's who!"

When the earl continued to stare, Timothy added, "At Almack's last night, don't you remember?"

The earl shrugged. "I was in a bad mood, old man, wishing I hadn't allowed myself to be cajoled into looking into that wretched Marriage Mart in the first place. And I'm sure no one remembers one careless comment of mine."

"You think wrongly, then," Timothy retorted. "I've heard it repeated twice today already, with more jests tacked on, and Emmaline is in tears, my aunt says. Aunt Mary hauled me out of bed—at any ungodly hour, let me tell you—to complain, although what she thinks I can do . . . But you're the mostly-eagerly heeded arbiter of the Ton since Beau Brummel took himself off to the Continent to evade his debtors. If you weren't so damned perfect, with your elegant neckcloths and impeccable tailoring, not to mention that perfect Grecian coin of a face the ladies swoon over—"

This time the earl shook his head, and a strand of dark hair fell back. For the first time, Timothy had a clear view of the ragged scar that marred the earl's left cheek. It started above the temple and ran past his ear and on beneath the erect shirt collar, the jagged line almost—but not quite—hidden beneath the earl's slightly too-long hair, and damned if that shaggy hair hadn't started a new fad among the calflings who aped Whitby's casual elegance . . .

"Perfect?" The earl's voice was icy.

Timothy swallowed. "Oh, that don't signify. It just adds a touch of the exotic, don't you know, romantic war wound, and all that—in fact, the ladies love it," he protested, but he knew his voice wavered. Damn, he always forgot.

"But that don't change my argument," he said, trying to recapture his momentum. "The Ton still looks to you, Whitby, and it ain't right—you misuse your power over Society's opinion."

"If I have any power, as you claim, it is quite unsought and totally irrelevant." Whitby lowered his face again to sip his wine.

Timothy swallowed, almost tasting his relief.

"Not to the persons you cut down, it ain't," he argued. "It's easy enough to put someone down, much harder to build someone up. Why don't you do something agreeable for a change?"

"I assure you, Galston, the next time I see Miss Mawper, I will be charm personified—"

But a new voice interrupted.

"Look, a woman—a lady, I should almost say!"

The earl turned back toward the bow windows of White's, where several younger gentlemen lounged, watching the street. This was male territory, and any respectable lady knew it and avoided St. James's Street with utmost care.

So why was a young and very pretty girl dashing down the pavement, pursued doggedly by a stout, red-faced female?

Even Timothy paused to stare. None of the onlookers could make out the words spoken outside the window, but they saw the older woman catch the girl by the arm and her lips move in what was obviously an energetic scold.

The young woman's expression twisted. Was she a lady or not? She was dressed decorously and with obvious expense, but her attitude to the older female—mother, aunt, governess, whatever—didn't seem in keeping with her youth, nor did she seem abashed by her social transgression. In fact, now she jerked away from the other's hold, and while the men watched, entranced, landed a passable left hook into the woman's rounded midriff. The woman staggered back. The girl's hands curled into fists, and her bonnet slid off her fair hair as she waited for the woman to recover.

"Ten pounds on the younger lady!" one of the watchers called.

"Done. But hardly a lady, I'd say," another of the gawkers suggested. He added a comment which made the other men guffaw and offer a few disparaging guesses of their own as to the girl's social status—or even profession.

The earl frowned. One of the men sitting closer to the window looked up to see it, and beneath Whitby's reproving glance, the laughter faded. The other men turned back to watch the mill in progress.

"See," Timothy muttered. "I told you people listen to you. All you have to do is frown or smile, and the Ton obeys . . ." He paused to stare out the window at the continuing struggle between the two women. He had obtained what he had come for, so why did he still feel dissatisfied? Someone ought to show Whitby just how misguided the arrogant earl was, he thought.

Outside, the stout woman—apparently thoroughly out of temper—slapped the girl's cheek. But the younger lady did not give in. She ducked and evaded the next blow. When she glanced up again, her cheek was reddened from the impact, and her eyes were wide with fear.

Timothy thought that the earl had stiffened. Timothy said, "I repeat, raising people up is much harder than cutting 'em down. For example, I'd bet you a hundred pounds you couldn't make a lady out of—out of—well, whoever that girl is."

"Probably some rich cit's daughter who hasn't heeded her lessons in deportment." The earl shook his head. "Or

mayhap some escapee from Bedlam, judging by her bar-
baric behavior. Can't make a silk reticule out of a sow's
ear. Anyhow, we don't even know who she is."

"And if I can find out her name? What about the bet?"

"I can't change her birth, and I'm sure as Hades no
damned governess to give lessons in ladylike conduct."
The earl's dusky eyes seemed to darken even more, but
there was something in his tone Timothy had not heard
before.

So this time Timothy, elated to at last observe a chink in
Whitby's armor, stood his ground.

"So you admit my point? You can cut down an aspiring
miss without a second thought, but you can't lift an awkward girl with, obviously, no sense of propriety, nor ex-
pend any real effort in the attempt? Afraid it will be too
difficult a task, eh?"

Whitby narrowed his eyes.

Timothy's surge of confidence faded just a little; he
tried not to gulp.

"If you learn her name, if she has any pretension to gen-
tility at all, I will see that she is the toast of the Ton. Are
you satisfied?"

Timothy grinned, looking up just in time to see that the
matronly woman had finally succeeded in pulling the still-
struggling girl back up the street. They were almost out of
sight.

One of the men in the window groaned as his mate urged,
"Pay up!"

"Oh, very." Timothy tried not to laugh in the earl's face.
"I'll let you know her name when I find it out."

And he hurried out of the club to follow the two women.

NICOLE BYRD

LADY IN WAITING
0-515-13292-6

A talented artist, Circe Hill has no interest
in the affairs of the heart—
until the man she secretly loves pretends to court her to
silence his matchmaking mother.

DEAR IMPOSTOR
0-515-13112-1

She's Psyche Hill, a lady in want of a fabulous
inheritance. There's only one way to secure it: by
marriage. There's only one problem.
She's not at all in love.
He's Gabriel Sinclair, a handsome gamester on the run
and in need of a place to hide. Psyche can offer him a
safe haven. There's only one problem.
He's falling in love far too fast.

"The real thing—a story filled with passion,
adventure, and the heart-stirring emotion that
is the essence of romance."
—Susan Wiggs

BERKLEY SENSATION
COMING IN MAY 2005

Hot Legs
by Susan Johnson
Curator Cassie Hill has sworn off men. But when a
painting is stolen, a hot-shot bounty hunter is called
in—and he's driving Cassie wild.

0-425-20355-7

Master of the Moon
by Angela Knight
A shape-shifting werewolf, Diana London is on the trail
of a killer vampiress. But her search takes an unexpected turn when erotic dreams lead her to Llyr, the king
of the faeries.

0-425-20357-3

The Moon Witch
by Linda Winstead Jones
Juliet Fyne has been kidnapped by the Emperor's
men—only to be rescued by a man whose animal
instincts tell him she's the only woman he will ever
love.

0-425-20129-5

Daring the Highlander
by Laurin Wittig
An independent young widow must help an unlikely
leader without losing her own cautious heart.

0-425-20292-5